Dog Heaven

KIT'S DOG, PONCH, took no more than a step forward, and without a moment's hesitation that darkness slammed silently down around them again. This time at least Kit was sure he had air around him and Ponch, and he had oxygenation routines ready to kick in if their bodies were affected by any kind of paralysis. Nonetheless, Kit still couldn't move, couldn't see anything.

He tried to speak out loud but again found that he couldn't. It didn't matter; the leash wizardry would carry his thoughts to Ponch. *What do we do now?* Kit said silently

Be somewhere.

Kit normally would have thought that that was unavoidable. Now he wasn't so sure. *Well, where did you have in mind?*

Here.

And something appeared before them. It was hard to make out the distance at first, until Kit saw what the thing was: a small shape, pale gray against that darkness, except for a whiter underbelly.

It was a squirrel.

Diane Duane's
Young Wizards Series

DIANE DUANE

The Wizard's Dilemma

Magic Carpet Books
Harcourt, Inc.
Orlando Austin New York San Diego
Toronto London

Requests for permission to make copies of any part of the work
should be mailed to the following address:
Permissions Department, Harcourt, Inc.,
6277 Sea Harbor Drive, Orlando, Florida 32887-6777.

www.HarcourtBooks.com

First Magic Carpet Books edition 2002
First published 2001

Magic Carpet Books is a trademark of Harcourt, Inc., registered in the
United States of America and/or other jurisdictions.

The Library of Congress has cataloged an
earlier edition as follows:
Duane, Diane.
The wizard's dilemma/Diane Duane.
p.   cm.—(The young wizards series; 5)
"Magic Carpet Books."
Sequel to: A wizard abroad.
Summary: Teenage wizard Nita travels to other universes to find
a cure for her mother, who has brain cancer.
[1. Wizards—Fiction. 2. Cancer—Fiction. 3. Fantasy.]
I. Title.
PZ7.D84915Wk   2001
[Fic]—dc21   00-12998
ISBN-13: 978-0152-02460-4 pb   ISBN-10: 0-15-202460-3 pb
ISBN-13: 978-0152-05491-5 digest pb   ISBN-10: 0-15-205491-X digest pb

Text set in Stempel Garamond
Designed by Trina Stahl

A C E G H F D B

Printed in the United States of America

For Jason Gamble,
the favorite nephew,

and

for Sam's friend's daughter…

both members of the next generation

Contents

The revelation of some uneasy secrets
would move most anything, even pigs and fishes,
to lift their heads and speak: and at such times
it furthers one to cross the great dark water
and learn the truth its silent shadows hide.

In the wet, reedy evening, birdsong echoes,
old calling young, eventually answered;
while another stands in the dark and calls its fellow,
hearing for answer only the ancient silence
in which tears fall, under a moon near-full.
The lead horse breaks the traces and goes astray
to cry its clarion challenge harsh at heaven.
Understandably. But can it understand in time
the danger that dogs immoderate success?...

> —*hexagram 61*
> *"a wind troubles the waters"*

If Time has a heart, it is because other hearts stop.

> —*Book of Night with Moon*
> *9.v.IX*

Friday Afternoon

"HONEY, HAVE YOU SEEN your sister?"

"She's on Jupiter, Mom."

There was no immediate response to this piece of news. Sitting at a dining-room table covered with notebooks, a few schoolbooks, and one book that had less to do with school than the others, Nita Callahan glanced over her shoulder just in time to catch sight of her mother looking at the ceiling with an expression that said, *What have I done to deserve this?*

Nita turned her head back to what looked like her homework, so that her mother wouldn't see her smile. "Well, yeah, not *on* Jupiter; it's hard to do that...She's on Europa."

Her mother came around and sat down in the chair opposite Nita at the table, looking faintly concerned. "She's not trying to create life again or something, is she?"

"Huh? Oh, no. It was there already. But there was some kind of problem."

The look on her mother's face was difficult to decipher. "What kind?"

"I'm not sure," Nita said, and this was true. She had read the mission statement, which had appeared in her copy of the wizard's manual shortly after Dairine left, but the fine print had made little sense to her—probably the reason why she or some other wizard had not been sent to deal with the trouble, and Dairine had. "It's kind of hard to understand what single-celled organisms consider a problem." She made an amused face. "But it looks like Dairine's the answer to it."

"All right." Her mom leaned back in the chair and stretched. "When will she be back?"

"She didn't say. But there's a limit to how much air you can carry with you on one of these jaunts if you're also going to have energy to spare to actually get anything done," Nita said. "Probably a couple of hours."

"Okay...We don't have to have a formal dinner tonight. Everyone can fend for themselves. Your dad won't mind; he's up to his elbows in shrubs right now, anyway." The buzz of the hedge trimmer could still be heard as Nita's dad worked his way around the house. "We can take care of the food shopping later...There's no rush. Is Kit coming over?"

Nita carefully turned the notebook page she'd been working on. "Uh, no. I have to go out and see him in a little while, though...Someone's meeting us to finish up a project. Probably it'll take us an hour or two, so don't wait for me. I'll heat something up when I get home."

"Okay." Her mother got up and went into the kitchen, where she started opening cupboards and peering into them. Nita looked after her with mild concern when she heard her mom's tired sigh. For the past month or so, her mom had been alternating between stripping and refinishing all the furniture in the house and leading several different projects for the local PTA—the biggest of them being the effort to get a new playground built near the local primary school. It seemed to Nita that her mother was always either elbow deep in steel wool and stain, or out of the house on errands, so often that she didn't have a lot of spare time for anything else.

After a moment Nita heaved a sigh. *No point in trying to weasel around it, though,* she thought. *I've got problems of my own.*

Kit...

But it's not his fault...

Is it?

Nita was still recovering from an overly eventful vacation in Ireland, one her parents had planned for her, to give Nita a little time away from Kit, and from wizardry. Of course, this hadn't worked. A wizard's work can happen anywhere, and just changing continents couldn't have stopped Nita from being involved in it any more than changing planets could have. As for Kit, he'd found ways to be with Nita regardless—which turned out to have been a good thing. Nita had been extremely relieved to get home, certain that everything would then get back to normal.

Trouble is, someone changed the location of "normal" and didn't bother sending me a map, Nita thought. Kit had been a little weird since she got home. Maybe some of it was just their difference in age, which hadn't really been an issue until a month or so ago. But Nita had started ninth grade this year and, to her surprise, was finding the work harder than she'd expected. She was used to coasting through her subjects without too much strain, so this was an annoyance. Worse yet, Kit wasn't having any trouble at all, which Nita also found annoying, for reasons she couldn't explain. And the two of them didn't see as much of each other at school as they'd used to. Kit, now in an accelerated-study track with other kids doing "better than their grade," was spending a lot of his time coaching some of the other kids in his group in history and social studies. That was fine with her, but Nita disliked the way some of her classmates, who knew she was best friends with Kit, would go out of their way to remind her, whenever they got a chance, how well Kit was doing.

As if they're fooling anyone, she thought. *They're nosing around to see if he and I are doing something else…and they can't understand why we're not.* Nita frowned. Life had been simpler when she'd merely been getting beaten up every week. In its own way, the endless sniping gossip—the whispering behind hands, and the passed notes about cliques and boys and clothes and dates—was more annoying than any number of bruises. The pressure to be like everyone else—

to do the same stuff and think the same things—just grew, and if you took a stance, the gossip might be driven underground...but never very far.

Nita sighed. Nowadays she kept running into problems for which wizardry either *wasn't* an answer, or else was the wrong one. And even when it was the right answer, it never seemed to be a simple one anymore.

As in the case of this *project, for example.* Nita looked down at the three notebook pages full of writing in front of her. *If I didn't know better, I'd think it was turning into a disaster.* Nita knew that wizards weren't assigned to projects they had no hope of completing. But she also knew that the Powers That Be weren't going to come swooping in to save her if she messed up an intervention. She was expected to handle it: That was what wizards were for...since the Powers couldn't be everywhere Themselves.

This left Nita staring again at her original problem: how to explain to Kit why the solution he was suggesting to their present wizardly project wasn't going to work. *He's so wrong about this,* she thought. *I can't believe he doesn't see it. I keep explaining it and explaining it, and he keeps not getting it.* She sighed again. *I guess I just have to keep trying. This isn't the kind of thing you can just give up on.*

Her mother plopped down beside her again with a pad of Post-it notes and peeled one off, sticking it to the table and starting to jot things down on it. "The sticky stuff on those is getting old," Nita said, turning to a clean page in her notebook. "It doesn't stick real well anymore."

"I noticed," her mother said absently, repositioning the note. "Milk, rye bread—"

"No seeds."

"Your dad likes caraway, honey. Humor him."

"Can't you just get me one of the little loaves without the seeds, Mom?"

Her mother gave her a sidelong look. "Can't *you* just...you know..." She attempted to twitch her nose in the manner of a famous TV "witch" of years past, and failed to do anything much except look like a rabbit.

Nita rolled her eyes. "Probably I could," she said, "but the trouble is, that bread was made *with* the seeds, and it thinks they belong there."

"Bread *thinks*? What about?"

"Uh, well, it— See, when you combine the yeast with the flour, the yeasts—" Nita suddenly realized that if this went on much longer, she was going to wind up explaining some of the weirder facts of life to her mother, and she wasn't sure that either she or her mother was ready. "Mom, the wizardry would just be a real pain to write. Probably simpler just to take the seeds out with my fingers."

Her mother raised her eyebrows, let out a breath, and made a note. "Small loaf of nonseeded rye for daughter whose delicate aesthetic sensibilities are offended by picking a few seeds out of a slice of bread."

"Mom, picking them out doesn't help. The *taste* is still there!"

"Scouring pads...chicken breasts..." Her mom gnawed reflectively on the cap of the pen. "Shampoo, aspirin, soup—"

"*Not* the cream-of-chemical kind, Mom!"

"Half a dozen cans of nonchemical soup for the budding gourmet." Her mother looked vague for a moment, then glanced over at what Nita was writing. She squinted a little. "Either I really *do* need reading glasses or you're doing math at a much higher level than I thought."

Nita sighed. "No, Mom, it's the Speech. It has some expressions in common with calculus, but they're—"

"What about your homework?"

"I finished it at school so I wouldn't keep getting interrupted in the middle of it, like I am here!"

"Oh dear," her mother said, peeling off another note and starting to write on it. "No seedless rye for *you*."

Nita immediately felt embarrassed. "Mom, I'm sorry—"

"We all have stress, honey, but we don't have to snap at each other."

The back door creaked open, and Nita's father came in and went to the sink.

Nita's mother glanced up. "Harry, I thought you said you were going to oil that thing. It's driving me nuts."

"We're out of oil," Nita's father said as he washed his hands.

"Oil," her mother said, and jotted it down on the sticky note. "What else?"

Her father picked up a dish towel and stood behind her mother's chair, looking down at the shopping list. "Lint?" he said.

This time her mother squinted at the notepaper. "That's 'list.'"

"Could have fooled me."

Nita's mom bent closer to the paper. "I see your point. I guess I really should go see the optometrist."

"Or maybe you should stop using the computer to write everything," her dad said, going to hang up the towel. "Your handwriting's going to pot."

"So's yours, sweetheart."

"I know. That's how I can tell what's happening to yours." Her father opened the refrigerator, gazed inside, and said, "Beer."

"Oh, now *wait* a minute. You said—"

"I lost ten pounds last month. The diet's working. After a hard day in the shop, can't I even have a cold beer? Just one?"

Nita put her head down over her notebook and concentrated on not snickering.

"We'll discuss that later. Oh, by the way, new sneakers for *you*," her mother said, giving her father a severe look, "before your old ones get up and start running around by themselves, without either of our daughters being involved."

"Oh, come on, Betty, they're not that bad!"

"You put *your* head in the closet, take a sniff, and tell me that again...assuming you make it out of there alive...If you can even *tell* anymore. I think all those flowers you work with are killing your sense of smell—"

"You don't complain about them when I bring home roses."

"It counts for more when somebody brings roses home if he's not also the florist!"

Nita's dad laughed and started to sing in off-key imitation of Neil Diamond, "Youuu don't bring me floooooowerrrs...," as he headed for the back bedroom.

Nita's mom raised her eyebrows. "Harold Edward Callahan," she said as she turned her attention back to her list making, "you are potentially shortening your lifespan..."

The only answer was louder singing, in a key that her father favored but few other human beings could have recognized. Nita hid her smile until her mother was sufficiently distracted, and then went back to her own business, making a few more notes on the clean page. After some minutes of not being able to think of anything to add, she finally closed the notebook and pushed it away. She'd done as much with the spell as she could do on paper. The rest of it was going to have to wait to be tested out in the real world.

She sighed as she picked up her copy of the wizard's manual and dropped it on top of her notebook. Her mother glanced over at her. "Finished?"

"In a moment. The manual's acquiring what I just did."

Her mother raised her eyebrows. "Doesn't it go the other way around? I thought you got the spells out of the book in the first place."

"Not all of them. Sometimes you have to build something completely new if there's no precedent spell to help you along. Then when you test the new spell out and it works okay, the manual picks it up and makes it available for other wizards to use. Most of what's in here originally came from other wizards, over a lot of years." She gave the wizard's manual a little nudge. "Some wizards don't do anything much *but* write spells and construct custom wizardries. Tom, for example."

"Really," Nita's mother said, looking down at her grocery list again. "I thought he wrote things for TV."

"He does that, too. Even wizards have to pay the bills," Nita said. She got up and stretched. "Mom, I should get going."

Her mother gave her a thoughtful look. "You know what I'm going to say…"

"'Be careful.' It's okay, Mom. This spell isn't anything dangerous."

"I've heard *that* one before."

"No, seriously. It's just taking out the garbage, this one."

Her mother's expression went suddenly wicked. "While we're on the subject—"

"It's Dairine's turn today," Nita said hurriedly, shrugging into the denim jacket she'd left over the chair earlier. "See ya later, Mom…" She kissed her mom, grabbed the manual from on top of her notebook, and headed out the door.

In the backyard, she paused to look around. Long shadows trailed from various dusty lawn furniture; it was only six-thirty, but the sun was low. The summer had been short for her in some ways—half of it lost to the trip to Ireland and the rush of events that had followed. Now it seemed as if, within barely a finger-snap of summer, the fall was well under way. All around her, with a wizard's ear Nita could hear the murmur of the birches and maples beginning to relax toward the winter's long rest, leaning against the earth and waiting with mild expectation for the brief brilliant fireworks of leaf-turn; the long lazy conversation of foliage moving in wind; and the light of sun and stars beginning to taper off to silence now, as the hectic immediacy of summer wound down.

She leaned against the trunk of the rowan tree in the middle of the backyard and looked up through the down-drooping branches with their stalks of slender oval leaves, the green of them slowly browning now, the dulled color only pointing up the many heavy clusters of glowing BB-sized fruit that glinted scarlet from every branch in the late, brassy light. "Nice berries this year, Liused," Nita said.

It took a few moments for her to hear the answer: Even with the Speech, there was no dropping instantly into a tree's time sense from human life speed. *Not bad this time out...not bad at all,* the tree said modestly. *Going on assignment?*

"Just a quick one," Nita said. "I hope."

Need anything from me?

"No, that last replacement's still in good shape. Thanks, though."

You're always welcome. Go well, then.

She leaned for a moment more to let her time sense come back up to its normal speed, then patted the rowan tree's trunk and went out into the open space by the birdbath. There she paused for a little to just listen to it all: life, going about its business all around her— the scratchy self-absorbed noise of the grass growing, the faint rustle and hum of bugs and earthworms contentedly digging in the ground, the persistent little string music of a garden spider fastening web strand to web strand in a nearby bush—repetitive, intense, and mathematically precise. Everything was purposeful... everything was, if not actually intelligent, then at least aware—even things that science didn't usually think were aware, because science didn't yet know how to measure or overhear the kinds of consciousness they had.

Nita took a deep breath, let it out again. This was the core of wizardry, for her: hearing it all going, and keeping it all going—putting in a word in the Speech here or a carefully constructed spell there, fixing broken things, helping what was hurt to heal and get going again...and being astonished, delighted, sometimes scared to death in the process, but never, ever bored.

Nita said a single word in the Speech, at the same time stroking one hand across the empty air in search of the access to the little pinched-in pocket of time space where she kept some of her wizardly equipment.

Responsive to the word she'd spoken, a little tab of clear air went hard between her fingers: She pulled it from left to right like a zipper, and then slipped her hand into the opening and felt around. A second later she came out with a piece of equipment she usually kept ready, a peeled rod of rowan wood that had been left out in full moonlight. She touched the claudication closed again, then looked around her and said to the grass, "Excuse me..."

The grass muttered, unconcerned; it knew the drill.

Nita lifted the rod and began, with a speed born of much practice, to write out the single long sentence of the short-haul transit spell in the air around her.

The symbols came alive as a delicate thread of pale white fire, stretching around her from the point of the rowan wand as she turned: a chord of a circle, an arc, then the circle almost complete as she came to the end of the spell, writing in her "signature," her name in the Speech, the long chain of syllables and symbols that described who and what she was today.

With a final figure-eight flourish, she knotted the spell closed, pulled the wand back, and let the transit circle drop to the grass around her, an arabesqued chain of light. Turning slowly, Nita began to read the sentence, feeling the power lean in around her as she did so, the pressure and attention of local space focusing in on what Nita told it she wanted of it, relocation to *this* set of spatial coordinates, life support set to planet-surface defaults—

The silence began to build around her, the sound of the world listening. Nita read faster, feeling the words of the Speech reach down their roots to the Power That had first spoken them and taught them what they meant, till the lightning of that first intention struck up through them and then through Nita, as she said the last word, completed the spell, and flung it loose to work—

Wham! The displacement of transported air always sounded loud on the inside of the spell, even if you'd engineered the wizardry to keep it from making a lot of noise on the outside. The crack of sound, combined with the sudden blazing column of light from the activated transit, left Nita momentarily blind and deaf.

Only for a moment, though. A second later the light died back, and she was standing near the end of a long jetty of big rough black stones, all spotted and splotched with seagull guano and festooned with washed-up seaweed in dull green ribbons and flat brown bladdery blobs. The sun hung blinding over the water to the west, silhouetting the low flat headlands that were all she could see of the Rockaway Beach peninsula from this angle. Somewhere beyond them, lost in mist and sun glare and half submerged beneath the horizon line, lay the skyline of New York.

Nita pulled her jacket a little more tightly around her in the chilly spray-laden wind and turned to look over her shoulder. Down at the landward end of the quarter-mile-long jetty, where it came up against the farthest tip of West End Beach, was a squat white box of a building with an antenna sticking up from it: the Jones Inlet navigational radio beacon. Beyond it there was no one in sight—the weather had been getting too cool for swimming, especially this late in the day. Nita turned again, looking southward, toward the bay. At the seaward end of the jetty was the black-and-white painted metal tower that held up the flashing red Jones Inlet light, and at its base a small shape in a dark blue windbreaker and jeans was lying flat on the concrete pediment to which the tower was fastened, looking over the edge of the pediment, away from Nita.

She headed down the jetty toward him, picking her

way carefully over the big uneven rocks and wondering at first, *Is he all right?* But as she came near, Kit looked up over his shoulder at her with an idle expression. "Hey," he said.

She climbed up onto the cracked guano-stained concrete beside him and looked down over the edge, where the rocks fell steeply away. "What're you doing?" Nita said. "The barnacles complaining about the water temperature again?"

"Nope, I'm just keeping a low profile," Kit said. "I don't feel like spending the effort to be invisible right now, with work coming up, and there've been some boats going through the inlet. Might be something happening at the Marine Theater later. It's been a little busy."

"Okay." She sat down next to him. "Any sign of S'reee yet?"

"Nothing so far, but it's only a few minutes after when we were supposed to meet. Maybe she got held up. Whatcha got?"

"Here," Nita said, and opened her manual. Kit sat up and flipped his open, too, then paged through it until he came to the "blank" pages in the back where research work and spells in progress stored themselves.

Nita looked over his shoulder and saw the first blank page fill itself in with the spell she had constructed that afternoon, spilling itself down the page, section by section, until that page was full, and the continued-on-next-page symbol presented itself in the lower right-hand corner, blinking slowly. "I had an idea," she said, "about the chemical-reaction calls. I thought that maybe the precipitates weren't going to behave right—"

"Okay, okay, give me a minute to look at it," Kit said. "It's pretty complicated."

Nita nodded and looked out to sea, gazing at the blinding golden roil and shimmer of light on the Great South Bay. These waters might *look* pretty, but they were a mess. New York and the bedroom communities around it, all up and down Long Island and the Jersey shore, pumped terrible amounts of sewage into the coastal waters, and though the sewage was supposed to be treated, the treatment wasn't everything it was cracked up to be. There was also a fair amount of illegal dumping of garbage and sewage going on. Various wizards, independently and in groups, had worked on the problem over many years; but the nature of the problem kept changing as the population of the New York metropolitan area increased and the kinds of pollution shifted.

Nita and Kit were more than usually concerned about the problem, as they had friends who had to live in this water. Since shortly before Nita had had to go away for the summer, they'd been slowly trying to construct a wizardry to take the pollution out of the local waters on an ongoing basis. If it worked, maybe the scheme could be extended up and down the coast. But the problem was getting it to work in the first place. Their efforts so far hadn't been incredibly successful.

Kit was looking at the second full page of Nita's work. Now he turned it over and looked at the third page, the last one. "This," he said, tapping a section near the end, "is pretty slick."

"Thanks."

"But the rest of this—" Kit shook his head, turned back to the first two pages, and touched four or five other sections, one after another, so that they grayed out. "I don't see why we need these. This whole contra-replication routine would be great—if the chemicals in the pollution knew how to reproduce themselves. But since they don't, it's a lot of power for hardly any return. And implementing these is going to be a real pain. If you just take this one—" he touched another section and it brightened—"and this, and this, and you—"

Nita frowned. "But look, Kit, if you leave those out, then there's nothing that's going to deal with the sewer outfall between Zachs Bay and Tobay Beach. That's tons of toxic sludge every month. Without those routines—"

Kit closed his eyes and rubbed the bridge of his nose in a way Nita had seen Tom, their local advisory wizard, do more than once when the world started to get to him. "Neets, this is all just too involved. Or involved in the wrong way. You're making it more complicated than it needs to be."

Oh no . . . here we go again. I thought he was going to get it this time, I really did . . . "But if you don't name all the chemicals, if you don't describe them accurately—"

"The thing is, you don't *have* to name them all. If you just take a look at the spell I brought with—"

"Kit, *look.* That stripped-down version you're suggesting isn't going to do the job. And the longer we don't *do* something, the worse the problem gets! Everything that lives along this shoreline is being affected... whatever's still alive, anyway. Things are *dying* out there, and every time we go back to the drawing board on this, *more* things die. Getting this wizardry running has taken too long already."

"Tell me about it," Kit said in a tone that struck Nita as a lot more ironic than it needed to be.

And after all the work I did! she thought. Nonetheless she tried to calm down. "All right. What do *you* think we should do?"

"Maybe," Kit said, and paused, "maybe it would be good if we let S'reee take a look at both versions. If she thinks—"

Nita's eyes widened. "Since when do we need a third opinion on something this straightforward? Kit, it'll either do what it's supposed to or it won't. Let's test it and find out!"

He took a deep breath and shook his head. "I can tell already, it's not going to do what we need."

She stared at Kit, not knowing what to say, and then after a moment she got up and stared down at him, trying to keep from clenching her fists. "Well, if you're so sure you're right, why don't you just do it yourself? Since my advice plainly isn't worth jack to you."

"It's not that it's not worth anything, it's that—"

"Oh, *now* you apologize."

"I wasn't apologizing."

"Well, maybe you need to!"

"Neets," Kit said, also frowning now, "what do you want me to do? Tell you that I think it's gonna be fine, when I don't really think so?"

Nita flushed. When you were working with the Speech, in which what you described would come to pass, lying could be fatal...and you quickly learned that even talking *about* spells less than honestly was dangerous.

"Energy is precious," Kit said. "Neither of us can just throw it around the way we used to a couple years ago. It's a nuisance, but it's something we have to consider."

"Do you think I wasn't considering it? I took my time over that. I didn't even put it through the spell checker. I checked all the syntax, all the balances, by hand. It took me forever, but—"

"Maybe the 'forever' was a hint, Neets," Kit said.

She had been trying to hang on to her temper, but now Nita got so furious that her eyes felt hot. "Fine," she said tightly. "Then you go right ahead and handle this yourself. And just leave me out of it until you find something you feel is simplistic enough to involve me in."

Kit's expression was shocked, and Nita didn't care. *Who needs this?* she thought. *No matter what I try to do, it's not good enough! So maybe it's time I stopped trying. Let him work it out himself, if he can.*

Nita turned and made her way back down the jetty, her eyes narrowed in annoyance as she slapped her claudication open and pulled out the rowan wand. In one angry, economical gesture, she whipped the wand around her, dropping her most frequently used transit circle to the stones, the one that would take her home. It was a little harder to speak the spell than usual. Her throat was tight, but not so much so that she couldn't say the words that would get her out of there. In a clap of imploding air, she was gone, and spray from a wave that crashed against the jetty went through the place where she had been.

Friday, Early Evening

KIT RODRIGUEZ JUST SAT there on the concrete platform at the bottom of the Jones Inlet light tower for some minutes, looking at the spot where Nita had vanished, listening to the hiss of the surf, and trying to work out what the heck had just happened.

What did I say? Kit went over their conversation a couple of times in his head and couldn't find any reason for her to have gotten so upset. *What is her* problem *these days? It can't be school. Nobody bothers her anymore; she does okay.*

It was a puzzle, and one he'd been having no luck solving. Maybe it was because he'd been so busy... and not just during the last couple of months, either. Granted, lately he'd been spending a lot of time on the bottom of the Great South Bay. And over the past couple of years, he'd also been to Europe, and had stopped off on or near most of the planets in the solar system, though only on the way to places much farther out, including some places that weren't exactly planets. Even Kit's mother, who initially had been really nervous about his wizardry, had eventually started to admit that all that travel was probably going to be educational, and theoretically ought to make him, if not smarter, at least more mature. But Kit was beginning to have his doubts. For the past few weeks, when he hadn't been in school, in bed, or a few hundred feet deep in water, he'd been spending a lot of his spare time sitting on a particular rock in the Lunar Carpathians, looking down on the green-blue gem that was Earth from three hundred thousand kilometers out, and coming back again and again to the question, *Are girls another species?*

The first time the thought had occurred to him, he'd felt embarrassed. He had been in places where members of other species had been present in their hundreds—sometimes in their thousands—tentacles and oozy bits and all. None of them had at the time struck him as all that alien; they were, when you got right down to it, just people. And though their differences from human beings were tremendous, sometimes making them completely incomprehensible, that still didn't undermine his affection for them. He liked the aliens he met, even when they were weird. *Come to think of it, I like them* because *they're weird.* But Nita, who theoretically was just as human as Kit was, had been pushing the weirdness-and-incomprehensibility envelope pretty hard lately. Her behavior was hard to understand, from someone who was usually so rational—

Something dark broke the dazzle of the water about a quarter mile away. Kit cocked an ear and heard a long high whistle, slightly muffled, and after that first shape—a short stumpy barnacle-pocked dorsal fin—came the sleek dark shining shape of the back of a humpback whale, rolling in the water as she breached and blew. One small eye set way down at the end of the long, long jaw regarded Kit as S'reee slid toward the jetty, back-finning expertly to keep from coming to grief on the rocks. *"Dai stihó,* K!t," she whistled and clicked in the Speech. "Sorry I'm late. Traffic…"

Uneasy as he was, Kit had to chuckle. "I know. I can hear it even up here." The main approaches to New York Harbor ran straight through this part of the Great South Bay, and for a whale, keeping clear of the ever-increasing number of ships—not so much the ships themselves but the inescapable sound of their engines and machinery, always a nuisance for a creature that worked extensively with sonar—was a problem and made getting around quickly a lot more trouble than it used to be. Noise pollution in the bay was as much a problem for the many species who lived there as was the sewage, and would probably be a more difficult problem to solve. It was one of a number of projects S'reee had been forced to tackle since her abrupt promotion to the position of senior cetacean wizard for these waters.

S'reee rolled idly in the water, looking down the jetty. "It's my fault; I should have left the Narrows earlier. But never mind. Where's hNii't?"

"I don't think she's going to be with us today," Kit said.

S'reee didn't reply immediately, but that thoughtful

little eye dwelt on Kit. As whales went, S'reee wasn't that much older than Kit or Nita, but the increased responsibilities she'd been pushed into had been making her perceptive—maybe more perceptive than Kit exactly cared for right now, especially since he still wasn't sure that he hadn't misstepped somehow.

"Well," S'reee said after a moment, "is that a problem? Can we manage, or should we reschedule?"

Kit thought about that. "I've got something that might be worth looking at," he said. "We may as well lay it out in place and have a look at it."

"All right."

Kit reached into the pocket of his jeans, which was also the way into his own storage pocket of space, and came out with a little ball of light, a spell in compacted form, which he dropped to the concrete he was standing on. As the compaction routine came loose and let the spell expand, he shoved his manual down into the pocket, then picked up the spell and shook it out.

It was a webwork of interconnected statements in the Speech, all of which briefly flared bright and then, dimming, settled and spread themselves into a form that could have been mistaken for a cloak made of plastic wrap. Kit whirled it around him, then held still while the spell sealed itself shut all about him and completed its access to its air supply, also tucked away in the spatiotemporal claudication in his pocket. Normally this spell was used as a space suit, for occasions when moving or working in a large "bubble" of air wasn't desirable, but Kit had adapted it for use as a wet suit. He glanced back at the beach to make sure no one was watching—the last thing he wanted was for someone to think some kid out here was suicidal—and jumped well away from the rocks, into the water next to S'reee.

The two of them submerged. Kit took a moment to adjust the wizardry he was wearing, to add weight as necessary so that it would counteract the buoyancy of the air in the wet suit and his lungs, then he took hold of S'reee's dorsal fin, and she towed him away from the jetty, southward.

The waters were getting murky this time of year, but not murky enough to hide something that Kit was beginning to get tired of looking at: an irregular cluster of humped, sinister shapes, half buried in sludge, not far from where the sewerage outfall from Tobay Beach tailed off. Half a century ago, some ship had dropped or dumped a cargo of mines on the bottom, in about fifty fathoms of water. But as far as Kit was concerned, that wasn't half deep enough.

"We really need to do something about that," Kit said, glancing at the mines as they passed them by. "Somebody seriously exceeded their recommended stupidity levels the day they dumped *those* here."

"I wouldn't argue the point," S'reee said as they headed out to the point where they had been preparing to anchor their wizardry. "But one thing at a time, cousin. Do you really think you have a solution for our present problem?"

"I've got *something*," Kit said. "You tell me."

"Shortly."

It took them a few minutes more to reach the spot,

due south of Point Lookout, where the three of them had been contemplating anchoring the wizardry once they'd settled on what it was going to be. Here the tides came out of Jones Inlet with most force, helping keep the dredged part of the ship channel clean; but here also the pollution from inside the barrier islands came out in its most concentrated form, and this, Kit and Nita had thought, would be a good place to stop it. "The day before yesterday, I spent a little while checking the currents here," S'reee said, as she paused to let Kit slip off, "and I'd say you two were right about the location. Also, the bottom's pretty bare. There isn't too much life to be inconvenienced by tethering a spell here, and what there is won't mind being relocated. Let's see what you've got."

Kit pulled out his manual, turned to the workbook section, and instructed it to replicate the structure of the proposed spell in the water, where they could see it. A few seconds later he and S'reee were looking together at the faintly glowing schematic, a series of concentric and intersecting circles full of the "argument" of the wizardry.

S'reee swam slowly around it, examining it. "I have to confess," she said at last, "this makes more sense than what the three of us were looking at earlier. All those complex chemical-reaction subroutines...they'd have taken us weeks to set up, and exhausted us when we tried to fuel them. Besides, it was too much of a brute-force solution. It's no good shouting at the Sea, as our people say; you won't hear what it has to say to you, and it won't listen until you do."

"You think it'll listen to this?"

S'reee swung her tail thoughtfully. "Let's find out," she said. "If nothing else, it's going to be quicker to test to destruction, if it fails at all. And between you and me—and I hate to say it—it's a more elegant solution than what Nita was proposing."

Kit felt uneasy agreeing with her. "Well," he said, "if it doesn't work, it won't matter how elegant it is. Let's get set up."

He started laying out the spell for real. It contained a simplified version of one of the circles he and Nita had been arguing about two days before—there was no point in wasting a perfectly good section of diagram that could be tied into the revision. Kit drew a finger through the water, and the graceful curves and curlings of the written Speech followed after as he drifted around in a circle about twenty yards across, reinstating the first circle as he'd held it in memory.

"Is this how the second great circle looks?" S'reee said, describing the circle with a long slow motion of body and tail. Fire filled the water, following her gesture, writing itself in pulsing curls and swirls of light—all the power statements and the conditionals that were secondary parts of the spell.

"You've got it," Kit said. "One thing, though…" He looked ruefully at the place where Nita's name was written. Carefully he reached out and detached the long string of characters in the Speech that represented Nita's wizardly power and personality, and let it float away into the water for the time being. A wizard doesn't just casually erase another wizard's name, any more than you would casually look down the barrel of a gun, even when you were sure that the chamber was empty. Changing a name written in the Speech could change the one named. Erasing a name could be more dangerous still.

"You'll need to knit that circle in a little tighter to compensate," S'reee said.

"Taking care of that now."

It took only a few moments to finish tightening the structure. Kit looked it over one more time; S'reee did the same. Then they looked at each other. "Well?" Kit said.

"Let's see what happens," said S'reee.

Together they began to recite—Kit in the human, prose-inflected form of the Speech; S'reee in the sung form that whale-wizards prefer. Kit stumbled a couple of times until he got the rhythm right—though the pace was quicker than that at which whales sing their more formal and ritual wizardries, it was still fairly slow by human standards. *One word at a time,* he thought, resorting to humming the last syllables when he needed to let S'reee catch up with him; and as they spoke together and fed power to it, the wizardry began to light up around them like a complex, many-colored neon sculpture in the water, a hollow sphere of curvatures and traceries, at the center of which they hung, waiting for the sense of the presence they were summoning.

And slowly, as the wizardry came alive around them, the presence was there, making itself felt more strongly each passing moment as Kit and S'reee worked together toward the last verse—the wizard's knot, in this case a triple-stranded braid, which would seal together three great circles' worth of spell. The pressure came down around them, the weight of tons of water and millions of years of time, hard to bear; but Kit hunched himself down a little, got his shoulders under the weight and bore it up. The water went from the normal dusky green of these depths to a flaring blue-green, like a liquid set on fire. All around them, if it was possible for water to feel wetter than water already was, it did. The personality of the local ocean, partly aware, washed through both Kit and S'reee, intent on washing away resistance over time, as it always had.

Kit had no intention of being washed anywhere. Slowly and carefully he and S'reee started to put their case, defining a specific area on which they desired to operate, telling the ocean what they wanted to do and why it was going to be a good thing.

They were reminding the ocean how things had once been: a long discussion, setting aside for the moment its outrage over having been systematically polluted. But then the local waters were a different issue from the greater, world-girdling Sea, which was a whole living thing, a Power in its own right and the conduit through which the whales' own version of wizardry came to them.

The Sea stood in the same relationship to the ocean as the soul stood to the body, and the ocean, merely physical as it was, had its own ideas about the creatures that had come over the long ages to populate it. To the ancient body of water, which had suddenly found itself playing host to the first and simplest organisms, everything biological looked suspiciously like pollution. The merely physical ocean, remembering that most ancient, blood-saline water, had for a long time resisted the idea of anything living in it. Many times life had tried to get started as the seas cooled, and many times it had failed before the one fateful lightning strike finally lanced down and stirred the reluctant waters to life.

Now, Kit was suggesting—with S'reee, a recently native form of "pollution," to back him up—a possible compromise. Here in this one place, at least, the ocean had an opportunity to return to that old purity, to water in which any chemical except salt was foreign. Maybe in other places this same intervention could be brought about, with wizards to power it and the ocean's permission. But first they had to get this initial permission granted.

It was a long argument, one which the ocean was reluctant to let anyone else win, even though it stood to benefit. Kit knew from his research in the manual and from a number of conferences with S'reee that there was always difficulty of this kind with oceanic wizardries. The waters themselves, far from being fluid and pliant to a wizard's wishes, could be as rigid as berg ice or as hostile as hot pillow lava to action from "outside." The discussion had to be most diplomatic.

But Kit and S'reee had done their homework, and they didn't have to hurry. They just kept patiently putting their case in the Speech, taking their time. And Kit thought he started to feel a shift....

I think it's starting to listen! S'reee said privately to Kit.

Kit swallowed and didn't respond...just kept his mind on the argument. But now he was becoming certain that she was right. Just this once, persistence was winning out. They'd both been hoping for this, for though the waters had flinched under those early lashes of lightning, they also had conceived a certain sneaking fascination for the wild proliferation of life that had broken loose in them over a mere few thousand millennia. Now, as Kit and S'reee hung in the center of the spell sphere they had constructed, they saw the light of the Sea around them start slowly, slowly to shift in color and quality as it began to accept the spell.

The shimmer of the wizardry's outer shell began to dissolve into splashes of green and gold brilliance, the catalytic reactions that would make the pollutants snow down as inert salts onto the ocean bottom as fast as they built up. That inert "garbage" would still have to be cleaned up, but the Sea itself had routines for that, older than human wizardry and just as effective for this particular job.

Kit and S'reee watched the wizardry spread away in great ribbony tentacles, diffusing itself, dissolving slowly into the water—one long current drifting away southward, another running up the channel, with the rising flood tide, toward the inland waters and the main sources of the pollution. After three or four minutes there was nothing left to be seen but the most subtle shimmer, a radiance like diluted moonlight.

Then even that was gone, leaving the waters nearly dark, but someone sensitive to the power they had released could still have felt it, a tingle and prickle on the skin, the feel of advice taken and being acted upon. The silence faded away, leaving Kit and S'reee listening to the wet-clappered *bonk, bonk* of the nun buoy half a mile away, the chain-saw ratchet of motorboat propellers chopping at the water as they passed through Jones Inlet.

Kit, hovering in the water, looked over at S'reee. The dimly seen humpback hung there for a long moment, just finning the water around her, then dropped her jaw and took a long gulp of the water, closing her mouth again and straining it back out through the thousands of plates of baleen.

"Well?" Kit said.

She waved her flukes from side to side, a gesture of slow satisfaction. "It tastes better already," she said.

"It *worked!*"

S'reee laughed at him. "Come on, K!t, a spell always works. You know that."

"If you mean a spell always does *something*, sure! It's getting it to do what you *originally* had in mind that's the problem."

"Well, this one did. It certainly discharged itself properly. If it hadn't, the structure of it would still be hanging here, complaining," S'reee said. "But I think we've done a nice clean intervention." She chuckled, a long scratchy whistle, and finned her way over to Kit, turning a couple of times in a leisurely victory roll.

Kit high-fived one of her ventral fins as it waved

past him, but the gesture brought him around briefly to where he saw Nita's name, detached from the spell, still hanging there, waving like a weed in the water and glowing faintly. Kit sighed and grabbed the string of symbols, wound them a few times around one hand, and stuffed them into his "pocket," then grabbed hold of that ventral fin again and let S'reee tow him back to the surface.

They floated there for a few minutes in the twilight, getting their breath again as the reaction to the wizardry began to kick in. "How long was that?" Kit said, looking at the shore, where all the streetlights down the parkway had come on and the floodlights shone on the brick red of the Jones Beach water tower and picked out its bronze-green pyramidal top.

"Two hours, I'd guess," S'reee said. "As usual it seems like less when you're in the middle of it. Maybe you should get yourself back onto land, though, K!t. I'm starting to feel a little wobbly already."

Kit nodded. "I'll go in a few minutes," he said, and looked around them. They were about three miles off Jones Beach. He looked eastward, to where a practiced eye could just make out the takeoff lights of planes angling up and away from Kennedy Airport. "I wonder, how soon could we expand the range of this closer to the city? There's a whole lot of dirty water coming from up there. Even though they don't dump raw sewage in the water anymore, the treatment plants still don't do as good a job as they should."

"You're right, of course," S'reee said. "But maybe we should leave the wizardry as it is for a while, and see how it behaves. After that, well, there's no arguing that the water around here can still use a lot more work. But we've made a good start."

"Yeah, the oysters should be happy, that's for sure," Kit said. There hadn't been shellfish living off the south shore of Long Island for many years now. After this piece of work, that would have a chance to change. Certainly the oystermen would be happy in ten or twenty years, and the fish who ate oysters would be, too, a lot sooner.

"True. Well, I don't see that we can do much more with this at this point," S'reee said, "except to say, well done, cousin!"

"Couldn't have done it alone," Kit said. But something in the back of his mind said, *But you* did *do it alone. Or not with the usual help . . .*

"Come on," S'reee said, "you've got to be feeling the reaction. We're both going to need a rest after that. I'll swim you back."

As they got close to the jetty, Kit said, "We should have another look at the wizardry again . . . When, do you think?"

"A week or so is soon enough," S'reee said, standing on her head in the water and waving her flukes meditatively in the air as Kit let go of her and clambered up out of the water onto the lowest rocks. "No point in checking the fueling routines any sooner; they're too charged up just now."

"Okay, next Friday, then. And I want to think about what we can do about those explosives down there, too."

"You're on, cousin. *Dai stihó.* And when you see hNii't'..." S'reee paused a moment, then just said, "Tell her we all have off days; it's no big deal."

"I will," Kit said. "*Dai,* S'reee."

The humpback slid under the water without so much as a splash. Kit spent a moment listening to the high raspy whistle of S'reee's radar-ranging song dwindling away as she navigated out of the shallows, heading for the waters off Sandy Hook. Then, in the flashing crimson light of the jetty's warning beacon, he unsealed the wet-suit spell, shook it out, wrapped it up tight, and shoved it back into his pocket along with Nita's written name and his manual. He shivered then, feeling a little clammy. *It's the interior humidity of the suit,* he thought, frowning. *I forgot to adjust the spell after I noticed the problem the last time.*

Kit grimaced, toying with the idea of doing a wizardry to dry his clothes out, and then thought, *Probably by the time I get home they'll be dry from my body heat already. No point in wasting power.*

He reached into the back of his mind and felt around behind him for his own preset version of what he referred to as the beam-me-up spell, found the one that was set for home, and pulled it into reality, shook it out in one hand, like a whip: a six-foot chain of multicolored light, a single long sentence in the Speech, complete except for the wizard's knot at the end that would set it going. He said that one word, and the wizardry came alive in his hand, bit its own tail. Kit dropped the chain of fire on the worn wooden decking of the fishing platform and stepped into it....

The blaze of the working spell and the pressure-and-noise *whoomp!* of displaced air blinded him briefly, but it was a result Kit was used to now. He opened his eyes again and saw streetlight-lit sidewalk instead of planking. Kit bent over, picked up the wizardry again, undid the knot and shook it out, then coiled it up and stuffed it into his pocket, and down still farther into the pocket in his mind, while simultaneously bracing himself for what he knew was going to hit him in a few seconds. Wobbly as he, too, was starting to feel now, he might not be able to keep it from knocking him over....

But nothing happened. Kit glanced around and then thought, *Whoops! Wrong destination,* for he was standing not outside his own house but two and a half blocks away. It was Nita's house he was looking at: He had grabbed the wrong spell, the only other one in his mind that got as much use as the take-me-home one. Nita's house's porch light was off; there were lights in the front windows, but the curtains were drawn.

I should go see if she wants to talk, he thought.

But her mood had been so grim, earlier...and now he'd found that he'd underestimated the dampness of his clothes. They were chilly, and he was getting still chillier standing here.

I really don't feel like it, Kit thought. *Let it wait until tomorrow. She'll be in a better mood then.*

He walked away into the dusk.

Friday Evening

KIT WALKED A COUPLE of blocks down Conlon Avenue to his own house, the usual kind of two-story frame house typical of this area. It was strange that he and Nita had lived so close together for so long and had never run into each other before becoming wizards; just one of those things, Kit guessed. Or maybe there was some reason behind it. But the Powers That Be were notoriously closemouthed about Their reasons. *Whatever. We both know where we are now.* Then Kit breathed out, amused. *Or at least most of the time we do...*

As Kit headed up the driveway to his house, he heard the usual *thump, wham-wham-wham-wham-wham* of paws against the back door, and he grinned and stopped. *CRASH* went the screen door, flying open, and a bolt of black lightning—or something moving nearly as fast as lightning might if it had four legs and fur—came hurtling out, leaped over the steps to the driveway without touching them, hit the ground with all legs working at once, like something out of a cartoon, and launched itself down the driveway at Kit. He had just enough time to brace himself before Ponch hit him about chest high, barking.

Kit laughed and tried to hold Ponch's face away from his, but it didn't work; it never worked. He got well slobbered, as Ponch jumped up and down on his hind legs and scrabbled at Kit's chest with his forepaws. The barking was as deafening as always, but there was, of course, more to it than that. Anyone who knew the Speech could have heard Kit's dog shouting, "You're late! You're late! Where were you? You're late!"

"Okay, so I'm late," Kit said. "What're you complaining about? Didn't anyone feed you?"

You smell like fish, Ponch said inside his head, and licked Kit's face some more.

"I just bet I do," Kit said. "Don't avoid the question, big guy."

I'm hungry!

Kit snickered as he pushed the dog down. Ponch was very doggy in some ways—loyal, and (as far as he knew how to be) truthful. He was also devious, full of plots and tricks to get people to feed him as many times a day as possible. *I should be grateful that that's as devious as he gets,* Kit thought as he made his way to the back door. "Come on, you," he said, and pulled open the screen door.

Inside was a big comfortable combined kitchen and dining room, where his mama and pop usually could be found this time of night. The only thing that happened in the living room at Kit's house was TV watching and the entertainment of family friends and guests—when that didn't drift into the kitchen as well. There was a big couch off to one side, under the front windows, with a couple of little tables on either side, one of which had a small portable TV that was blaring the local news; in the middle of the room was the big oval dining table, and on the other side of the room were the cooking island and, beyond it, the fridge and sink and oven and cupboards. On the cooking island was a pot, boiling, but as Kit went by he peered into it and saw nothing but water. He chucked his book bag over the back of one of the dining-room chairs and sidestepped neatly as Ponch, running in the slowly closing screen door after him, hit the tiled floor and skidded halfway across it, almost to the door that led to the living room. "Hey, Mama," Kit called, "I'm home. What's for dinner?"

"Spaghetti," his mother called from somewhere at the back of the house. "It would have been meatballs as well, but we didn't know which planet you were on."

Kit let out a small breath of relief, for spaghetti was not one of the things his mother could ruin, at least not without being badly distracted. She was one of those people who do a few dishes really well—her *arroz con pollo* was one of the great accomplishments of civilization on Earth, as far as Kit was concerned—but beyond those limits, his mama often got in trouble, and there were times when Kit was incredibly relieved to find his pop cooking. *Especially since it means I don't have to interfere...* He smiled ruefully. The last time he tried using wizardry to thicken one of his mama's failed gravy recipes had been memorable. These days he stuck to flour.

Kit's father came up the stairs from the basement into the kitchen—a big brawny broad-shouldered man, dark eyed, and dark haired except around the sideburns, where he claimed his work as a pressman at a Nassau County printing plant was starting to turn him gray. "He's gonna take that screen door off its hinges some day, son," Kit's father said, watching Ponch recover himself and start bouncing around the kitchen.

"Might not be a bad idea," said Kit's mother from the next room. "It's as old as the house. It looks awful."

"It's not broken yet," Kit's father said. "Though every time that dog hits it, you get your hopes up, huh?"

Kit's mother came into the kitchen and didn't say anything, just smiled. She was taller than Kit's dad, getting a little plump these days, but not so much that she worried about it. Her dark hair was pulled back tight and bunned up at the back, and Kit was slightly surprised to see that she was still in one of her nurse's uniforms—pink top and white pants. *Though maybe it's not "still,"* he thought as she paused to give Kit a one-armed hug and sat down at the end of the table.

"You have to work night shift tonight, Mama?"

She bent over to slip one of her shoes onto one white-stockinged foot, then laced the shoe up. "Just evening shift," she said. "They called from work to ask if I could swap a shift with one of the other nurses in the med-surg wing; he had some emergency at home. I'll be home around two. Popi'll feed you."

"Okay. Did anybody feed Ponch?"

"I did," said Kit's mother.

"Thanks, Mama," Kit said, and bent over to kiss her on the cheek. Then he looked down at Ponch, who was now sitting and gazing up at Kit with big soulful eyes and what was supposed to pass for a wounded look. *You didn't believe me!*

Kit gave him a look. "You," he said. "You fibber. You need a walk?"

"YEAH-YEAH-YEAH-YEAH-YEAH-YEAH!"

His mother covered her ears. "He's deafening," she said. "Tell him to go out!"

Kit laughed. "*You* tell him! He's not deaf."

"I'm glad for him, because *I* will be shortly! Pancho! Go *out!*"

Delighted, Ponch turned himself in three or four hurried circles and launched himself at the screen door again. *Thump, wham-wham-wham-wham-wham, CRASH!*

"I see," Kit's father said as he paused by the spaghetti pot, "that he's figured out how to push the latch with his paw."

"I noticed that, too," Kit said. "He's getting smart." And then he made an amused face, though not for his father to see. *Smart* didn't begin to cover the territory.

"So how did your magic thing go tonight?" his dad said.

Kit sat down with only about half a groan. "It's not

magic, Pop. Magic is when you wave your hand and stuff happens without any good reason or any price. Wizardry's the exact opposite, believe me."

His father looked resigned. "So my terminology's messed up. It takes a while to learn a new professional vocabulary. The thing with the fish, then, it went okay?"

Kit started to laugh. "You call S'reee a fish to her face, Pop, you're likely to remember it for a while," he said. "It wasn't the fish; it was the water. It was dirty."

"Not exactly news."

"It's gonna start getting cleaner. *That*'ll be news." Kit allowed himself a satisfied grin. "And you heard it here first."

"I imagine Nita must be pleased," his mother said.

"I imagine," Kit said, and got up to go to the fridge.

He could feel his mother looking at him, even without turning to see. He could hear her looking at his pop, even without so much as a glance in her direction. Kit grimaced, and hoped they couldn't somehow sense the expression without actually seeing it themselves. The problem was that they were parents, possessed of strange unearthly powers that even wizards sometimes couldn't understand.

"I thought maybe she was going to come over for dinner," said his pop. "She usually does, after you've been out doing this kind of work."

"Uh, not tonight. She had some other stuff she had to take care of," Kit said. *Like chewing the heads off her unsuspecting victims!*

The sudden image of Nita as a giant praying mantis

made Kit snicker. But then he dismissed it, not even feeling particularly guilty. "Where's Carmela?"

"Tonight's a TV night for her," Kit's pop said. "A reward for that math test. I let her take the other portable and the VCR; she's upstairs pigging out on Japanese cartoons."

Kit smiled. It was unusual for things to be so quiet while his sister was conscious, and the thought of sitting down and letting the weariness from the evening's wizardry catch up with him in conditions of relative peace and quiet was appealing. But Ponch needed walking first. "Okay," Kit said. "I'm gonna take Ponch out now."

"Dinner in about twenty minutes," his dad said.

"We'll be back," Kit said. As he went out the back door, he took Ponch's leash down off the hook where the jackets hung behind the door. Out in the driveway he paused and looked for Ponch. He was nowhere to be seen.

"Huh," Kit said under his breath, and yawned. The post-wizardry reaction was starting to set in now. If he didn't get going, he was going to fall asleep in the spaghetti. Kit went down to the end of the driveway, looked both ways up and down the street. He could see a black shape snuffling with intense interest around the bottom of a tree about halfway down Conlon.

Kit paused a moment, looking down where Conlon Avenue met East Clinton, wondering whether he might see a shadow a little taller than him standing at the corner, looking his way. But there was no sign of her. He made a wry face at his own unhappiness. *Just a fight.* Nonetheless, he and Nita had had so few that he wasn't really sure about what to do in the aftermath of one. In fact, Kit couldn't remember a fight they'd had that hadn't been over, and made up for, in a matter of minutes. This was hours, now, and it was getting uncomfortable. *What if I really hurt her somehow? She's been so weird since she got back from Ireland. What if she's so pissed at me that she—*

He stopped himself. *No point in standing here making it worse. Either go right over there now and talk to her or wait until tomorrow and do it then, but don't waste energy obsessing over it.*

Kit sighed and turned the other way, toward the end of the road that led to the junior-senior high school. He saw Ponch sniffing and wagging his tail near the big tree in front of the Wilkinsons' house. Ponch cocked a leg at the tree and, after a few seconds' meditation, bounded off down the street. Kit went after him, swinging the leash in the dusk.

From farther down the street came a sound of furious yapping. It was the Akambes' dog, whose real name was Grarrhah but whose human family had unfortunately decided to call her Tinkerbell. She was one of those tiny, delicate, silky-furred terriers who looked like she might unravel if you could figure out which thread to pull, but her personality seemed to have been transplanted from a dog three or four times her size. She was never allowed out of the backyard, and whenever one of the other neighborhood dogs went by, she would claw at the locked gate and yell at them in Cyene,

"You lookin' at me? I can take you! Come over here and say that! Stop me before I tear 'im apart!" and other such futile provocations.

Kit sighed as Ponch went past and as he followed, and the noise scaled up and up. There was no point in going over and talking to Grarrhah. She took her watchdog role terribly seriously, and would work herself into such a lather that she would already be lying there foaming at the mouth from overexcitement and frustration by the time you got to the gate. Making a poor creature like this more crazy than she was already was no part of a wizard's business, so Kit just walked by as Grarrhah shrieked at him from behind the gate, "Thief! Thief! Burglars! Joyriders, ram raiders, walk-by shooters; lemme at 'em, I'll rip 'em to shreds!"

Kit walked on, wondering if there was something he could do for her. Then he grinned sourly. *What a laugh! I don't even know what to do about Neets.*

All at once he changed his mind about letting things wait until the next day. Kit reached into his pocket and pulled out the manual. Among many other functions, it had a provision for print messaging for times when wizards were having trouble getting in touch with each other directly—a sort of wizardly pager system. He flipped to the back pages where such messages were written and stored. "New message," he said. "For Nita—"

The page glowed softly in the dusk and displayed the long string of characters in the Speech that was Nita's name, and the equivalent string for her manual.

There the book sat, ready to take down his message...and Kit couldn't think what to say. *I'm sorry?*

For what? *I didn't run her down. I told her what I thought. I don't think I was nasty about it. And I was right, too.*

He was strongly tempted to tell her so, but then Kit came up against a bizarre notion that doing that under the present circumstances would be somehow unfair. He spent another couple of minutes trying to find something useful to say. But he wasn't sure what was bothering Nita, and he was still annoyed enough at the way she'd behaved to feel like it wasn't his job to be the understanding one.

Kit frowned, opened his mouth…and closed it again, discarding that potential message as well. Finally all he could find to say was, "If you need some time by yourself, feel free."

He looked at the page as the words recorded themselves in the Speech.

More?

"No more," Kit said. "Send it."

Sent.

He stood there for a moment, half hoping he would get an answer right back. But there was no response, no hint of the subtle fizz or itch of the manual's covers that indicated an answer. *Maybe she's out. Maybe she's busy with something else.*

Or maybe she just doesn't want to answer…

He closed the manual and shoved it back into his pocket. Then Kit started walking again. When he reached the streetlight where Jackson Street met Conlon, he looked around. "Ponch?" he said, then listened for the jingle of Ponch's chain collar and tags.

Nothing.

Now where'd he go? Sweat started to break out all over Kit at the thought that Ponch might have gotten into someone's backyard and caught something he shouldn't have. Ponch's uncertain grasp of the difference between squirrels—which he hunted constantly with varying success—and rabbits—which he chased and almost always caught—had made him disgrace himself a couple of months back when one of the neighbor's tame rabbits had escaped from its hutch and wandered into Kit's backyard. Ponch's enthusiastic response had cost Kit about a month's allowance to buy the neighbor a new rabbit of the same rare lop-eared breed...a situation made more annoying by the fact that wizards are enjoined against making money out of nothing except in extreme emergencies connected with errantry, which this was not. Kit had yelled at Ponch only once about the mistake; Ponch had been completely sorry. But all the same, every time Ponch's whereabouts couldn't be accounted for, Kit began to twitch.

Kit started to jog down the street toward the entrance to the school, where Ponch liked to chase rabbits in the big fields to either side. But then he stopped as he heard a familiar sound, claws on concrete, and the familiar jingle, as Ponch came tearing down the sidewalk at him. Kit had just enough warning to sidestep slightly, so that Ponch's excited jump took him through air, instead of through Kit. Ponch came down about five feet behind where Kit had been standing, spun around, and started jumping up and down in front of him again, panting with excitement, "Come see it! Come see, look, I found it, c'mon c'mon c'mon c'mon, comesee-comeseecomesee!"

"Come see *what*?" Kit said in the Speech.

"I found something."

Kit grinned. Normally, with Ponch, this meant something dead. His father was still getting laughs out of the story about Ponch and the very mummified squirrel he had hidden for months under the old beat-up blanket in his doghouse. "So what is it?"

"It's not a *what*. It's a *where*."

Kit was confused. There was no question of his having misunderstood Ponch; the dog spoke perfectly good Cyene, which anyone who knew the Speech could understand. And as a pan-canine language, Cyene might not be strong on abstract concepts, but what Ponch had said was fairly concrete.

"Where?" Kit asked. "I mean, *what* where?" Then he had to laugh, for he was sounding more incoherent by the moment, and making Ponch sound positively sophisticated by comparison. "Okay, big guy, come on, show me."

"It's right down the street."

Kit was still slightly nervous. "It's not anybody's rabbit, is it?"

Ponch turned a shocked look on him. "Boss! I promised. And I said, it's not a *what*!"

"Uh, good," Kit said. "Come on, show me, then."

"Look," Ponch said. He turned and ran away from Kit, down the middle of the dark, empty, quiet side street...

... and vanished.

Kit stared.

Uhhh ... what the—!

Astonished, Kit started to run after Ponch, into the darkness ... and vanished, too.

Nita had come back from the Jones Inlet jetty that evening to find that her mother had left to go shopping. Her dad was in the kitchen making a large sandwich; he looked at Nita with mild surprise. "You just went out. Are you done for the day already?"

"Yup," Nita said, heading through the kitchen.

"Kit coming over?"

"Don't think so," Nita said, dropping her manual on the dining-room table.

Her father raised his eyebrows and turned back to the sandwich he was constructing. Nita sat down in the chair where she'd been sitting earlier and looked out the front window. She was completely tired out, even though she hadn't done anything, and she was thoroughly pissed off at Kit. The day felt more than exceptionally ruined. Nita put her head down in her hands for a moment.

As she did, she caught sight of a sticky-note still stuck to the table. "Uh-oh—"

"What?"

"Mom forgot her list—"

"You mean her 'lint'?" Her dad chuckled.

"Yeah. It's still stuck here."

"She'll call and get me to read it to her, probably."

There was a soft *bang!* from the backyard—a sound

that could have been mistaken for a car backfiring, except that there weren't likely to be cars back there. "Is that Dairine?" Nita's dad said.

"Probably," said Nita. It hadn't taken her parents long to learn the sound of suddenly displaced air—a sign of a wizard in a hurry or being a little less than slick about appearing out of nothing. At first it seemed to Nita as if her folks, after they'd found out she was a wizard, spent nearly all their time listening for that sound in varying states of nervousness. Now they were starting to get casual about it, which struck her as a healthy development.

But wait a minute. Maybe it's Kit, coming back to apologize— Nita started to get up.

The screen door opened and Dairine came in.

Nita sat down again. "Hey, runt," she said.

"Hey," said Dairine, and went on past.

Nita glanced after her, for this was not Dairine's normal response to being called runt. Her little sister paused by the table just long enough to drop her own book bag onto a chair, then went into the living room, pushing that startling red hair out of her eyes. It was getting longer, and, as a result, her resemblance to their mother was stronger than ever. *Has she started noticing boys?* Nita wondered. *Or is something else going on?*

Something scrabbled at the back door. Dairine sighed, came back through the dining room and the kitchen, went to the screen door, and pushed it open. A clatter of many little feet followed, as what appeared to be a little silvery-shelled laptop computer, about the size of a large paperback book, spidered into the kitchen on multiple spindly legs.

Nita peered at it as it followed Dairine back into the living room. "Am I confused," she said, "or is that thing getting smaller?"

"You're always confused," said Dairine as she headed for her room, "but yeah, he's smaller. Just had an upgrade."

Nita shook her head and went back to looking at her mom's list. Dairine's version of the wizard's manual had arrived as software for the household's first computer, and had been through some changes during the course of her Ordeal. Finally she'd wound up with this machine...if *machine* was the right word for something that was clearly alive in its own right. In the meantime the household's main computer continued to go through periodic changes, which made some of the neighbors suspect that Nita's father was making more money as a florist than he really was. For his own part, Nita's dad shrugged and said, "Your mom says it does the spreadsheets just fine. I don't want to know what else it might do...and as long as I don't have to pay extra for it..."

The phone on the wall rang. Her dad went over to it, picked it up. "Hello...Yes. Yes, you did, dopey...I am...Wait and I'll read it to you...Oh. Well, okay, sure...She just came in. No, both of them...Sure, I'll ask."

Nita's dad put his head around the corner. "Honey, your mom forgot a couple other things, too, so she's coming back. She says, do you want to go clothes shopping? They're having sales at a couple of the stores in the mall."

Nita couldn't think of anything else to do at the moment. "Sure."

Her dad turned his attention back to the phone. Nita went back to her room to change into a top that was easier to get in and out of in a hurry. From upstairs she could hear faint thumping and bumping noises. *What's she doing up there?* she thought, and when she finished changing, Nita went up the stairs to Dairine's room.

It was never the world's tidiest space—full of books and a ridiculously large collection of stuffed animals—but now it was even more disorganized than usual. Everything that had been on Dairine's desk, including chess pieces and chessboard, various schoolbooks, notebooks, calculators, pens, papers, paintbrushes, watercolor pads, compasses, rulers, a Walkman and its earphones, and much less classifiable junk, was now all over Dairine's bed. The desk was solely occupied by an extremely handsome, brushed stainless-steel cube, about a foot square, sitting on a clear Lucite base. Dairine looked over her shoulder at Nita as she came in. "Whaddaya think?" she said.

"I think it's gorgeous," Nita said, "but what is it?"

Dairine turned it around. There on one side was what could have been mistaken for the logo of a large computer company...but there was no bite out of the piece of fruit in question. The logo was inset into the side of the cube in frosted white and was glowing demurely. This by itself would not have been all that un-usual, except that there was no sign of any cord plugged into any wall.

"You mean this is a *computer*? Is this what you're replacing the old downstairs one with?" Nita said, sitting down on the bed. "It looks really cool. One of your custom jobs?"

"Nope, it's their new one," Dairine said. "Almost. I mean, the newest one in the stores looks like this. But those don't do what *this* one does."

Nita sighed. "Internet access?"

Dairine threw Nita a *you-must-be-joking, of-course-it-has-that* look. Wizards had had a web that spanned worlds for centuries before one small planet's machine-based version of networking had started calling itself World Wide. But that didn't mean they had to be snob-bish about it; and local technology, and ideas based on it, routinely got adapted into the business of wizardry as quickly as was feasible. "All the usual Net stuff, sure," Dairine said, "but there's other business...the new version of the online manual, mostly. I'm in the beta group." She glanced over fondly at her portable, which was sitting on the desk chair, scratching itself with some of its legs. "*They* voted me in."

Nita raised her eyebrows and leaned back. "Coming from the machine intelligences, that sounds like a com-pliment. Just make sure you don't mess up Dad's ac-counting software when you port it over." She cocked an eye at the portable, which was still scratching. "Spot here have some kind of problem?"

"If you're smart, you won't suggest he's got bugs!"

"No, of course not..."

Dairine leaned against the desk. "His shell's itching him from the last molt. But he's also been getting more like an organic life-form lately. I don't know whether it's a good thing or not, but there's nothing wrong with his processing functions, or his implementation of the manual, and he seems okay when we talk." Dairine looked at the laptop thoughtfully. "I thought Kit was going to be with you. He said he wanted to see the new machine when it came in."

"Huh?"

Nita's heart sank a little at the look Dairine was giving her. But her sister just picked the laptop up off the chair and put it on the desk. The laptop reared itself up on some of its legs and went up the side of the new computer's case like a spider, clambering onto the top and crouching there. Somehow it managed to look satisfied, a good trick for something that didn't have a face. Dairine sat on the end of the bed. "Something going on?"

Nita didn't answer immediately.

"Uh-huh," her sister said. "Neets, it's no use. Mom and Dad you might be able to hide it from for a while, but where I'm concerned, you might as well have it tattooed on your forehead. What's the problem?"

Nita stared at the bedspread, what she could see of it. "I had a fight with Kit. I can't *believe* him. He's gotten so—I don't know—he doesn't listen, and he—"

"Neets," Dairine said. "Level with me. By any chance...are you on the rag?"

Nita's jaw dropped. Dairine fell over laughing.

Nita gave Dairine an annoyed look until she quieted down. At last, when Dairine was wiping her eyes, she muttered, "I don't have that problem. Anyway, it's the wrong time."

"Well, you do a real good imitation of it," Dairine said. "If that's not it, what *is* the problem?"

Nita crossed her legs, frowning at the floor. "I don't know," she said. "Since I got back, it's like...like Kit doesn't trust me anymore. In the old days—"

"When dinosaurs walked the earth."

"Nobody likes a smart-ass, Dairine. Before I went away, if I'd given him the spell I gave him today, after all that work, he'd have said, fine, let's do it! Now, all of a sudden, everything's too much trouble. He doesn't even want to try."

"Maybe he doesn't want to blow energy on something that looks like it's going to fail," Dairine said.

"Boy, and I thought *he* was the winner of the tactlessness sweepstakes right now," Nita said. "You should call him up and offer to coach him."

"He'll have to make an appointment," Dairine said, pushing the pillows into a configuration she could lean on. "I've been busy." But her face clouded as she said it.

Aha, Nita thought. "I was going to ask you about that—"

The open window let in the sound of a car pulling into the driveway below. Dairine looked out the window. Below, a car door opened and shut, though the car's engine didn't turn off. "There's Mom," Dairine said.

Nita sighed and got up.

"But one thing," Dairine said. "Was Kit clear that the guy you were seeing over there—"

"I wasn't *seeing* him!"

"Yeah, right. Ronan. You sure Kit isn't confused about that?"

Nita stared. "Of course he isn't."

"You sure *you're* not confused about it?"

For that, Nita had no instant answer.

"Nita?" her mother called up the stairs.

"Later," Nita said to Dairine. "And don't think you're getting off easy. I want a few words with you about 'busy.'"

Dairine made a noncommittal face and got up to do something to the new computer as Nita went out.

In the darkness, Kit stood very still. He had never seen or experienced a blackness so profound; and with it came a bizarre, anechoic silence in which not even his ears rang.

"Ponch?" he said.

Or tried to say. No sound came out. Kit tried to speak again, tried to shout...and heard nothing, felt nothing. It was the kind of effect you might expect from being in a vacuum. But he knew that feeling, having been there once or twice. This was different, and creepier by far.

Well, hang on, Kit thought. *Don't panic. Nothing bad has happened yet.*

But that doesn't mean that it's not going to. Come to think of it, am I even breathing? Kit couldn't feel the rise of his chest, couldn't feel or hear a pulse. *What happens if there's nothing to breathe here? What happens if I suffocate?*

True, he didn't feel short of breath. *Yet,* said the back of his mind. Kit tried to swallow, and couldn't feel it happening. Slowly, old fears were creeping up his spine, making his neck hairs stand on end in their wake. It was a long time since Kit had gotten over being afraid of the dark...but no dark he'd had to cope with as a little kid had ever been as dark as *this.* And those darknesses had been scary because of the possibility that there was something hiding in them. This one was frightening, and getting more so by the minute, because of the sheer certainty that there was *nothing* in it. *I've had enough of this. Which way is out?!*

...But no! Kit thought then. *I'm not leaving without my dog. I'm not leaving Ponch here and running away!*

But how do you run away when you can't move? And how do you find something when you can't go after it? The horror of being trapped here, wherever *here* was, rose in him. *I'm not going to put up with this,* Kit thought. *I'm not going to just stand here and be terrified!* He tried to strain every muscle, tried to strain even *one,* and couldn't move any of them. It was as if his body suddenly belonged to someone else.

So I can't move. But I can still think—

There was a spell Kit knew as well as his transit spells, so well that he didn't even bother keeping it in compacted form anymore; he could say it in one breath. It was the spell he used to make a small light for reading under the covers at night. Kit could see the spell in his mind, fifty-nine characters in the Speech, twenty-one syllables. Kit pronounced them clearly in his mind, said the last word that tied the knot in the spell, and turned it loose—

Light. Just a single source of light, pale and silvery. There was no way to tell for sure if it was coming from near or far; it looked small, like a streetlight seen from blocks away. Just seeing it relieved Kit tremendously. It was the first change he had managed to make in this environment. And if he could do that, he could do something else. *Just take a moment and think* what *to do*—

Kit realized he was gasping for breath. He also realized that he was able to feel himself gasping. He tried to move his arms, but it was like trying to swim in taffy. As he concentrated on that light, he thought he saw a change in it. *The light's moving*— But that was wrong. Something dark was moving in front of it. *Oh no, what's that*—

Suddenly he could move his hand a little. He reached toward his pocket to fish out something he could use as a weapon if he had to protect himself. It was taking too long. The dark thing was blocking the light, getting closer. Kit strained as hard as he could to get his hand into his pocket, but there was no time, and the dark object got closer, flailing its way toward him. Kit felt around in his mind for one other spell he'd used occasionally when he had to. Not one that he liked to use, but when it came to the choice between surviving and going down without a fight...

The dark shape blotted out the light, leaving it visible only as a faint halo around whatever was coming. Kit said the first half of the spell in his mind and then waited. He wasn't going to use it unless he absolutely had to, for killing was not something a wizard did unless there was no choice.

The dark shape was closer. Kit felt the spell lying ready in his mind, turning and burning and wanting to get out and do what it had been built for. *But not yet,* Kit thought, setting his teeth. *Not just yet. I want to see*—

The black shape was right in front of him now. It launched itself at him. Kit got ready to think the last word of the spell—

—and the dark thing hit him chest high, and started washing his face as it knocked him over backward.

The two of them came down hard together on blacktop. Suddenly everything seemed bright as day in the single light of the streetlight down at the end of the side street. There Kit lay in the road, with a bump that was going to be about the size of a phoenix's egg starting to form on the back of his head, and on top of him Ponch washed his face frantically, saying, "Did you see it? Did you see what I found? Did you? Did you?"

Kit didn't do anything at first but grab his dog and hug him, thinking, *Oh, God, I almost blew him up; thank you for not letting me blow him up!* Then he sat up, looking around him, and pushed Ponch off with difficulty. "Uh, yeah," he said, "I think so ... But why are you all wet?"

"It was wet there."

"Not where *I* was," Kit said. "But am I glad you

came along when you did. Come on, let's get out of the street before someone sees us." Fortunately this was a quiet part of town, without much traffic in the evening, and the two of them had the additional protection that most people didn't recognize wizardry even when it happened right in front of them. Any onlooker would most likely just have seen a kid and his dog suddenly fall over in the middle of the street, where they'd probably been playing, unseen, a moment before.

Kit got up and brushed himself off, feeling weird to be able to move. "Home now?" said Ponch, bouncing around him.

"You better believe it," Kit said, and they started to walk back down the street.

"I'm hungry!"

"We'll see about something for you when we get in."

"Dog biscuits!" Ponch barked, and raced down the street.

Kit went after him. When he came in the back door, his father was just taking the spaghetti pot over to the sink to drain it. "Perfect timing," he said.

Kit looked in astonishment at the beat-up kitchen wall clock. It was only fifteen minutes since he'd left.

His father looked at him strangely. "Are you all right? You look like you've seen a ghost."

Kit shook his head. "Uh...I'm okay. I'll explain later. Leave mine in the pot for me for a few minutes, will you, Pop?" He headed into the living room and sat down by the phone.

That was when the shakes hit him. He just sat there and let it happen—not that he had much choice—and meanwhile enjoyed the wonderful normality of the living room: the slightly tacky lamps his mother refused to get rid of, the fact that the rug needed to be vacuumed. At least there *was* a rug, and a floor it was nailed to—not that terrifying empty nothingness under his feet. Finally Kit composed himself enough to pick up the phone and dial a local number.

After a few rings someone picked up. A voice said, "Tom Swale."

"Tom, it's Kit."

"Hey there, fella, long time no hear. What's up?"

"Tom—" Kit paused, not exactly sure how to start this. "I need to ask you something about your dogs."

"Oh no," Tom said, sounding concerned. "What have they done now?"

"Nothing," Kit said. "And I want to know how they do it."

There was a pause. "Can we start this conversation again?" Tom said. "Because you lost me somewhere. Like at the beginning."

"Uh, right. Annie and Monty—"

"You're saying they *didn't* do anything?"

"Not that I know of."

"Okay. This conversation now makes sense to Sherlock Holmes, if no one else. Keep working on *me*, though."

Kit laughed. "Okay. Tom, your dogs are always turning up in your backyard with...you know. Weird things."

"Including you, once, as I recall."

"Hey, don't get cute," Kit said.

He was then immediately mortified by the tone he had taken with his Senior wizard, a genuinely nice man who had a lot to do in both his jobs and didn't need thirteen-year-olds sassing him. But Tom simply burst out laughing. "Okay, I deserved that. Are you asking me how they do it?"

"Yeah."

"Then it's my reluctant duty to tell you that I'm not sure. Wizards' pets tend to get strange. You know that."

"But do they always?"

"Well, except for our macaw—who was strange to start with and who then turned out to be one of the Powers That Be in a bird suit—yes, mostly they do."

"Are there any theories about why?"

"Loads. The most popular one is that wizards bend the shape of certain aspects of space-time awry around them, so that we're sort of the local equivalent of gravity lenses...and creatures associated with us for long periods tend to acquire some wizardly qualities themselves. Is this helping you?"

There was a lot of barking going on in the background. "I think so."

"Good, because as you can probably hear, the non-weird part of our local canines' lifestyle has kicked in with a vengeance, and they say they want their dinners. But they can wait a few minutes. As far as wizards' dogs are concerned, the development of 'finding' behaviors seems to be relatively common. It may be an outgrowth of the retrieving or herding behaviors that some dogs have had bred into them. Does Ponch have any Labrador in him?"

"Uh, there might be some in there." This had been a topic of idle discussion around Kit's house for a long time, his father mostly referring to Ponch, when the subject came up, as "the Grab Bag." "But he's mostly Border collie. Some German shepherd, too."

"Sounds about right."

"But Tom—" Kit was wondering how to phrase this. "That the dogs might be able to find things, that I can understand. But how can they find *places*? Because Ponch has started finding them."

There was quite a long pause. "That could be interesting," Tom said. "Has he taken you to any of these places?"

"Just once. Just now."

"Are you all right?"

"Now I am. I think," Kit said, starting to shake again.

"You sure?"

"Yeah," Kit said. "It's all right. It was just...nothing. No sound, no light or movement. But Ponch got in there, and he knew how to get out again. He got *me* out, in fact, because I couldn't do much of anything."

"That's interesting," Tom said. "Would you consider going there again?"

"Not right now!" Kit said. "But later on, yeah. I want to find out where that was! And how it happened."

"Well, pack animals do prefer to work in groups. From Ponch's point of view, you two probably constitute a small pack, and maybe that's why he's able to share his new talent with you. But until now, to the best of my knowledge, no wizard's found out exactly where the dogs go to get the things they bring back, because no one's been able to go along. If you really want to follow up on this—"

"Yeah, I do."

"Then be careful. You should treat this as an unstable worldgating; you may not be able to get back the same way you left. Better check the manual for a tracing-and-homing spell to keep in place. And make sure you take enough air along. Even though Ponch seems unaffected after short jaunts, there's no guaranteeing that the two of you will stay that way if you linger."

"Okay. Thanks."

"One other thing. I'd confine the wizardry to just the two of you."

Kit was silent for a moment. Then he said, "You're saying that I should leave Nita out of this…"

Tom paused, too. "Well, it's possible that the only one who's going to be safe with Ponch as you start investigating this will be you. The semisymbiotic relationship might be what got you out of your bad situation last time. You don't want to endanger anyone else until you're sure what's going on."

"Yeah, I guess so."

"But there's something else," Tom said. "I just had a look at the manual. Nita's assignment status has changed. It says, 'independent assignment, indeterminate period, subject confidential.' You know what that's about?"

"I have an idea," Kit said, though he was uncertain.

"It sounds like she's chasing down something of her

own," Tom said. "Usually when there's a formal status change like that, it's unwise to interrupt the other person unless you need their help on something critical to an ongoing project."

"Uh, yeah," Kit said. *Now, how much does he know?* "We just wound up a project, so nothing's going on." He felt guilty at the way he'd put that—but there were lots of things that "we" could mean.

"Okay. I saw the précis on that last one, though. Nice work; we'll see how it holds up. But as regards Ponch, let me know when you find something out. The manual will want an annotation from you on the subject, though it'll 'trap' the raw data as you go. And if you find anything in Ponch's behavior that has to do with more-normal worldgating, tell the gating team in New York—though the fact that a dog's involved is probably going to make them laugh, if it doesn't actually ruffle their fur…"

"So to speak. Okay, Tom. Thanks!"

"Right. Best to Nita." And Tom hung up, to the sound of more impatient barking.

Ouch, Kit thought. The last few words made him hurt inside.

But he took a moment to get over it, then got up and went back into the kitchen to see about some spaghetti.

Friday Night

AFTER DINNER KIT WENT upstairs to his bedroom, pausing by the door to Carmela's room, at the sound of a faint hissing noise coming from inside. He knocked on the door.

"Come in!" his sister shouted.

Slightly surprised, Kit stuck his head in the door. His sister was lying on her bed, on her stomach, and the source of the hissing was the earphones she was wearing. On the TV, it looked as if a young boy in a down vest and baseball cap was being electrocuted by a long-tailed yellow teddy bear. "Oh," Kit said, now understanding why Carmela had shouted.

"What?" His sister pulled one of the earphones out.

"Nothing," Kit said. "I heard something going 'sssssssss' in here. Thought maybe it was your brains escaping."

His sister rolled her eyes.

"Isn't that kind of stuff a little below your age group?" Kit said.

Carmela ostentatiously put the earphone back in. "Not when you're using it to learn Japanese. Now go away."

Kit closed her door and, for once, did what she told him. Carmela was no more of a nuisance to Kit than she had to be at her age. She had even taken his wizardry pretty calmly, for an otherwise excitable fifteen-year-old, when Kit had told the family about it. After the shock wore off, "I always *knew* you were weird" had been Carmela's main response. Still, Kit kept an eye on her, and always put his manual away where she wouldn't find it; the thought of her turning into an older version of Dairine terrified him. *Still, wizardry finds its way. If it's gonna happen, there's no way I can stop it.* His older sister, Helena, seemed safe from this fate, being too old for even late-onset wizardry. She had just left for her first year of college at Amherst, apparently relieved to get out of what she described as "a genuine madhouse." Kit loved her dearly but was also slightly (and guiltily) relieved to be seeing less of her, for she was the only member of the family who seemed to be trying to pretend that Kit's wizardry had never really happened. *Maybe she'll sort it out over the next year or so.*

Meantime, I have other problems....

He pushed his door open and looked around at his room. It was a welter of bookshelves; the usual messy bed; a worktable, where he made models; the desk, where his ancient computer sat; and some rock posters, including one from a hilariously overcostumed and overmade-up metal group, which had been a present from Helena when she cleared out her room—"a souvenir," she'd said, "of a journey into the hopelessly retro."

Kit tossed his jacket onto the bed and plopped down into the desk chair, where he put out his hand and whistled for his manual. It dropped into his hand from the little pouch of otherspace where he kept it. Kit pushed the PC's keyboard to one side and opened the manual.

First he turned to the back page, the messaging area. There was nothing there, but he'd known there wouldn't be; he hadn't felt the "fizz" of notification when he picked up the manual. Then Kit paged backward to the active wizards' listing for the New York area. Yes, there it was, between CAILLEBERT, ARMINA, and CALLANIN, EOIN:

> CALLAHAN, Juanita L.
> 243 E. Clinton Avenue
> Hempstead, NY 11575
> (516) 555-6786
> power rating: 6.08 +/−.5
> status: conditional active
> independent assignment / research:
>   subject classification withheld
> period: indeterminate

Apparently the Powers had something planned for her...or were maybe just cutting her some slack. *Sounds like she can use it, too,* Kit thought, feeling brief irritation again at the memory of the afternoon. *Well, okay.*

He paused and then flipped back to a spot a few pages after Nita's listing, running his finger down one column. There it was: RODRIGUEZ, CHRISTOPHER R. Address, phone number, power rating, status, last assignment, blah, blah, blah....But there was something else after his listing.

Notes: adjunct talent in training

Kit sat back. *Now what the heck does* that *mean?*

He heard thumping on the stairs down the hall and glanced up in time to see Ponch hit his door, push it open, and wander in, waving his tail. The dog turned around a few times in the middle of the floor, then lay down with a thump.

Kit looked at him thoughtfully. Ponch banged his tail on the floor a few times, then yawned.

"You tired, big guy?" Kit said, and then yawned as well. "Guess I am, too."

"It's like chasing squirrels when I do what we did," Ponch said. "I want to sleep afterward."

"I understand that, all right," Kit said. "Got a little while to talk?"

"Okay."

"Good boy. Ponch, just where exactly were we?"

"I don't know."

"But that wasn't the first time you did that, was it?"

"Uh..." Ponch looked as if he thought he was about to confess to something that would get him in trouble.

"It's okay," Kit said, "I'm not mad. How long have you been doing that?"

"You went away," Ponch said. "I went looking for you."

Kit sighed. When Nita had been in Ireland over the summer, he'd "beamed over" there several times to help her out. Once or twice he'd been there long enough to get a mild case of gatelag, and he remembered Ponch's ecstatic and relieved greetings when he came back. "So...when? End of July, beginning of August?"

"I guess. Right after you went the first time."

"Okay. But where *did* you go? Since you didn't find me."

"I tried, I really tried!" Ponch whimpered. "I missed you. You were gone too much."

"It's okay; I'm not mad that you didn't find me! It was just an observation."

"Oh." Ponch licked his nose in relief.

"So where did you go?"

"It was dark."

"You're right there," Kit said. "The same place we were together?"

"We weren't there together all the time," Ponch said. "You're not there until you *do* something."

Kit wasn't terribly clear about what Ponch meant. He was tempted to push for more information, but Ponch yawned at him again. "Can we go there another time?"

"Sure." Ponch put his head down on his paws. "Whenever you want. Can I go to sleep now?"

"Yeah, go ahead," Kit said. "I wish *I* could."

Shortly, Ponch had rolled over on his side and was

emitting the tiny little snore that always sounded so funny coming from such a big dog. Kit stood up, yawning again. He couldn't put off the reaction to the evening's wizardry much longer, but first he wanted to look into a couple of things. Fortunately, tomorrow was Saturday, and he could sleep late. Kit sat down again, opened the manual once more, and soon found the section he wanted. *Tracking and location protocols…isodimensional…exodimensional…*

Kit found a pen and a pad and started making notes.

The mall was crowded that evening, but not so much so that Nita and her mother had any trouble getting their shopping done. The clothes came first, for Nita's mother was concerned that Nita didn't have anything decent to wear to school; and privately Nita agreed with her. At the first shop they went into, though, some differences emerged between their definitions of *decent.*

Nita's mom walked among the racks, shaking her head and trying to avoid looking at the two tops and three skirts Nita was carrying. "They're all so expensive," her mother said under her breath. "And they're not terribly well made, either. Such a rip-off…"

Nita knew this wasn't the problem. She trailed along behind, not saying anything. As she finished looking at the racks, her mother stopped and looked at Nita. "Honey, tell me the truth. Are the other girls really wearing stuff like this?" From the nearest rack, she picked up a black skirt identical to one of the ones Nita was carrying, holding it up with a critical expression.

"Stuff exactly like this, Mom. Some of them are shorter. This one's a little conservative." *Because I chickened out on the really short one.*

"And the principal hasn't been sending people home for wearing skirts this short? *Really?*"

"Really."

"You wouldn't be bending the truth in the service of fashion, here?"

Nita had to laugh at that. "If I was gonna lie to you about anything, Mom, don't you think I would have done it when it was about much bigger stuff? Great white sharks? Saving the world?" And she grinned.

"I begin to wonder," her mom said, putting the skirt back on the rack, "exactly how much you *aren't* telling me that I ought to know about."

"Tons of things," Nita said. "Where should I start? Did I tell you about the dinosaurs in Central Park?"

Her mother looked over her shoulder with one of those expressions that suggested she wasn't sure whether Nita was joking. But the expression shaded into one that meant her mom had realized this *wasn't* a joke and she didn't like the idea. "Is this something recent?"

"Uh, kind of. Except we made it so it never happened, and maybe *recent* isn't the right word."

Nita's mother frowned, perplexed. Nita ignored this; the translation of what she'd said was bothering her. "Potentially recent?" Nita said, to see how the substitution sounded. Unfortunately English lacked the right kind of verb tenses to describe a problem that could be easily expressed in the Speech. "No, it can't happen anymore, I don't think. At least, not that time, it can't. *Formerly* recent?"

"Stop now," Nita's mother said, "before this takes you, me, and the dinosaurs many places that none of us wants to go, and let's get back to the skirt." She picked it up again. "Honey, your poor old mom tries hard not to live entirely in the last century, but this thing's hardly more than a wide belt."

"Mom, remember when you trusted me about the shark?"

"Yeeees...," her mother said, sounding dubious.

"So trust me about the skirt!"

Her mother gave her a cockeyed look. "It's not the sharks I'm worried about," she said. "It's the wolves."

"Mom, I promise you, none of the 'wolves' are going to touch me. I just want to look *normal.* If I can't *be* normal, let me at least simulate the effect!"

Her mother looked at her with mild surprise. "You're not having problems at school, are you?"

"No, I'm fine."

"The homework—"

"It's no big deal. There's more than there used to be, but so far I'm not overloaded."

"You *are* having problems, though."

"Mom—" Nita sighed. "Nobody beats me up anymore, if that's what you're worried about. They can't. But a lot of the kids still think I'm some kind of nerd princess." She grimaced. Once Nita had thought that when she got into junior high, reading would be seen as normal behavior for someone her age. She was still waiting for this idea to occur to some of her classmates. "It's nothing wizardry will cure. Just believe me when I tell you that dressing in style will help me blend in a little. I know I didn't care much about clothes in grade school, but now it's more of an issue. As for the length, if you're worried that moral rot will set in, I'll promise to let you know if I see any early warning signs."

Her mother smiled slightly. "Okay," she said, put back the skirt she'd been holding, and reached out to take the one Nita was carrying. "Moral rot hasn't been much of a problem with you. So this is an experiment. But if I hear anything from your principal, I'm going to make you wear flour sacks down to your ankles until you graduate. You and the dinosaurs better make a note."

"Noted, Mom," Nita said. "Thanks." She went off to put the other two skirts back where she'd found them. *This one's a start. She'll soften up in a couple of weeks, and we can come back for the other ones.*

They went to the cash register and paid for the skirt. Then Nita's mom drove them to the supermarket, and as they tooled up and down the aisles with the cart, Nita began to feel normal, almost against her will. But then, while standing there with a bottle of mouthwash in her hand and working out if it was a better bargain than other bottles nearby, Nita's mother suddenly turned to her and said, "What *kind* of dinosaurs?"

Boy, Nita thought, *maybe it's a good thing I didn't mention the giant squid!*

When Nita and her mom got home, Nita and Dairine helped put away the groceries (and Nita helped her mom keep Dairine out of them); so it was half an hour before she could get up to her room and fish out her manual. As she picked it up, she felt a faint fizz about the covers, a silent notification that there was a message waiting for her. Hurriedly she flipped it open to the back page. At the top of the page was Kit's name and his manual reference. In the middle of the page were the words: *If you need some time by yourself, feel free.*

Just that. No annotation, no explanation. Nita flushed hot and cold, then hot again.

Why, that little— He wouldn't even pick up the *phone and call me!*

Or else he's really, really mad, and he doesn't trust himself to talk to me.

Or maybe he just doesn't feel like it.

Nita felt an immediate twinge of guilt…and then stomped on it. *Why should I feel guilty when* he's *the one who's screwing up? And then can't take the heat when someone tries to straighten him out about it?*

Time by myself? Fine.

"Fine," she said to the manual.

Send reply?

"Yeah, send it," Nita said.

Her reply spelled itself out in the Speech on the page, added a time stamp, and archived itself. *Sent.*

Nita shut the manual and chucked it onto her desk, feeling a second's worth of annoyed satisfaction…followed immediately by unease. She didn't like the feeling. Sighing, Nita got up and wandered back out to the dining room.

Now that the groceries were gone, computer-printed pages were spread all over the dining-room table. While Nita looked at them, her mother came in from the driveway with a couple more folders' worth of paperwork, dropping them on top of one pile. "Stuff from the flower shop?" Nita said, going to the fridge to get herself a Coke.

"Yup," her mother said. "It's put-Daddy's-incredibly-messed-up-accounts-into-the-computer night."

Nita smiled and sat down at the table. Her father was no mathematician, which probably explained why he pushed her so hard about her math homework. Her mom went into the kitchen, poured herself a cup of tea, and put it into the microwave. "You should make *him* do this," Nita said, idly paging through the incomprehensible papers, a welter of faxes and invoices and Interflora order logs and many, many illegible, scribbly notes.

"I've tried, honey. The last time he did the accounts, it took me a year to get them straightened out. Never again." The microwave dinged; her mother retrieved the cup, added sugar, and came back in to sit at the end of the table, sipping the tea. "Besides, I don't like to nag your dad. He works hard enough...Why should I make it hard for him when he comes home, too?"

Nita nodded. This was why she didn't mind spending a lot of time at home; with the possible exception of Kit, she seemed to be the only person she knew who *had* an enjoyable home life. Half the kids in school seemed to be worrying that their parents were about to divorce, but Nita had never even heard her parents raise their voices to each other. She knew they fought—they would vanish into their bedroom, sometimes, when things got tense—but there was no yelling or screaming. That suited Nita entirely. It was possibly also the reason her present fight with Kit was making her so twitchy.

Her mother paged through the paperwork and came up with a bunch of paper-clipped spreadsheet print-outs. "Though privately," she muttered as she took the papers apart and started sorting them by month, "there are times I wish I'd never given up ballet. Sure, you get sprains and strains and pulled muscles, and your feet stop looking like anything that ought to be at the end of a human leg, but at least there was never much eye-strain." She smiled slightly. "But if I ever went back to that, there would be all those egos to deal with again. 'Creative differences'... that being code for everybody shouting at one another all day." She shook her head. "This is better. Now where did the pen go?"

Nita fished it out from under the papers and handed it over. Her mother started writing the names of months on top of the spreadsheets. "How many days in May, honey?"

"Thirty-one." Nita started looking around under the papers and came up with another pen. "Mom..."

"Hmm?"

"If you had a fight with somebody... and they were incredibly wrong, and you were right... what would you do?"

"Apologize immediately," her mother said.

Nita looked at her in astonishment.

"If they mattered to me at all, anyway," her mother said, glancing up as she put one page aside. "That's what I always do with your dad. Particularly if circumstances have recently proved me to be correct."

"Uh…," Nita said, seriously confused.

Her mom labeled another page and turned it over. "Works for me," she said. "I mean, really, honey…" She glanced at the next page, turned it over, too. "Unless it's about a life-and-death issue, why make a point of being right? Of getting all righteous about it? All it does is make people less likely to listen to you. Even more so if they're close to you."

Nita gave her mother a sidelong look. "But, Mom, if it really *is* a life-or-death issue—"

"Sweetie, at your age, a lot of things look like life-and-death. Don't get that look; I'm not patronizing you," her mother added. "Or what you do—I know it's been terribly important sometimes. But think of the problem as a graph, where you plot the intensity of experience against total time. You've had less total time to work with than, say, your dad or I have. Things look a lot more important when the 'spreadsheet' is only a page long instead of four or five."

Nita considered that to see if it made sense. To her annoyance, it did. "I *hate* it when you sneak up on me by being objective," she said.

Her mother produced a weary smile. "I'll take that as a compliment. But it's accidental, honey. It'll take me days to get this sorted out, and right now my whole life is beginning to look like a grid. I don't see why yours shouldn't, too."

Nita smiled and put her head down on her arms. "Okay. But, Mom…what do you do if you find out that you're *wrong*?"

"Same thing," her mother said. "Apologize immediately. Why change a tactic that works?"

"Because it makes you look like a wimp."

Her mother glanced up from the papers again, raising her eyebrows. "Excuse me, I must have missed something. It's *not* right to apologize when you're wrong?"

Nita saw immediately why Dairine refused to play chess with their mother anymore. She was cornered. "Thanks, Mom," she said, and got up.

Her mother let out a long breath. "Nothing worthwhile is easy, honey," she said, and looked down ruefully at the papers, rubbing her eyes. "This, either. Come to think of it, I could probably use an aspirin about now." And she got up and went to get one.

Nita was starting to feel like she could use one herself. *She's probably right.*

And something's got to be done. The water situation out there isn't going to just fix itself—

But what am I supposed to do? I can't work with Kit when I'm pissed off at him! It's going to have to wait. The Powers That Be understand that wizards need room to be human, too.

But even as she thought it, Nita felt guilty. A wizard knew that the energy had been running slowly out of the universe for millennia. Viewed in that context, no delay was worthwhile. Every quantum of energy lost potentially could have been used to make some fragment of the cosmos work better. A relationship, for example...

Nita got up and wandered back to her room, thinking about what she might do to make herself useful, besides the project she and Kit and S'reee had been working on in the bay. It wasn't as if there weren't projects she'd been interested in that Kit hadn't been enthusiastic about. This would be a good time to start one of those.

Yet as Nita shut the door of her room, Dairine's point came back to her. *Is it possible that Kit and I really* do *still have unfinished business about Ronan?* Before, Nita wouldn't have thought it likely. Now she wondered. Dairine could be cunning and sly, and a pain in the butt... but she was also a wizard. She wouldn't lie.

But why wouldn't Kit have told me?

Unless he thought the idea was stupid. Or unless he really didn't think it was a problem.

She sat down at the desk and put her feet up on it, and picked up the manual, hoping to feel that fizz... but there was nothing. Nita dropped it in her lap and stared at the dark window. *I was stupid with him,* she thought. *But he wasn't being terribly open-minded, either. Or real tactful.*

She opened the manual idly. Life had changed so much since she'd found it; it now seemed as if she'd had the manual within reach all her life—or all the life that mattered. In some ways it seemed to Nita as if all her childhood had simply been an exercise in marking time, waiting for the moment when this book would snag her hand as she trailed it idly down a shelf full of books in the children's library. It was always handy now, either in her book bag or tucked away in her personal claudication. A couple years' use had taught Nita that the manual wasn't the infallibly omniscient resource she'd taken it for at the beginning. It *did* contain everything you needed to know to do your work... but it left deciding what the work *was* to you. You might make mistakes, but they were yours. The manual made it all possible, though. It was compendium, lifeline, communications device, encyclopedia, weapon, and silent adviser all rolled into one. Nita couldn't imagine what wizardry would be like without it.

And there was something else associated with wizardry that she couldn't imagine being without, either.

She riffled through the pages, let her hand drop. The manual fell open at a spot near its beginning, and as Nita looked down, she wondered why she should even be surprised that she found herself looking at this particular page.

In Life's name, and for Life's sake, I assert that I will employ the Art, which is Its gift, in Life's service alone, rejecting all other usages. I will guard growth and ease pain. I will fight to preserve what grows and lives well in its own way; I will not change any creature unless its growth and life, or that of the system of which it is part, are threatened or threaten another. To these ends, in the practice of my Art, I will ever put aside fear for courage, and death for life, when it is right to do so—looking always toward the Heart of Time, where all our sundered times are one, and all our myriad worlds lie whole, in That from Which they proceeded....

She let out a long unhappy breath as she gazed at the words. *I will ease pain....*

Nita had made her share of mistakes during her practice, but if there was one thing she prided herself on, it was taking the Oath seriously. *But lately maybe I haven't been doing a very good job. On the large things, yeah. But have they been blocking my view of the small ones?*

And what makes me think that being friends with Kit is something small?

Nita closed the book, put it down on the desk, and pushed it away. *It's too late tonight. Tomorrow. I'll go over and see him tomorrow...and we'll see what happens.*

Saturday Morning
and Afternoon

SLEEPING IN TURNED OUT to be an idle fantasy. Kit rolled over just after dawn, feeling muzzy and wondering what had managed to jolt him out of a peculiar dream, when suddenly he realized what it was. A cold wet nose had been stuck into his ear.

"Ohh, *Ponch...*" Kit rolled over and tried to hide his head under the pillow. This was a futile gesture. The nose followed him, and then the tongue.

Finally he had no choice but to get up. Kit sat up in bed, rubbing his eyes, while Ponch jumped up and washed the back of Kit's neck as if he hadn't a worry in the world. Kit, for his own part, ached as if someone had run him over lightly with a truck, but this was a normal side effect of doing a large, complex wizardry; it would pass.

"Awright, awright," Kit muttered, trying to push Ponch away. He glanced at the clock on his dresser—*Ten after six?!... What have I done to deserve this?*—and then looked over at the desk. His manual sat where he had left it, last thing. Closing it, finally getting ready to turn in, he had felt the covers fizz, had opened the book to the back page, and had seen Nita's response.

Fine.

He got up, went over to the desk, and opened the manual again. Nothing had been added since. Nita was plainly too pissed off even to yell at him. But Tom had been pretty definite about letting her be if she was working on some other piece of business. *Okay. Let her get on with it.*

He shut the manual and went to root around in his dresser for jeans and a polo shirt. Ponch was jumping for joy around him, his tongue lolling out and making him look unusually idiotic. "What're *you* so excited about?" Kit asked in the Speech.

"Out, we're gonna go out, aren't we?" Ponch said in a string of muffled woofs and whines. "We're gonna go *there* again, you can go with me, this is great, let's go out!" And Ponch abruptly sat down and licked his chops. "I'm hungry," he said.

There..., Kit thought, and shuddered. But now that the experience was half a day behind him, he was feeling a little less freaked out by it, and more curious about what had happened.

He put his head out his bedroom door. It was quiet; nobody in his house got up this early on a Saturday, unless it was his dad, who was an occasional surf-casting nut and would sometimes head out before dawn to fish the flood tide down at Point Lookout. No sign of that happening today, though.

"Okay," he said to Ponch. "You can have your breakfast, and then I want a shower...and then we'll go out. After I take care of something."

Ponch spun several times in a tight circle and then launched himself out into the hall and down the stairs.

Kit went after him, fed him, and then went back upstairs to take a shower and make his plans. When he came downstairs, Ponch was waiting at the side door to be let out.

"In a minute," Kit said. "Don't *I* get something to eat, too?"

"Oh."

"Yeah, 'oh.' You big wacko." Kit grabbed a quart of milk out of the fridge and drank about half of it, then opened one of the nearby cupboards and found a couple of the awful muesli-based breakfast bars that his sister liked. He stuck them in his pocket and then went to the write-on bulletin board stuck to the front of the fridge. The pen, as usual, wasn't in the clip where it belonged; Kit found it behind the sink. On the board he wrote: GONE OUT ON BUSINESS, BACK LATER. This was code, which Kit's family now understood. To Ponch he said, "You go do what you have to first...I have something to get ready."

Kit let the dog out and locked the door behind them. Then he and Ponch went out into the backyard. It wasn't nearly as tidy or decorative as Nita's. Kit's father wasn't concerned about it except as somewhere to sit outside on weekends, and so while the lawn got mowed regularly, the back of the yard was a jungle of sassafras saplings and blackberry bushes. Into this little underbrush forest Ponch vanished while Kit sat down on a creaking old wooden lounger and opened his manual.

He knew in a general way what he wanted—a spell that would keep him connected to Ponch in mind, letting him share the dog's perceptions. It also needed to be something that would keep them within a few yards of each other, so that if physical contact became important, Kit could have it in a hurry. He paged through the manual, looking for one particular section and finding it: *Bindings, ligations, and cinctures*—wizardries that dealt with holding energy or matter in place, in check, or in alignment with something else. *Simplex, multiplex... Here's one. First-degree complex aelysis... proof strength in m-dynes... to the minus four...* The original formula for the spell, Kit saw, had called for fish's breath, women's beards, and various other hard-to-find ingredients. But over many years the formula had been refined so that all you needed to build it now were knowledge, intention, a basic understanding of paraphysics, and the right words in the Speech.

Yeah, this is what I need. "All right," Kit said softly in the Speech. "This is a beta-class short-term interlocution." He pronounced the first few sentences, and the spell started to build itself in the air in front of him—a twining and growing chain of light, word linking to word in a structure like a chain of DNA, but with three main strands instead of two.

After a couple of minutes he was finished and the structure nearly complete. Kit plucked it out of the air, tested it between his hands. It looked faintly golden in the early morning light, and felt at least as strong as a steel chain would, though in his hands it was as light and fine as so much spun silk.

Not bad, Kit thought. But there was still one thing missing. The place down at one end of the spell where his own name and personal information went was now full; Kit had pasted it in from the wizardry he and S'reee had just done. But as for Ponch...

It embarrassed him to have to turn to his dog, who'd now returned from the bushes and was sitting and watching Kit with great interest. "Ponch," he said, "I can't believe I've never asked you this before. But what's your name?"

The dog laughed at him. "You just said it."

"But Grrarhah down the street uses a Cyene name."

"If the people you lived with named *you* Tinker-bell," Ponch said in a surprisingly dry voice, "so would *you.*"

Kit had to grin at that. "I don't mind the name you gave me," Ponch said. "I use that. It says who I am." He stuck his nose in Kit's ear again and started to wash it.

"Euuuu, Ponch!" Kit pushed him away... but not very hard.

"Okay, look, give it a rest," Kit said. "I have to finish something here."

"Let me see."

Kit showed him the wizardry. As Ponch watched, Kit pronounced the fifteen or sixteen syllables of the Speech that wound themselves into the visible version of Ponch's name, containing details like his age and his breed (itself a tightly braided set of links with about ten strands involved). Ponch nosed at the leash; it came alive with light as he did so. "There's the collar," Kit said, looping the end of the spell through the wizard's knot he had tied there, then holding the wide loop up. The similar loop at the other end, made up of Kit's name and personal information, would go around his wrist.

Ponch slipped his head through the wider of the two loops, then shook himself. The loop tightened down.

"That feel okay?" Kit said. "Not too tight?"

"It's fine. Let's go."

"Okay," Kit said, and stood up. He slipped his wrist through the other loop and pronounced the six words that got the environmental and tracking functions of the wizardry going, the parts that would snap them back here if anything life threatening happened. The "chain" flickered, showing that the added functions were working. "Right. Show me how."

"Like this—"

Ponch took no more than a step forward, and without a moment's hesitation that darkness slammed silently down around them again. This time at least Kit was sure he had air around him and Ponch, and he had oxygenation routines ready to kick in if their bodies were affected by any kind of paralysis. Nonetheless, Kit still couldn't move, couldn't see anything.

Or could he?

Kit would have blinked if he could have, or squinted. Often enough before, in very dark places, he'd had the illusion that he could see a very faint light when there was actually nothing there. This was like that—yet somehow different, not as diffuse. He could just make out a tiny glint of light, far away there in the dark, distant as a star....

It faded. Or maybe it wasn't truly there at all. *Oh well.*

Ponch?

Here I am.

And abruptly Kit really could see something, though he still couldn't move. Down just out of range of his direct vision, though still perceptible as a dim glow, he could tell that the "leash" was there, the long chain structure of the wizardry glinting with life as the power ran up and down it. It was unusual to be able to see it doing that, instead of as a steady glow; there was something odd about the flow of time here. Maybe that was the cause of the illusion of breathlessness.

Kit tried to speak out loud but again found that he couldn't. It didn't matter; the leash wizardry would carry his thoughts to Ponch. *What do we do now?* Kit said silently.

Be somewhere.

Kit normally would have thought that that was unavoidable. Now he wasn't so sure. *Well, where did you have in mind?*

Here.

And something appeared before them. It was hard to make out the distance at first, until Kit saw what the thing was: a small shape, pale gray against that darkness, except for a whiter underbelly.

It was a squirrel.

This was so peculiar that even if he hadn't been

frozen in place, Kit still wouldn't have done much but stand and stare. There it was, just a squirrel, sitting up on its hind legs and looking at them with that expression of interest-but-not-fear you get from a squirrel that knows you can't possibly get near it in time to do anything about it.

Okay, Kit said in his mind, completely confused. *Now what?*

Shhh.

The instruction amused Kit. He wasn't exactly used to his dog telling him what to do. But suddenly, a little farther away, there was another squirrel, rooting around in the grass, looking for something: a nut, Kit supposed.

And another squirrel…and then another. They were all doing different things, but each of them existed absolutely by itself, as if spotlighted on a dark stage. Next to him, Ponch shifted from foot to foot, whimpering in growing excitement.

There were more squirrels every moment…ten of them, twenty, fifty. But then something else started to happen. Not only squirrels, but other things began to appear. Trees, at first. *I guess that makes sense; where there are squirrels, there are always trees.* They were unusually broad of trunk, astonishingly tall, with tremendous canopies of leaves. And slowly, underneath them, grass began to roll out and away into what built itself into a genuine landscape—grass patched with sunlight, wavering with the shadows of branches. The sky, where it could be seen, came last, the usual creamy blue sky of a suburban area near a large city, spreading itself gradually up from horizon to zenith, as if a curtain were being lifted. Finally, there was the sun, and Kit felt a breeze begin to blow.

Ponch made a noise halfway between a whine and a bark and leaped forward, dragging Kit out of immobility, as he tore off toward the nearest squirrel. The whole landscape now instantly came alive around them like a live-action version of a cartoon: squirrels running in every direction, and some of them rocketing up the trees, all of them in frantic motion—especially the one that Ponch was chasing as he dragged Kit along. This was an experience Kit had had many, many times before in the local park, and all he could do now was try not to fall flat on his face as he was pulled along at top speed.

Kit laughed, finding that his voice worked again. Briefly he considered just letting Ponch off the spell leash. But then that struck Kit as a bad idea. He still had no sense of where they were, or what the rules of this place were. *Better just tell the spell to extend as far as it needs to, so he can run.*

It took a few seconds to change the loci-of-effect and extensibility variables—longer than it normally would have taken, but then, Kit thought he wasn't doing badly for someone who was being hauled along through a forest at what felt like about thirty miles an hour. Finally Kit was able to extend the leash, then slowed down from the run until he was standing there in the bright sun between two huge trees, watching his dog go tearing off across the beautiful grass, barking his head off with delight.

He's found Squirrel World, Kit thought, and had to

laugh. There was seemingly infinite running room, there was an endless supply of squirrels, and there were trees for the squirrels to run up, because there had to be some challenge about this for it to be fun. *He's found dog heaven. Or maybe Ponch heaven...*

Ponch was far off among the trees now. Kit sat down on the grass to watch him. This space had some strange qualities, for despite the increased distance, Kit's view of Ponch was still as clear and sharp as if he were looking at him through a telescope. Ponch was closing on the squirrel he'd been chasing. As Kit watched, the squirrel just made it to the trunk of a nearby tree and went up it like a shot. Ponch danced briefly around on his hind legs at the bottom of the tree, barking his head off, then spotted another squirrel and went off after that one, instead.

Maybe this isn't exactly Ponch heaven after all, Kit thought. *Could this be the dog version of a computer game?* For there didn't seem to be instant wish fulfillment here. Ponch still wasn't catching the squirrels; he was mostly chasing them.

Kit watched this go on for a while, as his dog galloped around over about fifty acres of perfect parkland, littered with endless intriguing targets. *The question is, where* is *this? Somewhere inside his mind? Or is it an actual place? Though it's a weird one.* Their entry here hadn't been anything like a normal worldgating. Normally you stepped through a gate, whether natural or constructed, and found another place waiting there, complete. Or sometimes, as he'd seen happen in Ireland over the summer, that other place came sweeping over you, briefly pushing aside the one where you'd been standing earlier.

But this was different. *It's as if Ponch was* making *this world, one piece at a time...*

He gazed down at the grass. Every blade was perfect, each slightly different from every other. Kit shook his head in wonder, looked up and saw Ponch still romping across the grass. There was always another squirrel to chase, and Kit noticed with amusement that the ones that weren't being chased were actually following Ponch, though always at a discreet distance. *So he won't be distracted?* When Ponch managed to pursue one closely enough that it actually had to run up a tree, there were always others within range when he was ready for them.

How is he doing *this?* Kit wondered. "Ponch?"

Ponch let off a volley of frustrated barks at the squirrel he was chasing, which had gone halfway up one of the massive tree boles and was now clinging to it head down and chattering at him. Kit couldn't make out specific Skioroin words at this point, but the tone was certainly offensive. Ponch barked at the squirrel more loudly. "Yeah, okay, get over it," Kit yelled. "There are about five thousand more like him out there! Can you give it a rest so we can have a few words, please?"

Ponch came galloping back to Kit a few seconds later. "Isn't it great, do you like it, do you want to chase some, I can make some more for you..."

"Sit down. Your tongue's gonna fall off if it waves around much more than that," Kit said.

Ponch sat down beside him and leaned on Kit in a

companionable manner, looking entirely satisfied with life, and panting energetically.

"Look," Kit said. "How are you doing this?"

"I don't know."

"You must know a little," Kit said. "You told me yesterday, 'You're not there until you do something.' What did you do?"

"I wanted you."

"Yes, but that was the first time."

"That's what I did."

Kit sighed and put his head down on his knees, thinking. "This," he said, "what you did just now. How did you do this? Where did all these squirrels come from?"

"I *want* squirrels."

"Yeah, and boy, have you got them," said Kit, looking around him in amusement. The two of them were completely surrounded by squirrels, an ever growing crowd of them, all sitting up on their little hind legs and staring at Ponch, all intent and quiet... as if someone in a whimsical mood had swapped them for the seagulls in *The Birds*. "Where did they all come from?"

Ponch sat quiet for a moment, and stopped panting as a look of intense concentration came over his face. Then he looked at Kit and said, "I wanted them here."

Suddenly Kit got it. The way Ponch used *wanted* was not the way it would have been used in Cyene; it was the form of the word used in the Speech. And in the wizardly language, the verb was not passive. The closest equivalent in English would be *willed*; in the Speech, the word implies not just desire but creation.

"You *made* them," Kit said.

"I wanted them to be here. And here they are." The dog jumped up and began to bounce for sheer joy. "Isn't it *great*?!"

Kit rubbed his nose and wondered about that. "What happens when you catch them?" he asked, to buy himself time.

"I shake them around a lot," Ponch said, "and then I'm sorry for them."

Kit grinned, for this was more or less the way things went in the real world. But then he paused, surprised. He'd slipped and spoken to Ponch in English, but the dog had understood him.

"Are you able to understand me when I'm *not* using the Speech?" Kit asked.

Ponch looked amused. "Only here. I made it so I would always know what you're saying."

"Wow," Kit said. He looked around him again at the patient squirrels. "Have you made anything else?"

"Lots of things. Why don't you make something?"

"Uh...," Kit said, and stopped. The ramifications of this were beginning to sink in, and he wanted to make some preparations. "Not right this minute. Look, you wanna go see Tom and Carl?"

Ponch began to bounce around again. "Dog biscuits!"

"Yeah, probably they'll give you some. And if they have a spare clue for me to chew on, that wouldn't hurt, either." Kit got up. "You done with these guys?"

"Sure. They wait for me. Even if they didn't, I can always make more."

"Okay. Let's go home."

Ponch acquired a look of concentration. A second later, the landscape went out, as if a light had simply been turned off behind it, and Kit felt a tug on the leash. He followed it—

—and they stepped out again into early morning in Kit's backyard: birdsong, dew, the sound of a single station wagon going down the street in front of the house as the newspaper guy threw the morning paper into people's driveways...

Kit took a deep breath of the morning air and relaxed. From above them came an annoyed chattering noise. Ponch wheeled around and began dancing on his hind legs and barking.

"Didn't you just have enough of those?" Kit said. "Shut up; you're going to wake up the whole neighborhood! Come on...We need to go see Tom."

Nita rolled over in her bed that morning, feeling strangely achy. At first she wondered if she was catching a cold; but it didn't seem to be that. *Probably it's just from being upset,* she thought. *Hey, I wonder...*

She got up and padded over to the desk, where her manual lay. Nita picked it up and flipped to the back page, hoping to see some long angry rant from Kit. But there was nothing.

She broke out in a sweat at the sight of the page with not a thing on it but the previous two communications. *He must be completely furious,* she thought. *This is gonna be awful...and when Dairine hears about it, she's going to laugh herself sick. I'll probably have to kill her.*

Nita put the manual down, pulled open a drawer in her dresser and extracted a clean T-shirt, then pulled it on along with yesterday's jeans and turned back to the desk. *I wonder what he's up to, though. Maybe he's out working on the water with S'reee.*

Nita flipped through to Kit's listing in the directory and glanced at it. *Last project: mesolittoral water-quality intervention, for details see reference MSI-B14-/XIiii/ βγ66384-67/1141-2211/ABX6655/3: other participants, Callahan, Juanita L., hominid / Sol III, S'reee a!hruuni-Aoul-mmeiihnhwiii!r, cetacean / Sol III; intervention status complete / functioning...*

Nita's mouth dropped open.

...anentropia rate 0.047255-E^8; effectiveness rating 3.5 +/- .10; review scheduled Julian date 2451809.5—

Oh, my God. It's working!

The initial reaction of sheer delight at the solution of a problem that had had them all literally running in circles for so long was now drowned by a nearly intolerable wave of combined embarrassment and annoyance.

They got it working without me.

He was right.

I was wrong.

Nita sat there in shock.

I am so stupid!

Yet she couldn't quite bring herself to believe it. And she was still listed as a participant in the spell. Nita paged back to the section where intervention references were kept, and shortly found a copy of the spell diagram that Kit and S'reee had been using.

Nita traced the curves and circles of it, all apparent in an enlarged hologrammatic format when you looked at the page closely. The basic structure of the wizardry was derived broadly from the last pattern she and Kit had worked on together, before they started disagreeing about the details. It was missing any of the extra subroutines she had insisted were absolutely necessary to make the spell work right. The detailed versions of the effectiveness figures were at the bottom of the page, updating themselves as she watched, demonstrating that the water coming out of Jones Inlet was indeed getting cleaner by the second....

Nita sat there in the grip of an attack of complete chagrin. *What an utter dork I've been,* she thought. *I'm going straight over there to apologize. No, I'm not going to wait even that long.*

She flipped back to the messaging pages, touched the message from Kit to wake up the reply function. "Kit?" she said in the Speech. "Can we talk?"

Send?

"Send it," Nita said.

Then she waited. But to her complete astonishment, the page just flashed once, leaving her message sitting where it was. *Message cannot be dispatched at this time. Please try again later.*

What?? "How come?"

The notification blanked out, replaced by the words: *Addressee is not in ambit. Please try again later.*

Nita stared. She had never seen such a description before and didn't have any idea what it meant.

She put the manual down on the desk. "Keep trying," Nita said, and went downstairs. It was quiet; there was no smell of anyone having been making breakfast down there. *I may be the only one up.*

Nita picked up the kitchen phone and dialed Kit's number. It rang a couple of times, then someone picked up. "Hello?"

It was Kit's sister. "Hola, Carmela!"

"'Ola, Nita," said Carmela, in a somewhat odd voice—she had her mouth full. There was a pause while she swallowed. "You missed him; he's not here."

"Where'd he go, do you know?"

"Nope. He left a note on the fridge; must've been early . . . said he was going out to do some wizard thing and he'd be back later."

"Today, you think?"

"Oh yeah, today. If he was gonna be gone longer than tonight, he sure would have told Pop and Mama, and they would've screamed, and I would've heard it."

Nita had to chuckle. "Okay, Mela. If he comes in, tell him I called?"

"Sure, Neets. No problem."

"Thanks. Bye-bye."

"Byeeee . . ."

Nita hung up. *He's out on errantry . . . but where? I should have been able to find him. It shouldn't matter if he was on the Moon, or even halfway out of the galaxy. His manual still would have taken the message. It's not like the manuals care about light speed, or anything like that.*

After a few moments Nita went back upstairs to see what the manual might be showing. The last page still hadn't changed.

I don't believe this, Nita thought. *I ought to call Tom and Carl and see what they say. Where is he that the manual can't find him?!*

She picked up the manual and started to take it downstairs to the phone with her, then stopped. She would have to tell Tom and Carl what had been going on, and she was too embarrassed.

But *where* was Kit?

Down the hall Dairine's door opened, and her sister wandered down toward her in the direction of the bathroom, wearing nothing but a huge Fordham T-shirt of their dad's. She looked at Nita vaguely. "What's for breakfast?"

"Confusion," Nita said, rather sourly.

"What?"

"Nothing yet. Nobody's up. And I can't find Kit."

Dairine stopped and stared at her, pushing the hair out of her eyes and yawning. "Why? Where is he?"

"Somewhere the manual can't find him."

"*What?*"

"Look at this!" Nita was concerned enough to show Dairine her manual, even though it meant she would see the messages above the strange new notification. Dairine looked at the back page and shook her head.

"I've never seen *that* before," she said. "You sure it's not a malfunction or something?"

Nita snorted. "Have you ever seen a manual malfunction?"

"I have to admit," Dairine said slowly, "if I did, I'd get worried...considering What powers them. Come on, let's see if mine's doing the same thing."

Nita followed Dairine to her room and glanced at where the pile of stuff from yesterday had mostly been dumped on the floor. "You'd better take care of this before Mom gets up," Nita said. "She'll have some new and never-before-seen species of cow."

"Plenty of time for that," Dairine said, going over to her desk and knocking one knuckle on the outside of the laptop's case. "She was up till half past forever last night with Dad's stuff."

The laptop sprouted its legs again and stood up on them, stretching them one after another like a centipede that thought it was a cat. "Morning, Spot," Dairine said.

"*Mrng,*" said the laptop in a small scratchy voice.

"Manual functions?"

"*Spcfy.*"

"Messaging," Dairine said.

The laptop popped open its lid, and its screen flickered on, showing the usual apple-without-the-bite logo, then blanking down again. A moment later the operating system herald displayed, a stylized representation of a book open to a small block of text. This was then replaced by a messaging menu, overlaid on a shimmering blue background subtly watermarked with the manual logo. "Main address list," Dairine said. "Test message." The screen blanked. "To Kit Rodriguez. Where are you? Send."

The words displayed themselves on the screen exactly as they had in Nita's manual, blinked out, and then reappeared with a little blue box underneath them in which was written in the Speech, *Error 539426010: Recipient is not in ambit. Please resubmit message later.*

"Huh," Dairine said. "More information."

The blue box enlarged slightly. *No further information available.*

"We'll see about *that*," Dairine muttered. "Thanks, cutie."

"*Yr wlcm*," said the laptop, and sat down on the desk again, stretching out its legs.

"Doesn't waste his words, does he?" Nita said, smiling.

"He's shy," Dairine said, with a wry expression. "You should hear him when we're alone. Let's try this."

She went over to the sleek cube of the new computer and waved a hand over the top of it. The light behind the apple came on. Nita cocked an ear. "Is its fan broken?"

"No, it doesn't have one. There's just some kind of little chimney that convects out the heat, so it doesn't need a fan."

"Or a plug…"

Dairine grinned, and waved over the top of the silvery case again. A second later the monitor, a suitably slick flat-screen model on a Lucite base, appeared to one side of the main processor case. "Mom may have some problems with that," Nita said.

"Oh, it won't do that when I get all the normal software installed and put it out downstairs. Meantime, I don't see why it should have to sit on the desk when there's umpteen billion cubic parsecs of perfectly good otherspace to stick it in."

On the screen appeared a manual herald like the one that had been displaying on the laptop, but this one had a discreet Greek letter β blazoned across the image of the book. Dairine waved once more over the top of the processor case, and the keyboard, also in brushed stainless steel, appeared. "What do you need that for?" Nita asked.

"I type faster than I talk."

"Impossible."

Dairine gave Nita a dirty look and started typing, while Nita looked in interest at the keyboard, the standard North American QWERTY type. "Not much good for the Speech."

Dairine hit the carriage return and shook her head. "Come on, Neets, really." She flicked a finger in the air over the keyboard; the keyboard stretched, and the keys shimmered and reconfigured themselves to display the 418 characters of the Speech. "Eventually we won't need this, but the wireless transparent neuro-translation routines are still in pre-alpha." She looked at Nita with a mischievous expression. "Getting interested finally? I can copy Spot for you and give you his twin, if you like."

"Thanks, but I'll stick with the manual I know."

Dairine shook her head in poorly concealed pity. "Luddite."

"Technodweeb," Nita said. "Call me sentimental. I like books. They don't crash."

"Huh," Dairine said, as the monitor blanked and then brought up a long, long list. Dairine glanced over at Spot. "You wanna pass it that last error?"

A moment later that same little blue screen appeared on the monitor. "Right," Dairine said. She glanced over her shoulder at Nita. "Sometimes the beta shows background information that the normal release version doesn't have in it yet, or doesn't routinely release. Any additional information on this?" she said to the desktop machine.

The blue box was partly overlapped by another one, in a lighter shade of blue. It contained the words:

> For accurate and secure message storage and delivery, manual messaging functions require each party's manual to supply a coordinate based on the intersection between each wizard's personal description in the Speech and his present physical location in a given universe. Message dispatch and storage cannot be achieved when one or both addressees are in transit or experiencing transitory states between universes. Please remessage when the condition no longer obtains.

"Oh, well, I guess that's okay, then," Dairine said in astonishment heavily tinged with irony. She looked at Nita. "Another *universe*? That's normally not a transit you make without permission from seriously high up."

"Yeah," Nita said. She opened her manual again and paged through to where Kit's status report was.

Dairine hit a couple of keys; the monitor changed to show the same view. Under the listing for the water wizardry, Kit's status report said:

Present project: access-routine investigation and stabilization, training assignment with adjunct talent; situation presently in development. Detail reference: in abeyance due to possible Heisenberg-related effects; update expected c. Julian day 2451796.6.

"Adjunct?" Dairine muttered.

The thought went through Nita like a spear: *He's working with someone else!* At first it seemed ridiculous. *But considering how I treated him...why* shouldn't *he want to work with other people? I've brought this on myself. Idiot! Idiot!*

"Whatever else is going on," Dairine said, "the Powers That Be know about it. Look, here's an authorization code. They must have some way of keeping tabs on him if They've even got a projected update time in there. Point six...that's after dinner, I guess. Try again then."

Nita closed her manual, feeling slightly relieved. "Yeah..."

"But Neets, look," Dairine said, "if you're worried, why not just try to shoot him a thought? No matter what the manual's doing, it's not like your brain is broken."

"Unusual sentiment from you," Nita said.

Dairine's smile was slightly sardonic. "So maybe I'm mellowing in my old age," she said. There was more of an edge than usual on the expression, but Nita got the feeling it wasn't directed at her...for a change.

She sat down on the bed, pushing the area rug around with her feet. "Never mind. If he's in another universe, I doubt I've got the range to reach him."

"Probably you're right," Dairine said. "But that's not the reason you're not going to try, is it?"

Nita looked at her sister and found Dairine regarding her with an expression that actually could have been described as *understanding.* "You're afraid you're gonna find that he's shut you out on purpose," Dairine said, "and you couldn't stand it."

Nita didn't say anything. Dairine glanced away, looking at the computer, and hit a key to clear the screen.

"Well...," Nita said at last, "lately it's been harder than usual to hear him thinking, anyway. And he's been having the same trouble with me."

There were things that that could mean for wizards, especially if they'd been working closely together for some time...and Nita knew Dairine understood the implications. "Neets," Dairine said at last, "if you're really that worried, you should take the chance, anyway. It's better than sitting here busting a gut."

"I hate it when you're right," Nita said finally.

"Which is always," Dairine said, "but never mind; I'm used to it by now." She went back to tapping at the keyboard.

Nita let out a long breath and closed her eyes.

Kit?

Nothing.

Kit? Where are you?!

Still nothing. Nita opened her eyes, as upset with herself, now, as with the situation. She must have sounded completely pitiful and helpless, if he'd heard her.

But I don't think he did. And that by itself was

strange. Even when you called someone mind to mind and they refused contact, there was always a sense that they were still *there*. This time there was no such sense. And the manual, as Nita opened it once more to the page she'd marked, and looked at it again, still reported Kit as out there, doing *something....*

"Nothing?" Dairine said.

"Not a refusal," Nita said, trying to keep relief out of her voice. "Just...nothing. Maybe he really is just out of range."

Dairine nodded. "Just have to wait till he gets back, then."

Nita sighed and headed downstairs. As she came into the dining room, she heard someone in the kitchen. Turning the corner, she saw that it was her mother, standing there by the counter and looking bleary as she drank a mug of tea and gazed out the window.

"Mom, you look pooped!" Nita said.

Her mother laughed. "I guess. Even after I went to bed last night I had numbers going around and around in my head...Took me a while to get to sleep. Never mind, I'll have a nap before dinner. Speaking of which, where *has* Kit been the past day or so?"

Nita tried to think of what to say. Her mother glanced at her, glanced away again. "Just so I can keep the leftovers from piling up," her mother said. "I just like to know when I'm supposed to be cooking for five. You think he might be along tonight?"

"I don't know for sure," Nita said. "I'll tell you when I find out."

"Okay. I'm going to the shop later, if you want me." Her mom had another drink of tea, then put the mug aside. "Some paperwork was missing from what your dad gave me yesterday, and I need to go root around in what *he* calls a filing system. Did we miss anything from shopping last night?"

"I think we need more milk."

"I think we need to buy your sister a cow," her mother said, and went off to get dressed.

Nita went up to her room to kill some time until she could reach Kit. It was annoying to be mad at someone, but it was even worse to discover that you were wrong to be mad at them, and worse yet not to be able to apologize to them and get it over with. *I'm never gonna make* this *mistake again!*

Or at least I sure hope I won't... because it just hurts too much.

When Kit got over to Tom and Carl's place with Ponch, he wasn't surprised to find Tom already working—sitting out on the patio in jeans and T-shirt and a light jacket, typing away on his portable computer at the table next to the big square koi pond. "It's the only quiet time I get before the phone starts ringing," Tom said, letting Kit in the side gate. "Come on in, tell me what you found..."

Over a cup of tea, while Ponch sprawled under the table, Kit described what Ponch had been doing, and Tom looked at the "hard" report in his Senior's version of the manual, which was presently about the size of a phone book. Tom shook his head, turning over pages and reading what Kit could see even from across the table was a very abstruse analysis indeed, in very small print.

"This is a new one on me," he said at last. "I'll ask Carl to have a look later; the worldgating and timesliding end of things is more his specialty. But I'm not even sure that what Ponch is doing *is* either of those. And I can't find any close cognates to this kind of behavior in any other wizards' reports."

"Really?" Kit said. "How far does that go back?"

"All the way," Tom said absently. "Well, nearly. Some of the material before the first hundredth of a second of the life of this universe is a little sketchy. Privacy issues, possibly."

He shook his head and closed the book. "Kit, I'm not sure *where* you were. I'm not sure it can even be classified as a *where*, as a physical universe that, given the right geometries, can be described in terms of its direction and distance from other neighboring universes. Ponch's place might be another dimension, another continuum even, completely out of the local sheaf of universes. Or an entirely different state of being, not physical the way we understand it at all." He shrugged. "He's found something very unusual that's going to take some exploring before we begin to understand it. At least your whole experience is stored in the manual, and you'll want to add notes to it later. It'll help the other wizards who'll be starting analysis on it."

"I thought your version of the manual was going to be able to explain this."

Tom leaned back. "There's never any guarantee of

that. We're told new things *about* the universe all the time. But we're not routinely told what they *mean*. Wizardry is like science that way. We're expected to figure out the meaning of the raw data ourselves."

"So what do I do?"

"Well, what were you thinking of doing?"

"What Ponch suggested," Kit said. "Going into that…that 'state,' I guess, and seeing if I could do what he was doing: make things."

"Probably not a bad idea," Tom said. "You seem to have come out of this all right…but don't get careless. Exploratory wizardry can be dangerous, even though you *are* working for the Good Guys."

The patio door slid open, and there was Carl, in jeans and flip-flops and an NYPD T-shirt. "I heard voices," he said.

"Sorry, we didn't mean to disturb you—"

"Not *your* voices," Carl said, rueful. "The voices of certain fur-bearing persons who're in the kitchen right now, eating anything that doesn't run away fast enough."

"Dog biscuits!" Ponch said, and immediately got up and went over to jump on Carl in a neighborly way.

"Go on in. They'll show you where the box is," Carl said, and Ponch ran into the house. "If there's anything they know, it's that."

"Where's *ours*?" came a chorus of voices from the koi pond.

"It's too early. And you're all overweight, anyway," Carl said, sitting down at the table.

A noise of boos and bubbly razzes came from the pond.

"Everybody's a critic," Carl said. "What have we got?"

"Take a look," Tom said, and pushed his copy of the manual over to Carl.

"Huh," Carl said after a moment's reading. Then he looked over his shoulder in the direction of the continuing racket. "Will you guys hold it *down*?" He glanced over at Kit. "See, if you'd waited half an hour, you could have had all the fish breath you wanted."

Kit laughed. "What do you make of this?" Tom said.

Carl shook his head. "Once again, the universes remind us of their most basic law; they're not only stranger than we imagine, they're stranger than we *can* imagine. Which is what makes them so much fun." He turned a page. "I really don't understand this, but there are a couple of people I can call later. You going to go back there?" he said to Kit.

"Yeah, when I get back home."

"All right. Try an experiment. Try to affect the space where you find yourself, the way Ponch did, and see how that works. But also, see if you can bring something back with you. It doesn't have to be anything big. A leaf, a pebble. But something to analyze might help us determine the nature of the space, or whatever, that it comes from."

"Just test it first to make sure it's not antimatter," Tom said.

"Uh, *yeah*," Kit said. He had no desire to be totally annihilated.

"It's just a thought," Carl said. "Antimatter universes are well outnumbered by orthomatter ones, but you can't tell just by looking."

"I'll make a note," Kit said.

"Anything from Nita?" said Tom.

"Uh...not yet," Kit said. "I think, besides whatever she's working on, she may be wanting to take a little holiday from group spelling. We were having a rough time there for a while."

"Happens all the time," Carl said, leaning back in his chair. "You get stuck at different stages of mastery, and things can get a little bumpy. It passes, as a rule. But it can be tough when one partner or member of a group is working faster than the other, or in a different paradigm."

Kit thought about that. "Look...do you guys ever fight?"

Carl and Tom looked at each other in astonishment, and then at Kit, and both laughed. "Oh, lord! Constantly!" Tom said. "And it's not just about the joint practice, either. There aren't enough hours in the day for all the stuff we have to deal with. Finding time just to be friends can be tough, but it has to be made...and when we don't make it, we get sore at each other more easily."

"It always came so naturally with Neets," Kit said. "I guess maybe I didn't think much about having to work on it."

"Believe it, you have to," said Carl. "And then we have what we laughably call 'normal lives' as well. I have a job and an office to go to, Tom has to sit here and hit his deadlines, and there are bills to pay and work to do around the house and everything else. But first and foremost comes the wizardry, and keeping it part of 'normal life' is always a challenge. Sure, we bite each other sometimes. Sometimes it takes a while to patch things up. Don't let it throw you. But don't let it take too long, either."

"No," Kit said. "It's funny. I'm glad I got this last job done. It's useful. But now I don't know what to do next. And Neets always knows; she always has an idea for something else that needs doing. Sometimes it drives me nuts. Now it feels weird not to have her bugging me about 'the next thing.'"

"You'll work it out," Carl said. "Sorting out the details of your practice in the early part of your wizardly career is the exciting part."

"Yeah." Kit got up. "I'll let you know how it comes out."

"Right."

He recovered Ponch from pigging out on dog biscuits and walked home from Tom and Carl's, giving Ponch a chance to run ahead and lose some of the excitement. The route took Kit past Nita's, not entirely accidentally. He knew that sometimes she got up early. But all the curtains at her house were still drawn, all the doors were closed, and the car was in the garage. Kit reached into his jacket pocket, slipped his hand around the manual. There was no fizz about its cover.

He sighed and went on by, and a few minutes later

they were back at Kit's house. It was still quiet inside as he went down the driveway and into the back, and he and Ponch took themselves into the back of the yard, among the sassafras trees, where they were out of view from the Macarthurs' and Kings' houses.

"You ready?" Kit said to Ponch.

"Let's go!"

And they stepped together once more into the dark....

For Nita, the afternoon took its own sweet time going by. There was still no sign of Kit. Her mother had gone off to the shop after lunch, and Dairine went off, too, and took Spot with her. Nita sighed and tried to watch TV, but there was nothing on. She tried to do some work with the manual, but every time she touched it, its cover was still and fizzless under her hands, and she put it down as quickly as she picked it up. She even dallied with the idea of doing some work on a science report that was due in a couple of weeks, but the thought of actually starting it before she needed to was repulsive. *When I first got into wizardry, I'd never have thought it was possible to be bored again,* Nita thought, *but it seems that a wizard really* can *do anything, given enough time.*

Around four o'clock she was back in her bedroom, having just finished a bologna sandwich, when she heard a *whoomp!* of displaced air in the backyard. Nita looked hurriedly out the back window but saw that it was only Dairine, with Spot spidering along behind her. She sighed, slumped a little, and took down a book to read.

She had read no more than a page or two when Dairine came in, looking out of sorts. "Where've you been?" Nita asked, chucking the book away, since it was obvious she wasn't going to get any reading done, either.

"Europa."

"Again?"

Dairine frowned. "Neets," she said wearily, and sat on her bed, "I'm having some problems."

"*You?*"

"Please," Dairine said. She was staring at the bedspread as if it were written over with the secrets of the universe instead of a slightly faded stars-and-moons pattern. After a while she said in a low voice, as if embarrassed, "I'm not getting the results I was getting a while ago."

Nita pushed back from her desk and folded her arms, putting her feet up. This was a problem she'd come to know all too well. "Dair, it happens to all of us. You get a little older...you lose your initial edge and your first big blast of power, and start feeling your way to where your specialty's going to be. It's not always what you first thought it'd be. Tom says it's real common for a first specialty to shift, and for your power levels to jump around a lot when you're new to the Art."

Her sister sat there, still staring at the quilt. This worn-down look wasn't something Nita was used to seeing in her sister. Dairine's energy levels were usually such that you wanted to hook her up to wires and make serious money by selling power to the electric company. "I don't care if it is normal," Dairine said. "I hate it."

"You think you're the only one? I wasn't wild about my first flush wearing off, either. But you get used to it."

"Why do we *have* to get used to it?" Dairine burst out. "What good am I if I'm not effective?"

"You mean, what good are you if you can't solve every problem you come up against in three seconds?" Nita said. "Well, obviously, none at all. Guess you'd better go straight to the bathroom and flush yourself."

Dairine stared at her sister. "Or find a black hole and jump in," Nita said, leaning back and closing her eyes. "Tom says there's a lot of interest in the time-dilation effects, especially on the middle-sized ones. Be sure to file a report with the Powers when you get back. Assuming this universe is still here."

Nita waited for the explosion. There wasn't one. She opened her eyes again to find Dairine staring at her as if she were something from Mars. Actually, Dairine had stared at things from Mars with a lot less astonishment.

"What?" Dairine said.

Nita had to smile, even though Dairine's whining was annoying her. "Sorry. I was going to say, you remind me of me when I was your age."

Dairine made a face. "*There's* a horrible thought."

She wrapped her arms around her knees, and put her face down against them. "The last thing I want is to be that normal again." She produced an elaborate shudder, turning *normal* into a swear word.

"You want to watch that, Dari," Nita said. "Just because we're wizards doesn't mean we're any better than 'normal' people. The minute you start acting like there's a 'them' and an 'us,' you're in trouble. The only thing that makes wizards different is that we have the power to do more than usual to help. And helping other people, as part of keeping the world running, is the only reason the power exists in the first place." It was a lesson Nita had learned at some cost, having done enough dumb things in her time until she got it straight.

Dairine gave Nita a noncommittal look. "Edgy, aren't we? Still nothing from Kit?"

Nita made a face. "No. But just let it sit for the time being, okay? Meanwhile, what was their problem? The amoebas or whatever they are?"

"They call themselves *hnlt*," Dairine said. "And how they manage to do that when they've only got one cell each, I don't know."

"'Life knows its way,'" Nita said, quoting a proverb commonplace to wizards in more than one star system. "And personality arrives right behind it. Sooner than you'd think, a lot of the time."

"Yeah. Well, they have this—I mean, there's a—" Then Dairine made a wry face at how ineffective English was for describing this kind of problem. She dropped into the Speech for a couple sentences' worth of description of something that seemed to be happening to the gravity on Europa. Apparently the sea bottom far down under the surface ice was being catastrophically shifted in ways that were destroying some of the *hnlt* habitats.

After a moment, Nita nodded. "That's a nasty one. So what did you do?"

Dairine looked glum. "I suggested they wait a little while and see what happens," she said. "The Sun's real active now, and the activity is pushing Jupiter's atmosphere around a lot harder than usual, even the densest parts down deep. That's what's causing the gravitational and magnetic anomalies. It'll probably quiet down by itself when the sunspot cycle starts to taper off."

"Makes sense. Good call."

"But Neets, what's the *point*? I couldn't do anything. I *couldn't*! Only a few months ago I could— I could do everything up to and including pushing planets around. And now, because I can't, a lot of the *hnlt* are going to die before the Sun quiets down. All I can do is help them relocate their habitats elsewhere on Europa. But those other places are going to be just as vulnerable. No matter what I do, I'm not going to be able to save them all…"

Nita shook her head; not that she didn't feel sorry for her sister. "Dari, it's just the way things go. You started at a higher-than-usual power level, so you're having a bigger-than-usual crash."

"Why don't you try finding some *more* awful way of putting that?" Dairine muttered. "Take your time."

Nita understood how Dairine felt; she'd been down this road herself. "You'll be finding your next few years' working-level in a while. But as for the way you were last month…" Nita sighed at the memory of the way *she'd* been when she got started. "Entropy's running. The energy runs out of everything…even us. We have to learn not to blow it all over the landscape, that's all."

Dairine was silent for a few moments. Finally she leaned against the wall and nodded. "I guess I'll just have to keep working on it. Where's Mom?"

"Late," Nita said. "She's probably still looking for Dad's paperwork. She said he started burying it all in those old carnation boxes in the back again."

"Uh-oh. And after she got him the new filing cabinets." Dairine snickered. "I bet he got yelled at."

They heard someone pulling into the driveway. Nita cocked an ear at her bedroom window, which was right above the driveway, and could tell from the sound that it was her dad's car. Her mom had walked to town. Nita glanced at the clock. It was a little before five, the time their dad usually shut the store on Saturdays. "There they are. Bet he closed up early to get her to stop giving him grief."

The back door opened, closed again. Nita got up, yawning; even after the sandwich, dinner was beginning to impinge on her mind, and her stomach was making sounds that could have passed for a polite greeting on Rirhath B. "Mom say anything to you about what she was going to make tonight? Maybe we can get a head start."

"I don't remember," Dairine said as they headed

through the living room. This answer was no surprise; Dairine's normal response to food was to eat it first and ask questions later.

"Huh," Nita said. "Dad—"

She stopped. Her father stood in the kitchen, looking down at the counter by the stove as if he expected to find something there, but the counter was bare, and her father's expression was odd. "You forget something, Daddy?" Nita said.

"No," he said. And then Nita saw his face working not to show what it felt, his hands not so much resting on the edge of the counter as holding it, holding on to it, and heard his voice, which pushed its way out through a throat tight with fear.

"Where's Mom?" Dairine said.

Nita's stomach instantly tied itself into a horrible knot. "Is she all right?" she said.

"She's—" her father said. And then immediately after that, "No. Oh, honey—"

Dairine pushed her way up beside Nita, her face suddenly as pale as her father's. "Daddy, *where's Mom*?!"

"She's in the hospital." He turned to them, but he didn't let go of the counter, still hanging on to it. As his eyes met Nita's, the fear behind them hit her so hard that she almost staggered. "She's very sick, they think—"

He stopped, not because he didn't know what to say, but because he refused to say it, to think it—it was impossible. Nonetheless Nita heard it, as her dad heard it, repeating over and over in his head:

They think she might die.

Saturday Afternoon and Evening

IN A PLACE WHERE directions and distances made no sense, Kit and Ponch stood in the endless, soundless dark, the leash spell hanging loose between them and glowing with silent power.

So here we are. You feel okay?

I feel fine.

So what should I make?

Anything, Ponch said, as he had before.

Kit thought about that...and discovered that he couldn't decide what to do first. *Typical,* he thought. *Presented with the possibility to create anything you can think of, your mind goes blank.*

He tried to take a breath and found that his breathing now seemed to be working properly. "Am I getting used to this place?" Kit said softly in the Speech, and found that he could actually hear himself.

No answer; but then if one *had* come, he'd have jumped out of his skin.

"Okay," he said then. "Lights..."

And suddenly Kit found himself standing unsupported in the midst of interstellar glory. "Wow," he said softly. He and Ponch were apparently somewhere in the fringes of a gigantic globular cluster, all the nearby darkness blazing with stars of every possible color—and the farther darkness was peppered with not just thousands but hundreds of thousands of galaxies, little globes and ovals and spirals everywhere, a megacluster of the kind that astronomers were sure existed but had never seen.

It's bright, Ponch said.

"No argument there," said Kit, as he wondered why producing all this had been so easy. He was used to wizardry taking a good deal more effort. Is *this even wizardry?* he wondered. It had needed no construction of spells, no careful and laborious plugging in of words and variables, and no sudden drain of energy after the wizardry was fueled from your own power and turned loose. That last factor was what made Kit mistrust this process. He was used to the concept that every wizardry had its price, and one way or another, you paid; and its corollary: that any wizardry that doesn't charge you a decent admission fee usually isn't worth anything.

All the same, it would be smart to play around in here a little and see what it *was* worth. Kit also thought he could guess why Carl wanted him to try to bring back some small physical artifact. It would confirm whether or not this space was simply some kind of illusion or mirage, amusing but otherwise not terribly useful.

"Okay," he said, "let's take this from the top. A sun, first..."

And one appeared, though he hadn't even asked for it in the Speech: a deep yellow-orange star, a vast, roiling, heaving landscape of blinding flame, directly below his feet. For a second Kit flinched at the roar and turmoil of burning gas beneath him, all dancing with prominences and loops and arches of radiant plasma—inexhaustible fountains of fire half a million miles high, leaping away from the star's seething limb and pouring themselves back into the surface again in slow-motion grace. *In vacuum you wouldn't normally get sound, I guess,* Kit thought. But he seemed to be in some kind of peculiar rapport with this space that let him sense things he ordinarily wouldn't, and the tearing basso wind-roar of superheated ions blasting upward past him was strangely satisfying. Ponch, sitting beside him, squinted down at the ravening brilliance but didn't comment.

"Not bad, huh?" Kit said.

Ponch yawned. "The squirrels are more fun."

"You've got a one-track mind," Kit said. "Okay, now we need a planet..."

And the star receded into the distance, reducing itself to proper sunlike size. Below Kit was his planet, all covered in cloud, muttering softly to itself as it rotated, already coasting away from them along its orbit. Kit thought he could actually feel the heat pouring off it, a feverish sensation. *A lot of heat trapped under those clouds*, he thought. *It's a "supergreenhouse," like Venus...* There was no telling how big this world was, without anything to give him a frame of reference. *Have to go down there and take a closer look*, Kit thought—

—and suddenly he was standing on a rocking, shaking, stony surface. All around him rocks tumbled down low cracked cliffs, and a wind as brutal as the solar one but laden with a stinging drizzle of acid instead of fire shrieked past him. In a more normal reality, Kit knew this terrible supersonic fog would have eaten the unprotected flesh off his bones in seconds, but here he seemed immune. *Because I imagined it?*

Kit grinned and waved one hand in front of him airily. "Lose the acid," he said, "lose the wind, lose the clouds." The instant he spoke, the air went clear, fell silent, and the dull, overarching, brassy canopy faded away to dark clarity. The stars showed through again, and the high, hot, golden sun. But sound vanished as well, and it started to get very cold.

"No, no; atmosphere is okay!" Kit said. "Something I can breathe. Landscape..."

Green rolling grassland spread itself away in every direction under a blue, blue sky. Ponch leaped up in delight. "Squirrels!"

"No squirrels," Kit said. "Don't overdo them or you'll get bored." He rubbed his hands together in delight. "You know what this is, Ponch? It's magic-crayon country."

"Crayons? Where?" Ponch had conceived a weird fondness for the taste of crayons when Kit was younger, and had always gone out of his way to steal and eat them.

"Not that way," Kit said, turning around and gazing all about him at the total wilderness. "But if I thought of an elephant with three hairs in its tail here— *Uh-oh.*"

Ponch began barking deafeningly. The elephant, large and purple-gray, as in the original illustration from that old children's book, looked around in surprise, then looked over at Ponch and said, a little scornfully, "Do you have a problem?"

"Sorry," Kit said. "Uh, can I do something for you?"

"Trees are generally better for eating purposes than grass," the elephant said. "A little more variation in the landscape would be nice. And so would company."

Kit thought about that. A second later the grassland looked much more like African veldt, with a scattering of trees and an impressive mountain range in the distance, and another elephant stood next to the first one. They looked each other up and down, twined their trunks together, and walked off into the long grass, swinging their three-haired tails as they went.

Kit paused then, wondering whether they were a boy and a girl, and then wondering whether it mattered. *Maybe it's better not to get too hung up on the minor details right now,* he thought.

He glanced down at Ponch. "Want to try another one?"

"You sure you don't want to think again about the squirrels?"

"Yes, I'm sure." Kit folded his arms, thinking. He took a step forward, opened his mouth to speak—

—and found he didn't have to do even that. The two of them were standing in a waste littered with reddish rocks; an odd springy green mosslike growth was scattered here and there around them. The strangely foreshortened landscape ran up to a horizon hazed in red-violet dust, where low mountains reared up jagged against an amethyst sky; and so did an outcropping of delicate towers, apparently built of green glass or metal, gleaming faintly in the setting of a small, remote-seeming, pinky-white marble of a sun.

"*Yes,*" Kit said softly. It was Mars, but not the Mars of the real world, which nowadays, as he'd seen for himself, was unfortunately short on cities. This was the romantic Mars of stories written a hundred years ago, where fierce eight-legged thoats ran wild across dead sea bottoms, and displaced, sword-swinging warriors from Earth ran around after very, very scantily clad Martian princesses.

Ponch glanced around, looking for something.

"What?" Kit said.

"No trees."

"You can hold it in till we get home. Come on…"

He took another step forward, thinking. One step and he and Ponch were in the darkness; another, and they were in what looked like New York City but wasn't, because New York City was not under a huge glass dome, floating through space.

"Aha," Ponch said, immediately heading toward a fire hydrant.

"Uh-uh," Kit said. Another few steps and they were in darkness; another step after that, in a landscape all veiled in blowing white, whiteness crunching under-foot, and up against an indigo sky, great crackling curtains of aurora, green and blue and occasionally pink-ish red, hissing in the ferociously cold air. Something shuffled past in the blowing snow, some yards away, paused to swing its massive head around toward Kit, looking at him out of little dark eyes: a polar bear. But a polar bear the size of a mammoth....

Ponch jumped and strained at the leash, barking. "Oh, come on; let him live," said Kit, and he took an-other step, into the dark. Reluctantly, Ponch followed. Kit was getting the rhythm of it now. A few steps in darkness, to do a few moments' worth of thinking... and then one step out into light, into another landscape or vista or place. The last step, this time, and he and Ponch were wading up to Kit's knees and Ponch's neck in some kind of long, harsh-edged beach grass clothing a vista of endless dunes. Off to their right the sea rolled up to a long black beach in an endless muted roar. Kit looked up into the shadow of immense wings going over, ruffling his hair and making the grass hiss around him with their passing—one huge shape silhouetted against the twilight, then two, five, twenty, with wings that seemed to stretch across half the sky. They soared in echelon toward a horizon over which a long violet evening was descending, and beyond which the distant and delicate fire of a barred spiral galaxy, seen almost face on, was rising slowly behind a glittering haze of nearer, lesser stars.

He had the hang of it now. *Just let the mind run free, let the images flow.*

A few steps more and Kit came out into the middle of a vast plane of what looked like black marble, stretching away to infinity in all directions, and above it light glinted, reflected in the surface: not a sun or a moon, but an artificial light of some kind, almost like a spotlight. Far away, on a patterned place in the floor, small figures stood, some of them human, some not— some of them alien species that Kit had seen before in his travels, others of which he had never seen the like. One moved, then another. There was a pause, and then several moved at once, and one of them vanished. Kit started to go closer, until he saw the great shadowy shapes bending in all around him in the upward-towering dimness, to look more closely at the one piece that seemed to have escaped the game board.

Kit smiled slightly, waved at them, and took another step. The darkness descended, then rose once more on some long, golden afternoon on a rise of land over-looking a lake. A pointy-towered palace lay all sun gilded down by the water, banners flying from every sharp-peaked roof, and knights on horses clattered along a dusty road toward the castle gate, the late sun glittering sharp off lance heads and armor, the colors of the knights' surcoats as vivid as enamel. Another step, quicker, as Kit started pushing the pace: out into the aquamarine light of some underwater place, white sand under his feet, lightwaver playing in broad patterns across it, and an odder, bluer light glimmering against the depths ahead of him as the rippling, ribbony crea-tures of some alien abyss came up out of shadows ten miles deep to peer curiously at the intruder.

Kit found he could do without the darkness between worlds. It was a new vista at every step now, and Ponch padded along beside him on the wizardly leash as calmly as any dog being taken for a walk in the park. Forests of massive trees, all drowned in shadow, bare sand stretching away to impossible distances and suggesting planets much larger than Earth, gleaming futuristic cityscapes covering entire continents; a step, and night under some world's overarching greenish rings, a single voice chanting in the air, like a nightingale saluting them; a step, and the time before dawn in a vast waste of reedy waters reflecting the early peach-pink of the sky, everything still except for the flop of a fish turning, then putting its head up to look thoughtfully at them as they waded past; a step, and the blurring, whirling uncertainty of the vast space between an atom's nucleus and the silvery fog of its innermost electron shell—

—and a step out into a place where, if he had taken another step, Kit would have fallen some thousands of feet straight down. There, on the top of a mountain imperially preeminent among its fellows, Kit paused, looking down through miles of blue-hazed air at lakes held between neighboring peaks like silent jewels under a rosette of suns—three small pinkish stars riding high in a morning sky—and all the snow on all the mountains from here to the horizon stained warm rose, so they all looked lit from within. Kit breathed that high chill air—which no one besides him and Ponch had ever breathed before, the air of a world made new that moment—and shook his head, smiling the smallest smile.

He thought of the darkness. *What a place to play. Neets has got to see this.*

He stood there looking down on the immense vista for a few moments longer. "We should get back," he said.

"Why?"

"I'm not sure about the time difference yet," Kit said. "And I don't want to worry Mom."

Another thought niggling at the back of Kit's mind was: *If this...state...is as easy to shape and reshape as it seems, it'd be real easy to get hooked on it.* He'd had a phase, a couple years back, when he'd been hooked enough on a favorite arcade game to give himself blisters and blow truly unreasonable amounts of his allowance money in the process. Now Kit remembered that time with embarrassment, thinking of all the hours he'd spent on something that now bored him, and he watched himself, in a casual way, for signs that something similar might happen again.

But I almost forgot. Kit reached down and picked up something from the mossy rocks at his feet: a single flower, a little five-petaled thing like a white star. Kit slipped it into his pocket, and farther in, right down into the space-time claudication, sealing it there. Then he turned around to glance at Ponch—the top of the peak was so narrow that they hadn't had room to stand side by side. "Ready?"

"Yes, because I don't think I can hold it in much longer."

Together they stepped straight out into the air, out into the darkness—

—and out into Kit's backyard.

He looked around. Twilight was falling. *Guess I was right to be a little concerned about the time,* Kit thought. *Looks like it wasn't running at the same rate in all those places. Something else to tell Tom…*

He took the leash off Ponch, wound up the wizardry, and stuffed it into his pocket. Ponch immediately headed off toward the biggest of the sassafras trees to give it a good "watering."

Kit went into the house. His mother and father were eating; his dad looked up at Kit, raised his eyebrows, and said, "Son, can't you give us a hint on how long you're going to be when you go out on one of these runs? Tom couldn't tell me anything."

"Sorry, Pop," Kit said as he went past his dad, patting him on the shoulder. "I wasn't sure myself. I didn't think it'd be this long, though, and now I know what the problem is… I'll watch it next time."

"Okay. You want some macaroni and cheese?"

"In a minute."

Kit headed up the stairs in a hurry; Ponch hadn't been the only one with "holding it" on his mind. Then he went into his room to check his pocket and was delighted to find the flower right where he'd put it. Kit placed it carefully on his desk, traced a line around it with his finger, and said the six words of a spell that would hold the contents aloof from the local progress of time for twenty-four hours.

This was not a cheap spell, and the pang of the energy drain the spell cost him went straight through him. Kit had to sit down in his desk chair and get his breath back. While he sat there, he reached farther into his pocket, touched his manual...and felt the fizz.

He grinned, pulled it out, paged to the back of it... and let out a long breath. The manual was showing a message that had come in only a few minutes before. *I can't talk now. But can we talk later? I've got some apologizing to do.*

All right, Kit thought, relieved. *She's seen sense at last, and I'm not gonna rub her nose in it. There's too much serious neatness going on here.* "Reply," he said to the manual. "Call me anytime: I'm ready."

And he ran down the stairs, exhilarated, to feed Ponch and have his own dinner. *Just wait till she sees! Whatever's been going on with her, this is gonna take her mind off it.*

I can't wait.

Saturday Evening

HOW SHE AND DAIRINE got their dad into the dining room and sat him down, Nita couldn't afterward remember, except for a flash of horror at the awful topsy-turviness of things. It was the parents who were supposed to be strong when the kids were scared. But now there were just the three of them, sitting there close, all of them equally scared together. Her father was hanging on to his control, and Nita held on to hers as much out of her own fear as out of sympathy; if she broke down, he might, too.

"She collapsed as she was leaving the store," her father said, staring at the table. "I thought she was kneeling down to look at one of the plants in the window, you know how she would always fuss over the display not being just right. She just seemed to kneel down... and then she leaned against the doorsill. And she didn't get up."

"What was it?" Dairine cried. "What happened to her?"

"They're not sure. She just passed out, and she wouldn't wake up. The ambulance came, and we took her over to the county hospital. They did some physical tests, and then they X-rayed her chest and her head, and put her in the ICU..." Her father trailed off. Nita saw the frightened look in his eyes as he relived some memory that terrified him. "They said they'd call when they had some news."

"I'm not waiting for that!" Dairine said. "We have to go to the hospital. Right now!" She turned as if intending to go get her jacket.

Her father caught hold of her. "*Not* right now, honey. The doctor told me that they need a few hours to get her stable. She's okay, but they need to do some tests, and—"

"Dad," Nita said.

He looked at her.

The terror in his eyes was awful, worse than what Nita was feeling. She wanted to grab him and hold him and pat his back and say, "It's going to be all right." But she had no idea whether it was going to be all right or not. Nita settled for grabbing him and holding him, and Dairine, too.

Then they began to wait.

The time until they went to the hospital passed in a kind of horrible disturbed silence, most of the disturbance coming from the phone, as it rang and rang and rang again, and every time, Nita's father lunged for it, hoping it was the hospital, and every time, it wasn't.

There were always people on the other end who'd heard from someone they knew about Nita's mom or had seen the ambulance at the shop. Every time Nita's dad had to explain to someone what had happened, he got more upset.

"Daddy, *stop answering it*!" Nita cried at one point.

"They're your mother's friends" was all he would say. "And mine. They have a right to know. And besides, what if the hospital calls?" And there was no arguing with that.

"Let us answer it," Dairine said.

"No," said their dad. "Things are hard enough for you two. You let me handle it." The phone rang again, and he went to answer it.

After that, it seemed that the phone just went on ringing all evening.

Nita was terrified. She wasn't used to not knowing what was happening, not being able to *do* anything—and her shock was such that she wasn't even able to make any kind of plan about what to do next. Dairine paced around the house like a caged creature, her face alternately frightened and furious, and she wouldn't talk to anybody, not even Spot, who crouched mutely near one of the chairs in the living room and simply watched her go back and forth. Nita felt actively sorry for it but didn't know what to do; Spot's relationship was exclusively with Dairine, and she didn't know how it would take to being comforted by someone else.

If comforted *is even the word*, Nita thought, *because I wouldn't know what to say or do to make it* comfortable...*any more than I know what to say to Dairine. Or Dad.* That was the worst of it: not being able to do anything for either of them. Again and again, after her dad hung up the phone, that deadly quiet would descend, emphasizing the voice that was *not* there, all of a sudden. And then the phone would ring into the silence again...and Nita felt certain that if it rang once more, she'd scream.

But finally the hospital called. Nita watched her father answer, his face naked in its changes, shifting every second between fear and uncertainty and greater fear. "Yes. This is he. Yes." He paused, turning away from where Nita sat at the dining-room table.

"She is?"

Nita's heart seized.

"Uh, good."

She breathed again. *And I don't even know why; I don't even know what's happening!*

"Yes...sure we can. About half an hour. Yes. Thanks."

He hung up, turned to Nita. Dairine was standing there by the living-room door, as intently as Nita had been. "She's still in intensive care," her dad said, "but they say she's stable now, whatever that means. Let's go."

Shortly, Nita found herself walking into a setting entirely too familiar to her from too many TV shows: all the people in pastel uniforms with stethoscopes hanging around their necks and shoved into their breast pockets, all the white jackets, the metal beds and the stretcher-trolleys in the corridors, people going places in a hurry and doing important but inexplicable things. What the TV shows had never gotten across, and what now struck itself deeply into Nita's mind, was the smell of the place. It wasn't a bad smell. It was clean enough...but that cleanliness was cold, a chilly distancing scent of disinfectant and other chemicals. The faces of the people working there were kind, mostly, but a lot of them had a strange preoccupied quality, unlike the faces of the actors on the TV shows. These people weren't acting.

Nita and Dairine stuck close to their father as they made their way through the hospital corridors and to the reception desk, where someone could tell them where to go. "They've moved her out of ICU, Mr. Callahan," the lady at the desk said. "She's over in Neurology now. If you go down that hall and turn right—"

Her father nodded and led them off down the hall. About three minutes' walking brought them through swinging doors and up to a nurses' station.

One of the nurses there, a large, cheerful-looking lady in a pink scrub-style uniform, with her brown hair pulled back tight in a bun, looked up as they approached. "Mr. Callahan?"

"Yes."

"The doctor would like to see you—that's Dr. Kashiwabara, she's the senior neurologist. If you can go into that room across the hall and wait for a few minutes, she'll be with you shortly."

They went into the plain little room—white walls, beige tile floor, noisy orange sofa that was also literally noisy, with plastic-covered cushions that wheezed when you sat down on them—and waited, in silence. Nita's dad put an arm around her and Dairine, and Nita hoped she didn't look as stiff with fear as she felt. *I can't believe this,* she thought, bizarrely angry with herself. *I'm so scared, I can't even think. I wasn't this afraid when I thought a* shark *might eat me! And this isn't even about* me. *It's someone else—*

But that makes it worse. That was true, too. There'd been times when Kit was in some bad spot, and the terror had risen up and had nearly choked the breath out of her. And that was just Kit—

Just! said the back of her mind in shock. Nita shook her head. Kit was so important to her ... but he wasn't her mother.

The door opened, and the sound made them all jump. "Mr. Callahan?" said the little woman in the white coat who was standing there. She was extremely petite and pretty, with short black hair, and had calm, knowledgeable eyes that for some reason immediately put Nita more at ease. "I'm sorry to have kept you waiting. These are your daughters?"

"Nita," said Nita's dad, "and Dairine."

"I'm pleased to meet you." She shook their hands and sat down on the couch across from them.

"Doctor, how's my wife? Is she any better?"

"She's resting," said the doctor. "I don't want to alarm you, but she had several minor seizures after we admitted her, and sedation was necessary to break the cycle and allow us to find out what's going on."

"Do you know?"

The doctor looked at the chart she was carrying, though she didn't open it. "We have some early indications, but first I want to talk to you about some things we didn't have time to discuss while we were admitting Mrs. Callahan. Has she been having any physical problems lately?"

"Physical problems—"

"Double vision, or problems with her sight? Headaches? Any trouble with coordination—a little more clumsiness than usual, perhaps?"

"She's been saying she needed to get reading glasses," Dairine said softly.

Nita looked at her dad. "Daddy, she's been taking a lot of aspirin lately. I didn't realize until just now."

Their father looked stricken. "She hadn't mentioned anything to me," he said to the doctor. "The hours I've been working lately, sometimes the kids have been seeing more of her than I have."

Dr. Kashiwabara nodded. "All right. I'll be going over these issues with Mrs. Callahan myself when she's more lucid. But what you've told me makes sense in terms of what we've found so far. There's been time to do an X ray, anyway, and there seems to be a small abnormal growth at the base of one of the frontal lobes of her brain."

Nita swallowed.

"What kind of growth?" her dad said.

"We don't know yet," said Dr. Kashiwabara. "I've scheduled her for a PET scan this evening, and an MRI scan tomorrow morning; those should tell us what we need to know."

"This is a brain tumor we're talking about," said Nita's father, his voice shaking. "Isn't it?"

Dr. Kashiwabara looked at him, then nodded. "What we need to do is find out what kind it is," she said, "so that we can work out how best to treat it. What we do know at this point is that the tumor seems to have grown large enough to put pressure on some nearby areas of Mrs. Callahan's brain. That's what caused the seizures. We've medicated her to prevent any more. She's going to be pretty woozy when you see her; please don't be concerned about that by itself. For the time being, while we run the tests, she's going to have to stay very quiet to keep excess pressure from building up in her skull and brain. It means she needs to stay flat on her back in bed, even if she feels like she's able to get up."

"For how long?" Dairine said.

"Depending on how the tests go, it may be only a couple of days," Dr. Kashiwabara said. "We'll do the scans that I mentioned, and then there'll have to be a biopsy of the growth itself—we'll remove a tiny bit of tissue and test it to see what kind it is. After that, we'll know what our next move needs to be."

The doctor folded her hands and rubbed them together a little, then looked up. "I'll be doing that procedure myself," she said. "I don't want to trouble your wife about signing the permissions, Mr. Callahan. Maybe we can take care of that before you leave."

"Yes," Nita's dad said, hardly above a whisper, "of course."

"I want you to call me if you have any questions at

all," Dr. Kashiwabara said, "or any concerns. I may not be able to get back to you immediately—I have a lot of other people to take care of—but I promise you I will always call you back. Okay?"

"Yes. Thank you."

"All right," said the doctor, and got up. "Why don't you go see her now? But, please, keep it brief. The seizures will have been very fatiguing and confusing for her, and she won't be fully recovered from them until tomorrow. Come with me; I'll show you the way."

They walked down the corridor together, and Dr. Kashiwabara led them into a room where there were four of those steel beds: two of them empty, the third with a cloth curtain pulled partway around it, under which they could see a nurse in white shoes and pink nursing sweats doing something or other. In the fourth bed, beyond the partway-pulled curtain, their mom lay under light covers, with one arm strapped to a board, and an IV running into that arm. She was in a hospital gown, and someone had tied her hair back and put it up under a paper cap. Her eyes suddenly looked sunken to Nita; it was the same tired look she had been wearing this morning, but much worse. *Why didn't I notice?* Nita's heart cried. *Why didn't I see something was wrong?!*

"Mrs. Callahan?" said Dr. Kashiwabara.

It took Nita's mom's eyes a few moments to open, and then they seemed to have trouble focusing. "What...oh." She moistened her lips. "Harry?"

It was as if she couldn't see him properly. "I'm here, honey," he said, and Nita was astonished at how strong he sounded. He took her hand and sat in the chair by the bed. "And the girls are here, too. How're you feeling?"

There was a long pause. "Like...bats."

Nita and Dairine looked at each other in poorly concealed panic. "Baseball bats," their mother said. "Very sore."

"Like somebody was hitting you with baseball bats, you mean?" Nita said.

"Yeah."

From the seizures, Nita thought. Her mother turned her head toward her, across from her dad. "Oh, honey...," she said, "I'm sorry..."

"What're you sorry for, Mom? This isn't your fault!" Nita said. And even as she said it, she knew exactly whose fault it was.

There was only one of the Powers Who at the beginning of things had insisted on inventing something never contemplated before in the universe: entropy, disease...death. That Lone Power had been her enemy more than once, but suddenly it seemed to Nita that she hadn't done It nearly as much damage as she should have.

Dairine, next to Nita, leaned over the bed. "Mom, why didn't you tell us your head was hurting you?"

"Honey, I *did.*" She shook her head on the pillow. "I thought...I thought it was stress." She smiled. "Seems I miscalculated..."

She drifted off then, her eyes closing. Nita and Dairine exchanged a glance. Nita took her mom's hand and closed her eyes, trying something she had never tried with her mother. She slipped her consciousness a little way into her mother's body, gingerly, carefully. Without a wizardry specifically built to the purpose, she could get nothing clear—just a fuzzy, muzzy feeling, a faint vague pain at the edge of things, an odd sense of dislocation...

...and one other thing. A small something. A *lot* of small somethings that were *not* her mom. They were all gathered together into something little and hot and strange, burning against the cooler, "normal" background: something alien...and malevolent.

Nita gulped, and opened her eyes. *I could be wrong. I didn't do that exactly by the book. But boy...will I, later.*

Her mother opened her eyes. "I don't want you to worry," she said, very clearly.

Her dad actually managed to laugh. "Listen to you," he said. "Worrying about *us*, as usual. You concentrate on getting rested up, and help these people do whatever they need to do."

"Don't have much choice," Nita's mother said. "Got me outnumbered." She closed her eyes again.

Nita met her dad's eyes across the bed. "We should go," he said softly. "Sleep's probably the best thing for her."

"Mom," Dairine said, "we'll see you tomorrow, okay? You have a nap."

"'nt to extremes...to get one," her mother whispered. "Sorry."

They sat there for a few minutes more, saying nothing. Finally one of the nurses looked in the door at them, put his finger to his lips, then gestured out into the hall with his head and raised his eyebrows.

Nita got up, bringing Dairine with her. "Dad…," she said.

His eyes had been only for their mother's face. Now he turned, saw the nurse, who looked at their dad and tapped his watch. Nita's father nodded, got up. It was hard for him to let go of their mom's hand. Nita had to look away from that, as she felt the tears welling up in her. *I'm not going to cry here,* she thought. *The whole world can hear me, and Dad—*

She headed for the door. Behind her came her dad and Dairine, and they stood lost for a moment in the hall. There was nothing they could do but go home.

It was dark, it was late, when they got back. *Where did the evening go?* Nita thought as her dad locked the back door. Somehow hours had fleeted by as if in a few minutes, leaving only pain and a feeling of having been cheated of time, somehow…not that Nita wanted *that* particular slice of time back. Going through it once was enough. Dairine apparently agreed; she went upstairs to her room, and Nita heard the door shut.

"Daddy," Nita said.

He was sitting in his chair in the living room, with only one lamp on, everything else in shadow, his face rigid and stunned-looking in the dim light. "What?"

"Daddy…what they told us," Nita said softly, "it's scary, yeah…but maybe it's not what you were thinking."

He didn't ask how she knew. "Nita," her father said, reluctant, "you didn't see them when they first brought her in, after the X ray, before I came back. I saw the doctor looking at the X ray. I saw her face…"

Nita swallowed. Her dad put his face in his hands, then raised it again. His cheeks were wet. "They're being careful," he said. "They're right to be: They have to do the tests. But I saw the doctor's face." He shook his head. "It's not… it's not good."

Then he clenched his fists. "I shouldn't be frightening you," he said. "I could be wrong."

"You always say we have to tell each other when we're scared," she said. "You have to take your own advice, Dad."

He was silent for a long time. "It's stupid," he said. "I keep thinking, 'If I hadn't been working so hard, this wouldn't have happened. If she hadn't been working so hard on the accounts, this wouldn't have happened.' It's like it has to be all my fault, somehow. As if that would help." He laughed, a short, bitter sound. "And even when I know it's not… I *feel* like it is. Stupid."

Nita swallowed. "I keep thinking," she said, "I should have seen it, that she wasn't feeling okay."

"So do I."

Nita shook her head. "But I guess that… when someone's been there forever… you stop looking at them, some ways. It's dumb, but it's what we do."

Her father wiped his hands on his pants and looked up at her with an expression that was considering, and full of pain. "You know," he said, "you sound a lot like your mom sometimes."

It was the best thing he could have said to her. It was the worst thing he could have said to her. When the shock wore off, all that Nita could say was "You should try to get some sleep."

Her father gave her a look that said, *You must be kidding.* But aloud he said, "You're right."

He got up, gave her a hug. "Good night, honey," he said. "Get me up at eight." He went off to the back bedroom and closed the door.

Nita went to bed, too, but there was nothing good about her night at all. She lay awake for hours, rerunning in her mind all kinds of things that had happened the previous week, especially conversations with her mother—trying to see what had gone wrong, what could have gone differently, how she could have predicted what had happened today, how she could have prevented it somehow. It was torment—and she didn't seem able to stop doing it—but it was better than going on to the next set of thoughts that Nita knew was lying in wait for her. The past, at least, was fixed. The only alternative was the future, in which any horrible thing could happen.

The sound of a hand turning the knob of her bedroom door brought Nita sitting up straight in bed in absolute terror. *Of what?* she thought a second later, scornful and angry with herself, while also trying to breathe deeply and slow down her pounding heart, which seemed to be shaking her whole body. But she knew what she was afraid of. Of hearing the phone ring downstairs in the middle of the night, of having her father come in and tell her...tell her—

Nita gulped and struggled for control. In the darkness, she heard a couple of steps on the floor. "Neets," said a small voice. Then the bedsprings creaked a little.

Dairine crept into Nita's bed, threw her arms around Nita, buried her face against her chest, and began to sob.

Nita suddenly found herself looking at a moment long ago: a small Dairine, maybe five years old, running down the sidewalk outside the house, oblivious— then tripping and falling. Dairine had pushed herself up on her hands and, after a long pause, started to cry...but then came the laughter of the kids down the street, the ones toward whom she'd been running. Nita had been struck then by the sight of Dairine's face working, puckering, as she tried to decide what to do, then steadying into a downturned mouth and thunderous frown, a scowl of furious determination. Dairine got up, and said just one thing: *"No."* Knees bleeding, she wiped her face, and walked slowly back to the house, shoulders hunched, her whole body clenched like a small fist with resolve.

I don't think I've seen her cry since, Nita thought. And so Dairine had gone on, for so long, expressing herself almost entirely through that toughness. But now the shell had cracked, and who would have ever known that there was such pain and fear contained inside it?

But Nita knew now, and there was nothing she could do but hang on to her sister and let Dairine sob herself silent. *It's not fair,* Nita thought, the tears leaking out as she hugged Dairine to her. *Who do I get to cry on? Who's going to be strong for me?*

If any Power listened, It gave her no answer.

Sunday Morning

BEFORE DAWN NITA FOUND herself awake and sitting up in bed, looking at the faint blue light outside her window. There had been no transition from sleeping to waking: just that unsettling consciousness, and a feeling that the world was wrong, that *everything* was wrong. She had no idea how long it had taken her to get to sleep last night after Dairine, silent and drained, had finally slipped away.

Drained. That was the word for how Nita felt, too. But some energy was beginning to coil back into that void as the shock wore off. Nita looked at her manual, and saw the words in front of her eyes without even having to touch it: *I will fight to preserve what grows and lives well in its own way; I will not change any creature unless its growth and life, or that of the system of which it is part, are threatened—*

She swallowed. *I am a wizard. And if my mom's life isn't "threatened" right now, I don't know when it will be. There has to be another way to fight this than just what they've got in the hospital.*

And I'm going to find out what it is.

She got up, dressed, grabbed the manual, and took it back to bed with her. Its covers were fizzing. Nita settled herself up against the wall at the head of the bed and flipped the book open to read the message waiting for her, then glanced out the window at the bleak predawn light. *I'll get in touch with him later. No point in waking him up early just to get him upset. I've done enough stupid stuff to him lately.*

She paged through the manual to the section with information on the medical and healing-related wizardries. That section was much larger this morning than she had ever found it before. Nita began reading what was there with intensity and with a concentration she could hardly remember having expended since she first found this book and understood what it meant. She had a couple of hours to spare before the time her dad had told her to wake him up.

She used them, pausing only once, to go to the bathroom, taking the book with her when she did. To say that the subject was complex was understating badly. There was just too much information. She had the manual stop displaying everything that had to do with injuries and trauma, chronic diseases and afflictions… and though she narrowed and narrowed her focus, the section she was reading didn't get any thinner. Finally there was almost nothing between the covers except pages and pages of material concerning abnormal growths and lesions, and still she found more every time she targeted a specific condition. Nita also saw a lot of a word in the Speech that she didn't much like—a word that translated into English as *intractable*. There was a lot of discussion of theory here, but not many spells. Nita got nervous when she noticed that, but she didn't stop reading. There had to be a way. There was *always* a way, if you could just push through to the core of the matter....

The light grew in her room; she hardly noticed. Birds began singing the restrained songs of early autumn, but Nita shut their voices out. She read and read...and suddenly her alarm clock went off, at eight-thirty.

Nita scrambled out of bed, shut the noisy thing off, and went to see if her dad was up yet. Pausing outside the master bedroom, listening, she couldn't hear any sound of anyone stirring in there.

She knocked softly on the door. No answer. "Dad..."

Still nothing. Nita eased the door softly open and peeked in.

Her father was asleep in the reading chair in the corner between the two bedroom windows. He sat slumped over, his mouth hanging open a little, a slight snore emitting from him—almost the same sound Ponch made when he lay on his back with his feet in the air and snored; the thought almost made her smile. But smiling about anything right now seemed like some kind of betrayal.

She glanced at the bed, which had not been slept in, and let out an unhappy breath, then went over to her dad and crouched down beside the chair. "Daddy," she said.

His eyes opened slowly; he looked at her as if he couldn't understand what he was doing here.

Then it all came back to him. She saw the pain fill his eyes. Nita clenched her jaw and managed to keep from getting any weepier than she already felt. "It's eight-thirty, Dad," she said. "You said we should go to the hospital in an hour or so."

"Yeah." He slowly sat upright and rubbed his face. "Yeah." He looked at her then. "How are you doing, honey?"

"Better. Maybe better," she said. "Daddy, I guess I was so scared, I forgot for a minute."

"Forgot what?"

"Maybe I can do something."

Her father looked at her, uncomprehending.

"Daddy," Nita said, "I *am* a wizard. In fact, we've got two of them in the house. And we know a bunch more of them, all over the place. Wizardry's *about* fixing broken things, healing hurt things...saving lives. We must be able to do *something.*"

Her dad's expression went curiously neutral. "Honey," he said, sounding slightly embarrassed, "you know, that's the kind of thing I...try not to think about. It still seems like a fairy tale, sometimes. Even when everything's all right, I don't think about it much. And right now...now I'd be afraid it'll..."

Fail, Nita thought. It was the thought that had been nagging at her, too. "Dad, in Mom's case, it's really complicated. I've barely had time to start working out what to do. But there has to be *something.* I'm not going to do anything else until I find out what."

Her father rubbed his face again. "Well...all right. In the meantime, we'd better get ourselves over there. Have you had your shower?"

"Not yet."

"You go ahead. I'll make us some breakfast. Is Dairine up?"

"I don't know. She had trouble getting to sleep last night."

"She wasn't alone," her father said softly.

He reached out to Nita and hugged her. "Oh, honey..." He ran out of words for a few moments. Then he hugged her harder. "You hang in there. We'll all keep each other going somehow, and it'll be all right."

"Yeah," Nita said, hoping that it was true.

When they got to the hospital, Nita's mother was sleeping, having been up early for the MRI scan. "She was awake late last night," the head nurse, that large lady with the bun hairstyle, told Nita's dad, "and it seems like a good idea for her to get caught up on her sleep now. But her doctor's finishing another procedure, and she asked me if you could wait for half an hour or so. She'd like to see you."

"No problem," Nita's father said. In reality it wasn't even that long; after she and Dairine went up to take a quick look in at their mom, and Nita saw that she was indeed sleeping peacefully, Nita left Dairine there to have a moment with their mom by herself, and made her way back to the little waiting room, where she found her dad already talking to Dr. Kashiwabara. The doctor looked up as Nita came in.

"Good morning," she said as Nita sat down. "Well, your mom had a quiet night—except for the scans, of course. She's been doing the sensible thing, and sleeping when we weren't actually running her in and out of the machines. In fact, she fell asleep during the MRI this morning, which I wouldn't normally have thought possible; it's like sleeping in a garbage can while someone's banging on it."

"If you lived long with our daughters," Nita's dad said, "you'd be surprised what you'd learn to sleep through."

Dr. Kashiwabara smiled faintly. "Come to think of it," she said, "where's the younger one?"

Nita looked around in surprise. Dairine should have come back from their mom's room by now. "Be right back," she said.

Nita retraced her steps. Slipping quietly into the room, she found Dairine standing there, her back against the wall near the door, looking across the closer, empty bed at the curtained one where their mother lay. In her arms she was holding Spot—which Nita hadn't noticed Dairine bringing to the hospital in the first place—and the whole room was sizzling with the electric-air feel of a wizardry on the ebb, either newly dismantled or incomplete.

"What are you doing?" Nita whispered, and grabbed Dairine by the upper arm. "Come *on!*"

Dairine didn't resist her; she didn't have the energy. Nita was sure she knew why, but there was no dealing with it right now. She hustled Dairine back to the little conference room and sat her down.

Nita's father gave Dairine one of those looks that said, *Misbehaving again, I see,* but said nothing aloud. The doctor greeted Dairine, then turned back to their father.

"Well," she said, "Mrs. Callahan's status is pretty stable. And now we've had the scans that I wanted. I've had a chance to look at them, and this morning I had a couple of my colleagues look at the results. We're all in agreement."

She took a long breath. "Mr. Callahan," she said, "I don't know; you'll have to tell me whether you think it's better that you and I should discuss this alone first."

"Not a chance," Nita said. Dairine shook her head.

Her father swallowed. "They're both intelligent girls, Doctor," he said. "They're going to have to hear, anyway. Better they should get the explanation from you than secondhand from me."

The doctor nodded, then got up, shut the door to the corridor, and sat down again. "All right," she said. Her voice was measured, gentle. "Mr. Callahan, the growth in your wife's brain is definitely a tumor. We're ninety percent sure that it's a growth of a type called glioblastoma multiform. This kind of growth is very invasive, very fast growing. It invades nearby tissue quickly and destructively. And it is usually malignant."

They all sat still as statues.

"The only way we're going to be a hundred percent sure of the assessment is to do a biopsy," Dr. Kashiwabara said. "We'll do that in a day or two, so that we can determine our course of action. But I want to stress to you that the tumor itself can be removed. That will relieve the pressure on the surrounding structures."

"But that's not everything, is it?" Nita said.

The doctor shook her head. "I said that this kind of growth is invasive. It has a tendency to spread—to seed itself throughout the body, to other organs: the lymph nodes, the liver and spleen, the bone marrow. Because glioblastomas grow so quickly at this stage in their development, it's hard to tell how long the tumor may have been there in 'silent' mode, seeding itself. The important thing is going to be to start chemotherapy as soon as possible after the surgery to remove the tumor. Possibly radiotherapy as well."

Nita's father nodded. "Have you discussed this with my wife?" he said.

"Not yet," said the doctor. "That comes next. I wanted a chance to prepare you first, since you two will want to talk about it together, and it's important that you both have all the facts."

"The 'seeding,'" her father said. "It's cancer that you mean. Spreading."

"Yes," said Dr. Kashiwabara.

Nita felt as if she had been turned to ice where she sat. *Cancer* was a word that she had come across repeatedly in her reading that morning, but she had been trying to ignore it. Now she realized her folly, for the most basic tool of wizardry is words, and a wizard who ignores words willfully is only sabotaging herself.

"What are her chances?" Nita's father said.

"It's too soon to tell," said the doctor. "Right now

our priority is to get that tumor out of there. Afterward there'll be time to look at the long-term options."

"Is the operation dangerous?" Nita said.

Dr. Kashiwabara looked at her. "There's a certain risk," she said. "As in any surgical procedure. But the tumor's in an area where it won't be too hard to get at, and for this kind of surgery, we use a technique that's more like the way we fix people's noses than anything else. It's not nearly as invasive or traumatic as brain surgery was years ago. I'll sit down with you and show you some diagrams, if you like."

"Thanks," Nita said. "Yes."

The doctor turned back to their dad. "Is there anything else you want to ask me?"

"Only when you think the surgery will be scheduled."

"As soon as possible. There's a team of local specialists that we put together for this kind of surgery. I'm getting everyone's schedules sorted out now. I think it'll be Wednesday or Thursday."

"Okay," Nita's dad said. "Thanks, Doctor."

The doctor went off, leaving them together. *I saw her face,* Nita remembered her dad saying. She was shaking. *He was right...*

"There's no point in us hanging around here," her father said. "Why don't we look at the diagrams Dr. Kashiwabara has for us. Then I'll drop you two home, and come back a little bit later, so I can talk to Mom."

"Daddy, no!" Dairine said. "I want to stay and—"

Dari, Nita said silently, *shut up. We need to see Tom, in a hurry. And you and I need to talk.*

"No, honey," their father said. "I want to see her first. Okay?"

"All right," Dairine said, subdued, but she shot Nita a rebellious look. "Let's go."

Nita held her fire until they were home, and all had had something to eat. When her father was getting ready to go out, she stopped him at the door and said, "We may be going out, Dad. Don't be surprised if we're not here when you get back. There are visiting hours tonight, right?"

"Yes, I think so. You can go then." Her dad exhaled. "I guess it's a good thing that the surgery will happen quickly. We can start...coping, I guess."

"Yeah. And we'll do more than that." She gave him a hug. "Give that to Mom for me."

"I will."

She watched him pull out of the driveway and drive off.

Nita started up the stairs and met Dairine halfway down them, shrugging into her jacket, with Spot under her arm. "Not so fast," Nita said. "I want you to tell me what you were doing in there."

"Something," Dairine said. "Which was more than *you* were."

Nita was tempted to hit her sister—to *really* hit her, which shocked her. Dairine brushed by her and headed for the back door. Nita grabbed her own jacket and her manual, locked the back door, and went after her.

Dairine was halfway down the driveway already. "Were you crazy, doing a wizardry right there?" Nita whispered as she caught up with her. "And you *bombed*, didn't you? You crashed and burned."

Dairine was walking fast. "I don't want to talk about it."

"You'd better talk about it! She's my mother, too! What were you trying to do?"

"What do you think? I was trying to cure her!"

Nita gulped. *"Just like that? Are you nuts?* Without even knowing exactly what *kind* of growth you were operating on yet? Without—"

"Neets, while I've still got the power, I've got to try to do something with it," Dairine said. "Before I lose the edge!"

"That doesn't mean you just do any old thing before you're prepared!" Nita said. "That wizardry just came *apart*! What if some piece of it got loose and affected someone else in there? What if—"

"It doesn't matter," Dairine muttered, furious. "It didn't work." Nita looked at her, as they crossed the street and headed down the road that led to Tom and Carl's, and saw the tears starting to fill Dairine's eyes again. "It didn't work," Dairine said, more quietly. *"How can it not have worked?* This isn't even anything *like* pushing a planet around; this isn't even a middle-sized wizardry— It…" She went quiet.

Nita could feel the tension building all through Dairine, like a coil winding tighter and tighter. "Come on," she said.

When they rang Tom's doorbell, it was a few

moments before he answered, and as he opened the screen door, Nita wasn't quite sure what to make of his expression. "It's Grand Central Station around here this morning," Tom said, "in all kinds of ways. Come on in."

"Is this a bad time?" Nita asked timidly.

"Oh, no worse than usual," said Tom. "Come on in; don't just stand there."

He quickly closed the front door behind Nita and Dairine as they went by, which was probably just as well, because otherwise a passerby might have seen the six-foot-long iridescent blue giant slug sitting in the middle of the living-room floor, deep in conversation with Carl. At least it would have looked like a giant slug to anyone who hadn't been to Alphecca VI, but slugs weren't usually encrusted with rubies of such a size. "Hey, ladies," Carl said as they passed, and then went back to his conversation with his guest.

Tom led them into the big combined kitchen–dining room. "Are you two all right?" Tom said. "No, I can tell you're not; it's just about boiling off you. What's happened?"

Briefly Nita told him. Tom's face went blank with shock.

"Oh, my God," he said. "Nita, Dairine, I'm so sorry. This started happening when?"

"Yesterday afternoon."

Tom sat down at the table. "Please," he said, gesturing them to seats across from him. "And you say they've got the scans done already. That helps." He looked up then. "It also explains something Carl noticed an hour or so ago..."

Carl had just said good-bye to the Alpheccan, who had vanished most expertly, without even enough disturbance of the air to rustle the curtains. "Yeah, I thought that was you earlier," Carl said, coming over to sit down at the table and looking at Dairine. "It had your signature, with that kind of power expenditure. But something went real wrong, didn't it?"

"It didn't work," Dairine said softly.

"There are only about twenty reasons why it shouldn't have," Carl said, sounding dry. "Inadequate preparation, no concrete circle when so many variables were involved, insufficiently defined intervention locus in both volume and tissue type, other unprotected living entities in the field of possible effects, inadequate protection for the wizardry against 'materials' memory of past traumas in the area; shall I go on? *Major* screwup, Dairine. I expect better of you." He was frowning.

Nita tried to remember if she'd ever seen Carl frown before, and failed, and got the shivers.

"I thought I could just *fix* it," Dairine said, looking pale. "I mean—I've done that kind of thing before."

Carl shook his head. "Yes, but you can't go on that way forever. Your power levels are down nine, maybe ten points from mid-Ordeal levels. That's just as it should be. But hasn't it occurred to you that there's another problem? You started very big. This is a small wizardry by comparison—and you haven't yet mastered the reduction in scale to make you much good at the small stuff. Sorry, Dairine, but that's the price you pay for such a spectacular debut. Right now Nita's the only one in your house who's got the kind of control to attempt any kind of intervention on your mother at all. You're going to have to let her handle it. And I warn you not to interfere in whatever intervention Nita may elect. It could kill all three of you. It's going to be hard for you to sit on your hands and watch, but that's just what you're going to have to do."

"It's not fair," Dairine whispered.

"No," said Tom. "So let's agree that it's not, then move past that to some kind of solution. If indeed there is one."

"*If!*" Nita said.

Tom looked at her steadily, an expression inviting her to calm herself down. "Maybe a Coke or something?" Carl said.

"Please," Nita said. Carl got up to get the drinks. To Tom, Nita said, "I was doing a lot of reading this morning. I kept running into references to spells that had to do with cancer being difficult because the condition is 'intractable,' or 'recalcitrant.'" She shook her head. "I don't get it. A spell *always* works."

"Except when the problem keeps reconstructing itself afterward," Tom said, "in a different shape. It's like that intervention you and Kit were working on, the Jones Inlet business. If the pollution coming out of the inner waters was always the same, the wizardry would be easy to build. But it's changing all the time."

Nita grimaced. "Yeah, well," she said, "I blew a whole lot of time on detail work on that one, and the spell worked just fine without it. I think I'm having a lame-brain week." She rubbed her face. "Just when I most seriously don't need one!"

"There's not much point in beating yourself up about that right now," Tom said. "The foundations of the wizardry were sound, and it did the job, which is what counts. And you may be able to recycle the subroutines for something else eventually."

Carl came back with four bottles of Coke, distributed them, and sat down. He exchanged glances with Tom for a second longer than absolutely necessary, as information passed from mind to mind.

"Oh boy," Carl said. "Nita, Tom's right. The basic problem is the structure of the malignancy itself—"

"Look, let's take this from the top," Tom said. "Otherwise there are going to be more misunderstandings." He held out his hand, and a compact version of his manual dropped into it. He put it down on the table and started leafing through it. "You've done some medical wizardry in the past," he said to Nita.

"Yeah. Minor healings. Some not so minor."

Tom nodded. "Tissue regeneration is fairly simple," he said. "Naturally there's always a price. Blood, either in actual form or expressed by your agreement to suffer the square of the pain you're intending to heal—that's the normal arrangement. But when you start involving nonhuman life in the healing, things get complicated."

Nita blinked. "*Excuse* me? My mother was human the last time I looked!"

Carl gave Tom an ironic look. "What my distracted colleague here means is that it's not just your mother you have to heal, but also whatever's attacking her. If you don't heal the *cause* of the tumor or the cancer, it just comes back somewhere else, in some worse form."

"What could be worse than a brain tumor?!" Dairine said.

"Don't ask," Tom said, still leafing through the manual. "There are too many ways the Lone Power could answer that question." He glanced up then. "Your main problem is that cancer cells are tough for wizards to treat because they're neither all inanimate nor all biological life. They're a hybrid...which causes problems when trying to write a spell that will eradicate them without hurting normal cells. It's exactly the same thing that makes chemotherapy slightly dangerous. It poisons the good cells as well as the bad ones unless it's very carefully managed."

"The other part of the problem," Carl said, "is that the viruses and malignant cells mutate as they spread. That makes cancer as intractable for wizards to treat as for doctors. Even if you could wave your hands in the air and say, 'Disease go away!' all you can do is make the disease go away that's there *today*. After that, all it takes is one virus that you missed, hidden away in just one cell somewhere, to start breeding again. They get smarter and nastier after an incomplete eradication. What comes back will kill you faster than what was there originally. Worse, you can never get them all. A spell complex enough to do that, accurately naming and describing each and every cell, and what you think might be hiding in it, would take you years to write. By which time..." He shook his head.

"I thought maybe *you* did spells like that," Nita said in a small voice.

Tom smiled, even though the smile was sad. "That's a much higher compliment than I deserve. No, a wizardry *that* complex is well beyond my competence... which is a shame, because if it wasn't, I wouldn't rest by day or night until I had it for you."

Nita gulped.

"A lot of wizards have spent a lot of time on this one, Nita," said Carl. "There are ways to attempt a cure, but the price is high. If it weren't, there wouldn't be much cancer; we'd be stomping it out with ease wherever we found it. As it is, look at the world around you, and see how far we've got."

That thought wasn't one she cared for. "You say there are ways to 'attempt' a cure," Nita said. "It sounds like it doesn't work very often."

"That's because of the most basic part of the problem," Carl said. "It leaves us, in some ways, even less able to do anything than the medical people. We're wizards. Viruses, though they're not exactly *organic* life, are life regardless. And we cannot just go around killing things without dealing with the consequences, at every level."

"Oh, come *on!*" Dairine said.

"Not at all," Carl said. "Where do you draw the line, Dairine? Where in the Oath does it say, 'I'll protect this life over here but not *that* one, which is just a germ and happens to be annoying me at the moment?' There's no such dichotomy. You respect *all* life, or none of it. Of *course*, that doesn't mean that wizards never kill. But killing increases entropy locally, and it's always to be resisted. Sometimes, yes, you must kill in order to save another life. But you must first make your peace with the life-form you're killing."

"If I'm just going to be killing a bunch of viruses," Nita said, "I should be able to manage that."

Carl shook his head. "It may not be so easy. Viruses have their own worldview: 'Reproduce at any cost.' Which also can mean 'kill your host.' In dealing with that kind of thing, a wizard is handicapped right from the start."

"Blame the Speech," Tom said. "It's the basis on which every wizardry is predicated...but here, it's also our weak spot, if this *is* a weakness. Everything that lives knows the Speech and can use it to tell you how life feels for it, how its universe makes it behave..."

Nita stared at the table, her heart sinking. Tom was right. It was hard to be angry at something—a rock, a tree—that you could hear saying to you, *This is how I'm made; it's not my fault; you see how the world is, the way things are; what else can I do?* And for the simplest things—and viruses are about as simple as things get—it would be hard to explain to them why they shouldn't be doing this, why they should all just stop reproducing themselves and essentially commit suicide so that your mother didn't have to die. Their world was such a simple one, it wouldn't allow for much in the way of—

Nita's eyes went wide.

She slowly looked up from the table at Tom. "What

about— Tom, is it possible to change a cancer virus's perception of the world—change the way the universe seems for them, *is* for them—so that they're more sentient? So that a wizard *could* deal with them to best effect? Talk them out of being there…talk them out of killing? Something like that?"

Tom and Carl looked at each other. Tom's look was dubious. But Carl's expression was strangely intrigued. He nodded slowly.

"You know the rules," he said. "'If they're old enough to ask…'"

"'…they're old enough to be told.'"

Tom folded his hands and looked at them. "Nita," he said, "I couldn't ask about this before. Who are you thinking of doing this wizardry for? Your mother or you?"

Nita sat silent, then she opened her mouth.

"Don't," Carl said. "You're still in shock; you can't possibly have a clear answer to the question yet. You're going to have to find out as you do your work. But the question matters. Wizardry, finally, is about service to other beings. Our own needs come second. If you start fooling yourself about that, the deception is going to go straight to the heart of any spell you write, and ruin it. And maybe you as well."

"Okay," Tom said. "Let that rest for the moment." To Nita he said, "Are you clear about what you're suggesting you want to do?"

"I guess it would mean changing the way things behave in the universe, locally," Nita said. "Inside my mom." And she gulped. When she put it that way, it suddenly became clear how many, many ways there were to screw it up.

"Changing the structure of the universe itself," Tom said. "Yes. You get to play God on a local level."

"You're going to tell me that it's seriously dangerous," Nita said, "and the price is awful."

"Anything worth having demands a commensurate price," Carl said. "What is your mother's life worth to you?...And yes, this option has dangers. But I see that's not likely to stop you in the present situation."

He leaned back a little in his chair, folding his arms, looking at Nita. "We have to warn you clearly," Carl said. "You think you've been through a lot in your career so far. I have news for you. You haven't yet played with *anything* like this. When you start altering the natural laws of universes, it's like throwing a rock into a pond. Ripples spread, and the first thing in the local system to be affected, the first thing the ripples hit, is *you.* You're going to need practice handling that, keeping yourself as you are in the face of *everything* changing, before trying it for real...and unfortunately, in this universe, everything *is* for real."

"I don't care," Nita said. "If there's a chance I might be able to save my mom, I have to try. What do I need to do?"

"Go somewhere it's *not* for real," Carl said. "One of the universes where you can practice."

Nita stared at him, confused. "Like learning to fly a plane in a simulator?"

"It wouldn't be a simulation," Tom said. "It'll be real enough. As Carl said, figures of speech aside, it's *always* for real. But if you have to make mistakes while you're learning how to manipulate local changes in universal structure, there are places set aside where you can make them and not kill anybody in the process."

"Or where, if you kill yourself making one of those mistakes, you won't take anyone else with you," said Carl.

There was a moment's silence at that.

"Where?" Nita said. "I want to go."

"Of course you do, right this minute," Carl said, rubbing his face. "It's going to take time to set up."

"There may not *be* a lot of time, Carl! My mom—"

"Is not going to die today, or tomorrow," Tom said, "as far as the doctors can tell. Isn't that so?"

"Yes, but—" Nita stopped. For a moment she had been ready to shout that they weren't being very considerate of her. But that would have been untrue. As her Senior wizards, their job was to be tough with her when she needed it. Anything else would have been *really* inconsiderate.

"Good," Carl said. "Get a grip. You're going to need it, where you're going. The aschetic continua, the 'practice' universes, are flexible places—at least the early ones in the sequence—but if you indulge yourself in sloppy thinking while you're in one, it can be fatal."

"Where are they?" Nita said. "How do I get there?"

"It's a worldgating," Tom said. "Nonstandard, but you'd be using existing gates." He glanced at Carl. "Penn Station?"

"Penn's down right now. It'd have to be Grand Central."

Nita nodded; she had a fair amount of experience with the worldgates there. "What do I do when I get there?"

"Your manual will have most of the details," Carl said. "You'll practice changing the natures and rules of the nonpopulated spaces that the course makes available to you. You'll start with easy ones, then move up to universes that more strenuously resist your efforts to change them, then ones that will be almost impossible to change."

"It's like weight lifting," Nita said. "Light stuff first, then heavier."

"In a way."

"When you finish the course," Tom said, "if you've done it correctly, you'll be in a position to come back and recast your mother's physical situation as an alternate universe...and change its rules. If you still want to."

If? Nita decided not to press the point. She'd noticed over time that sometimes Tom and Carl spent a lot of effort warning you about things that weren't going to happen. "Yes. I want to do it."

Tom and Carl looked at each other. "All right," Tom said. "You're going to have to construct a carrying matrix for the spells you'll take with you—sort of a wizardly backpack. Normally you'd read the manual and construct the spells you need, on the spot, but that won't work where you're going. In the practice universes, time runs at different speeds, so the manual can be unpredictable about updating...and you can't wait for it when you're in the middle of some wizardry where speed of execution is crucial. Your manual will have details on what the matrix needs to do. What it looks like is up to you."

"And one last thing," Carl said. He looked sad but also stern. "If you go forward on this course, there's going to come a time when you're going to have to ask your mother whether this is a price *she* wants you to pay."

"I know that," Nita said. "I'm used to asking my mom for permission for stuff. I don't think this'll be a problem." She looked up at them. "But what *is* the price?"

Tom shook his head. "You'll find out as you go along."

"Yeah," Nita said. "Okay. I'll get started as soon as I get home."

And then, to Nita's complete shock, she broke down and began to cry. Tom and Carl sat quietly and let her, while Dairine sat there looking stricken. After a moment Tom got up and got Nita a tissue, and she blew her nose and wiped her eyes. "I'm sorry," she said, "that keeps happening all of a sudden."

"Don't be sorry," Tom said. "It's normal. And so is not giving up."

She sniffed once or twice more and then nodded.

"Go do what you have to," Tom said.

She and Dairine got up. "And Nita," Carl said.

On her way to the front door, she looked back at him.

"Be careful," Carl said. "There are occupational hazards to being a god."

Sunday Afternoon and Evening

NITA AND DAIRINE WALKED home, and Nita went up to her room and settled in to work. The moment she sat down at her desk, she saw that her manual already had several new sections in it, subsequent to the usual one that dealt with worldgatings and other spatial and temporal dislocations.

The first new section had general information about the practice universes: their history, their locations relative to the hundreds of thousands of known alternate universes, their qualities. *They're playpens,* Nita thought as she read. *Places where the structure that holds science to matter, and wizardry to both of them, has some squish to it; where the hard corners on things aren't so hard, so you can stretch your muscles and find out how to exploit the squish that exists elsewhere.* There was no concrete data about how the practice universes had been established, but they were very old, having apparently been sealed off to prevent settlement at a time almost too ancient to be conceived. *One of the Powers That Be, or Someone higher up, foresaw the need.*

While it was useful that no one lived in those universes to get hurt by wizards twisting natural laws around, there seemed to be a downside as well. You couldn't stay in them for long. The manual got emphatic about the need not to exceed the assigned duration of scheduled sessions—

> Universes not permanently inhabited by intelligent life have only a limited toleration for the presence of sentients. The behavior of local physics within these universes can become skewed or deranged when overloaded by too many sentient-hours of use in a given period. In extreme cases such over-inhabition can cause an aschetic continuum to implode....

Boy, there's *a welcome I won't overstay,* Nita thought, though not without a moment's curiosity about what it was like inside a universe when it imploded. *Something to get Dairine to investigate, maybe.* Nita managed just a flicker of a grim smile at the thought.

> Access scheduling is arranged through manual functions from the originating universe. Payment for the gating is determined by duration spent in the aschesocontinuum and deducted from the practitioner at the end of each session. Access is through local main-line gating facilities of complexity level XI or better; the gating type is a diazo-Riemannian timeslide, which, regardless of duration spent in the aschetic continuum, returns practitioners to the originating universe an average of +.10 planetary rotations along duration axis, variation +/- .005 rotation.

Nita did the conversion from the decimal timings, raised her eyebrows. *So you go in, then come out more* or less two hours after you went...no matter how much time you spend there.

Could get tiring.

Ask me if I care!

There were many other details. Nita spent the rest of an hour or so absorbing them, then passed on to what seemed the most important part of the work in front of her: constructing the matrix to hold the spells she'd be using in the practice universes. The matrix would hold a selection of wizardries ready for use until she could get back to where the manual could be depended on for fast use.

The thought of a place where you couldn't depend on the manual made Nita twitch a little. But that was where she had to go to do her mother any good, so she got over it and started considering the structure of the matrix. It was complex; it had to be in order to hold whole ready-to-run spells apart from one another, essentially in stasis, so that they couldn't get tangled. The matrix structure that the manual suggested was straightforward enough to build but fiddly—like putting chain mail together, ring by ring and rivet by rivet, each ring going through three others.

Nita cleared her desk and laid the manual out where she could keep her eye on the guide diagram it provided. Then she put out her hands and pronounced eighty-one syllables in the Speech. Once complete, the sentence took physical form, drifting like a glowing thread into her hands. She said the sentence again, and again, until she had nine of the strands. Then Nita wound them together and knotted the ends of the ninefold strand together with a wizard's knot, creating a single sealed loop, which she scaled down in size. The next loop of nine strands was laced through that one, as were the next two. When it was finished, there would be three-to-the-sixth links in the matrix: seven hundred twenty-nine of them....

Nita didn't allow the numbers to freak her out. She kept at it, making each set of nine strands, winding them together, looping them, linking them through the other available links, and fastening them closed. The work was as hypnotic in its way as crocheting—a hobby that Nita had taken up a couple of years ago at her mother's instigation, then promptly dumped because the constant repetition of motions made her hands cramp. But this was not about making a scarf. This was about saving her mother's life...so Nita found it a lot easier to ignore the cramps.

Gradually the delicate structure began to grow. Several times Nita missed hooking one of the substructures into all the others it had to be connected to, and the diagram in the manual flashed insistently until she went back and fixed it. Slowly, though, she started to get the rhythm down pat, and the eighty-one syllables, repeated again and again, came out perfectly every time, though they started becoming meaningless with the repetition. *I'm going to be saying these things in my sleep,* Nita thought, finishing one more unit and moving on to the next.

About an hour into this work, Nita heard her dad come home. The back door shut, and she heard him moving around downstairs in the kitchen, but she kept doing what she was doing. A few minutes later there was a knock at her door, and he came in.

Nita looked up at him, grateful for the interruption, and flexed her hands to get rid of the latest bout of cramps. The steady energy drain that came with doing a repetitive wizardry like this was really tiring her out, but that couldn't be helped. "How's Mom?" she said.

"She's fine," her father said, and sat down wearily on her bed. "Well, not fine; of course not. But she's not in pain, and she's not so full of the drugs this afternoon... We talked about the surgery. She's okay about that."

"Really?" Nita said.

Her father rubbed his face. "Well, of course not, honey," he said. "Who *wants* anybody monkeying around with their brain? But she knows it's got to be done."

"And the rest of it?"

Her dad shook his head. "She's not exactly happy about the possibility that the cancer might have spread. But there's nothing we can do about that, and there's no point in worrying about it when there's something so much more important happening in a few days."

He looked at the faint line of light lying on Nita's desk. "What's that?"

She picked it up, handed it to him. "Go ahead," she said when he hesitated. "You can't hurt it."

He reached out and took the delicate linkage of loop after loop of light into his hands. "What's it for?"

"Helping Mom."

"You talked to Tom and Carl?"

"Yeah." Nita wondered whether to get into the details, then decided against it. *When he's ready to ask, I'll be ready to tell. I hope.* "There are places I can go," she said, "where I can learn the skills I need to deal with the...cancer." She had trouble saying the word. *I'm going to have to get over that.* "I won't be gone for long, Dad, but I'll be going to places where time doesn't run the same way. I may be pretty tired when I get back."

He handed back the partly made matrix. "You really think this has a chance of making a difference? Of making your mom well?"

"It's a chance," Nita said. "I won't know until I try, Daddy."

"Is Dairine going with you?"

Nita shook her head. "She's got to sit this one out."

Her father nodded. "All right. Sweetheart...you know what I'm going to say."

"Be careful."

He managed just the slightest smile. "When are you going to tell Mom about this?"

"When I've tried it once. After I see how it goes, I'll tell her. No point in getting her worried, or excited, until I know for sure that I *can* get where I have to go and do what I have to."

"One other thing, hon..."

Nita looked at her father with concern.

"For tomorrow and Tuesday, anyway, I think you and Dairine should go to school as usual. It's better for us all to stick to our normal routines than to sit around home agonizing over what's going on."

Nita wasn't wild about this idea, but she couldn't find it in her heart to start arguing the point with her father right now. "Okay," she said after a moment.

"Then I'll go get us something to eat," her father said, and went out.

Nita turned back to the desk, let out a long sad breath at the pain and worry in her dad's face, and said the eighty-one syllables one more time....

Kit spent the day adding notes to his manual on where he had been. Once or twice during the process he checked the back of the book to see if there was anything from Nita but found nothing. At first he thought, *Maybe she's busy. It's not like she doesn't have her own projects to work on.* But as the evening approached, Kit began to wonder what she was up to. *I guess I could always shoot her a thought.*

He pushed back in his desk chair, leaned back—
"Ow!"

Kit turned around hurriedly and realized that Ponch was lying right behind him, half asleep...or formerly half asleep. He wasn't now; not with one of Kit's chair legs shoved into his gut. "Sorry," Kit said, pulling the chair in a little.

"Hmf," Ponch said, and put his head down on his paws again.

Kit sighed and closed his eyes once more. *Neets?...*

...Nothing. Well, not quite. She was there, but she wasn't in receiving mode right now, or just wasn't receptive. Additionally, coming from her direction, Kit could catch a weird sort of background noise, like

someone saying something again and again—a fierce in-turned concentration he'd never felt in her before. *What's she doing?...* The noise had a faint taste of wizardry about it, but there was also an emotional component, a turmoil of extreme nervousness, but blocked, stifled—he couldn't make anything of it.

Weird, he thought. *Neets? Anybody home?*

Still no reply. Finally Kit sighed and leaned forward to his work again. The manual had presented him with a detailed questionnaire about his experiences in the places he'd been, and there were still a lot of sections to fill in. *I'll walk over there after I'm done and see what the story is.*

It was after eight before Kit got up. He went downstairs to get his jacket, for it was chilly; fall was setting in fast. As Kit went by, his pop looked up from the living-room chair where he was reading, and said, "Son, it's a school day tomorrow. Don't be out late."

"I won't," Kit said. "Just gonna drop in on Nita real fast."

With a scrabble of claws on the stairs, Ponch threw himself down them and turned the corner into the living room. "Whereyagoin'-whereyagoin'-whereyagoin'!"

"Mr. Radar Ears strikes again," Kit's father said. "Can't move around here without that dog demanding you take him out for a walk."

"He has his reasons," Kit said, amused, and headed out.

The streetlight at the corner was malfunctioning again, sizzling as its light jittered on and off. Kit didn't mind the "off"; as he crossed the street with Ponch, he could see more plainly the stars of autumn evening climbing through the branches of the trees. Already there were fewer leaves to hide them. At the rate this fall had been going, with sharp frosts every night, there would be few leaves, or none, left in a couple of weeks. Past the faint glints of Deneb and Altair in that sky were Uranus and Neptune. Kit couldn't see them with the naked eye, but to a wizard's senses they could be felt, even at this distance, as a distant tang of mass in the icy void. Kit smiled at the thought that they seemed even more like the local neighborhood than usual, compared to the places he'd been today.

He came to Nita's house and, to his surprise, found it dark and Nita's dad's car gone. *Maybe they all went out somewhere, to the movies or to visit somebody, something like that. Oh well, Mela said she called. And she got my message. She'll get back to me.*

Kit walked Ponch for a little while more, then went home and settled once again at his desk to finish that report in the manual, but first he used it to leave Nita another message. *Tried to reach you earlier, but you sounded busy. Call when you can.* He would have added *See you at school tomorrow,* except that this was less likely than it used to be. Their classes were all different, and at the moment they didn't even have the same lunch period.

He sent the message, then paged through the manual to finish his report. Ponch curled up behind Kit's chair, muttering a little to himself as he groomed his paws after their walk. "If you were going to tell someone your gut feeling about the places where we went yesterday," Kit said to Ponch, reading him one of the questions he still had to answer, "what would it be?"

"They smelled nice," Ponch said slowly. "But smell isn't everything..."

Kit raised his eyebrows, made a note of that, and went back to work.

Monday Morning and Afternoon

NITA SAW DAWN COME in again…this time because she hadn't bothered to go to sleep after coming back from the hospital. She had been too busy working on the spell matrix. Now, worn out, she sat at her desk in the vague morning light and looked at it as it lay in her hands.

To a wizard far enough along in her learning to think in the Speech, and used to seeing the underpinnings of power beneath mere appearance, it looked two ways. One was a complex, interwoven glitter and shimmer of strands of light with nine prominent "knots" showing, each one a receptor site into which a "free" wizardry could be offered up. But the other semblance, which had made it easier for Nita to work with the wizardry in its later stages, was a charm bracelet, though one with no charms on it as yet. The manual suggested it would take time for her to choose the spells she needed and mate them successfully to the matrix. Nita hoped it wouldn't take as long as the manual suggested it might. She needed to hurry.

She poured it through her fingers, feeling the virtual mass she had bound into the matrix's structure. It now looked and felt enough like an ordinary charm bracelet that no one would find it strange Nita was wearing it. It was also a convenient shape; she wouldn't have to keep it in a pocket.

"Didn't think you'd be done with it already," Dairine said from right behind her.

Nita started, nearly falling right out of her chair, then looked over her shoulder. "Yeah, well, think about that the next time you accuse me of not doing anything."

Dairine nodded. She looked wan, in that early light, and her dad's big T-shirt hanging off her made her look more waiflike and fragile than usual. Nita regretted having spoken sharply to her. "You okay?"

"No," Dairine said, "and why should I be? Terrible things are happening, and there's nothing I can do. Worse, I have to sit around and hope that *you* get it right." She glowered.

This, at least, was a more normal mode of operation for Dairine. Nita poked her genially. "We'll see what Carl says," she said. "Go on."

Dairine went off. Nita got up and opened a drawer, to choose her clothes for that day, picked up that new skirt and almost decided not to wear it. Then she thought, *Why not? If I get sent home, it'll just give Mom an excuse to feel like she was right. Probably cheer her up, too.* She fished around for a top to go with it, then went off for her shower.

Half an hour later, showered and dressed, Nita felt slightly better, almost as if she hadn't been up all night. She went downstairs to have a bite of breakfast and found her father finishing a bowl of cereal. He glanced at Nita as she rummaged in the fridge, and said, "Isn't that a little short?"

Nita snickered. "Mom bought it, Dad. It was long enough for *her.*"

Her father raised his eyebrows. He normally left this kind of issue to Nita and her mom to resolve; now he seemed to be having second thoughts. "Well, I suppose... Come by the store when you're out of school and we'll go straight over and see Mom."

"Okay." She put the milk down and hugged him. "See you later."

Her father went out, and Nita watched him get into the car and drive off. It felt to her as if he was just barely holding it all together, and that tore at Nita. *Well, if I can make this work, he won't need to be that way for long.*

Please, God, let it work!

She drank a glass of milk and then sat down at the kitchen table with her manual, flipping to the back of it. There she saw the new message from Kit and was immediately guilt stricken. *I'll catch up with him at school today,* she thought. *Right now, though, I've gotta take care of this first.* She opened a new message on a clean page. *Carl?*

The answer came straight back; he was using his manual, too. *Good morning.*

Got a moment?

If it's just a moment, yes.
I'm done. Want to check it out?
Okay. Come on over.

Nita reached into her claudication-pocket, pulled out the transit spell she used for Tom and Carl's backyard, and tweaked the ingress parameters so that there'd be no air-displacement bang. Then she dropped it to the floor and stepped through.

Carl was standing in the doorway from the house to the patio, tying his tie and looking out at the garden. Nita paused for just a moment to admire him; she didn't often see him dressed for work. "Nice tie, Carl."

He glanced down at it. It was patterned all over with bright red chilies, a surprising contrast to the sober charcoal of the suit. "Yeah, it was a gift from my sister. Her ideas of business wear are unique. What've you got for me?"

"Here," Nita said, going over to hand him the charm bracelet. He raised his eyebrows, amused by the shape, and then dissolved the appearance to show the matrix itself, enlarged until it stretched a couple of feet in length, shimmering and intricate, between his hands.

"Yeah," Carl said, examining it section by section. "Right..." He showed her one spot where the linked strands didn't come together quite the same way they did elsewhere. "Open receptor site there..."

"I know. I left it that way on purpose, in case I need to expand it later." Nita pointed at the spell strands around the spot. "See, there's reinforcement around it, and a blocker."

"Hmm..." He looked at the rest of the matrix.

"Yeah, I see what you've done; it makes sense. Okay, I'll sanction it."

Carl took the two ends of the matrix strand and knotted them with a slightly more involved version of the wizard's knot. The whole length of the matrix flashed briefly with white fire as Carl set his Senior's authorization into the structure of the wizardry. Though the flash died away quickly, for a few moments the whole backyard hummed with released and re-bound power. Nita was distracted from the sight of a small, complex structure now hanging from the strand, like a tangled knot of light, by a sudden annoyed voice that said:

> *"Any chance you might*
> *hold it* down *out there? People*
> *in here are still sleeping."*

Nita looked around. One of the koi in the fishpond had put its head up out of the water and was giving them both a cranky look.

Carl sighed. "Sorry, Akagane-sama." He bowed slightly in the fish's direction.

The koi, a big handsome one spotted in dark orange-gold and white, rolled halfway over on the edge of the pool, and caught sight of Nita with one golden eye. It looked at her thoughtfully, then said:

> *"If half a loaf is better*
> *than no bread, then at least*
> *I want the crumbs now."*

"It's blackmail, that's what it is," Carl said, and vanished into the house. A few moments later he came back out and dropped some koi pellets and toast crumbs into the water.

The fish let out a bubble of breath, glancing at what Carl was holding. "All the drawing lacks," it said,

> *"is the final touch: to add*
> *eyes to the dragon..."*

Then it slipped back into the water with a small splash, and started eating.

Nita glanced at Carl. He shrugged. "Sometimes I don't know whether I have koi or koans," he said. "Anyway, you're all set now. The Grand Central gate will acknowledge this when it comes in range." He handed Nita the matrix, and it looked like a charm bracelet again. But there was something added: a single golden charm— a tiny fish. "So when're you going to start?"

"Uh, this afternoon, if I can stay awake that long."

"Go well, then," Carl said. "Speaking of which, I have to go, too." He patted her on the shoulder. "Good luck, kiddo." He went into the house.

Nita slipped the bracelet onto her wrist, and headed back to her transit circle.

Kit went to school that morning still excited about what he'd brought back from his dog walk. He'd transited the little flower, still in stasis, over to Tom's Sunday night, and he spent all his morning classes wondering what Tom would make of it. At lunchtime Kit managed to get out to where the pay phones were ranked in front of the Conlon Road entrance, and waited in line for nearly ten minutes before one was free.

Tom answered right away. "You get it okay?" Kit said.

"Yup. And I've been going through a précis of the raw data from your walk—the whole capture is about a thousand pages, maybe more. The really interesting thing about your jaunt, though, is that the places you went, the places you made, *are still there.*"

Kit wasn't sure what to make of that. "I thought they would just go away afterward."

"Seems not."

"What does that mean?"

"That I need an aspirin, mostly," Tom said. "Well, it means a few other things, too."

Kit glanced around—none of the other kids nearby was paying him the slightest attention—and whispered, "But...you can't just make things—planets, whole universes—out of *nothing*!"

"Strangely enough, that's how it was originally done. What's unusual is that it's not usually done that way any*more*. Received wisdom had it that the grouped khiliocosms, or 'sheaf of sheaf of universes,' the whole aggregate of physical existence, had a stable and unchanging amount of matter and energy. What you and Ponch have been doing would seem to call that into question."

"Uh, then I guess we're sorry," Kit said. "We didn't mean to make trouble for anybody."

Tom burst out laughing. "The only ones it's trouble for are the theoretical wizards, most of whom are probably now pulling out their hair, scales, or tentacles. You get transitory changes in the structure and nature of wizardry every now and then. Mostly they're situational ripples in the fabric of existence, and mostly they pass. But they're going to have a party explaining *this* one."

"Is it going to be a problem?" Kit said.

"For the average wizard in the street? No," Tom said. "But I think you should have a talk with Ponch to keep him from running off and creating universes on his own. We don't know how stable these universes are...and we don't know if they might not be able to proliferate."

"Proliferate?"

"Breed," said Tom.

Kit was taken aback. "Universes can *breed*?" he whispered.

"Oh yes. I could get into the geometries of it, the mechanics of isoparthenogenetic *n*-dimensional rotations and so on, but then I'd need *three* aspirins, and my stomach'll get upset. Just have a word with Ponch, okay? I'd rather not wake up and discover that one of Ponch's creations has self-rotated and left our home space hip-deep in squirrels. It would cause talk."

"Uh, yeah."

"Meanwhile, what you brought back is safe, and

lots of people are going to want to look at it. So on behalf of research wizards everywhere, thanks a lot. What's the rest of your day look like?"

"Geometry, social studies...and gym." Kit made a face. He was not a big gym fan; wizardry can keep you from falling off the parallel bars, but it can't make you good at them.

"Uh-oh," Tom said, picking up on Kit's tone of voice. "Every now and then I think, *In the service of my Art I may accidentally drown in liquid methane or have my living-room rug slimed by giant slugs, but no one can* ever *make me climb one of those ropes again.*"

"Must be nice," Kit said.

"It will be, you'll see. Meanwhile, I think you've impressed Somebody with how you handled yourself out there. I was told to authorize you for further exploration. When you two go for your next walk, though, leave the manual on verbose reporting. It'll be useful for the researchers."

"No problem."

"Thanks again..." Tom hung up.

Then there was nothing to do with the rest of the day but go through classes as usual. While changing periods, Kit looked for Nita but didn't see her. Once, as he was just going into his math classroom before the bell rang, he caught sight of someone from behind, way down the hall, who he thought was her. But then Kit dismissed the idea; Neets didn't wear skirts that short. *And it's a shame,* said some unrepentant part of his mind.

Kit made an amused face. That part of his mind had been getting outspoken lately. His dad had reassured him that this was nothing to be concerned about—"revving up," he called it—but he wouldn't say much more. That made Kit want to laugh. His father, big and tough and worldly wise though he was, had a core of absolute shyness that few people outside the family recognized—but Kit knew it was the source of his own quiet side. He suspected that when it came to the facts of life, *he* was going to have to ask his dad to sit down and explain it all, to get the chore out of the way.

Kit went through the rest of the day, looking around for Nita again when school finished, but he couldn't find her. He went home, checked his manual, and found no new message from her, so he walked over to her house but found no one home. It made Kit want to laugh as he looked at the empty driveway. There'd occasionally been times when he didn't want to see Nita about anything specific, and she couldn't be avoided. Now, when he *did* want to talk to her, she couldn't be found. . . .

Kit went home, had dinner, and did his homework. By the time he was finished with the miserable geometry, he was ready to take all the blame for their fight, if only to get things back the way they ought to be—anything to distract himself from the horror of cosines and the Civil War. He pushed all the schoolbooks on his desk aside and shot her a thought: *Neets! Earth to Nita!*

Nothing. But this time it was a nothing he recognized—a faint mutter of distant low-level brain activity.

Nita was deeply asleep. Kit glanced at the clock in mild bemusement. *At eight at night?!*

Never mind. Tomorrow morning early I'll meet her before she goes to school; we'll walk over together.

He wandered down the hall to his sister's room, peered in. Carmela was not there, but the TV and the tape deck were, and from the earphones lying on the bed, he could faintly hear someone singing in Japanese. The VCR was running, and on the TV, some kind of cartoon singing group—three slender young men with very long ponytails—seemed to be appearing in concert, while searchlights and lasers swept and flashed around them. *It's not like the house isn't full of her weird J-pop half the time to start with,* Kit thought, *but she's got cartoon J-pop, too? Oh well. It's an improvement on the heavy metal.*

Carmela emerged from the upstairs bathroom and brushed past him. "Looking lonely, little brother," she said, flopping down on her stomach and putting the earphones back in. "Where's Miss Juanita been lately?"

"Good question," Kit said, and headed down the stairs.

"Where ya goin'?" she shouted after him.

He smiled. "Out to walk the dog."

Monday Night, Tuesday Morning

![*]

NITA WOKE UP AFTER midnight. She felt a flash of guilt for having fallen asleep straight after coming home from the hospital. But no matter how much she might have felt that precious time was slipping by, she'd been completely worn out, and there was no point in trying to do anything wizardly. Now the charm bracelet was satisfyingly heavy around her wrist, glinting in the light of the lamp on her desk, and she was rested and ready. *So let's get to work...*

She went downstairs to check where people were, and found that her dad had gone to bed. Nita made herself a sandwich and brought it back upstairs with her, pausing by Dairine's door to listen.

Silence. Softly Nita eased the door open, peered inside. In the darkness she could make out a tangle of limbs, pillows, and T-shirt on the bed—Dairine, in her usual all-night fight with the bedding. Nita shut the door and went into her room again.

She ate the sandwich with workmanlike speed and changed into jeans and sneakers and a dark jacket. Then she went to her desk to pick up the few small stand-alone wizardries that she thought would be useful for this exercise. One at a time she hooked each of them to a different link of the charm bracelet: a small gold house key, a little silvery disc with the letters *GCT* intertwined on one side and the number twenty-five on the other, a tiny stylized lightning bolt, a pebble, a little megaphone.

Nita pulled out her transit wizardry and changed its time-space coordinates, triggering the fail-safe features that would abort the spell if anyone was standing in the target area. Then she dropped the circle to the floor and stepped through, pulling it after her as she went.

The side doorway into which Nita stepped normally serviced one of the food stands in the Graybar Passage on one side of the terminal. Now there were only some black plastic garbage bags there, and Nita stepped over them and came out into the big archway dividing the passage from the Main Concourse. It would be a while before Grand Central shut down; a few trains were still moving in and out…and so was other traffic. Nita made her way to the right of the big octagonal brass information center, heading for the doorway that led to track twenty-five.

No train stood at the platform this late. Nita paused under the archway at the bottom of the platform, behind some iron racks and out of view of the control center far down the track on the right. She felt around in the back of her mind for another wizardry she'd prepared earlier, lying there almost ready to go. Nita said the thirty-fifth word, and the air around her rippled and misted over in a peculiar half-mirrored way. Whoever looked at her would see only what was directly behind her; she was effectively invisible now.

Nita walked on down the platform. Grand Central's most-used worldgate was down here, hanging in the space between tracks twenty-five and twenty-six, and accessible from either side for those who knew how to pull it over to the platform. Quite a few wizards used it for long-distance transport in the course of any one day—

Nita stumbled. *"Auuw!"* said someone down by her feet.

She recovered herself and stood still, looking around but unable to see what she'd tripped on. "Uh...sorry!"

"Oh," a voice said. "I see what you're doing. Wait a minute."

Suddenly there was a small black cat standing down by her foot, looking up at her. "Better," the cat said in the Speech. "Sorry about that. We were invisible two different ways."

"Dai, Rhiow," Nita said. Rhiow was the leader of the Grand Central worldgate supervision group, all of whose members were cats, since only feline wizards can naturally see the hyperstring structures on which worldgates are constructed. "I'm on errantry, and I greet you—"

"Aren't we all?" Rhiow said. "Nice to see you, too." She was looking at the opening in the air, filled with an odd shimmering darkness, which had manifested itself at Nita's approach. "Now, there's a configuration you don't see every day."

"Carl okayed it."

"Of course he did. It wouldn't be here otherwise. Good timing on your part, though." Rhiow looked back toward the scurrying people in the Main Concourse with a put-upon expression. "This gate's been getting three times the usual use while the others are moving around."

"Moving!" Nita's eyes widened. She'd seen more than once now what happened when a worldgate dislocated itself improperly. The results could vary from simply disastrous to extremely fatal.

"No, it's all right; it's our idea, not the gates'!" Rhiow said. "But Penn Station is being moved into a new building, across Eighth Avenue, and the gates have to go, too. We've had our paws full."

"It was nice of you to take the time to see me off."

"Not a problem, cousin," Rhiow said. "I wanted to make sure this behaved itself when you brought it online. Meanwhile, watch how you go, and watch how you handle what you find. We can bring danger with us even to a training session, so you be careful."

"I will."

"*Dai stihó* then, cousin."

"*Dai...*"

Manual in hand, Nita stepped through.

At first there was only a second's worth of darkness and the usual feel of the brushing of the worldgate across and through her, a feathers-on-mind feeling—strange as always but swiftly over. And then she broke out into light again, as if through the surface of water...

...and found herself on the opposite platform, next to track twenty-six.

Nita glanced around, confused. *Uh-oh. Am I still invisible?* She was. But then she realized that she needn't have worried. There was no one in sight at all.

She walked slowly back up the platform under the long line of fluorescent lights, going softly to avoid attracting any attention in this great quiet. *Now where'd Rhiow go?* Nita thought, glancing back at the platform to make sure she hadn't missed her somehow. But there was no sign of her, no movement, no sound anywhere—nothing but the soft cool breath of the draft coming up out of the dark depths of the tunnel through which the trains came into the station from under Park Avenue.

In the archway that led out into the Main Concourse, Nita paused, looking around her cautiously. There was no one out there, and all the lights were low. That was really bizarre, for even when the station was closed in the middle of the night, the lights were always up full, and there were always *some* people here: cleaners, transit police, workers doing maintenance on the trains and tracks. The lightbulb stars still burned, distant, up in the great blue backward sky of the terminal's ceiling, but below them the terminal was empty, drowned in a silence even more peculiar than the twilight now filling it.

Nita stood there and listened hard…not just with the normal senses, but with those that came with wizardry and were sharpened by its use. She tried to catch any hint of something wrong, the influence of the Lone Power or other forces inimical to a wizard. But there was no glimmer of danger to be sensed, no whisper of threat. *Okay,* she thought. *Mere weirdness I can handle.*

Softly Nita went out across the huge cream-colored expanse of the Main Concourse floor and up the ramp to the doors that led out onto Forty-second Street. She pushed one brass door open, stepped out onto the sidewalk.

There was no one here, either, and it wasn't one in the morning. It was midafternoon. The sun was angling westward, not even out of sight behind the skyscrapers yet.

Nita looked up and down Forty-second. No traffic, no cars, no people anywhere in sight; only the traffic lights hung out over the street, turning from red to green as she watched. A thin chill wind poured down the street past her, bearing no smells of hot-dog vendors, no voices, no honking horns…no sounds at all.

This was so creepy that Nita could hardly bear it. Once before she'd been in a New York that was nearly this empty…and she and Kit had had a bad time there. But here Nita got no sense of the Lone Power being in residence. She'd have instantly recognized that cold hostile tang in the air, the sense of being watched and overshadowed by something profoundly unfriendly.

Nita reached into her pocket of space, pulling out

her manual and flipping it open to the new section about the practice universes. *Aschetic Spaces Habituation and Manipulation Routine,* it said: *Introduction:*

> You have now successfully entered the first of a series of "aschesis" or "live proof" continua that have been made available to you. Successful handling and manipulation of this continuum will result in your being offered the next one in the series.

> You are cautioned not to remain past your assigned time. Time warnings embedded in your manual may not function correctly.

A smaller block of text appeared underneath:

> A timepiece based on the vibratory frequency of one or more crystalline compounds or elements has been detected on your person. Please use this timepiece for temporal measurements until further advice is given. Please do not change the vibratory frequency of [QUARTZ] in this universe.

"Gee, that was the first thing on my list," Nita muttered, glancing at her watch. She did a double take; the face of the watch, which until then had been plain white with black numerals, was now showing a red half-arc around the face, from the numbers 1 to 7. Nita glanced back at her manual.

> Your total permitted time for this session has been marked.

> *YOUR GOAL:*

> Each universe or continuum possesses a "kernel," or core, which contains a master copy of its physical laws and the local laws of wizardry. This master copy is a single complex statement in the Speech that lists all properties of matter

and energy in the local universe, and the values for which these properties are set. To manipulate physical law on a universal scale, whether temporarily or permanently, the universe- or continuum-kernel first must be located.

To avoid easy alteration of natural laws by local species, world-kernels are normally hidden. This universe's kernel has been concealed in a routine manner. You must find the kernel before your allotted time elapses. You must then use the kernel to change the local environment. If you cannot find the kernel within the time allowed, this assignment will be offered to you again in one planetary rotation of your home world or one idiopathic cycle appropriate to your species....

Just once a day. Nita swallowed. Wednesday was coming fast. "All right," she said to the manual, "the meter's running; let's go!"

The red arc on her watch began to flash softly; as she watched, it subtracted a tiny bit of itself from the point at which it had started.

Okay, she thought, *where do you begin?*

Nita walked away from the terminal, down that empty street, to pause at the corner of Forty-second and Lexington, looking up and down the avenue. Nothing moved anywhere. She leaned her head back to look up at the spire of the Chrysler Building, glittering in the westering sun against an unusually clear blue sky.

If I were this universe's heart, where would I be?

If it was a riddle, it was one whose answer wasn't obvious. So for a long time Nita walked north on Lexington Avenue through the windy afternoon, looking, listening, trying to get the feel of the place. It was missing something basic that her own version of New York had, but she couldn't put her finger on what was missing. At Eighty-fourth Street, on a hunch, she turned westward, heading crosstown, and started to page through the manual again for some hint of what she was doing wrong. She found a lot of information about the structures of aschetic universes, and one piece of this caught her attention, for she'd been wondering about it.

> Entire universes and continua are by definition too large and often too alien to allow quick kernel assessment and location while their genuine physical structures are displaying. Wizards on assessment/location duties therefore routinely avail themselves of a selective display option that screens out distracting phenomena, condenses the appearance and true distances of the space being investigated, and identifies the structure under assessment with a favorite structural paradigm already familiar to the wizard. Early assessment exercises default to this display option....

So it gave me someplace I'm used to working, Nita thought. *Probably just as well.* She paused at the corner of Fifth Avenue and Eighty-fourth, looking across the street and downtown at the Metropolitan Museum of Art, and then went across the street and into Central Park, continuing to read through the manual. There were no more hints, and two hours were gone already. Nita looked at some of the spells she'd used for detection in the past, but they didn't seem much good for this. They were mostly for finding physical things, not other spells.

And the spells in the book don't seem to be working right, anyway, Nita thought as she came out at Eighty-sixth and Central Park West, turning south. She wasn't getting the usual slight tingle of the mind from the wizardries as she read. It was as she'd been warned: The manual's normal instant access to the fabric of wizardry didn't seem to be working here.

Either way, Nita started to feel that spells weren't the answer. *If that's not it, there has to be another way. Besides just wandering around!* But the silent streets in which nothing moved—no sound but the wind— made everything seem a little dreamlike, the stuff of a fairy tale, not a real place at all.

But it is real. The only thing missing…

…is the sound.

Nita stopped at the southwest corner of Central Park West and Eighty-first and thought. Then she went down the path from the corner to the planetarium doors, and cut across the dog run to go up the steps to the nearby terrace, where the "astronomical" fountain was. There she sat on a bench under the ginkgo trees, near where the water ran horizontally over the constellation-mosaicked basin, and looked at her watch. She had only two hours left. Part of her felt like panicking. *This isn't working; I don't have time to spend another day doing this; what about Mom!* But Nita held herself quiet, and sat there, and listened.

Water and the wind; nothing else. But even those sounds were superfluous. She could tune them out, the way she tuned out Dairine's CD player when she didn't want to hear it. That didn't take a spell.

And maybe I don't need to tune them out, anyway. For this place to be normal, for real, she needed to tune things *in.* She needed those sounds, the sounds that to her spelled out what life was like in the city, what made it its own self.

Traffic, for example. The horns that everybody honked even though it was illegal. The particular way the tires hissed on the road in hot weather, when the surface got a little sticky in the sun. The sound of trucks backing up and making that annoying high-pitched *beep-beep-beep*. Air brakes hissing. Car engines revving as the lights changed. Sirens in the distance. One by one, in her mind, she added the sounds to the silence. There was a kind of music to it, a rhythm. Footsteps on the road and on the sidewalks created some of that; so did the rattle of those bikes with the little wagons attached that the guys from the stores used to deliver groceries.

And so did the voices. People talking, laughing, shouting at one another in the street; those sounds blended with the others and started to produce that low hush of sound, like a river. It wasn't a steady sound. It ebbed, then flowed again, rising and falling, slowly becoming that long, slow, low, rushing throb that was the sound of the city breathing.

Not even breath. Something more basic. A pulse...

Nita held still. She could hear it now. It was not a pulse as humans thought of such things. It was much too slow. You would as soon hear a tree's pulse or breathing as this. But Nita was used to hearing trees breathe, and besides, their breath was part of this bigger one. Slowly and carefully, as if the perception was something she might break if she moved too suddenly, she turned her head.

The "sound" was louder to the south. If this place had a heart, it was south of her.

Nita got up carefully and, concentrating on not losing the way she was hearing things now, made her way back to the stairs and down from the fountain terrace, back toward Central Park West, then started heading south again. Within a block she knew she was going the right way. *It's stronger.*

Within another block she was so sure of what and how she was hearing that she didn't need to walk carefully anymore. Nita began to alternate jogging and walking, heading for the source of that heartbeat. Even in the silence, now that she'd let that recur, she could hear that slow rush of cityness underneath everything, like the sound she'd once heard of blood flow in an artery, recorded and much slowed down, a kind of windy growl. She got as far as Central Park South and realized that the source of the pulse was to her right and ahead of her: downtown, on the West Side somewhere.

Nita followed the pulse beat, feeling it get stronger all the time, as if it was in her bones as well as the city's. She went west as far as Seventh Avenue, then knew she was on the right track. The pulse came from her left, and it was much closer now. Another ten blocks maybe?

It turned out to be fifteen, but the closer Nita got, the less she cared about the distance, or the fact that she was dog tired. *I'm going to do it. It's going to be okay. Mom's going to be okay!*

She came out in Times Square, and smiled as she perceived the joke—there were lots of people who would have claimed that this was the city's heart. But her work wasn't done yet. The kernel was hidden here somewhere. Now that she knew what to listen for, Nita could feel the force of it beating against her skin, like a sun she couldn't see. Nita stopped there in the middle of a totally empty Times Square, all blatant with neon signs and garish, gaudy electric billboards along which news of strange worlds crawled and flashed in letters of fire, in the Speech and in other languages, which she didn't bother to translate. She turned slowly, listening, feeling...

There. A blank wall of a building. It was white marble, solid. But Nita knew better than to be bothered by mere physical appearance, or even some kinds of physical reality. She went to the wall, passed her hands over it.

It was stone, all right. But stone was hardly a barrier to a wizard. Nita jiggled the charm bracelet around on her wrist until it showed one spell she had loaded there, the charm that looked like a little house key. It was a molecular dissociator, a handy thing for someone who'd locked themselves out or needed to get into something that didn't have doors or windows. Nita gripped the charm; it fed the wizardry into her mind, ready to go. All she had to do was speak the words in the Speech. She said them, put her hands up against the stone, feeling the molecules slip aside...then reached her hands through the stone, carefully, since she wasn't sure if what she was reaching for was fragile.

She needn't have worried. Her first sense of it as her fingers brushed it was that it was not only stronger than the stone behind which it was hidden but stronger than anything else in this universe, which might reach who knew how many lightyears from here in its true form rather than this condensed semblance-of-convenience. What Nita pulled out through the fog that she had made of the stone was a glittering tangle of light about the size of a grapefruit, a structure so complex that she could make nothing of it in a single glance... and that was just as it should be. This was a whole universe's worth of natural law—the description of all the matter and energy it contained and how they worked together—gathered in one place the same way that you could pack all of space into a teacup if only you took the time to fold it properly. The kernel burned with a tough, delicate fire that was beautiful to see.

But she didn't have time for its beauty right this moment. *Next time I'll have more time to just look at one of these,* Nita thought. *Right now I have to affect the local environment somehow.*

The longer she held the kernel in her hands, the more clearly Nita could begin to feel, as if in her bones, how this core of energy interacted with everything around it, was at the heart of it all. Squeeze it a little this way, push it a little that way, and this whole universe would change—

Nita squeezed it, and the sphere of light and power grew, and her hand sank into it a little, the "control structures" of the kernel fitting themselves to her. Her mind lit up inside with a sudden inrush of power, a webwork of fire—the graphic representation of the natural laws of this universe, of its physics, mathematics, and all the mass and energy inside it—and she knew that it was hers to command.

For a moment Nita stood there just getting the feel of it. It was almost too much. All that kept her in control was the fact that this was not a full-fledged universe but an aschetic one, purposely kept small and simple for beginners like her—a kindergarten universe with all the building blocks labeled in large bright letters, the corners on all the blocks rounded off so she couldn't hurt herself.

Still, the taste of the power was intoxicating. *And now to use it.* Through the kernel, Nita could feel the way all energy and matter in this universe interrelated, from here out to the farthest stars... and while she held what she held, she owned all that power and matter. She *ruled* it. Nita smiled and squeezed the kernel harder, felt her pulse increase as that of local space did—energy running down the tight-stranded webwork, obedient to her will.

In that clear afternoon sky, the clouds started to gather. The day went gray in a rush; the humidity increased, and the view of the traffic lights down the street misted, went indistinct. She felt the scorch and sizzle of positive ionization building in the air above the skyscrapers as the storm came rolling and rumbling in.

Nita held it in check for a while, let the clouds in that dark sky build and curdle. They jostled together, their frustrated potential building, but they couldn't do anything until Nita let them. Finally the anticipation and the growing sense of power was too much for her. *Do it!* she said to the storm, and turned it loose.

Lightning flickered and danced among the sky-scrapers and from cloud to cloud as the rain, released, came instantly pouring down. The Empire State Building got hit by lightning, as it usually did, and then got hit several more times as Nita told the storm to go ahead and enjoy itself. Thunderclaps like gigantic gunfire crashed and rattled among the steel cliffs and glass canyons, and where Nita pointed her finger, the lightning struck to order. She made it rain in patterns, and pour down in buckets, but not a drop of it soaked through her clothes—the water had no power over *her*. And when some of the electrical signs started to jitter and spark because of all the water streaming down them, Nita changed the behavior of the laws governing electricity, so that current leaped and crept up the rain and into the sky, a slower kind of lightning, sheeting up as well as down.

In triumph Nita splashed and jumped in the flooding gutters, like a kid, then finally ran right out into the middle of the empty Times Square and whirled there in the wet gleam and glare all alone—briefly half nuts with the delight of what she'd done, as the brilliant colors of the lights painted the puddles and wet streets and sidewalks with glaring electric pigment, light splashing everywhere like Technicolor water. The feeling of power was a complete blast...though Nita reminded herself that this was just a step on the way to something much bigger. Curing her mother was going to be a lot more delicate, a lot more difficult...and the wizardry was going to cost her. But the innocent pleasure of doing exactly as she pleased with the power she'd come so far to find was something she badly needed.

The novelty took a while to wear off. Finally Nita banished the storm, sweeping the clouds away and right out of the sky with a couple of idle gestures—exactly the kind of thing a wizard normally couldn't do in the real world, where storms had consequences and every phrase of every spell had to be evaluated in terms of what it might accidentally harm or what energy it might waste. *It'd be great if wizardry were like this all the time,* Nita thought. *Find the heart of power, master it, and do what you like; just command it and it happens; just wish it and it's done...*

But that was a dream. Reality would be more work. And it would be more satisfying, though not all that different—for bioelectricity was just lightning scaled down, after all, and every cell in the body was mostly water. Now Nita stood there in the cool air, as the sun started to set in the cleared sky behind the skyscrapers, and looked again at the tangle of power that she held, this whole universe's soul. On a whim as she looked down at it, Nita altered its semblance, as she'd altered the look of the spell matrix she wore. Suddenly it wasn't a tight-packed webwork of light she was holding, but a shiny red apple.

Nita looked at it with profound satisfaction, and resisted the urge to take a bite out of it. *Probably blow me from here to the end of things,* she thought. She brought the kernel back over to where she'd found it, and held it up to the stone wall. It didn't leap out of her hand back to its place, as she'd half expected it would;

it was reluctant. *It enjoys this kind of thing,* she thought. *It likes being mastered…being used.*

It likes not being alone.

Nita smiled. She could understand that. Carefully she said the words that would briefly dissolve the stone, and slipped the kernel back in.

Wait till Kit sees this, she thought, pulling her hands out of the stone and dusting them off, *when it's all over and Mom is better at last. He's gonna love it.*

She checked her watch. *Half an hour to spare; not too bad. I'll do better next time.* She turned the charm bracelet on her wrist to show the little disc that said GCT/25, her quick way back to the ingress gate. "Home," Nita said, and vanished.

She came out on the platform at Grand Central, invisible again; a good thing, for just as she stepped out of the gate, a guy went by driving a motorized sweeper, cleaning the platform for the rush hour that would start in just a couple of hours. Nita glanced at her watch. It was three in the morning; as predicted, the return gating routine had dropped her here two hours after she'd left. But she was six hours' worth of tired. She fished around in her pocket and came up with her transit circle…

…and couldn't bear to use it for a second or so yet. Nita walked off the platform out into the Main Concourse—where a guy with a wide pad-broom was pushing some sweeping compound along the shiny floor—and out past him, invisible, and up the ramp, to push open the door and stand on Forty-second Street again. *This* time there was traffic, and garbage in the gutter, and horns honking; this time the streetlights were bright; this time the sidewalks were full of people, hurrying, heading home from clubs or a meal after the movies, hailing cabs, laughing, talking to each other. As Nita dropped her transit circle onto the sidewalk, out of the way of the pedestrians, the wind coming down Forty-second flung a handful of rain at her, like a hint of something happening somewhere else, or about to happen.

Nita grinned, stepped through her circle, and came out in her bedroom. She pulled the circle up after her, and had just enough energy to pull her jeans off, crawl into bed, and pull the covers up before the darkness of sheer exhaustion came down on her like a bigger, heavier blanket.

"Nita?"

"Huh?!" She sat up in bed, shocked awake. Her father stood in the doorway, drying his hands on a dish towel, looking at her with concern.

"Honey, it's eight-thirty."

"Omigosh!!" She leaped out of bed, and a second later was amazed at how wobbly she felt.

"Don't panic; I'll drive you," her dad said. "But Kit was here ten or fifteen minutes ago. I thought you'd gone already—you don't usually oversleep—and then he went so he wouldn't be late." Her dad looked at her alarm clock. "Didn't it go off? We'll have to get you another one."

"No, it's okay," Nita said, rummaging hurriedly in

her drawer. "What time are we going to see Mom today?"

"When you get back from school."

"Good. I've got something to tell her." And Nita smiled. It was the first time in days that she'd smiled and it hadn't felt wrong.

It's going to work. It's going to be okay!

Tuesday Morning
and Afternoon

✳

NITA'S FATHER TOOK THE blame for her lateness
when he delivered her to the school's main office, and
when her dad left, Nita went to her second-period social studies class feeling more or less like she'd been
rolled over by a steam shovel—she was nowhere near
recovered from the previous night's exertions. She
waved at Jane and Melissa and a couple other friends in
the same class, sat down, and pulled out her notebooks,
intent on staying awake if nothing else.

This was going to be a challenge, as the Civil War
was still on the agenda, and the class had been stuck in
1863 for what now seemed about a century. Mr. Neary,
the social studies teacher, was scribbling away on the
blackboard, as illegibly as ever. *He really should have
been a doctor,* Nita thought, and yawned.

Neets?

She sat up with a jerk so sudden that her chair
scraped on the floor, and the kids around her looked at

her in varying states of surprise or amusement. Mr. Neary glanced around, saw nothing but Nita writing industriously, and turned back to the blackboard, talking about Abraham Lincoln at his usual breakneck speed while he wrote.

Nita, for her own part, was bending as far over as she could while she wrote, trying to conceal the fact that she was blushing furiously. *Kit—*

I was starting to think you were avoiding me!

No, I—

Where've you been? Don't you answer your manual anymore?

She could have answered him sharply...then put the urge aside. That was what had started this whole thing. *Look,* she said silently. *I'm really sorry. It was all my fault.*

All of it? Kit said. *Wow. Didn't think you were gonna go that far. The Lone Power's gonna be real surprised when It finds out you let It off the hook.*

His tone was dry but not angry...as far as she could tell. *Please,* Nita said. *I'd like to be let off it, too.*

There was a pause at Kit's end. *Where've you been? I've got some stuff to show you.*

It's, uh, it's been busy. I—

Look, Kit said, *save it for later. Wait for me after school, okay?*

Okay.

She felt him turn away in mind to become engrossed in the test paper that had just been put down in front of him. Nita turned her attention back to what her social studies teacher was doing at the blackboard...and was astonished to find that she *could.* Just that brief contact had suddenly lifted from her mind a kind of grayness that had been hanging over it since before her mom went into the hospital. *And now,* she thought, *even if Dairine can't help, maybe Kit can.*

But could he? *And what even makes me think that after the pain in the butt I've been, he's going to want anything to do with what I'm planning?* She desperately wanted to believe that he *would* want something to do with it, but she'd been pretty good at being wrong about things lately. *And even if I asked him, would he think I was just asking because—*

"Nita?"

Her head jerked up again. This time there was some subdued laughter from the kids around her. "Uh," she said, "sorry ... what was the question?"

"Gettysburg," said Mr. Neary. "Got a date?"

"Yeah, but he'll have to stand on a box to reach," said a voice in the back of the room, just loud enough for Nita to hear, and for the kids around her to snicker at.

"July first through July third, eighteen sixty-three," Nita said, and blushed again, but more in annoyance this time. There were a number of guys in her classes who thought it weird or funny that Nita hung around with a boy younger than she was, and Ricky Chan was the tallest and handsomest of them. His dark good looks annoyed her almost as much as his attitude, and Nita couldn't think which satisfied her more: the fact that everyone around her knew she thought he was intellectually challenged—which drove Ricky nuts— or that if he ever *really* annoyed her, she could at any moment grab him by his expensive black leather jacket and dump it, and him, into one of several capacious pockets of otherspace that numerous alien species were presently using as a garbage dump. *Except that wizards don't do that kind of thing.*

But boy, wouldn't it be fun to do it just once!

Mr. Neary turned his attention elsewhere, and Nita went on taking notes. That class, and the rest of the day, passed without further event; and when the last bell rang at three-thirty and she went out into the parking lot, Nita saw Kit loitering by the chain-link fence near the main gate.

Nita headed for the gate, ignoring the voices behind her, even the loudest one: "Hey, Miss *WAH*-Neeta, where'd you send away for those legs?"

"Yeah, nice butt, nice face…shame about the giant bulging brain!"

The usual laughter from behind ensued. Nita began to regret her belief that changing out of jeans was going to make the slightest difference to her life at school.

Do you want to, or should I?

Want to what? Nita asked silently. *We're supposed to be above this kind of thing.*

Kit's expression, as she caught up with him, was neutral. *There are species who would love these guys,* he said. *As a condiment.*

She made a face as they walked up to the corner together, turning out of sight and out of range of the guys behind them. "Yeah," she said, "I was thinking about that. Among other things. Such as that I'm a complete idiot."

Kit waved the sentiment away.

"No," Nita said, "I mean it. You're not supposed to make this easier for me."

"Oh," Kit said. "Okay, suffer away."

She glared at him. Then when Kit turned an expression on her of idiot expectancy, like someone waiting to see a really good pratfall, she managed to produce a smile—yet another one that to her surprise didn't feel somehow illegal. "You won't even let me do *that* right," Nita said.

"My sister won't let me do it, either," Kit said. "I don't see why *you* should get to." He lowered his voice. "Now, what the heck have you been *doing* that you're sound asleep at eight o'clock?"

All the things she'd been intending to say when this subject came up now went out of her head. "My mother has a brain tumor," Nita said.

Kit stopped short. "*What?*"

She told him, fighting to keep her face from crumpling toward tears as she did so. She'd meant to keep walking while she told him, but she found it impossible. Everything came out in a rush that paradoxically seemed to take her entire attention. Kit just stood there staring at Nita until she ran down.

"Oh, my God," he said in a strangled voice.

"Hey, lookit, he's not wasting any time," said a voice from down the street behind them.

Other voices laughed. "Yeah, where's the box for him to stand on?" said one. The laughter increased.

Kit frowned. The laughter suddenly broke off in what sounded like a number of simultaneous coughing fits.

"Kit!" Nita said.

Kit didn't stop frowning, just took Nita discreetly by the elbow and started to walk. "If they're gonna sneak out behind the bleachers in the field at lunchtime and smoke," he said, "it's not *all* my fault if it starts catching up with them. Come on— Neets, why didn't you *tell* me?"

"I just did," she said, confused.

"I mean, when you found out!"

"Uh—"

"God, you weren't kidding; you *are* an idiot! Why didn't you *call* me? Even if you were mad at me!"

"I *wasn't* mad at you! I mean—"

"Then, why didn't you—"

"I didn't want to call you just because I *needed* you!"

Then Nita stopped. Earlier that had seemed to make some kind of sense. Now it seemed inexpressibly stupid.

"You're right," she said then. "I've been having a complete brain holiday. Sorry, sorry—"

"No," Kit said. They turned the next corner, into Kit's street, and he shook his head, looking more furious than before. "They didn't tell me. They didn't even *tell* me. I'm gonna—"

"Who?"

"Tom and Carl. I'm gonna—"

"Gonna *what*?" Nita said, exasperated. "They're our Seniors. They *couldn't* tell you anything. It was private stuff; you know that has to be kept confidential, and they can't even deal with it at all unless it affects a wizardry. They didn't tell me what *you* were doing, either. So forget it."

Kit was silent as they walked down the street. Finally he said, "What're we going to do?"

We.

Nita held out her arm to show him the charm bracelet. Kit looked at it, seeing what was under the semblance. "That's what I heard you making. How'd you get it done so fast?"

Fear, Nita thought. "You need it for the practice universes," she said, "and I don't have much time. They operate tomorrow, or Thursday at the latest. That's the best time to do the wizardry, when she's not awake—"

"You're going to need someone to backstop you," Kit said.

That thought had been on Nita's mind. Strange, though, how she now felt some resistance to the idea. "Look, if I can just—"

"Neets." Kit stopped, looked at her. "This is your *mom.* You can't take chances. You're gonna have to spend almost all your free time in those other universes, and you're gonna be wrecked. And I bet Tom and Carl told Dairine to butt out, didn't they?"

"Uh, yeah."

"*Well?*"

"Yeah, of course...yeah." *What was I going to do, tell him I don't want his help? What's the matter with me?* "Thanks."

Suddenly Nita felt more tired than she'd been even in school. "Look, we're going to the hospital to see her as soon as I get home. You want to come to the hospital with us?"

Kit looked stricken. "I can't today. We have to go clothes shopping; can you believe it? Dad says we absolutely have to. But you'll go tomorrow, right?"

"Yeah, we go every day. Dad goes a couple of times."

"So I'll go with you then. It'll give me time to read up on what you've been doing." They stopped outside Kit's house. "As long as it's okay with you," he said suddenly.

"Huh? Yeah," Nita said.

"Okay. You going to go straight off and practice when you get back?"

"Yeah, I have to."

"All right. Just *call* me when you get back in, okay? Don't forget." He punched her in the arm.

"Ow! I won't forget."

"Then tell your mom I'll see her tomorrow."

And Kit headed up the driveway and vanished into the house.

Nita let out a long breath of something that was not precisely relief, and went home.

Her dad was hanging up the phone in the kitchen. He looked unhappy. "Daddy," Nita said, "are you okay?"

Dairine came around the corner as her dad got his jacket off one of the dining-room chairs. "Yes," he said, "but I could be happier. That was Dr. Kashiwabara. She says they're going to have to reschedule Mom's surgery for Friday or Saturday. One of the specialists they need—the doctor who does the imaging—had some kind of emergency and had to fly to Los Angeles." He sighed. "He'll be back in a day, they said, but I'm not wild about the idea of your mother being operated on by someone who might be jetlagged."

Nita threw a look at Dairine, who just nodded once. There were ways to add so much energy to another human being that they might have a whole solar system's worth of lag and not be affected. This was one of the simplest wizardries, and not beyond Dairine's abilities right now, no matter what else might be going on. "I think it'll be okay, Daddy," Nita said, dumping her schoolbooks on the table. "Let's go see Mom."

They drove to the hospital and found her mother, surrounded by a large pile of paperbacks, talking brightly to the lady in the next bed. "The only good thing about this," her mom said as they pulled the curtain around her bed for some privacy, "is that I'm really getting caught up on my reading."

Nita was about to throw a small silence-circle around them all, until she noticed that Dairine was walking quietly around the bed, doing it already. She made a mental note to herself to let Dairine do everything wizardly that she was capable of right now. As her dad pulled a chair over to the bed, Dr. Kashiwabara stuck her head in past the curtain and greeted them all, and Nita's dad immediately went out into the hall with her.

Nita sat down in the chair, looking idly at the books as she took her mom's hand. Many of them were of a type of techno-thriller that her mother didn't usually read. "Your tastes changing, Mom?"

"No, honey." Her mother's smile was a little rueful. "I just read the parts with all the shooting and blowing things up, and then I imagine doing that to the tumor…when I'm not hitting it with lightning bolts and setting it on fire. Guided imagery's a good tool to use to help deal with this, they say. Whether it actually makes it go away or not, it's a way to constructively use the tension. One of the therapists has been coaching me in how to do it. It gives me something to do when my eyes give out."

Nita nodded, feeling her mom's pulse as Dairine sat down on the other side of the bed. There was a faint resonance to that other pulse she'd felt and heard in the practice universe, not merely a sound or sensation but a direct sensation of the inner life—under threat, but still strong. "So what have you been doing?" her mother said.

"A lot." Nita explained to her mother as quickly and simply as she could about the practice universes, and the work she was doing there so that she could learn how to rewrite the rules inside the mini-universe that was her mom's body, and then talk the cancer cells out of what they were doing. Her mother nodded as she listened.

"In a way it sounds like what the therapist's been showing me how to do," said Nita's mom. "Though your version might be more effective. Okay, honey, I don't see that it can hurt…You go ahead. But you realize that they're still going to have to operate."

"Yeah, I know. I thought about trying to take the

tumor out, but it makes more sense to let the doctors do it. They've had more practice."

Her mother gave her a slightly cockeyed look. "Well, I think it's considerate of you to let them do something." She reached over to the other side of the bed and ruffled Dairine's hair. "Are you helping with this, sweetie?"

"No," Dairine said, and abruptly got up and went out through the curtain.

Her mother looked after Dairine with concern. "Oh no... what did I say?"

"Uhm," Nita said. "Mom, she can't help." Softly she explained the problem. "She's really upset; she feels useless. And helpless."

"*That* I can sympathize with," Nita's mother said, squirming a little in the bed. "Poor baby." She sighed. "I guess it's tougher to deal with than running around from planet to planet, having fun."

Nita found this idea more than usually exasperating. "Uh, excuse me... 'fun'? Mom, I've nearly had a ton of bricks dropped on me by a white hole, I've nearly been eaten by a great white shark, and the Lone Power's nuked me, dropped a small star on me, and tried to have me ripped apart by perytons. And Dairine may have had even more 'fun' than I have, not that I'd admit it to her. Wizardry has its moments, but it's not just fun. So gimme a break!"

Nita's mother looked at her thoughtfully. "If I haven't been taking it seriously enough, I'm sorry. It's still kind of hard to get used to. But, honey... if wizardry is so scary for you, so painful...why do you keep on *doing* it?"

Nita shook her head, not knowing where to begin. The rush you got from talking the universe out of acting one way and into acting another, with only the Speech and your intention for tools; to know what song the whales sing, and to help them sing it; to stand in the sky and look down on the world where you worked, and to be able to make a difference to it, and to *know* that you did—even in the Speech there were no words for that. And helping others do the same thing—particularly when spelling with a partner— "It doesn't always hurt," Nita said. "There's so much about it that's terrific. Remember when we took you to the Moon?"

Her mother's gaze went remote with memory. "Yes," she said. Her glance went back to Nita then. "You know, sweetie, sometimes I wake up and think I just dreamed that. Then Dairine comes in with that computer walking behind her..."

Nita smiled. "Yeah. There's a lot more like the Moon where that came from, Mom. And here, too. Life on Earth isn't a finished thing. New kinds of life keep turning up all the time. We have to be here for them, to help them get settled in."

"New kinds of life," her mother murmured.

"It just keeps on finding a way," Nita said.

And so does death, said a small cold voice in the back of her mind.

Nita gulped. "The hurt—I guess it balances out, even though you have to work at seeing it that way.

But, Mom, a lot of energy goes into making wizards what they are. We have a responsibility to life, to What made it possible for us to be wizards in the first place. If you just take that power and use it while everything's going okay, and then, afterward, decide you don't like the hard part, and just dump it all and walk off—" She shook her head. "Things die faster if you do that. And it does happen. 'Wizardry does not live in the unwilling heart.' But sometimes...sometimes it's real hard to stay willing."

"Like now," her mother said.

"I am not going to just let this thing kill you without doing something to stop it," Nita said to her mother in the Speech, in which it is, if not impossible, at least most unwise to lie.

Her mother shivered. "I heard that. Good trick when it's not in a language I know."

"But you *do* know it," Nita said. "Everything knows it. On some level, even your cancer knows it... and I'm gonna do everything I can to talk it out of what it's doing to you." Nita tried hard to sound certain of what she was doing.

Her mother looked at her. "That's why you're looking so tired."

"Uh, yeah. You spend time in those other universes, which you don't spend here...and it wears you out a little."

"I suppose I shouldn't ask you if you've been doing your homework," her mother said.

Nita swallowed. "Mom, right now I'm doing the only homework that matters."

Her mother was silent. Then, softly, she said, "Honey, what if—what you're planning—"

Doesn't work? Nita couldn't bear to hear it, wouldn't have it said. "Mom, we won't know if that's a problem till I've done it. Meanwhile, let the doctors do their thing. If nothing else—"

"It might buy you some time?"

Nita's smile was slightly lopsided with pain. "I've bought too much time as it is," she said. "It's how I spend it that counts now."

Just then one of the nurses put her head in the door. "Mrs. Callahan, your medication..."

"Laura, can it wait half an hour? I still haven't seen my husband and my other daughter, and I'd like to be able to speak English to them, for a little while at least."

The nurse looked at her watch. "I'll check. I think that'll be all right." She went off.

"Is this the stuff to prevent the seizures?"

Her mother winced. "It's not just that now, honey. My eyes are bothering me, and the headaches are getting bad. They try to keep me from reading, but if I can't at least do that, I'll go completely nuts just lying here. Do me a favor? Go find Dairine and let me spend some time with her before Daddy comes back."

A nervous expression passed across her mother's face, which she wasn't able to hide.

"It's about the biopsy, isn't it?" Nita said.

Her mother closed her eyes, and Nita felt the fear that went right through her. "Yup," her mother said.

Nita didn't even have to ask, *Was it positive?* She knew. "I'll go find her," Nita said. But she didn't let go of her mother's hand. "Mom," she said, "I really hate this."

"I hate it, too."

"All I want is for you to be home again."

Her mother opened her eyes and gave Nita a sly look. "Yelling at you to clean your room?"

"Sounds like paradise."

"I'm going to remind you of that later."

Nita found a smile somewhere. "You do that."

"I will. Go on, sweetie. Do your work...and we'll see what happens."

Nita kissed her mom and got out of there in a hurry, before the mood changed. She went out into the hall and saw Dairine leaning in the doorway of a little alcove where there were some vending machines—her gaze trained on the floor, her arms folded.

Thanks for the circle, she said silently to Dairine as she went over to her. *You got a couple of minutes? Mom wants to talk to you.*

About what? I can't do anything. Dairine didn't look up. *All this power, and it's not enough.*

Nita leaned against the same wall, folded her arms, stared down at the same undistinguished gray linoleum. *I know,* she said. *It'd be nice to be able to just make this vanish...but...*

But what can I do?!

Don't let her go through this alone was all Nita could think of to say.

Dairine nodded and went off down the hall. Nita watched her sister go, small and quick and tense, shoulders hunched, into their mother's room.

Tuesday Evening

WHEN KIT GOT HOME at last and lugged his share of the shopping into the kitchen, it was nearly seven.

Neets? Kit said silently as he started unpacking the contents of too many plastic bags onto the sofa. There were some T-shirts and some new jeans, but mostly the contents of these bags seemed to be socks, socks, and more socks.

Nothing. *Nope, she's off doing her training-universe stuff already. Can't blame her.*

"...and it's all got to be washed separately," his mother said, sounding less than enthusiastic, as she came in from the car. "Kit, honey, just make two piles, dark stuff and light stuff. This is going to take me forever."

Ponch came bounding in from outside, released from the backyard. "I think certain people want a walk," Kit's dad said as he entered and started unpacking another bag onto the kitchen table. "You go do that, son; I'll take care of these— Did you leave *any* socks in the store for the rest of humanity?" he called after Kit's mother.

"No. You're going to be wearing these till you die. Where did you hide the laundry basket?"

Kit gladly left his father in the company of all the world's socks, went to the back door, looked at the leash...then picked up the other one he'd left hanging beside it, invisible to nonwizardly eyes. "Ponch?"

"Yeah-yeah-yeah-yeah-yeah-yeah!"

They went down the street together, Ponch running ahead to take care of business while Kit went along behind him, paging through his manual as twilight deepened toward full dark. He found a good-sized section discussing the theory and structure of the practice universes but no information on how to get into them. *Access to the aschetic continua and to more detailed information is released on a need-to-go basis,* the manual said. *Consult your Area Advisory or Senior for advice and assessment.*

Yeah, and what if they say no? Kit closed the manual and shoved it into his "pocket." *And what if Nita gets pissed about my asking, because she thinks I think she can't handle it?*

Better not to get involved.

But I am involved.

It wasn't just that he liked Nita's mother. He couldn't imagine a world without her, and knew Nita couldn't, either. The shock of finding out what was happening was giving way to the fear of what life would be like afterward...after—

He didn't even want to think it. *And neither does Neets...*

Her fear was on Kit's mind. The two of them had been in some frightening situations. Mostly, though, these hadn't involved the kind of fear that lingered; they'd been over with in a hurry. What Kit had felt in Nita today, by contrast, had settled deep into her and made her something of a stranger. *And there's nothing I can do to help, really. She's got to get over it herself.*

If she can.

Ponch came running back to Kit. *Let's go!*

They headed down the street, to the side gate of the school. It was usually locked, but this was hardly a problem for Kit; he and the padlock through the gate's latch were old friends. As he reached the gate he reached out and held the padlock briefly. "Hey there, Yalie," he said in the Speech.

It wasn't as if inanimate objects were intelligent, as such, but they didn't mind being treated that way. *Who goes there?*

"Like you don't know."

The padlock popped open in his hand. Kit slipped it out, softly opened the gate and let himself and Ponch through, then locked up again. "You keep an eye on things now."

You can depend on me.

Kit smiled. Ponch had launched himself away across the grass, in the general direction of the school buildings. Kit let him run awhile, then whistled to call him back. All the lights in the school were off except for the exit lights at the ends of the hallways, and the houses nearby were all screened from the road and parking lot on this side by hedges. No one could see them in the near-darkness.

He shook out the wizardly leash and put the shorter loop around his wrist. Ponch ran back to him, jumped up, and put his forepaws against Kit; Kit braced himself and slipped the bigger loop around the dog's neck.

"Ready?"

"Ready."

Together they stepped into the deeper dark—

—and walked several steps more through it before breaking out into the light. There wasn't *much* light, though. A dim gray illumination inhabited the space, a thunderstorm twilight, with a greenish tinge like a bruise. A fog swirled around them, too, of the same color as the light. *Where is this?* Kit said silently to Ponch, down the leash. *I wasn't thinking of this.*

Neither was I. I don't always come out where I'd planned to.

They walked on through the grayness together. Ponch was sniffing at the featureless ground as they went. *Not very exciting,* Kit said. *How about if we—*

Not yet.

This assured tone from his dog was strange enough, but there was also something urgent about it. *You smell something?*

Always. But here—Ponch smelled the air, then went forward again with his nose to the ground—*it's something different.*

Like what?

Like— The light was getting dingier, fading away—an odd, slow effect, as if the universe were hooked up to a dimmer, and the whole thing were being turned slowly, slowly down. *It's you, but it's not you,* Ponch said, perturbed.

Dimmer and dimmer...and then Kit caught his first sight of them in the dark. A rustling, a shifting in the shadowless light that was fading away all around him...and the sudden thought, as the hair went up on the back of his neck was: *I don't want to be in the dark with* them*!*

He had never really seen them, when he was little. *Well, of course not! I was imagining them.* But his early childhood had been haunted by these creatures themselves by night, and the fear of them by day. Kit took a step backward. Beside him Ponch held his ground, but he whimpered softly, the same eager sound he made when he had a squirrel in his sights.

The rustling sound got louder and seemed to come from all around him. Kit glanced about, getting more nervous by the minute. His childhood night fears hadn't been anything like what some adults seemed to expect: unlikely things hiding somewhere specific—under the bed, in the closet, or behind a dresser. They'd been nowhere near so easy to nail down, or to ridicule. Silly monster-shapes would have been infinitely preferable to his tormentors, which had had no shapes at all. Shadow had been their element, twilight their breeding place; and if summer had been Kit's favorite season when he was little, it was because in summer the nights were shortest and the twilight a long time coming. It had been years since he'd thought of these creatures. *But maybe they haven't forgotten me.* And now, in a place where things that weren't real could become that way, his fears had come looking for him.

But have they? Kit thought. *Or did I find them… make them… the way I made those other worlds?*

He clenched his jaw as the scrabbling sound of jaws munching and chewing around him got louder. *It doesn't matter,* he thought. *If I run away now, they win. No way I'm going to let that happen.* His eyes narrowed. *I'm a wizard. And more than that, I'm* thirteen*! I got over these things years ago!*

But would that make a difference? The shadows grew deeper, the scrabbling noises louder than before, closer. The thought of dead eyes staring at him out of the dark, no-color eyes that were black holes even in the night, brought the hair up on the back of his neck. Kit turned, thinking he saw something—the old familiar way the shadow turned and writhed against his bedroom wall when a car went by in the street, flinching from the headlights, then wavering up and out into the dark again when the lights died, the shape towering up against the wall and dissolving its features. Kit gasped, felt around in the back of his mind for a wizardry that would save him—

—then abruptly stopped, because nothing was towering up anywhere. The scrabbling noises were still going on all around him and getting louder, but whatever these things were, they weren't his night terrors. Now he caught the first real glimpse of one of them as it came close enough to be clearly seen through the dimness...and what Kit saw was something that looked more like a giant centipede than anything else. It didn't seem to have a front or back end, just a middle, and about a million legs, but that was all.

Millipede, Kit corrected himself, watching the shiny gray-black creature, about a yard long, come chittering and skittering along this space's streaky gray floor, at the head of a group of maybe twenty of them. This whole scenario was looking more and more like a bug's-eye view of a kitchen floor late in the day, before anyone turned the lights on. The surface on which he and Ponch and the millipedes stood even started to look like linoleum.

Kit listened to his pulse starting to go back to normal as the first millipede came cruising along toward him, all those little feet whispering against the floor— a completely innocuous sound, now that he knew what it was. Ponch looked suspiciously at the creature, and a growl stirred down in his throat.

No, it's okay, Kit said. *Let it go. It won't hurt us.*
Are you sure?

Kit had a spell ready just in case. *I think it's all right,* he said. *Just let it go. Unless—*

"I'm on errantry, and I greet you," Kit said in the Speech.

The millipede creature paused, reared half its body up off the ground, and faced the two of them, its little legs working in midair. But there was no sense of recognition, no reply. The creature dropped down again and went flowing on past him and Ponch, all those legs making a tickly shuffling sound as it went. All its friends went flowing away after it, the little legs rustling and bustling softly along on the floor. Kit watched them vanish into the still-growing shadows, and slowly relaxed.

Now why did you make those? Ponch said, looking after them with a disapproving expression.

Did I make them?

I know I *didn't,* Ponch said in a reproachful tone. *And I don't care for the way they smelled. Don't make any more, all right?*

I think we're in agreement on that. Kit went forward, walking but not with intention to make another universe, or anything else, right this second. He just wanted to recover a little.

Ponch padded along beside him, his tongue hanging out. *Those were like the things I see sometimes when I'm asleep and it doesn't go right.*

Kit knew that Ponch dreamed, but it hadn't occurred to him that dogs might have nightmares. *So what do you usually do when you see them?*

Bite them . . . and then run away.

Kit laughed. *I think if I bit one of those, it wouldn't have tasted real wonderful.* But once he'd seen the creature clearly, it hadn't seemed terribly threatening. In the past he'd seen aliens that had looked much more horrendous. *If it was a nightmare, it was someone else's.*

Though if things had gone a little differently, it could have been mine. If I'd run, for example. Kit was suddenly certain of that. *I need to watch what I think in here, not let my mind wander.*

He looked down at Ponch. *You want to make some-thing first?*

Squirrels, Ponch said.

Kit rolled his eyes. *Look, I changed my mind. Let me go first. We can do the squirrels last, and you can have yourself a big run around while I rest.*

All right.

They walked through fifteen or twenty universes more. It was getting easier for Kit now to imagine them quickly, but despite that he spent a little more time in each one, making sure the small details looked correct. *After all, if these things are going to be here after I'm gone, I should take a little more care.* In one of them he spent a long while under that world's Saturn-like rings, watching to make sure they behaved as they really should when they rose and set. In another he stood on a long narrow spit of land pushing out into a turbulent sea, while the waves crashed all around him, and waited what seemed like nearly an hour for what he knew was coming: a fleet of huge-sailed ships that came riding up out of a terrible storm and with difficulty made landfall by that strange new shore.

As the last of the strangers came up out of the sea and into their new home, bearing their black banner with its single white tree, Kit glanced down at Ponch, who sat beside him, supremely unconcerned, scratching behind one ear.

The dog looked up as he finished scratching. *Aren't you done yet? Why don't you find one you like and* stay *there?*

Kit had to laugh. *Like* you *want to.*

Well, yes!

Come on, then. Squirrels…

Ponch leaped forward, and the sea and sky vanished as that universe flowed around them, full-formed—a great grove of those huge trees suddenly standing around the two of them as if it had been there forever. A veritable carpet of squirrels shrieked and leaped away as Ponch came plunging down into the middle of them.

Kit chuckled and went strolling off among the trees while the barking and squeaking and chattering scaled up behind him. *Maybe Neets'll be back by the time I get home,* he thought, heading into the depths of the green shade. *She's got to see this.*

The greenness went darker around him, the trees becoming fewer but much taller, and their high canopy becoming more solid. Kit stuffed his hands into his pockets and gazed down at the grass as he scuffed through it. He was feeling oddly uncomfortable. Until now any thought of Nita would have been perfectly ordinary. But now thinking about her unavoidably brought up the image of her mother.…It was as unavoidable as the idea of what might happen to her.

Imagine if it was my mama. Or my pop…

But Kit couldn't imagine it. His mouth went dry just at the thought. *It's no wonder she didn't call me. She's been completely freaked out.*

The shadows fell more deeply around him as he went, and though Kit could still feel the grass under his feet, he noticed that it was becoming indistinct. *At least*

Neets is working on an answer, he thought. But there was no avoiding the thought that no matter what any of them did for Nita's mother, wizards or not…finally, there was always the possibility that *nothing* would work.

He passed the last of the trees and came to a place where there was only the vaguely seen grass left. Kit walked slowly toward the edge of this, and slowly the light around him faded down toward darkness again—a clean plain empty darkness, not like the place where the millipedes had been: simply space with nothing in it. He paused there, turned to look behind him. Distant, as if seen through a reducing lens, all the trees were gathered together in their little halo of sunlight and glowing green grass, and Kit could just make out a small black shape running back and forth and being avoided, and then chased, by many little gray forms.

Kit turned around and looked out into the dark again. Now it was just an innocent void—no millipedes, and no ghosts of childhood fears, either. *I wonder how I got so scared of the dark, anyway?* It all seemed such a long time ago, and that phase of his life had come to an end, without warning, when he was eight. He could remember it vividly, those first heady nights when he *realized* that he wasn't afraid anymore and could lie there in the dark and stare at the ceiling of his room and not be afraid of falling asleep—not have to lie there shaking at the thought of what lay waiting for him on the other side of dream.

Before that, the sight of this would have left me

scared to death. But now there was something intriguing about this imageless emptiness. Kit stood there for a long while, and then felt something cold and wet touch his hand. He looked down. Ponch was sitting there beside him, gazing up at him.

Bored already?

Bored? Oh, no. But it isn't good to leave you by yourself a long time. It's rude.

Kit smiled. *It's okay...I coped.* He looked back toward the trees. There was a gray line beneath the nearest trees: the squirrels, looking for Ponch.

Ponch looked back, too. *It happened faster that time,* Ponch said, *this world.*

Yeah, Kit said.

I think it was because you'd seen it before.

Kit looked down at his dog, briefly distracted. It wasn't as if Ponch wasn't normally fairly smart. But this kind of thought, or interaction, even when the Speech was involved, wasn't exactly what Kit would have expected. *Is he getting smarter? Or am I just getting better at understanding him?*

Or is it a little of both?

There was no telling. Now Kit looked back into the darkness again and found not even the shadows of fear in it. The only things that now seemed to lie hidden there were wonder and possibility. What Kit found inexpressibly sad, considered together with this, was the thought of what was happening to Nita's mother, the limits of possibility in his own world all too clearly delineated.

Are we done? Ponch asked after a moment.

Not just yet, Kit said. *I think I want to take it a little further.*

What will you make?

Kit thought about that, and then, for no particular reason, about the millipedes.

If I can make fears real...

... could I make hopes real, too?

He looked out into the dark, and found nothing there for the moment but uncertainty.

Kit shook his head. *I don't want to make anything just yet,* he said to Ponch. *Let's just walk.*

They headed into the darkness. Kit let the light fade slowly behind them, until the two of them went forward together in utter blackness. There was no way to judge how far they went except by counting paces. Kit soon lost count, and stopped caring about it. There was something liberating about not knowing where you were going, just surrendering yourself to the night— and not making anything, either, but just being there, and letting the darkness be there, too, not trying to fill it with form but letting it exist on its own terms.

The blackness pressed in around them until it seemed to Kit to almost have a texture, like water, becoming a medium in its own right—not something unfriendly, just something *there*. It slowly became enjoyable. *If I had any scared-of-the-dark left in me,* Kit thought, *it's definitely cured now.* But after a while he began to lose interest, and once again he prepared to say good-bye to the dark for the time being.

Then Kit paused, for he thought he saw something.

Often enough, on this trip and the last, he'd had the illusion of seeing something in the blackness when nothing was there. Now Kit tried to see more clearly, and couldn't get that tiny glitter of light—for it *was* light—to resolve. *Not in front of us, though.*

Under us?

He couldn't be sure. *Ponch, you smell anything?*

No. What is it?

Look down there.

Kit got down on his hands and knees. This brought him closer to the minuscule glint of light, but not close enough. He passed his hands over the surface he'd been walking on. The light was underneath it...inches down, or miles, he couldn't tell.

I wonder...

Kit pressed against the surface. Did it give a little? It hadn't ever actually felt springy under his feet, but now Kit found himself wondering if this was because he'd been taking it for granted as a hard surface, and it had accommodated him.

He pressed harder against it. A strange feeling, as if the surface was giving under his hands, or under his will. *Let's see...*

Slowly, slowly Kit's hands sank into the darkness as he pushed. He slipped one out, rested it where the surface was still hard, and concentrated on the other hand, sliding it further and further down into that cool, resistant darkness. Faintly he could see the glow from that tiny spark or grain of light silhouetted against his fingers. He reached even further down, having to lie flat on the surface now, pushing his arm in up to the shoulder.

Got it—

Kit closed his fist on the light, started to withdraw his arm. It was difficult. The blackness resisted him. As he exerted himself, beginning to breathe hard, he felt a faint stinging sensation between two of his fingers. Looking down, he saw the spark escape between them and slip down into the dark again.

He pushed his hand down into the darkness once more, recovering the spark. It did sting, a sharp little sizzle like licking the end of a battery. Kit closed his hand again, pulled upward. Once more the spark slipped free, drifting lower, out of his reach.

Kit took a deep breath, not sure why he had to have this thing…*but I'm going to, and that's all there is to it.* He reached down as far as possible, but couldn't quite reach it. Finally he took a breath, held it, and pushed his face and upper body right down into that cool liquid blackness. By stretching his arm down as far as it would go, Kit just managed to get his hand underneath the spark. This time he didn't try to grasp it, just cupped it in his palm, and slowly, slowly brought his hand up through the pliant darkness. After a few seconds Kit dared to lift his face out, gasping, and pushed himself to his knees, while ever so slowly lifting his cupped hand.

The little glint of light almost slipped out of his hand, just under the surface. Kit stopped, let it settle, then slowly pulled his hand up toward him. The liquid darkness drained out of his hand, pouring away, and abruptly the spark flowed away with it…

…into Kit's other hand, which he'd put under the one that had the spark in it. As the last ribbons of darkness flowed away, there that tiny glint of light remained.

Kit sat down on the dark surface, getting his breath back. He could feel Ponch's breath on his neck as the dog looked curiously over his shoulder. *What is it?*

I don't know, Kit said. *But I'm going to take it home.*

They both gazed at it. It was not bright: an undifferentiated point source of light, faint, with a slight cool green cast to its radiance, like that of a firefly. Kit was briefly reminded of an old friend, and smiled at the memory. On a whim, he leaned in close to the little spark, breathed on it. It didn't brighten, as a spark of fire would have, but it stung his hand more emphatically.

Kit reached sideways to his claudication, pulled it open, and with the greatest care slipped the little spark in. When he was sure it was safe, he closed the pocket again and got to his feet, wobbling.

You all right, boss?

I think so. That took a lot out of me. Let's go home.

All right. The leash wizardry tightened as Ponch pulled Kit forward. *What was that about?*

Kit shook his head. *I'm not sure,* he said. The light of the normal world, nearly blinding by contrast to where they'd been, broke loose around them. *I think it was because it was…all alone.*

They stood there under the streetlight, and then Kit

undid the leash and let Ponch go sprinting down the road. A late blackbird repeated a few solitary notes up in a tree. *Just me*, it sang, *just me*.

Kit stood listening in the dark...then went after Ponch.

Late Tuesday Evening

✳

IT WAS A QUIET drive home from the hospital for Nita and Dairine and their dad. It was as if they'd all been hoping that when the tumor was removed, a closer look at it would prove the diagnosis wrong. But it wasn't going to happen that way. *I can't waste a minute, now,* Nita thought. *Every second I'm not working on this, those things are multiplying inside her. Kit'll understand. I've got to get going…and I can't wait for him.*

Nonetheless she tried to contact Kit before she left. She couldn't find him; the manual gave her the same subject-is-not-in-ambit message as before. *He never did get a chance to tell me just where he was, or how he's doing that,* she thought, dropping her transit circle to the floor and watching it flare with the brief shiver of life and light that meant the spell was ready. *Gotta find out…*

Along with several other wizardries, Nita had added her invisibility spell to her charm bracelet, as a small dangling ring with nothing inside it. Now she activated it and a moment later stepped through the transit ring, popping out once more in that vacant doorway in Grand Central. This time of day there were a lot more people around, and a fair number of trains coming in and out. It took Nita some minutes to get down to the worldgate end of the platform, as she had to sidestep in one direction or another about every three paces to keep from being run over by commuters who couldn't see her. At least the gate was idle and ready for her when she reached it. She went through in a hurry.

On the other side she found the platform empty again, and everything quiet. Nita walked down to the gateway on the Main Concourse and paused there to look at the painted sky. The figures of all the constellations were strange—the center of the "sky" not a bull, here, but a strange cat-shape, like a jaguar leaping with outstretched paws. Other odd forms shared the ecliptic with it: lizards and frogs and birds with long curling tails. Even this sky's color was different, a deep violet blue rather than the creamy Mediterranean color of the ceiling that Nita was familiar with.

She went up the ramp across the empty, shining floor and past the information booth—which was a brass ziggurat here—and came out into what at first she took for early evening. Then Nita got a glimpse of the sun and realized that it was afternoon...but in a Manhattan that was definitely not her usual one.

The skyscrapers all around were capped with stepped pyramids of the kind she had just seen substituted for the usual information booth inside the terminal. Uniformly the buildings seemed to be made of a golden stone—or maybe this was just the effect produced by that strange sun, which was bigger than it should have been, and was orange gold, though it stood at a height more like that of noon than sunset.

Down the center of the street ran a green strip of grass that reminded Nita of the built-up flower beds running down the middle of each block of Park Avenue. She looked across the street, and up; from high on the tops of some of the buildings south of Forty-second, Nita saw blinding orange light reflecting back. *Mirrors?* she thought. And the sky was very dark blue, almost a violet color. She was reminded of the way the sky looked on Mars. *Maybe not as much oxygen in the atmosphere?* Nita thought. *An old Earth, maybe; a tired one...*

It didn't matter. Her job was to find the place's kernel. And it would be better hidden, here.

She sat down on the curb of that empty Forty-second Street and listened. A slower pulse this time, fainter...like a place running down, a heart beating more out of habit than from any desire to go on living. Resignation? Could a whole universe feel resigned, ready to let go of life? It was an odd sensation. *But ours is old, too. Does it feel that way?*

After a few seconds she put the thought aside. There was something about the light here that was affecting her, maybe, or just the influence of this place's great age. But the realization itself could be useful. She'd listen for a slower pulse, a more leisurely beat...

Nita closed her eyes, held still, and felt for the kernel, the heart. She had no idea what this city sounded like when it was inhabited. But the wind, breathing down between the skyscrapers, didn't change. She listened to it, and let it give her hints.

Very slowly, they came. Strange hornlike sounds, not the wind but something else ... also the muted cries of birds and animals, the clatter of machinery. Nita put her hands flat down on the sidewalk on either side of her, feeling it, listening through the touch.

The sidewalk was stone, not concrete. Its gray-black basalt was quarried out of the island itself—brought here in great slabs by mechanical means of which Nita got glimpses—then carved to size, set in place, and fastened by some physical process that she didn't understand, again sensed only obscurely and at a great distance in time. There was a characteristic scent to the stone, sharp, hot—*They used lasers on it, maybe?*— then a glimpse of some kind of crystal, maybe not exactly the lasers Nita understood but similar enough.

She started to think that this approach might have been typical of the people who built this place, simple techniques and very advanced ones combined—an "old science," more like wizardry than anything else, and a "new science," far ahead of anything her own world had. And this world would have been that way because of the way its own universal law ran, a combination of some kind of science actually left over from some other universe—*That's weird!*—with something newer, homegrown: the two sorts of law tangled together but never perfectly melded, the ancient tension between them defining a particular feeling, unique to this world, a vibration like what a wizard could hear in a crystal's heart, a pulse not slow but actually very fast—

Then Nita heard it, a buzz, a faint whine like a bee going by. *Got it!*

She opened her eyes and turned slowly where she sat, checking what she "heard" and felt against the evidence of her other senses—

—and caught a sudden motion of something down the street. Nita stared in surprise. Something moved there, going across Forty-second Street and heading uptown; crossing the street, low...

...*rolling* across the street? Nita stood up to see better but got only a glimpse as whatever it was went up Lexington Avenue and vanished behind the building at the corner. If what she'd seen was a machine, it was one the likes of which Nita had never seen before. And while there *was* some machine-based life that had become sentient, this didn't look like any member of the various mechlife species with which Nita was familiar. From where she'd been sitting, this looked more like a long stretched-out Rollerblade—

Weird, but it can wait. Nita stood still and listened again, shutting everything out but this place's own pulse. *Uptown*... The sense was fainter this time, which didn't surprise her; she knew the tests would be getting harder. Nonetheless, it was clear enough to follow, and whatever Nita had seen down the road was heading in the same direction.

She went after it, not with any concern for her safety—after all, the practice universes were limited to wizards—but with considerable curiosity. As she came around the corner of Forty-second and Lex, Nita looked uptown, where the ground rose slightly, and saw something rolling up the sidewalk on the left-hand side of the avenue. It wasn't a single object at all, but a number of them, rolling away from her in a loose cluster. In this strange, rich light, they gleamed a dark bluish metallic color. Most of them looked about the size of tennis balls, at this distance, but there were two or three of them that were larger, maybe soccer-ball size. They were approaching the corner of Forty-fourth and Lex. As Nita watched, they rolled out onto the ornate pavement of Lexington Avenue, here all covered up and down its shining white length with characters in some alien language, then crossed the avenue and headed east down the side street.

Nita began to jog after them, crossing Lexington and looking down as she did at the huge colored characters inlaid in slabs of stone into the surface of the street. The workmanship was beautiful; you couldn't see so much as a crack between the inlay and the road itself, all done in a pearly white stone like alabaster. *I wonder what this looks like from a height,* she thought. *And what the letters say...* She grinned as she headed toward the corner where the blue spheres had turned. *Be funny if it wasn't some incredibly significant message, but just the name of the street.* She came to the corner of Forty-fourth, headed around it at a run—

—and instantly found herself tripping over several perfectly spherical shiny blue objects, which had been in the act of rolling back up the sidewalk toward her.

Nita spent the next three seconds trying not to fall,

trying not to bang into the beautifully and bizarrely carved wall of the building to her left, and trying not to step on the spheres, several of which were still rolling toward her. She finally got her balance back and stood there bracing herself against the wall and breathing hard for a few seconds, while the five spherical things, like blue-metal ball bearings of various sizes, rolled around her and then paused, one after another.

"Dai stihéh," they said to her, five times over.

Nita's jaw dropped.

"Uh, *dai,*" she said.

The giant blue ball bearings looked at her with mild interest. At least Nita *felt* that she was being looked at, but with exactly what, there was no telling. The spheres had no features of any kind; the only thing she could see in them was the reflection of the skyscrapers behind her, the sky, and her own face, wearing an embarrassed expression.

"Where's the rest of you?" said one or another of the ball bearings.

Confused, Nita looked around her. "'The rest'? There's just one of me. I mean, I have a—I mean, there's another wizard I work with, but he's—"

"'He'? There's just one of them?" The ball bearings sounded disappointed.

"Uh, yeah," she said. "We come in ones, where I come from."

The ball bearings seemed to be regarding her with faint disappointment. "But there *are* more of you," one said.

Nita hadn't previously heard the Speech spoken

with nothing but plural endings, even on the adjectives, and she was getting more confused every moment. "Well, in general, yes."

"Look, it's another singleton, that's all," one of them said to the others. "Looks like we're unusual in this neighborhood; the rest of us need to get used to it. It doesn't matter, anyway. We're all wizards together... that's the important thing."

"Uh, yes," Nita said. "Sorry, but what exactly *are* you?"

"People," said the blue ball bearings, in chorus.

Nita smiled. "Something else we have in common. Do you have something that other people call you?"

The spheres bumped into one another in sequence, and with their striking produced a little chiming chord, like a doorbell saying hello.

Nita took a breath and tried to sing it back at them. After a pause the spheres bumped together again, creating a soft jangling noise, which Nita realized was a regretful comment on her accent. "Sorry," she said. "Sometimes I'm not much good at staying in one key."

The spheres jangled again, but there was a humorous sound to it. "So call us Pont," one of them said.

Nita grinned a little; in the Speech it was one of the adjectival forms of the word for the number five. "Sure. It's nice to meet you. I'm Nita."

The spheres bumped themselves cordially into her ankles. "You guys here to practice looking for the kernel?" she said.

"Yes," one of them said.

"Well, no," said another.

"What we mean is, we've done this one already," said a third. "But the others have a head start, and they're running against time, so if you want to get in on it, you'd better hurry."

Pont started to roll down the street, and Nita followed them. "Others? How many more people are here?"

"Oh, just a few on this run," Pont said. "Some of them are repeating a secondary exercise—their time wasn't good enough the last cycle out."

"I haven't done this one before," Nita said. "Is it hard?"

The spheres looked at her. Two of them, to Nita's surprise, melded into one, running together exactly the way two drops of water become one, without even ceasing to roll. "How many of these have you done before?"

"Just one."

"Huh," Pont said. Nita couldn't repress a snort of laughter; the spheres' tone of voice was almost identical to one of Dairine's. "That's not bad. Usually you get a couple between this one and the starter scenario. You must have found the first one pretty quickly."

"I don't know," Nita said. "The manual was vague about the projected solution times—"

"Oh, the manuals," they said, and a couple of them bounced up and down in midroll, a shrug. "They're not much good in these spaces...and even outside them, they don't always correctly predict what's going to happen in here. You learn not to pay too much attention to them in testing mode. And you figure things out yourselves...but you're doing that already." They were looking up at Nita's charm bracelet, she could tell.

They paused at the corner of Third and Forty-fourth, and Nita looked up and down the street, listening. That high whining buzz was still perfectly audible if she stopped to listen for it, and still coming from the north, but also east a little more. "At least another block over," she said.

"Lead the way."

She trotted across Third and looked down at the patterns in the pavement again. "You know what these mean, Pont?"

"Not a clue," Pont said as they rolled across the avenue after her. "I think we're lacking the necessary cultural referents."

"You're not alone." They headed northward again, past the sleek, polished goldstone frontages of the buildings. It was odd that though these had doorways every now and then, there were no windows at street level, or lower than about thirty feet off the ground. This feature was doubtless expressive of some truth about this universe, but Nita didn't have the slightest idea what that might be.

"This is definitely one of the odder practice universes," Pont said as they made their way across Forty-fifth and on past more blind walls.

Nita raised her eyebrows. "Oh? What makes you say that?"

"Well, the way the space here is curved is unusually acute. The lack of entasis makes it—"

"Oh, come on, the entasis level is fine. It's just that everything looks odd to *you*," said another of the balls.

"It does not. It's perfectly obvious that *you* just don't know—"

"You're both crazy," yet another of the balls chimed in. "If you just—"

Nita had had plenty of arguments with herself in her head, but now she thought she was hearing one in a form she'd never imagined. "Look, don't fight about it," she said. "It wastes time. Pick just *one* of you to tell me, or something."

This astonished Pont so much that they stopped rolling and stared at one another. Nita stood still and waited for them to sort themselves out, while making a mental note that when she got back to where the manual worked at its normal speed, she was going to look up this life-form in a hurry.

"Well?" Nita said.

One of the five—the two who had combined themselves had come apart again as they were all crossing Forty-fifth—now said, "You could put it this way—"

Its surface shimmered. Without any warning at all, Nita found herself seeing the world the way Pont, or one of it, did—a landscape so alien that she could make almost nothing of it. Everything had a metallic sheen to it, and everything was fluid and in constant motion, running or rolling down one surface or another. And every surface was curved. It was like a world made of mercury, not just silvery but in a hundred different colors. Every single thing Nita could see was shaped like some version of a sphere, tiny or massive, everything either already perfectly spherical or working hard to get that way. There were no straight lines anywhere. Where it could be seen, even the horizon was curved.

Nita blinked. More than mere vision was involved in what she was perceiving. This space was acutely curved, so that its sky seemed to bend down and cover you like an umbrella. It was a perspective both claustrophobic and oddly big, giving you the illusion that you could wrap that universe around you like an overcoat, an absolutely huge one.

"Wow," Nita said. At first she was eager to break out of this way of seeing things. But then she caught herself, and looked a little harder. *This is weird, but—I wonder...* She held still, watched, and listened. Listening didn't do much good in this worldview; all the motion happened in silence. But the motion had a trend in one general direction. Everything Nita could see, everything that slid or rolled or pulsated around her, had a slight drift toward the direction in "front" of her—northward and eastward, though a little more eastward than the way she'd originally been heading.

Aha, Nita thought. *One point of view is good, but a second one from another mind helps you fine-tune your first one. It's like triangulating.* "Okay, okay," Nita said, and the image of the world-as-mercury oozed and flowed away, leaving her looking around her again, with relief, at edges and straight lines. She listened again for that buzz, heard it, and put it together with the direction in which things had been slipping and oozing.

"Are you all right?" Pont asked, sounding anxious.

Nita smiled; the "you" was plural. "I'm okay. Come on; you helped. We're closer than I thought—"

She headed down Forty-fifth at a trot and turned the corner onto Second Avenue, and paused there. All of Pont ran into her ankles, she'd stopped so suddenly. "What?"

Nita looked up and down Second, perplexed, for she hadn't expected it to be a canal. Where the curb would normally have been was now a sheer drop, and water reflecting that dark blue sky ran down between the white stone walls of the two sides of the avenue.

"We could roll across," said one of Pont.

"No, we couldn't. We left the wizardry home," said another.

"I told you we should have brought it," said the third.

"*You* said we should bring the multistate compressor," said the fourth, "and so we did. *We* were the one that wanted to bring the solidifier, but—"

Nita began to wonder what these creatures' family life was like. Just by *themselves*, if that was the right term, they seemed to have trouble getting along. "Look, guys," she said, "there's a bridge across at Forty-second."

"We'll have to go all the way down there and retrace our tracks."

"Better than going all the way up to Fifty-seventh," Nita said, peering up the avenue-cum-canal, "because that's the next one. Or we could swim."

Pont looked at her with all of itself. "'Swim'?"

She looked at the spheres. They lacked anything to swim with. "Okay, maybe not. Come on."

Nita jogged downtown as far as Forty-second, with Pont rolling after her, fast. The bridge arched up in a smooth ramp across the water, coming down on the opposite sidewalk, and they all headed north again. Nita could hear the little buzzing whine at the back of her mind getting stronger and stronger and followed it more quickly, while checking her progress against her memory of Pont's view of the world. Pont rolled along behind, arguing genially about their last timing in "the exercise" and how it might have been improved.

Just north of Fifty-fourth, Street Nita realized that she had come a little too far north. "East from here," she said to Pont, as they came up behind her.

The spheres looked at themselves, and made a little musical sound that translated itself, via the Speech, into "Uh-oh."

"What's the matter?" Nita said. She backtracked to the corner of Fifty-fourth, and headed east toward First Avenue.

"Nothing."

"That's easy for *you* to say," said another of Pont.

"Yes, well, you didn't like it much last time," said a third.

"And we don't like it much now, either," said the fifth one, which surprised Nita; she'd been starting to think of it as the quiet one. "We thought they would have moved it significantly. It almost always gets moved for a redo. But it looks like somebody has a little surprise for us."

Nita gave up trying to figure out what they were talking about, and headed toward First Avenue. She stopped at the corner, Pont rolling up alongside her. Nita's sense of the location of the kernel placed it right out in front of her, near where the block of Fifty-fourth between First and York should have been. But here there were no more streets at all. Directly in front of them was a huge stepped pyramid of golden stone, incomplete at its top, and behind it the East River flowed by. Sticking out into the river from one side of the pyramid was a long jetty or pier of that white stone.

"There they are," Pont said. "They didn't waste their time."

Nita squinted down at the jetty, bright in the sun, and saw down near the end of it what appeared to be a woolly mammoth, a second object of roughly cylindrical shape that wavered oddly around the edges, and a third small shape, elongated and six-legged, which was heading toward the end of the jetty while the other two faced off against each other.

"It's down there," Nita said. "Down in the water."

"We *told* you we should have left the compressor home," said Pont to one of themselves.

"And what we said was—"

"Come on, guys," Nita said. "Give it a rest. I can do water." She headed past the pyramid, toward the jetty.

The smallest of the creatures was slipping into the water. Nita jogged down the jetty, and saw that the bigger of the two creatures looked like a woolly mammoth only in terms of the bulk of its body. Seen up close, it looked much more like a giant three-legged football with green-and-brown shag carpeting stapled to it. Its companion, which faced it silently, was a bundle of bright purple tentacles about six feet high, waving gently, and changing colors as they did.

"*Dai stihó,* guys," Nita said as she went by the two wizards. They gazed at her as she passed—the tentacly wizard with one of several stalked eyes attached to the top of it, and the furry football apparently with its fur, which "followed" Nita as she went by.

She went to the end of the jetty, where the other wizard had vanished, and looked down at the water. Down there she could clearly feel the kernel's tight small buzz of power. It wasn't even all that far down. *No point in floating,* Nita thought. She flicked the charm bracelet around on her wrist, came up with the charm that was shaped like a little glass bubble, took hold of it, and jumped in.

As Nita sank, the air-and-mass spell came to life around her, holding the water away but at the same time counteracting the buoyancy of the air she'd brought with her to breathe. Because it was so compact, the spell's validity was limited, but she was sure she'd have time to do what she needed to do. *It's almost right underneath me. All I have to do is—*

—and then she saw, right under her, the sleek form swimming up toward her. Her first thought was *It's an otter*—and indeed it looked like one. But otters have fewer legs. This creature, golden-pelted, was stroking strongly along toward Nita with its front and back paws; and in the middle ones it held a tangle of light and power, small and bright, from which came the singing whine she'd been tracking.

As the creature flashed past, dark cheerful eyes blinked at her, and it grinned. Then it was heading toward the blue-lighted roil of surface. Nita let out a breath of slight annoyance and went after it, bobbing up to the surface in her bubble of air.

The other wizard was already clambering up out of the water with the kernel. This it showed to the other wizards, and one of them said, "All right, you've proved your point."

"Twenty-four minutes," the otter creature said to the furry three-legged wizard. "But it nearly didn't do me any good!" It turned its long sleek head to look at Nita as she climbed up onto the jetty and banished the bubble wizardry. "Look what I passed on the way up!"

"Dai stihó," Nita said. "Hey, you beat me fairly. I just got here late."

"Didn't think They were going to let anybody else in here, this cycle," said the furry creature. "Oh well. *Dai,* cousin!"

"Here's Pralaya," said Pont, indicating the "otter." "And that's Mmemyn"—one of Pont rolled over to the massive three-legged creature with the strange fur— "and here's Dazel. What was the matter with you two?" Pont said to them. "Why'd you just let Pralaya take the kernel?"

I did not wish to dissolve, said a slow silent voice that seemed to come from Mmemyn in a diffuse sort of way. *I did not anticipate the replay of this scenario putting the kernel under water.*

Nita realized that Mmemyn's voice came from the weird patchy fur that mostly covered it.

"Neither did I," said Dazel. "But it was plain by the time I got here that no effort would have brought me to the kernel before Pralaya got to it. Next time out, though, the outcome will be different."

"It will if Nita here does as well next time as they did on this run," Pont said. "They got the scent of that kernel right away and went straight across the city—a downhill roll all the way. Very direct."

"In this continuum, that's not easy," Pralaya said, putting down the kernel on the stone, where it lay glowing. "You've made a good start, cousin! What project are you working on that They've let you in for practice?"

"I'm...I'm trying to save my mother's life," Nita said. And suddenly the strangeness of it all caught up with her, as it hadn't done almost since she first became a wizard—the alien feel of another space and creatures all around her who were strangers to her in a way that few humans ever had to deal with. She found it hard to look at them; she couldn't do anything but stand there, trying to hang on to her composure.

The other wizards looked at one another, silent. Pont said, "In the Five's names, why are we keeping them standing here like this when they're distressed? It's all too new for them! Come on, everyone—if this run's done, let's go to the playpen for a while. We can show them the rest of us, and replay a couple of other runs, and let them get a feel for how it's done."

Pont bumped against Nita's legs. She looked down.

They said, "Come with us, Nita. There's more to this sheaf of universes and dimensions than just places to play hunt-the-kernel. Come relax; tell us the why of what you're hunting, and maybe we can help with the how."

Pont are right, said Mmemyn. *Will you come?*

"Uh, yes," Nita said. "Sure, let's go."

And instantly the world faded around them all and vanished.

Late Tuesday Night, Wednesday Morning

NITA BLINKED AND LOOKED around her. It was dark.

Not entirely dark, though. It was as if she and Pont and the others were standing on a shining white dance floor—one that was miles and miles from one side to the other. If the curvature of the last space had surprised Nita, this place had a similar effect, but exactly in reverse. You could feel the flatness of this place in the air, on your skin, in your bones. You could practically see the ruler lines embedded in everything.

Next to her, sitting up on his hind legs, Pralaya made a little raspy chuckle. "Yes, it's a good thing it never rains here," he said, glancing around. "You'd go crazy waiting for the water to run off."

"Don't know what *you're* complaining about," Pont said, rolling past them toward a light source off to one side, where Nita could see shapes silhouetted. "Lovely place, this: no ups, no downs. Paradise." The rest of Pont went past Nita, making a feeling like a shrug. "You always could find a square thing where a round one should be, Pralaya."

"Just a natural talent," Pralaya said, looking after Pont with amusement. He gave Nita a wry look.

The two of them went after Pont, Dazel and Mmemyn bringing up the rear. "You two obviously have history," Nita said.

"Oh, some," Pralaya said, pattering along six-footedly beside Nita as they made their way toward the light. "We're neighbors. Their home universe isn't too far from mine, the way the local sheaf of worlds is presently structured. We started running into one another pretty frequently in here when I began this series of workouts. If you're here more than once or twice, you'll start recognizing the present batch of regulars pretty quickly."

"I think it's going to be more than once or twice," Nita said. "I don't have much time left, and I'm a long way from where I need to be."

"You're new at this, to be so sure," Pralaya said, as they got closer to the light. "Feel the kernel?"

"Huh?" Nita paused. She hadn't realized this was another practice universe.

"Don't stop," Pralaya said. "Some places you're not going to have the leisure. You have to learn to sense on the move. Come on!"

Nita tried "listening" as they went. It was hard to do while your other senses were interfering, but this discovery obscurely annoyed her; she could just hear Dairine saying, *Can't walk and chew gum at the same time, huh?*

The annoyance focused her just enough to let Nita "hear" the kernel, just for a second, as a sort of difference in texture in the feel of the local space. "It's right there in front of us," Nita said, surprised. "Right in the middle of everybody."

"Not bad," Pralaya said. "This kernel's tough to sense; it's a fairly low-power one. We usually keep it locked in one spot—there are so many of us in and out of this space that no one feels like hunting for it every time."

"I thought everybody's time here was really limited."

"Oh, in the aschesis-universes proper, of course it is," Pralaya said. He paused for just a moment to scratch behind his ear with the middle set of paws, bending himself nearly into a half circle as he did so, then picked up the pace again. "But this isn't one of those. This is a pocket of space pinched off from the main aschesis sheaf. The Powers let us use it to relax in between finishing up a seeking run and going home again. It's useful, since sometimes when you finish a run, you're almost too tired to gate straight..."

They came to the fringes of the lighted area. Fifteen or twenty creatures of various sorts were standing or sitting around on what would have passed for nice furniture on several planets Nita knew. On one piece of furniture, an ordinary-looking occasional table done in shiny metal, sat this space's kernel, a brilliant and compact little webwork of light about the size of a baseball.

Pont were presently rolling under that table toward a group standing together and talking on the far side of the table, and the wizards assembled there had turned toward them and were greeting them.

"We've got more victims," Pont were saying to them. "Look, all; here's Nita."

All those strange eyes turned on her, and there were polite bows and limbs waving and wings flapping and a lot of voices saying "*Dai stihó*, cousin!"

"Uh, I'm on errantry, and I greet you," she said.

A chorus of replies, mostly amused variants on the theme "So are we!' went up around the group. Pont came rolling back to her and said, "You're in luck: a lot of the present class of practicers are here. Here are Lalezh; they're from Dorint. And that's Nirissaet; they're from Algavred XI—watch the tails! And that's Buerti, they're from Ilt. And this is Kiv..."

It went on that way for a while, and Nita despaired of remembering more than a few of the wizards' names, let alone those of planets or universes. But shortly she was surrounded by people talking in the Speech and arguing amiably about the best way to find a world kernel in a hurry, and someone brought her what she at first thought was a glass of water, except that there was no glass involved—just the water, holding a tumbler shape by itself. Pralaya raised his eyebrows in amusement as he caught her glance, waggling them in the general direction of the kernel where it sat on the coffee table. Apparently the kernel in the playroom often was used for just that: play.

While Nita was working out where the rim of her

invisible glass was, she heard a lot of information and gossip from the alien wizards around her, and she quickly realized that in even a fairly short time she could find out all kinds of useful things, any one of which could possibly help her save her mother. Nita actually had worked up her courage enough to ask a few questions of the most senior of the group that had collected around her—a wizard called Evrysss, who looked more like a giant spiny python than anything else—when her attention was suddenly grabbed by someone walking by at the edge of the group. But what really got Nita's attention was that it wasn't an alien. It was a pig. It wasn't one of the spotty breeds, but plain pink-white, with bristles that looked slightly silvery in this light, so that it glinted a little.

"—and so I said to Hvin, 'Now, just look here, if you keep straining your shael out of shape trying to get the kernel to deform its laws like that, you're never going to—'" Evrysss blinked at Nita's sudden astonished look. "Oh, haven't you been introduced? Chao?" The pig stopped, looked at the group, glanced up at Nita. "He'neet', this is the Transcendent Pig."

Nita's eyes opened wide as the pig stepped toward her, and she saw that little shining ripples seemed to spread out in the floor from where it stepped, as if solid things went briefly uncertain where it trod. About six possible responses to what Evrysss had said now went through Nita's head, but fortunately, before she blurted one of them out, she remembered the right one. She looked down at the Pig, and said, "What's the meaning of life?"

The other wizards chuckled, or hissed or bubbled with laughter, and the Pig gave Nita a wry look out of its little piggy eyes "I'll tell you the meaning of my life," it said, "if you'll tell me the meaning of yours."

"Uh...that might take a while. Even assuming I knew."

"It would for me, too," said the Pig, "so let's put it aside for the moment. Come on, sit down, make yourself comfortable."

She did, settling onto a nearby chromy framework that looked more or less like a human chair. Nita had first come across a reference to the Transcendent Pig when she was doing her earliest reading in the manual, just before she went on Ordeal. The Pig was classified as one of the "insoluble enigmas," a sort of creature that fell somewhere between wizards and the Powers That Be. Indeed the term *creature* was possibly inaccurate, for (so the manual said) no one responsible for creation could exactly remember *having* created it in the first place. At least the Pig's motives appeared to be benign, and it had been proved again and again to be immensely and inexplicably knowledgeable. Nita thought this was why the manual insisted that every wizard immediately ask the meaning-of-life question when meeting the Pig. There was always a chance the Pig might slip and actually answer it.

Well, not this time, she thought. "Do you come here often?" Nita said, and then cracked up at herself; hearing it, it seemed like about the most witless thing she could have found to say.

"Don't feel too silly," the Pig said dryly. "Everybody tends to concentrate so hard on the mandated question that their minds go blank on anything else. But I wander in and out of here every now and then. I like being at the cutting edge, and out here where no one has to be too afraid of making a mistake, some interesting work's being done. Not all of it as personal as yours, maybe, but it's all valuable."

"You mean you know?" Nita suddenly felt slightly embarrassed.

"Knowing is most of my job," the Transcendent Pig said. "But then there's a long tradition of oracular pigs. I should know: I started it." It paused. "That is, assuming you're into sequential time."

"It works all right for me," Nita said, rather cautiously.

"Well, preference is everything, as far as time's concerned; you can handle it however you like."

Nita had to smile at that. "*You* can, maybe. But you're built to be everywhen at once."

It gave her a sly look. "I suppose you might be right," the Pig said. "If everyone started to believe they could handle it the way I do, everywhen might get crowded."

Nita laughed. There was something about the Pig that put her at her ease—one thing being that, to her astonishment, it had a New York accent. She spent a while chatting with it about Earth and then about various other planets where her errantry had taken her, and soon realized there was absolutely nowhere she'd been that the Pig didn't know—it had been there, seen that, and left the T-shirt behind. "Or, rather, I'm there now," it said. "Or *have* been there now."

Nita smiled, reminded of trying to explain the tenses of conditional time to her mother. "My own language isn't much good for this kind of thing. Guess we should keep it in the Speech."

"No problem. Who did you come in with?"

"A bunch of people," Nita said. "Mostly Pralaya and, uh, Pont."

The Pig smiled at Nita's slightly embarrassed look as she used the "slang" version of Pont's name. "Oh," the Pig said, "you're another one who can't manage the music of the spheres? Don't worry about it, cousin. No one expects anybody else to handle home languages perfectly. The Speech is all anyone here really needs."

Nita nodded. "You hear that word so much around here," she said then, "and with wizards generally: *hrasht...*" It was the word in the Speech that translated as "cousin."

"Oh, the term's accurate enough," the Pig said. "We're all children of brothers and sisters, of kindred creatures who're children of that odd couple Life and Time. All related, mostly by just trying to live our lives and get by in the face of tremendous odds. But in a lot of cases, trying to do *more* than just get by." The Transcendent Pig looked around. "This is one of the places where you come to push past the usual definitions of what's possible." It gave her a thoughtful look. "And if you're lucky, you both pull off what you're seeking and get to enjoy it afterward."

"That's what I'm here for," Nita said.

"Trying to save a life is always worthwhile," said the Pig. "But the bigger work can be a lot easier sometimes. Nonetheless, I'd say you're in the right place for advice." It looked over at the wildly assorted group of beings standing around a tall table, all in the light, waving their manipulatory appendages at one another and talking at high speed.

"Got any to spare?" Nita said.

The Transcendent Pig waggled its eyebrows at her. "Not for free. You know the price."

"Uh, yeah. I'll pass." Nita still wasn't completely clear about the price she would pay for *this* particular work of wizardry. Taking on another obligation seemed unwise, especially when it was known to be— in wizardly terms—an extremely expensive one.

"So will we all," the Pig said, and got up, quirking its tail at her. "Keep your ears open, all the same. You never know what one of your cousins'll mention that could turn out to be really useful later on."

The Transcendent Pig wandered off. In her turn Nita got up off the more-or-less chair she'd been sitting on and went over to listen again to some of the other wizards who were talking in a group. What she had come to think of as "the kernel," they were calling by as many other names as there were species in the group: the World-Soul, the Cosmic Egg, the Shard, and numerous others. Some of the wizards were knowledgeable about the structure of the kernel itself, in ways Nita was certain she would never have time to master. Pont, in particular, were in the midst of a long talk with one of the other wizards—a storklike alien about six feet tall who seemed to have had some kind of accident in a paint store, one where they sold iridescent paint that didn't keep the same color for more than a minute. "If you're having so much trouble dealing with the place's kernel," Pont were saying, "you should get help. Go in as a team! It's always an option for any of us, once we're done with the orientation runs."

The other wizard, Kkirl, stretched her wings in a sudden blaze of scarlet and green, then folded them again. "I have concerns," she said. "The kernel of the planet in question is unstable. It won't stay where it's put; whether the turmoil on that world is itself a reflection of the kernel's instability, or the other way around, I cannot tell, though I have been working with it for many cycles now—"

"*Planets* have kernels?" Nita said.

"Not of the same power and complexity you would find in a universe-type kernel," Kkirl said, "but much smaller, more delicate ones, easily deranged if mishandled. I've spent as long as I dare assessing the situation and trying to make small adjustments. There's no more time, for the planet is inhabited by some hundreds of thousands of my people, and if that world's destruction by earthquakes and crustal disturbances is to be avoided, something must be done now. In the past two cycles, the quakes have become severe enough to threaten large parts of the surface of the planet. The Powers sanctioned an intervention that would deal with the kernel itself, and I was here to prepare one final test sequence. I don't really need it. But I'm still not sure it's safe to go on with the intervention by myself, let alone with—"

"Kkirl, what use is a meeting like this unless you use it to your advantage?" Pont said. "The Powers Themselves might have thrown us in your way. Let us—some of us, anyway—help you out! You can tell us how to proceed, and we'll be guided by you. Or, if nothing else, we can just lend you power. These aren't circumstances where anyone would be tempted to improvise."

Kkirl looked around, her feathers a little ruffled, uncertain. Several other wizards had been listening to their conversation, Pralaya among them. Now Pralaya stood up on its hindmost legs in order to look Kkirl in the eye more easily, and said, "Cousin, if your people's lives are in danger, letting your uncertainty hobble you is playing right into the Lone Power's desires. And delay could be fatal. Judging from what you've told us, it's becoming fatal already. You have to move past the uncertainty. What else are we all here for?"

Kkirl stood there silent. Finally she looked up, rustled her wings, and said, "You're right. I see no other way. And there's no point putting it off anymore. Who will come?"

"We will," Pont said. "What about you others?"

"I'll come," Pralaya said. "Of course. Who else?"

Mmemyn said, *I am free to come*; and another wizard that Nita had met only briefly, a long graceful silvery fishlike creature in a bubble of water, said, "I, too."

"Well enough. I'll draw up the transit circle, then," Kkirl said. "You will want to plug in your names and bring appropriate breathing media: The atmosphere is a reducing one, and there's a lot of oxygen." She glanced over at the "fish." "Not a problem for you, Neme, except for the acid in the air."

The various wizards started to get ready, adjusting their life-support wizardries, and Nita was surprised when one of Pont rolled over to her. "You know," it said, "you might come along as well."

Nita looked down at it, and over at the others, surprised. "Me? I'm just getting started. I didn't even get the kernel this time."

"Just an accident of timing," Pralaya said, glancing up.

Kkirl paused in the act of starting to pace out the circle. "And you're probably the youngest of us here," said Kkirl, "so that whatever you might lack in expertise, you'd surely make up in power. Do come, hNeet. The kernel won't be where I left it in any case; looking for it will be extra practice for you."

Her mother's predicament went through Nita's mind. But these people were trying to help her, to help her mom. It was the least she could do to help them. "Yeah," she said. "Sure, I'll come."

Kkirl went back to pacing out her transit circle, and it appeared on the floor before them. The wizards who were going produced their names in the Speech and started plugging them into the spell, in the empty spots Kkirl was now adding for them.

Nita looked over the diagram carefully as it completed itself. The coordinates for the solar system in question had an additional set of vector and frame coordinates in front of it, which Nita thought must be the determinators for an entirely different universe. Otherwise the diagram made perfect sense, and the long-form description of the planet itself made it plain why Kkirl was working on it. *It's tearing itself apart,* Nita thought, bending down to look at it closely. *The planet was big to start with, and then it captured all these moons, even a little "wandering planet" passing through its solar system…and now the gravitational stresses from some of the more massive moons have thrown everything out of whack.* This was a problem of the same kind as Dairine's, just as insoluble by brute force. Inherent in the transit circle, though, and written as an adjunct to it, Nita could see Kkirl's intended solution. The planet itself was going to have both its crust structure and its gravitational and magnetic fields reorganized and rebalanced. That could be done only by using the kernel, which when itself rewritten would in turn rewrite the whole under-crust stucture of the planet. *It's like the kernel is the master copy of a DNA molecule. Rewrite it and turn it loose, and every other molecule in a body gets changed in response.* This was fairly close to what Nita had in mind for her mother, and her heart leaped as she saw from Kkirl's diagram that she'd been on the right track, and began to see how she could implement a similar solution herself.

"See something that doesn't work?" Kkirl said, coming around behind her and looking over Nita's shoulder at the diagram.

"No." Nita said. "It looks fine."

"I'm glad. It's taken awhile. But the conditional statements there were the worst part. Fortunately the solution is adjudged to be ethical—see the GO/NO GO toggle down at the end? If that one tiny little knot won't knot, you might as well give up and go home."

Nita nodded. "Okay," she said, and reached into the back of her mind to pull out the constantly updated graphic version of her personal description. It manifested itself in the usual long graceful string of glowing writing in the Speech, but as she ran it briefly through her hands, Nita noticed some changes here and there, particularly in the sections that had to do with family and emotional relationships. *Mom...*, she thought. She let the written version of her name slide glowing to the floor and snug itself into the spot waiting for it in Kkirl's wizardry.

Then, suddenly getting the feeling that someone was behind her, Nita looked over her shoulder. Dazel was towering up behind her and leaning over her, looking down at her with a number of its eyes, while its many, many pink and dark-violet tentacles wreathed slowly in the air. It said nothing. The rest of its eyes were arching down over her to look carefully at her name in the Speech.

"Uh, hi," Nita said.

"Yes," Dazel said. It said nothing further, but more and more of its eyes curled down in front of her to look at her name, where it lay glowing against the white floor, until only eye was left still looking at Nita, hanging there on its thin, shiny pink stalk about three inches in front of her nose. The eye's pupil was triangular, and the rest of the eye was bloodshot, if blood were purple.

"Uh, right. Excuse me," Nita said, and slowly and carefully edged sideways out from underneath all those overarching eyes, trying hard not to make it look as if she was creeped out.

The eyes watched her go, but otherwise Dazel didn't move, except for those tentacles, which never seemed to stop their silent wreathing and twisting in the air. Nita made her way over to where Pralaya and Pont were settling some final details with Kkirl and a couple of other wizards, and sat down on a little stepstool-looking piece of furniture near Pralaya. As several of Pont rolled off to say something to a couple of wizards on the other side of the gathering, Nita bent over with her elbows on her knees and looked sideways at Pralaya. "Is it just me," Nita said softly, "or is there something a little...I don't know...*unusual* about him?" She glanced at Dazel.

Pralaya looked casually over his shoulder, then back toward Nita, scrubbing his face thoughtfully with one paw. "I don't really know," he said. "He does have this way of just standing there and looking at you with all those eyes for minutes on end. I mean, it's not as if there's anything *wrong* with lots of eyes. Or none, for that matter. Maybe it's the multiple brains." Pralaya started scrubbing the other side of his face. "I did ask him once if there was something bothering him, but the answer didn't make much sense."

Nita shook her head. "But the Speech *always* makes sense."

"If you're using it with the intent to be understood, yes," Pralaya said. He waggled his whiskers, an expression Nita took as a shrug. "Whatever; it's not my business."

Nita was starting to feel boorish at having even mentioned it. These people were, after all, wizards, except for the Pig, and had all been extremely kind to her. "Never mind," she said, "probably it *is* just me. So much has been happening—"

"Now what was *that* about?" said one of Pont, rolling out from under another of the tables.

"*That* what?" Nita said.

"Dazel there," said Pont, and a couple of them split apart in an uneasy way and then recombined, while "looking" across at Dazel. "They're leaving, apparently. We said to them, 'Go well,' and they said, 'Some of us may, but one of us will not.'"

Nita and Pralaya and all of Pont looked across at Dazel. It gazed back at them with some of those waving eyes, and then vanished.

"Ready now," Kkirl said, straightening up from checking the wizardry one last time. "Shall we?"

They all stepped into position, each into his, her, or its allotted place in the diagram. Nita gulped as she realized she was about to do a wizardry with almost no preparation, with beings she'd met hardly an hour before. But it was too late now. There were Pont, in their part of the circle, their five spheres bumping into one another and chiming a little nervously; Pralaya, sitting up on his haunches, his four other paws with their delicate little fingers now folded, expectantly, over his tummy; Neme, the fish-wizard, hanging in its globe of water like a Siamese fighting fish in a bowl, all gauzy silver fins and big eyes; Mmemyn, standing there seemingly eyeless and expressionless, like a giant, badly upholstered gymnastics horse; and Kkirl, her wings spread a little as she stepped into the control circle of the transit wizardry and began reciting the triggering sequence in the Speech, the words drowning out all other sound, including the tiny hissing feel of the playroom space's own kernel.

Nita took a breath, made sure her own personal atmosphere was in place around her and secured by the wizardry attached to her charm bracelet. Then she joined in the chorus of other voices, birdlike, moaning, chiming, growling. The sound of the Speech rose up in their conjoined voices and leaned in close around them, pressing in on all of them as the power built, down on them, squeezing them out of this space and, with a sudden explosive release, into another—

The sourceless radiance of the playroom space vanished, replaced by the high, hard, bright light of a sun high in a pale blue sky, all streaked with wind-torn, sulfurously yellow cloud. Nita and the other wizards stood in a saffron-stained wilderness of ice and blowing snow. Around them blasted a screaming wind that would have been not only bitterly cold—if a temperature-opaque forcefield hadn't been holding

Nita's air around her—but also unbreathable, laden with a stinging acid sleet.

The other wizards looked around with dismay. "There has been a lot of discharge of poisonous gas into the atmosphere because of the earthquakes," Kkirl said. "It's getting worse all the time."

"This isn't the seismically active area," Pont said, their spheres dividing up into numerous smaller ones and rolling out of the diagram.

"No, this is where I left the kernel," Kkirl said. "I was hoping it would stay anchored near the planet's magnetic pole. But as you see, it's gone again."

Nita looked out into that snow and listened once more. The wind was screaming in her ears, distracting her, and she wasn't perceiving this universe as artificially compressed, like the ones she'd practiced in. It stretched out all around her, vast to both her normal and her wizardly senses, real and challenging. At the same time, Nita was aware of Pralaya's eyes on her, thoughtful but also a little impatient and challenging, and she was reminded of Dairine again. Nita concentrated on listening. In the shriek of the wind, or behind it, something caught Nita's ear, and she looked over at Kkirl in confusion.

"Are you *sure* it's not here?" Nita shouted over the wind.

"What?"

"There's— I don't know, it's kind of an echo. Can you hear it?"

Kkirl listened. "No..."

Nita turned, looking all around her. There was nothing to see in this howling wilderness, but she could hear it now, she was sure. "Pont," she said, "can you give me a— Can you help me out here?" for Pont were short of hands. "Do what you did before?"

"What? Oh—"

Pont's surface shimmered. Suddenly overlying Nita's own perceptions was that odd, tightly curved view of the world: downcurving sky, the golden-hued ice curving away and down all around them, the wind blasting the snow past the wizards and away from them in great chilly clouds. Nita didn't fight the perception but leaned into the curvatures, staring around her, listening.

All the others were doing so, too, Nita could tell, though her perceptions of them were conditioned by Pont's. All the other wizards looked spherical, though all in different ways, as distinctive as basketballs from soccer balls from baseballs. Some hint of Kkirl's flamboyant colors showed, in the tight and elegant way she curved space around her; as did Mmemyn's slightly slow and scattered personality, in a sphere that was a little diffuse in the way it reflected its surroundings; as did Pralaya's, in a neat and compact roundness. Nita could sense everyone using their own wizardry-altered senses to search through the space around them for the kernel, as she was doing. Again Nita thought she felt a prickling tangle of unseen power rolling away from her, not far away, in a slow twisting path, downward—

Is it moving? Pralaya said in her mind.

That's what I thought, Nita said. *Pralaya, can you do what Pont's doing here? If three of us, or you and I and however many of Pont there are, all look at the same time—*

Yes.

And the look of the world changed again. The icy golden surface underneath them was still the same, as was the wind howling past, but now the wind had a voice, eloquent, upset. Nita's companions were once more wearing forms that looked much like Nita's own way of seeing them, but with something added. Now there were depths of texture and mind that hadn't been there before, as if you could put out a hand and feel thought, warm like fur—a livelier, more animate sense of the others than Pont's slightly chilly perception. *Maybe it's because Pralaya and I are both mammals,* Nita thought. *Or something like mammals…*

In the moment it took her to see through Pralaya's eyes and mind, Nita perceived many things quickly: glimpses of a blue-green forested home world with much water running under the shadows of the trees, a golden-eyed mate with an amused look, pups tumbling and squeaking in some dimly lighted den—a warm and affable outlook on a world that felt challenging and complex but basically friendly. Then everything steadied down to ice and snow and complaining wind again, and one more sense of the kernel, sharper and more precisely targeted: something trickling, running, down under the ice, where it was warmer and liquid was possible, where heat and other energy channeled narrowly up through veins in the crust, and that fizzing, writhing, unbalanced knot of local law was burrowing down in deep—

Down! Nita said.

The others looked down with her, inside the glacier on which they all stood, through it to the underlying stone, through that to the first boundary layer where the stone changed—and Kkirl laughed angrily, and said, *Powers' names, trust it to more or less stay put this one time! Come on, cousins, if it gets itself down into the mantle in this state, it'll derange the whole place before we can operate on it!*

They all knew the Mason's Word spell. That word gives new life to stone, but the more complex version of the spell reminds stone of previous states of being, times when the fourth element was mostly air or fire, or stone in some other phase—dust floating in space before coalescing into a planet, only an atom or two sticking together here and there. Nita used that spell now, pulling the words out of storage in the "pebble" charm on her bracelet, telling the ice and stone beneath her that their atoms were far enough apart for hers to slip between with no trouble.

The ice rose past Nita and swallowed her up like a blur of fog, and the stone like darker fog, hotter, resisting a little, as the whole group dropped down in pursuit of the kernel. Further down they plunged, the shadowy mist of stone rushing up past Nita as if she'd jumped feet first into dark water. But it wasn't happening fast enough; the kernel was well ahead.

Nita turned herself, swimming through the stone, diving through it as if it were the water off Jones Inlet, where she'd spent so much time lately. Far behind, she could sense the kernel more clearly, dropping toward the discontinuity level, where the crust became the mantle and the lava under the planet's skin seethed. *Can't let it get in there!* Nita laid her arms back along her sides and let the increasing pull of gravity take her, worked to make an arrow or torpedo of herself. She was the smallest, the lightest of the pursuing wizards— *Or maybe just being the youngest is enough,* she thought, as slowly, slowly she got closer to the kernel's tangle of light. It was losing speed, as if the stone through which it sank was getting denser. It felt that way to Nita now, the stone more like water than mist, and then more like mud than water, but she didn't let that stop her. The kernel was just ahead of her now, just out of reach. The others were nowhere near it. *Don't wait for them; they're not going to be here in time, just* get *it!*

With difficulty, as she arrowed down through the seething, thickening, darkening fire, Nita got her arms down and in front of her again, reached out. The kernel was slowing more…but so was she, and then the shock waves started to hit her. She'd known the boundary between crust and mantle would be like a wall, but she hadn't expected it to be as much a wall of violent vibration as one of heat. Now Nita could feel how the world shook where the rotating stony liquid of the upper core dragged itself against the underside of the relatively static crust in small rotating storms of liquid fire, like the spots in the atmosphere of Jupiter, just as dense, just as furious. The worst earthquakes imaginable were just the side effects of these, and Nita went straight through one after the kernel, blinded by the roaring swirling tumult of the fire.

Something caught her from behind, braced her for just a precious moment and lent her power. The world went clear and hard and sharp as it had done earlier, and so did the kernel, a bright fierce tangle of power, just long enough for Nita to grab it in both hands. It fought her, unstable and willful as Kkirl had warned her, jumping and bucking and stinging in her hands as if trying to get away. Nita wouldn't let it, wouldn't drop it.

Pralaya, Nita thought, knowing where that jolt of power had come from and not sure whether there was another one available. *Where's Kkirl? What does she want to do with this thing?*

Hang on. She's coming.

Together they hung on, though the storm of molten fire tore at them and tried to blow them around like leaves in a wind. Pralaya was feeding her strength, and Nita was glad of it. She wasn't sure how much longer she could hold on to the kernel, but abruptly the fire around her was disturbed by another presence, a swirl of color that wasn't so blinding, and the crooked little claw fingers hidden under the bends of Kkirl's wings caught hold of Nita's hands and the kernel, both at once.

An eyeblink later Nita was seeing the kernel as Kkirl saw it, complex and dangerous, yes, but not too much so to never be mastered. Kkirl had been studying this problem for a long time, and she was ready. Those delicate little claws sank deep into the force-crackling knot of that world's heart and froze the kernel's processes in place for just the few seconds it would take to enact what Kkirl had been planning all this while.

Nita could see and feel how she was doing it, how Kkirl was reshaping the way the kernel called for the planet's upper mantle and lower crust to interact—thinning out some of the more massive areas near the core, redistributing the mass so that the planet's continental plates would move more slowly and evenly and resist the uneven tidal effects of the planet's moons. Nita watched what Kkirl was doing—manipulating the kernel like a Rubik's Cube and setting in place the changes she wanted, one after another, but not actually triggering them until they were all set up. Nita realized this technique was what she would need for her mom—using the kernel inside her mother to reshape the cancer viruses and render them harmless, or maybe even helpful. *I'm so glad I came.*

Kkirl, better get on with it! Nita heard Pralaya thinking. He was running out of power to feed them.

Ready in a moment, Kkirl said.

I don't think we have that long! Nita said. She was still hanging on to the kernel along with Kkirl, but just barely; the thing was jerking and shaking in their hands and claws like a live thing, trying to tear free, resisting what was being done to it—

Now!

Kkirl turned loose the changes she had set into the kernel. A roar, a rumble all around as the old structures and energy flows tried to hang on just a little longer, as the new ones, shaky at first, started to assert themselves—then a terrible sudden shudder of that world, from the heart out, as everything started to fall into place. *Let's get out of here!* Pralaya shouted from behind them, and Nita let go of the kernel and started to struggle back up through the fire toward the surface, as the planet began restructuring itself.

Getting up and out of the fiery turmoil seemed to take infinitely longer than getting down into it. The smoky fog of molten stone gradually lightened, then abruptly vanished as Nita broke up out of the ice and back into normal physical form, and her normal life-support sphere reasserted itself around her. She collapsed to her knees, gasping for air. The other wizards erupted out of the ice around her, each doing the same, as the reaction to the wizardry hit. Underneath them the ground shook, and the air was full of the groans, shrieks, and crashing noises of ice shattering for miles in every direction. Nita saw Kkirl stagger to her long thin feet, fling her wings up, and shout into the snowy air one long sentence in the Speech.

The ground reared up, and Nita found herself sliding sideways down a slab of ice. Everything went dark, then bright again, the recall spell grabbing Nita and all the others and dumping them unceremoniously back onto the floor of the playroom. There they all slumped, lay, sloshed, or rolled gently from side to side for some moments, until one by one they started to recover.

Kkirl was a bright, collapsed bundle of feathers, rising and falling gently in the middle with her breathing, but not moving otherwise. Nita managed to get to her feet, and went shakily over to put an arm around Kkirl. "You all right?"

A faint squeaking noise was all that came from inside the feathers, as Nita was joined by Pralaya, who put out a paw to one of Kkirl's splayed-out wings. "Thanks," Nita said to him. "I'd have dropped the kernel back there if you hadn't helped."

"At least you caught it before it fell straight down into the core," Pralaya said.

Kkirl's head came up on its long neck out of the huddle of bright feathers; she was blinking.

"I don't know if that went the way it was supposed to...," Nita said, uncertain.

"Oh, it did! It did!" Kkirl said, staggering to her feet again. She shook her feathers out and back into place, looking unsteady but cheerful. "It's going to take some hours for the planet's crust to quiet down; it was never going to start looking better right away. But the intervention worked; that world's saved at last! Thank you, cousins," she said, turning to all the others. "Thank you all!"

There was a gradually rising hubbub of voices as the group who'd gone out with Kkirl recovered from what they'd done and other wizards still in the playroom came over to congratulate them. Nita, standing next to Pralaya, said to him, "I should head home...They're gonna be wondering what happened to me."

"Don't be a stranger, cousin," Pralaya said. "We haven't had much time to deal with *your* problem today, after all."

"Don't worry about that," Nita said. "I'll be back here tomorrow...I want to try out what I saw Kkirl do. I think it may work for my mom."

"Then maybe I'll see you," Pralaya said, patting her with one of the middle paws. "Go well...and I hope you find her better."

Nita nodded, shook out her transit-circle spell, and took herself home.

After what she'd been through, her bedroom looked almost too ordinary and normal to be believed—so much so that tired and hungry as she was, and though she plopped right down onto her bed, she couldn't go to sleep. She tried briefly to get in touch with Kit but found that he was asleep. Then, out of curiosity, Nita paged through the manual to see what the listings on the other wizards looked like. They were all interesting enough—she had a brief chuckle over the concept of Pralaya having had thirty-six pups with his mate, nine at a time. But even after twenty minutes or so of reading, she didn't feel sleepy.

Finally, still feeling listless and jangly, Nita got up again and went downstairs to get something to drink. As she turned the corner into the dining room, she was unnerved to find her dad sitting in a dining-room chair, in the dark, with the phone's receiver in his hand. It was beeping disconsolately, in the manner of a phone that should have been hung up a long time before.

Nita swallowed hard with sudden fear, took the receiver away from him, and hung it up. "Daddy, what is it?"

He looked up at her, as scared as she was. "It was the hospital." Nita's stomach instantly tied itself into a knot. "Mom had some more seizures after we left," her father said.

"Oh no," Nita said. Whatever small feelings of success she had had after the long evening's work had run out of her in about a second, leaving her completely terrified again. "Is she okay?"

"They got them to stop, yeah," her father said. "But it took longer this time. Honey, she's got to have that surgery as soon as she can."

"It's still going to be Saturday?"

"Yes. But is that going to be soon enough?"

Nita didn't know what to say. Her father looked up at her. "How was...whatever you were doing?"

"It was pretty good," Nita said, but now she wasn't so sure. "I need some more practice before Saturday, but I think I'm going to be able to help."

Her father didn't answer, just rubbed his face with both hands. *He doesn't believe me*, Nita thought. *But he doesn't want to say so.* "Daddy," she said, "you should go to bed. If Mom sees you're tired out, it's gonna get her worried."

He sighed, looked up at her. "You really do remind me of her sometimes," he said. "You two nag in exactly the same way."

"Thanks loads," Nita said. "Go on, Dad. Get some sleep. We'll go see her tomorrow afternoon."

He nodded, got up, went off to bed. *But he won't sleep*, Nita thought.

And for a long time, neither did she.

Wednesday

NITA MORE OR LESS sleepwalked through school the next day. She got spoken to several times for not paying attention. All she could really think about during school was seeing her mom in the hospital that afternoon, and then getting back into the practice universes and following up on what she'd seen Kkirl do with the kernel the day before.

She looked for Kit during the day but didn't see him, and there was no sign of him at the school gates when she started for home, and no note for her in the manual. *Maybe he's at the other gates,* Nita thought, and retraced her steps to the gates on the north side of the school. But he wasn't there, either. She'd tried shooting him a thought earlier, without response; now she tried it again. Still nothing....

For a change of pace, and on the off chance she might find Kit coming back from one of his other friends' houses, Nita went home the back way. It was a slightly longer route than her usual one, but it gave her a little time to mull over what she'd seen and felt Kkirl doing with the kernel. *But there's no way to tell if Mom's kernel is going to behave like that one did,* Nita thought. She really hoped it wouldn't. Without Pralaya's help and Kkirl's, she wouldn't have been able to hold the kernel for long—and Kkirl had had lots of time to plan what she was going to do. *Help is going to be a real good idea on this,* she thought. *Glad Kit's gonna be there.*

Yet she remembered Kkirl's initial reluctance to let the other wizards help with her own intervention, and Nita could understand where it had come from. *Suppose the one helping you messes up somehow?* It would be awful being in a situation where you might wind up blaming someone you knew well for...for—

She wouldn't even think it. *But it would be better if there was no one to blame but yourself if something went wrong. Or no one you were close to...*

Nita paused at the corner, gazing across the street while waiting for traffic to pass. *Pralaya wanted to help,* Nita thought. And Pralaya's entry in the manual, when she'd taken a look at it, had been impressive. He was old as wizards went—a part-time local Advisory on his planet, with a lot of experience. *But still...* It was hard to let anybody else get involved in this, whether she knew them or not. There was so much riding on it, so much that could go wrong.

She let out a long breath. There was no more traffic, and across the street from her was the church where Nita's mom went on Sundays.

Nita paused, then crossed the street. When she and Dairine had been much younger, they had routinely been dragged here. Then Nita's mother had had some kind of change of heart and had stopped insisting the kids go. "I don't think it's right to try to make you believe what I believe just because *I* believe it," she'd said. "When you're old enough, I want you to make up your own minds." And so church had become a matter of choice in the years that followed. Sometimes Nita didn't go to church with her mom, and sometimes, for reasons she found hard to describe to herself, she did— possibly it was exactly *because* her mother had made it optional. The things she heard in church sometimes seemed exactly right and true to Nita, and sometimes seemed so incredibly stupid and wrong that she was tempted to snicker, except that she knew better. And also, she had no desire for her mother, when they got home, to pull her head off and beat her around the shoulders with it for acting so rude. But by and large the issue of belief or disbelief in what went on in church didn't seem as important to Nita as the issue of just sometimes being there with her mom. It was simply part of the way they were with each other.

As a result of this Nita didn't go to the church by herself all that often. Now, though, as she came down the sidewalk in front of it, she stopped and stood there.

Why not, Nita thought. *After all, it's the One.* And no wizard worthy of the name could fail to acknowledge his or her most basic relationship with the uttermost source of wizardry, the Power most central to the Powers, Their ancient source.

She went in. She was half terrified that she would run into somebody her family knew or that, indeed, she would run into anybody at all. But there was no one there this time of the afternoon.

The place was fairly modern: high white ceiling, stained glass with a modern-art look to it, simple statues, and an altar that was little more than a table. Generally Nita didn't pay much attention to the statues and pictures; she knew they were all just symbols of something bigger, as imperfect as matter and perception were liable to make such things. But today, as she found a pew near the back and slipped into it, everything seemed, somehow, to be looking at her.

Nita pulled down the kneeler and knelt, folding her hands on the back of the pew in front of her. Then after a moment, she put her head down against her hands.

Please, please, don't let my mother die. I'll do whatever it takes.

Whatever.

But if You do let her die—

She stopped herself. Threatening the One was fairly stupid, not to mention useless, and (possibly worst of all) rude. Yet her fear was slopping back and forth into anger, about once every five minutes, it seemed. Nita couldn't remember a time when her emotions had seemed so totally out of her control. She tried to get command of herself now. It was hard.

Just…please. Don't let her die. If You don't, I'll do… whatever has to be done. I don't care what it is. I'm on Your side, remember? I haven't done so badly before. I can do this for her. Let what I'm going to do work…let me help her. Help me help her.

I haven't asked You for much, ever. Just give me this one thing. I'll do whatever it takes if You just let me save her, help me save her, let her live!

The cry from her heart left her trembling with her emotion. But the silence around her went on, went deep, continued. No answers were forthcoming.

And I was expecting what, exactly? Nita thought, getting angry—at herself, now—and getting up off her knees. A wave of embarrassment, of annoyance at her own gullibility and hopelessness, went through her.

She got up and went out the front door…and stopped. A long black hearse had driven up and was now parking down at the end of the church sidewalk. Someone was getting ready for a funeral.

For a moment Nita stood there transfixed with horror. Then she hurried away past the hearse, refusing to look at it more than once, and more determined than ever to make all of this work.

That afternoon when she and her dad and Dairine got to the hospital, they made it no farther than the nursing station. The head nurse there, Mrs. Jefferson, came out from behind the desk and took them straight into that little room across the hall, which Nita irrationally was now beginning to fear.

"What's the matter?" Nita's father said, as soon as the door was closed.

"Your wife's had another bout of seizures," Mrs. Jefferson said. "About an hour ago. They were quickly controlled again—no damage was done as far as we can tell—but she's exhausted. The doctor wanted her kept sedated for the rest of the day, so she's sleeping again. She'll be better tomorrow."

"But she won't be *that* much better until the surgery happens," Nita's dad said, sounding bleak.

Mrs. Jefferson just looked at him. "It's been scheduled for Friday now," she said. "Did Dr. Kashiwabara get through to you?"

"About that? Yes." Nita's father swallowed. "But between now and then—"

"We're keeping a close eye on her," Mrs. Jefferson said. "One of us was with her when it started this morning, which is why we were able to stabilize her so quickly." She paused. "She'd been hallucinating a little..."

Nita's dad rubbed his eyes, looking even more stricken. "Hallucinating how?"

The nurse hesitated. "Is Mrs. Callahan interested in the space program? Or astronomy?"

"Uh, yes, somewhat," Nita's father said warily.

"Oh, good." The nurse looked slightly relieved. "She was talking about the Moon a lot, when she first came to, after the seizures last night. Something about walking on the Moon. And she also kept repeating something about looking for the light, needing to use the light, and how 'all the little dark things' were trying to hide the light from her. That seems to have something to do with some of the guided imagery work that her crisis counselor was doing with her, or it may have been a response to some of the optical symptoms she's been having." The nurse shook her head. "Anyway, it's common enough for people to be confused afterward. I wouldn't worry too much about it."

Nita's heart was cold inside her.

"Can we sit with her for just a few minutes?" Nita's father said. "We won't try to wake her up."

The head nurse was about to say no... but then she stopped. "All right," she said. "Please keep it brief; if the doctor finds out that I let you..."

"We won't be long."

The three of them slipped into the room where Nita's mom was staying. Her roommates were gone; there was just the single bed now that had its curtains drawn around it. They slipped in through the curtains, stood there quietly.

Nita looked silently at her mom and thought about how drawn her face looked, almost sunken in; there were circles under her eyes. It was painful to see her like this. *Got to hurry with what I'm doing,* Nita thought, though she felt as tired as her mother looked. *Got to.*

Her dad was looking down at her mom as if she was the only thing in the world that mattered. Her mom and dad had known each other for a long time before they got married; apparently it had been a joke among their friends, that all of them knew her mom and dad were an item long before they knew it themselves. Here were two old friends, and suddenly one of them was really sick, might even—

Nita forcibly turned away from the thought and looked at her father's face. *No,* she thought.
No.

She was back in the practice universes almost as soon as she could get upstairs to her room and through her transit circle to Grand Central. Now that she knew where the playroom was, too, she made that space her first stop. On her next-to-last chance to practice, having another wizard along to give her a few last-minute pointers would be welcome.

But the playroom was empty when she got there. The central area still shone with that sourceless pale radiance, and the assorted alien furniture still sitting around glinted in the light. As she walked, Nita felt around her for the kernel and sensed it immediately. It had wandered away from the seating area, rolling out into the huge white expanse of the floor.

Nita went after it, only partly to have a little more practice in manipulating it. The glance she had had at her manual before leaving had made it plain that the next practice universe she encountered was going to be much more difficult, more closely tailored to her own problem. Whatever Power handled access to the practice universes had noticed Nita's looming deadline and was forcing the pace ... and she was feeling the tension. She was also aware that she was stalling. *But only a little,* she thought, as she spotted the kernel's vague little star of light, maybe a quarter mile away.

Nita hiked toward it, hearing nothing but its faint buzz in all that great, flat empty space. In this darkness, bare of the sounds of fellow wizards, it was all too easy to hear other things: the machines around her mother's bed in the hospital, the whisper of the nurses saying things to each other that they thought—incorrectly—Nita and Dairine couldn't hear. Nita reached the kernel, picked it up, and turned it over in her hands, holding it carefully; for all its power, it looked like such a fragile thing. Holding it she could feel how every little detail of this "pocket" universe was anchored in it, endlessly malleable. The more you believed in that malleability, the more easily the kernel could be changed. *That's something I've got to exploit,* she thought. *Not be afraid to improvise.*

But she *was* afraid. *It'd be dumb not to admit that,* Nita thought. *All I have to do is push through the fear. And at least Kit'll be there to help.*

The kernel in her hands sang softly, like a plucked string, as someone else came into the playroom. She turned to see who it was. Way back among the furniture, a golden-furred form sat up on its haunches and peered around. "Pralaya?" Nita called.

Abruptly he was right beside her. "That was quick," Nita said.

"Microtransit," Pralaya said, dropping down on all six feet again. "When you know a kernel's signature, if it's not too complex or unstable, you can home on it. Most of us learn this one pretty quickly; it's fairly simple." He yawned.

"You sound tired," Nita said as they started to walk back toward the furniture.

"I just finished a next-to-last workout," Pralaya

said. "Shortly I'll have to do the real piece of work, but not right this moment. I'm considering a few last options. What about you?"

"I've got to do my next-to-last, too," Nita said. "Or I think it will be. There's not much time left. They're going to be operating on my mom the day after tomorrow."

"How are you holding up?"

There were moments when the darkness here seemed to press in unusually closely around Nita. This was one of them. "Not so well," she said. "I'm scared a lot of the time. It makes it hard to work." She made a face. "Just another of the Lone One's favorite tactics—to use your own fear to make what you do less effective."

"It's a tactic that has another side, though," Pralaya said. "One you can use to your advantage. Fear can keep you sharp and make you sensitive to solutions you might not have seen otherwise."

"I guess. But I could do without Its tactics, at the moment, or Its inventions. Especially the first one It came up with."

"Death…," Pralaya said, musing. "Well, it's struck me that the Powers have been fairly philosophical about Their dealings with death and entropy. What They can't cure, we must endure, or so They say."

Nita nodded. "I guess we all wonder about *why* sometimes. Why the Powers That Be didn't just reverse what the Lone Power had done. Or trash everything and start all over if They couldn't repair the damage."

They got back to the furniture, and Nita dropped the kernel to its more usual place on the table. "Well,"

Pralaya said, "the manual is sparing with the details. But I think the other Powers had only a limited amount of energy left to Them afterward. The Lone One wasn't just another Power; It was first among equals, mightiest of all the Subcreators. Terrible energies were entrusted to It when things got started, and when It had expended those energies, they weren't available for use elsewhere by the Others."

Nita looked down at the kernel. "The Lone Power's changing now, though," she said. "Ever so slowly…"

"So they say. Not that that does us much good, here and now. Falling's easy. Climbing's hard, and It has a long climb ahead. And meantime, we have to keep on fighting Its many shadows among the worlds, and in our own hearts, as if no victory'd been won."

"The shadows in our hearts…," Nita said softly. She'd had too close a look at her own shadows when Dairine passed through her Ordeal, and since then she had wished often enough that there were some way to get rid of them. But there wasn't; not even wizards can make things happen just by wishing.

"I've got to get going," she said. "I'll stop in when I've finished my run."

"I'll probably still be here," Pralaya said. "I wanted to talk to Pont about a couple of things."

"Or…" Nita hesitated. "No, never mind; you're tired."

Pralaya gave her an amused look. "You're thinking that another point of view to triangulate with might not be a bad idea."

"Seriously, if you're tired, though—"

"You are, too," Pralaya said, "and you're not letting it stop you." He got up. "Why not, if you like? I may as well spend the time, till Pont shows up, doing something useful."

Nita hesitated just a moment more, then smiled. "Yeah," she said. "Let's go."

She got her transit circle ready. *Lucky he was here,* she thought. While Pont was friendly enough, there was a congenial quality about Pralaya that made him easier to work with, and the sharpness of his mind and the way he saw the aschetic universes were advantages.

Luck, though? said something at the back of her mind, something faintly uneasy. *Is there really such a thing?*

"Ready?" Pralaya said, dropping his own transit circle to the ground.

"Ready," Nita said.

They vanished.

Two hours by the playroom's time, much later by Nita's watch, she and Pralaya returned to the playroom—and Nita was never so glad to see such a boring, bland worldscape in her life, after the turbulent one she and Pralaya had just come out of. And that one had been, so her manual had warned her, more like the inside of a human body than anything else she'd worked with.

"I still feel silly for having expected to see tubes and veins and things," Nita said, as she flopped down into one of the chairs, which, though made for a hominid, had legs that bent in different places than hers did.

Pralaya reached over to the table, picked up the kernel in two paws, and tossed it to her. Nita turned it over in her hands, found the mass-manipulation part of the construct, and twiddled with it until the chair changed shape beneath her. "And I wasn't expecting all that sand," she said.

"The symbolism's a good-enough reflection of how a malignant illness like your mother's works," Pralaya said, curling up on the lounger next to Nita's chair. "Scrape it away in one place...the cells just keep breeding, filling in the gaps. And as for the tubes and organs and so on, working with them as such wouldn't help you. It's not your mother's tubes you're trying to cure; it's all of her. A big job."

Nita nodded, and rubbed her eyes. Finding the kernel had not been difficult, much to her relief, though it had been hidden in what seemed a world's worth of desert, with only the occasional eroded skyscraper-peak sticking up out of the sand.

But the practice malignancy that the aschetic universe had created for her had been much more than she could handle. She had managed to get rid of the viruses in a large area of it, but only by brute force, rather than talking them out of what they were doing. There had been billions of them, as many of them as there had been grains of sand, and their response to Nita had been furious, a storm of self-preservation. More than once they had almost buried her under dune after rolling dune...and when she had run out of both energy and time that could be spent in that universe, even after blasting clean a large part of that huge waste, she could feel the rest of it lying under the scorching, un-friendly sky, simply waiting for her to leave so that it could get on with what it had been doing...killing someone.

I can't give up now, Nita thought. Yet the thought of her mother's situation was really starting to scare her.

What if it's all for nothing? she thought. *What if even this—*

She hadn't wanted to say it to her mother, hadn't wanted to hear it said. But half the power inherent in wizardry lay in telling the truth about things. To deny the truth was to deny your own power.

"Problems?" Pralaya said quietly.

Nita paused, then nodded.

"I'm getting scared," Nita said. "I'm beginning to think...think that if what's wrong with my mom is as bad as things were in that last universe, then I may not be able to do it." It was hard to say, but it had to be said.

Pralaya made a little sideways tilt of his sleek head, which Nita had started to recognize as the way his people nodded.

"And willpower may not be enough," Nita said softly. "Trying my best...still may not be enough." She swallowed hard. "Loving her...no matter how much...it doesn't matter. It still may not be enough."

There was a long silence. In a slightly remote-sounding voice, Pralaya said, "Running into that hard wall of impossibility is something we all do eventually."

"It hurts," Nita said softly. "Knowing there's wiz-ardry...knowing that it can do so much...but not this. It would almost have been better not to know at all."

"That can happen," Pralaya said to her.

She looked up, shocked, for his tone was not precisely cautionary.

"Wizardry doesn't live in the unwilling heart," Pralaya said, again with that slightly remote tone, "as you know. If it starts to hurt too much, you can always give it up."

Nita sat silent in the unchanging radiance. "If I do that," she said, "then what's been given to me's been wasted. The universe would die a little faster because I threw away what the Powers gave me to work with."

"Of course, you're the only one who can say whether it's worth it," Pralaya said. "And afterward, you wouldn't know. Forgetfulness would come soon enough. Your mother might still die, but at least you wouldn't feel guilty that you couldn't stop it."

Nita didn't answer. She was beginning to hear more clearly something in Pralaya's voice that she hadn't been able to identify, really, until now, when they were alone here, in the quiet.

"But also," Pralaya said, "you're acting as if your mother was doing something she wasn't going to do, anyway."

"What?"

"Die," Pralaya said.

Nita just looked at him. *There's something about his eyes,* she thought. At first she had dismissed it as just another part of his alienness. Now, though…

"We're all mortal," Pralaya said. "Even the longest

lived of us. Sooner or later, the bodies give up, wear out, run down. Matter-energy systems have that problem, in the universes where living beings reside. I don't know of any solutions for that problem that are likely to do your species—or mine, for that matter—much good."

"But it wasn't supposed to happen *now*!" Nita cried. "I'm just a kid! My sister's even more of one! She's going to be..." She trailed off. It was indeed going to be worse for Dairine, as if Nita could even imagine, yet, how bad it was going to be for *her*. "She's going to be completely miserable," Nita said.

"'Wasn't supposed to happen'?" Pralaya said. "According to whom?"

Nita couldn't think of an answer to that.

"Twist and turn as we may," Pralaya said softly, "sooner or later we all come up against it. We do our service to the Powers That Be...but They do not always treat us in return as we feel we deserve to be treated. And then...then we look around us and begin to consider the alternatives."

Nita looked at Pralaya, uneasy again. He looked at her with those great dark eyes, and Nita saw a change in expression, as if someone else was looking out at her.

And suddenly she knew, understood, and her mouth went dry.

"I know who you are," Nita said, not caring now whether she was wrong or would feel stupid about it afterward.

"I thought you'd work it out eventually," the Lone One said.

They sat there in the silence for a few moments. "So that's it?" the Lone One said after a long pause. "You're not going to go all hostile on me?"

Nita's mind was in a turmoil. She knew her enemy... and at the same time, she'd never seen It like this before. *It* has *been changing*, she thought. *We gave It the chance to do that, right from the start.* But there was more to her reaction than just that realization. She had to admit that even through her fear and unease she was curious.

"Not right this minute," Nita said. "Not until I understand some things. I was in Pralaya's mind, once or twice. He's a real wizard. He has a real life. He has a mate, and pups, and..." She shook her head. "How can you be *you*... and Pralaya, too?"

It looked at her with mild amusement in those big dark eyes. "The same way I do it with you," the Lone One said.

Nita gulped.

"You know the rule: 'Those who resist the Powers... yet do the will of the Powers. Those who serve the Powers... themselves become the Powers.' And if you serve Them... then, if you're not careful, you also sometimes may serve me. I'm still one of Them, no matter what They say."

Nita didn't move, didn't say anything. She was remembering some more of the stricture It had quoted: *Beware the Choice! Beware refusing it!* She hadn't been quite clear about what that had meant before. Now she was beginning to get an idea.

"Sooner or later," It said, "every wizard leaves me a

loophole through which I can enter. Sooner or later every wizard just wants to make a deal, just one time. Sooner or later every wizard gets tired of always having it go the way the Powers That Be—the *other* Powers, I mean—insist it has to go. No room for flexibility in Their way of thinking. No room for compromise. So unreasonable of Them. But wizards have free will, and they don't always see things the Powers' way. When they come around to that line of thinking, I'm always here."

It stretched and scratched Itself. "For Pralaya, the loophole was curiosity. It still is; we've coexisted for some time. His people's minds are constructed differently from yours. They don't see an inexorable enemy when they see me, but part of the natural order of things. They've learned to accept death. Very civilized people."

Nita had her own ideas about that.

"He's useful," the Lone One said. "Pralaya is a very skilled, experienced wizard. He's had a long life; during it, various troubles have avoided him. That's been my doing. In return, occasionally I can exploit his acceptance of me, to slip in when he lets his guard down, and handle some business of my own."

"Like dealing with me," Nita said.

She was controlling herself as tightly as she could, waiting for any sense that her mind was being overshadowed by the Lone One's power against her will. But she couldn't feel any such thing.

"Among other things," the Lone Power said. "And if there's going to be a deal, the structure of it is simple enough. One less wizard in the world is worth something to me. Your mother's life is worth something to you." Pralaya shrugged. "Over your short career, you've been something of an irritant to me. But not so much so that I'm not willing to do you a favor in order to get rid of you."

Nita stared at it. "You're telling me that if I give up my wizardry...you'll save my mother's life."

"Yes."

Nita swallowed. "Why do I have a real hard time believing you?"

It gave her a whimsical look. "So I bend the truth sometimes. One of the minor uses of entropy. What do you expect of me? I use what tools I've been left...and the one I invented always works the best. It's working here and now, while we sit here talking. The cancer cells are spreading all through your mother's body right this minute, eating her alive." It smiled slightly. "Cute little machines that they are. Life thinks it can overcome everything...but in some ways, it's too strong for its own good. This is one of them."

Nita's mouth was bone-dry with fear. "Why should you keep your word once you've given it?"

It laughed. "Why shouldn't I? You think one ordinary mortal's life means that much to me? But a wizard...that's another story. You people cause me no end of grief, even over your little lifetimes. I run around and try again and again to kill you, or just to keep you from undoing my best work. It takes up too much of my time. Now here's a thing that's easy for me to do. You come to terms with me, and I call off the viruses.

Because you've willingly, consciously come to terms with me, by the Oath you swore, you then lose your wizardry. One less problem for me in the universe, afterward. Maybe more than just one less."

"It's a trick," Nita said.

"Not at all," the Lone Power said. "You don't believe me? Fine. You go right on inside your mother as planned. Take Pralaya with you, even; he'll be glad to help. But I'm telling you, you're still going to find it too much for you. The viruses will win in the end." The Lone One shrugged again. "But I'm even willing to let you try to beat me fair and square, and fail, and I'll *still* do you that last favor afterward...if you agree to the price."

The price. The words echoed. Suddenly Nita found herself wondering whether this encounter itself was the price that the manual had so far failed to specify.

And she was becoming cold inside at the thought that perhaps just by sitting here this long and listening to the Lone One, she had already paid it.

"What if I refuse?" Nita said.

"I couldn't care less," the Lone Power said. "Stretch your power to the uttermost. It won't help. The operation will end, and the doctors will get that tumor out, all right. But even in the short run it won't matter, because the viruses in your mother's body won't have listened to anything *you* have to say, and the secondary tumors will already be forming in her bone marrow and her pancreas and her liver. You'll have maybe a few more weeks with her. Or maybe you'll overextend yourself in the wizardry and leave your mother having to deal with the reality of *your* death, while her own is creeping up on her. Nice going-away present, that."

If Nita had felt cold before, it was nothing to how she felt now. She could find nothing to say.

"Don't make up your mind right away," the Lone Power said. "Think about it. You've got plenty of time...until the morning after next, at least. And then you can slip inside your mother, find her kernel, the software of her soul, and do your best."

"And you'll make sure I fail!"

"Far be it from me to be so unfair," the Lone Power said, and folded Pralaya's middle arms, leaning back in the lounger. "There's, oh, a chance in a million or two that you can save her...but your inexperience means that you'll have to do it by brute power, fueled by despair...and you'll almost certainly die, either doing it or trying to."

Nita was silent.

"It'll be a lot easier my way," the Lone Power said. "You go in, you fail...and then you agree to my price and I call off my little friends. Spontaneous remission, the doctors will all say afterward. Miracle cure. Everybody will be happy...most especially your dad." Nita gulped again. "And as for you, you just don't do any more wizardry. Your mother doesn't even have to know about it. Or you can tell her that you had to use up all the wizardry in you for this one big job, while you still remember what you were, anyway. And you'll be amazed how soon she stops bringing up the subject at all."

Pralaya scratched his tummy with his middle legs. "But then mortals always get so twitchy about magic, anyway. No matter what you've told your mother since she found out about it, she's never been entirely sure that you didn't get the wizardry somewhere...let's just say, somewhere unhealthy." It smiled at her, and the look was supremely ironic. "You'll be able to relieve her and your father of their concerns once and for all. And indirectly, their concerns about your little sister. I doubt even Dairine is going to rub their noses in her continued practice of wizardry when *you've* forgotten all about it. She'll go undercover and you'll all be just a normal happy family again."

Except for all the things that will never again be right...no matter how normal we seem.

Nita sat there feeling numb. "Just how are the other Powers letting you get away with this kind of thing?" she asked at last.

"They can't stop me," It said. "Not without undoing all of creation. And They're not willing to do that. Oh, there are some pocket universes where They have one or another of my aspects bound. You've seen one of those—on your Ordeal." It shrugged. "But I can't be confined to such places. The power of creation was given into my hands, once, and the willing gifts of Gods cannot be taken back after they are given...so I am still part of everything created, one way or another. And will be, until it all ends. But that's a long way ahead of us." It stretched. "There are more immediate concerns. You'll let me know what you decide, sooner or later…and if you pay my price, your mother will live."

It got up and stretched again. "I'll take my host home," the Lone One said. "It doesn't do for me to overshadow him for too long at a time; he might get suspicious. You'll decide what to do. And when you head out to do your final intervention, you'll find Pralaya waiting for you, ready to help you out—one way or the other."

Pralaya's transit circle appeared at his feet. "But one way or another," the Lone Power said, "I suggest you make your peace with the other Powers That Be. Your relationship with them isn't likely to last in its present form for much longer."

And Pralaya stepped through his circle, and vanished.

Nita sat there alone in stunned silence for a long, long while, thinking. Finally she got up and prepared her own transit circle, wanting more than anything else just to go home, where things would seem normal again, where she could get a little rest and try to work out where the truth lay.

But the image of her mother lying pale and stricken in the hospital bed kept coming before her eyes, and Nita was afraid that she had already made up her mind.

It was late when she got back, and the sight of her darkened bedroom seemed to suck the energy out of her. Nita fell onto the bed and lay there in desperate weariness, while her mind raced. For what seemed like hours, though it was probably only a few minutes, she tried to find a way out of the bargain she was being of-fered...*any* way out.

She couldn't find one. *I need another viewpoint,* she thought. But it was too late to talk to Kit.

And I need Pralaya, she thought. *That extra dose of ability, his talent at seeing and analyzing the alternate universes.* He was good at it, there was no question of that. She was going to need all the help she could get.

But Kit is going to want to come, she thought. *I can't stop him. And, oh, I do need his help.*

But he was even less experienced at this business of manipulating kernels than she was. *And if he does come along, when he sees Pralaya, what if he realizes who's hiding inside him?*

The details of this bizarre relationship were still making her head go around in circles. Up until now the Lone Power usually had manifested itself in displays of brutal and destructive power. Nita knew perfectly well that It could be subtle when It pleased. But she hadn't pictured anything like *this.* And regardless of the mechanism by which It had subverted this wizard, if Kit recognized Its presence in Pralaya, he was going to be furious that Nita was still working with him. *He's not going to understand what I'm up against here,* she thought.

He will if you explain it to him, said the back of her mind.

But Nita was already beginning to try to frame that explanation in her head, and the more she tried, the more it sounded like something that would simply make Kit think she had sold out to the Lone Power.

And what if he's right?

She turned over and stared at the ceiling, her mind noisy with tentative dialogue, and with anguish.

To save her mother...and lose her wizardry.

Was it worth it? Once, when Nita's wizardry was new, maybe she would have said *No!* right away. The Oath seemed so clear-cut then, the lines between good and evil very thickly drawn.

But now...

Her mother.

She simply could not imagine a life without that serene, dancing presence sailing through it. Her mother was always there, behind everything, involved in everything. The idea of a life without her, of an emptiness where she had been: never again to hear her voice, joking, yelling, singing to herself, never again.

Not this side of Timeheart, anyway.

Normally it was a comfort thinking of Timeheart, where everything that existed was preserved in perfection, close to the center of things. But the Heart of Time was remote—a remote certainty at best, a remote possibility when you were in a more cynical or suspicious mood. It was an abstract, nothing like the concrete reality of the woman who had been genially cursing at her Cuisinart just a week or so ago. The woman who had always been there with a hug for Nita, who had been able to understand about everything—about being bullied, about doing well or badly at school—even, to a certain extent, about wizardry itself.

And now...if I do this...I'll have to give that up. But she would still be here.

Yet...to give it up— The idea was bitter. A window on a hundred thousand other worlds, and a most intimate window on this one, closed forever—even the memory of it slowly ebbing away until there was just a small nameless ache at the bottom of her that she would learn to ignore with time, the place where wizardry had been and wasn't anymore. So many people had that ache and thought it was normal. Eventually Nita would be just one more of them. She would remember—if she remembered anything—"those great games she used to play with Kit." That was all they would be: memories of childhood fantasies.

And *he* would still remember the reality, while Nita would pass him on the street, maybe, or in school, and not know what he had been to her...not *really*.

But at least nobody would be dead.

Except the part of you that the Powers gave the wizardry to, Nita thought. *Murdered, just as if you'd shot it with a gun.* How could it possibly be a good thing to do that, no matter *whose* life it saved?

She put her face in her hands. It was a dilemma.

But, then, that's what a dilemma is, Nita thought. *A two-horned problem.*

A thing split in two.

Like me.

Like me and Kit, whispered a thought that had been lying unspoken in the back of her mind for a while now, for fear that speaking it might make it come true.

She moaned out loud with the sheer unfairness of it. Yet what use was keeping wizardry and partnership, and all the rest of it, when her mother wouldn't be there to see it and roll her eyes and insist that she do her homework? All the hospital talk of chemotherapy and radiotherapy and so on, after the surgery, could not hide from her what it took no wizardry at all to see: the looks on the faces of the doctors and nurses who were caring for her mom. They usually would not even say the name of the thing that had attacked her mother from within. They merely said "C.A." or used long Latin and Greek words, all of which had the ominous "oma" ending clinging to them, like a dark shadow trailing away behind. The doctors were as afraid of what was going to happen to her mom as Nita was. For all the magic that was medical science, there was precious little hope in their eyes.

If anything's going to save her, Nita thought, *it's going to have to be something I do.*

But which *something?*

The weariness was beginnning to catch up with her. Nita put her face into her pillow. She wanted to cry, but she felt too tired to do even that.

Mom. Kit. Her mind went back and forth between the two of them.

I'm just going to have to go ahead and get what help I can get out of Pralaya.

And then... if it doesn't work...

She was afraid now to try to see that far ahead in her life. But she was considering the options—and the idea of what Kit would think of this scared Nita. Yet she knew that keeping her options open was the right thing.

Like you were right about Jones Inlet? said another small voice in the back of her mind.

She gripped the pillow with both hands and ground her face into it. *Tell me what to do!* she begged whoever might be listening. *Give me a hint!*

But the night was silent around her, and no answers came. And the only Power That had spoken to her so far had been the One she had sworn never to deal with.

Finally sleep took her. But her dreams were all bad, and even in the midst of them, she knew that when she woke up, things would be no better.

Thursday

THE AWAKENING WAS SUDDEN, and Nita lay there with her heart pounding, knowing something was wrong but unable to work out what it was. Finally her eyes focused as she looked over at her alarm clock, and she realized it was eleven-thirty in the morning.

Didn't it go off? What happened? she thought, sitting bolt upright in bed.

"Dad called school," Dairine's voice said. Nita looked up and saw Dairine sitting in her chair with her feet up on Nita's desk, wearing nothing but one of her dad's T-shirts, and looking small and miserable. "He asked them to let us both off today because of the operation tomorrow."

Nita lay down again, wishing that she could just go back to sleep...except that it was hardly any better than being awake.

"Dair," she said, "if giving up your wizardry would make Mom better, would you do it?"

Her sister looked at her in complete shock and didn't say anything for at least a minute. For Dairine this was something of a record.

"Is that what you're going to have to do?" she said at last.

"I don't know."

"I'd...," Dairine said. "I'd..." And she trailed off, her eyes going haunted.

Nita nodded.

"Are you sure it would work?" Dairine said after a while.

Nita shook her head. "Nothing's sure," she said.

Dairine pulled her knees up under the baggy T-shirt and hugged them to her for a long time. Then she looked up.

"And then it would all be gone?"

"Everything," Nita said. "All the magic, gone forever."

Dairine sat with her forehead on her knees, minute after minute. When she looked up, her face was wet. "If you were sure..."

Nita shook her head again.

"I'd miss you," Dairine said.

"I wouldn't be gone," Nita said.

"You know what I mean."

Nita nodded. "Yeah," she said. "I'd miss you, too."

And Dairine got up and went out of Nita's room, heading downstairs.

Nita could do little else that day but work with the manual, trying to evaluate the effectiveness of her work with the kernels and fine-tuning the spells she would have with her while working on her mother. But the problem that she could not solve kept intruding itself between her and her preparation, and there was no respite from it, nowhere to hide.

The sound of the discreet *bang!* in the backyard brought Nita's head up—almost a welcome distraction. But then her heart went cold. *Kit. How am I going to explain this to him?*

It just isn't fair, she thought. *What's happened to Mom has spoiled everything. Even things I should be glad about hurt now.*

She heard the back door open and the faint sound of Kit saying something to Dairine in the kitchen, then his footsteps on the stairs, and a scrambling noise behind him as Ponch ran up. The dog was first into her room; he burst past Kit and ran up to Nita and put his forepaws up on her. "We went bang!" he said.

"Yeah, I heard you, big guy," Nita said, and looked at Kit as he came in and sat down on the bed.

"How'd it go?" Kit said. "You get your practice done?"

"Yeah...the last one, I think."

He looked concerned. "Is that going to be enough? Are you ready?"

At that she had to put her face in her hands, rubbing her eyes in an attempt to keep from looking like she was hiding her face. "I don't know," she said. "But it can't wait any longer."

"I guess you couldn't really put it off," Kit said, sounding like he could tell perfectly well that Nita wanted to.

"No," she said, unhappy. "When Mom's anesthetized is the best time to do this; even during sleep there's a chance she could be conscious enough to get caught up in what's going on, and that'd be a problem."

"Well," Kit said, "if you've done all the preparation you can...I guess there's nothing to do now but wait."

"Yup," she said.

"And while we're doing that, we can talk about exactly what you want me to be doing to help."

She didn't answer right away. Kit looked at her sharply, and she noticed Ponch's eyes on her, too, an expression more subtle and considering than you usually got from him. "Neets," Kit said, "why're you so twitchy all of a sudden?"

"Well, why on Earth wouldn't I be twitching!" Nita said.

Kit and Ponch just looked at her. "Neets," Kit said, "give me a break. This is *me*, remember? You're twitching more than usual. More than makes sense even for what you're going through, not that it's not awful enough. What's *happened* to you since we talked last?"

"Kit...," Nita said at last. "We've saved a lot of lives in our time. A *lot*."

"Millions," Kit said. There might have been some pleasure in the way he said it, but no pride.

"So how come I may not be able to save the one who matters?"

"Like those other times didn't matter, really," Kit said, with mild scorn. "But Neets, the key word here is *we*. You don't have to go through this alone."

She didn't say anything for a long while. "You don't

understand," Nita said at last. "This time, I think I *have* to do it alone." And she tightly controlled her mind so that he wouldn't hear her thought: *Because I couldn't stand it if somehow you wound up paying the same price I might have to... and losing your wizardry, too!*

Kit's look got suddenly even more concerned. "Neets. Tell me what you've been doing. I don't want a précis. I want the details. All of them."

She was silent for some moments. Then Nita told him.

It took a while, though doing some of the explaining mind to mind sped things up. But toward the end of it, as she began telling him about Pralaya, Kit's expression turned grave. When she told him about that last conversation she and Pralaya had had, Kit's eyes went cold. He didn't say anything for a good while.

"I'm still not sure how He was doing that," Nita said.

"As an avatar," Kit said. "Neets, *all* the Powers That Be can do that when They need to, when They're on the job. For cripes' sake, if the One's Champion can live inside a macaw for years at a time, why should it surprise you that the Lone Power can pull the same stunt every now and then?"

Slowly she nodded, feeling cold inside.

"Neets, I hate to say it, but this really looks like the Lone One's been getting at you. Even before It fell, It preferred to work by Itself. Then It got isolated and proud, and after that came the Fall... and now that pride is still Its favorite way of tripping people up. It makes them think they can handle everything by themselves."

"Kit, in this case there's actually something to it! You just don't have the experience at what I'm going to have to be doing—"

"As if that matters! Neets, you're not thinking straight right now. You even missed something as simple as the mechanism the Lone One's using to hide inside Pralaya. How can you be so sure about your thinking on everything else?"

That was something she couldn't bear to hear. Followed to its logical conclusion, that line of reasoning would suggest that everything Nita had been planning was possibly useless, doomed to failure from the start.

"If you accept Its help," Kit said, "you're probably going to lose your wizardry! But what's more important is that doing that is just *wrong.*"

Now she did hide her face in her hands. "Kit," she said softly, "it looks more and more like, to save my mom, I'm going to lose it no matter what I do. Or die trying. But I have to *try.*"

"Not alone," Kit said. "And not this way, Neets! You come to any kind of deal with that One, it's gonna backfire somehow. Believe me!"

"All this is real easy for *you* to say, but *your mother's not dying!*"

Kit's expression was pained, but he just shook his head. "You think I haven't imagined about a hundred times how this must be for you? But it doesn't change the rights and wrongs of it, Neets. It says right there in the Oath, 'I will defend life *when it is right to do so.*' It's *never* right to do it on the Lone Power's terms, and if you let It sucker you into this—"

"Kit, you've got to believe me. It's not like that. You don't really understand what's going on here."

"I understand that you're messing around with the Lone Power, and you're going to get burned! What makes you think It has the slightest intention of doing what It says It's going to? It's gonna find some loophole to exploit, just the way It always does, and leave you out in the cold."

He stopped. There was a long, long silence as he and Ponch watched her.

Nita discovered that she was actually starting to shake. *He's right. But I'm right, too. What do I do—?*

"Look," she said. "I can't take much more of this right now. Tomorrow morning is getting closer every minute, and I'm not sure I'm ready yet."

"When are you going to start work in the morning?" Kit said.

Nita rubbed her eyes again. "Around eight. The doctors said that's when they're starting."

"I'll be here," Kit said. "Neets, please . . . Get some rest. Get your brains straightened out. *You're not going to do this alone.*"

He got up and headed out hurriedly, almost as if something was making him nervous. Ponch licked her hand and trotted out after Kit.

Nita sat there for a long while. *There's no way I'm going to be able to keep him from coming along . . .*

...if I wait for him.

But Nita *did* want to wait for him. She knew his help would be invaluable. At the same time, she knew that the minute Kit set eyes on Pralaya, there would be trouble. She would lose Pralaya's help. And she needed that, too, regardless of who might live inside Pralaya from time to time.

And at the end of it all, if she could not cure her mother herself, then Pralaya had to be there to implement the bargain.

There were no answers, and time was running out. The only consolation was for Nita to keep telling herself that tomorrow around this time, it would all be over. Her mother would have been saved or else she wouldn't have been, and if she hadn't, Nita wouldn't be in any position to worry about anything else.

It was not much consolation at all.

The rest of the day was a waking nightmare. Nita was tempted to go back into the practice universes one last time, but she wasn't sure what difference that would make—and she was tired, tired. She needed her rest but couldn't seem to get any. Details of the spells she would need to take with her, last-minute ideas, and the constantly returning thought that Kit might be right and she might be completely wrong kept going around and around in her head, and gave her no peace.

It seemed like about five minutes after Kit had come over that Nita's dad came home from work, and they all went to the hospital together. Her mother hadn't had any more seizures, for which Nita was profoundly thankful. Except the thought kept creeping in: *Is this the Lone One just giving me more time to think... and to be grateful to It?* The idea made her shudder.

When they went into Nita's mom's room, Nita saw that a number of machines had been moved in by the bed. One apparently was to make sure there was warning if she had any more seizures—there were ugly little pink and blue contact pads glued all over her head, with the hair held down around them in a hopeful sort of way by one of the "turbans" Nita had seen some of the nurses wearing. Her mom looked unnatural, drawn, more tired than ever, and her smile was wearing thin at the edges.

"Oh, honey, don't look at me like that," her mom said, seeing Nita's expression. "I look like the bride of Frankenstein, I know that. It's all right. I was due for another haircut, anyway."

Two things hit Nita at once. The first thing was that, as always, her mother was trying to take care of her, even when she herself was sick. The second, which struck Nita with a terrible inevitability, was that what her mother was saying was not true: It would never be all right, never again. Her mom was really going to die.

For several long seconds, Nita could find nothing at all to do or say, and she didn't dare look her mom in the eye; she knew her mother would see instantly what was the matter. Fortunately, Dairine got between her and her mom, and Nita disentangled herself and turned away, never more grateful for her sister's inborn ability to get in the way.

But the moment decided her. Kit or no Kit, Lone One or not, she would do anything she had to do to save her mother: give up her wizardry, agree to whatever had to be agreed to. She was lost.

But at least I know now, she thought. The rest of the visit passed in a kind of cheerful fog of small talk, all of it forced; none of them felt much like discussing what was going to happen the next day. After a while Nita's dad asked Nita and Dairine to give him a few moments alone with their mom.

Nita went down the hall, down by the soft-drink machine, and Dairine followed her slowly.

"Is it gonna be all right?" Dairine said. Suddenly she didn't sound like her usual competent self. Suddenly she sounded very young and scared, really wanting her older sister to tell her that things were going to work.

"Yeah," Nita said. "One way or another."

And there was nothing else to say and nothing else to do but wait for the morning.

Friday Morning

HOW NITA SLEPT THAT night she never knew; she assumed it must have been exhaustion. At six that morning, her dad, fully dressed and ready to leave, awakened her.

"Dad," Nita said, and got out of bed.

He looked at her with a terrible stillness. She would almost have preferred him to cry or yell; but he was now reduced to simply waiting.

"Are you ready?" he said.

There was almost no way to answer him and still tell the truth. "I'm going to start work when they do," Nita said. "It may take me as long as Mom spends in the OR, or even longer, so don't panic if I'm not here when you get home."

"All right," her father said.

He reached out and put his arms around her. All Nita could do was bury her face in his shoulder and hang on, hang on hard, trying not to cry, much though she wanted to; she was sure it would frighten him if she lost her control now.

"Be careful, honey," he said, still with that terrible control. "I don't want to—" He stopped. *Lose you both,* she heard him think.

"I'll be careful," Nita said. "Go on, Daddy. I'll see you later."

She let go of him and turned away, waiting for him to leave. He went out the back door; a moment later, Dairine came into her room.

"Did you hear from Kit?" she asked.

Nita nodded. *Oh, please, don't ask me any more.*

Dairine didn't say anything. "Look," she said then, as outside, their dad started the car. "Come back," Dairine said. *"Just come back."*

Nita was astonished to see tears in her sister's eyes. For a split second she wanted desperately to tell Dairine that she was afraid she might not come back... or that she might come back and not be a wizard anymore—and Nita wasn't sure which possibility was more awful. But she didn't dare say anything. If Dairine got any real sense of what was going on inside Nita's head, there was too much of a danger that she might interfere...and Tom and Carl had been emphatic about what would happen then.

Nita just nodded and hugged Dairine. "You ready to give the surgeons whatever energy they need?"

"All set."

"Then go on," she said. "Dad's waiting. Keep an eye

on him, Dari." She swallowed. "Keep him from getting desperate. It's going to matter."

Dairine nodded and went downstairs.

Nita waited to hear the car drive away. Then she got herself ready, checking the charm bracelet one last time for the spells stored there. A couple of openings remained, and she spent a few minutes considering what she might add. Finally, thinking of that first meeting with Pont and the other wizards, she added the subroutine that let the wizard using it walk on water. *If there was ever a day I needed to believe I could do that,* she thought, *it's today.*

Then she opened her manual to the pages involving access to the practice universes.

Let's go, she said to the manual. *The playroom first... and then the main event.*

The page she was looking at shimmered, and then the print on it steadied down to a new configuration, a more complex one than she'd seen so far. It flickered, and then said: *Secondary access to nonaschetic "universe" analog has been authorized. Caution: This "universe" is inhabited. Population: 1.*

Nita pulled her transit-circle spell out of the back of her mind, dropped it to the floor, took one last deep breath, and stepped through.

At seven-fifteen that morning, Kit was sitting on the beat-up kitchen sofa, eating cornflakes out of an ancient beat-up Scooby-Doo bowl in a studied and careful way. It was partly to steady his stomach—cornflakes were comfort food for him, inherently reassuring on some strange level—and partly his standard preparation for a wizardry. All your power wouldn't do you much good if your brains weren't working because your blood sugar was down in your socks somewhere.

He finished the bowl he was working on, contemplated a second one, and decided against it. Kit took his mom's favorite bowl to the sink and washed it out carefully, going over his preparations one last time in his head. He knew as much about the aschetic universes as the manual would tell him without approval from a Senior. He knew that Nita's authority and agreement would be enough to get him inside her mother with her; and beyond that, he had every power-feeding technique he could think of ready to go in the back of his head.

"I want to come along," Ponch said from behind him.

Kit sighed as he finished washing the spoon, and he put it in the rack, too. "I don't think you can," he said. "It's going to be complicated enough as it is."

"I want to be with you. And I want to see her."

Kit sighed again. Ponch had caught some of his boss's nervousness about what Nita had gotten herself into. "Look," Kit said. "You can come over and see her off, okay? Then you have to go home and wait for me."

Ponch wagged his tail. "And *no* coming after me once I've left you," Kit said. "You have to stay here."

Ponch drooped his head, depressed that Kit had anticipated what he'd been thinking.

Kit went to get his jacket from the hooks behind the

door. He checked his jacket pocket for his manual, though he wasn't sure how useful it would be inside Nita's mom. *Better to have it, though.* As he was running through his checks one last time, his mom, wearing what his dad referred to as the "Tartan Bathrobe of Doom," wandered into the kitchen, looked back at Kit and Ponch, and caught the dog's sad expression. "He hasn't been bad again, has he?" she said.

Ponch drooped his head some more and wagged his tail again, an abject look that fooled Kit not at all. "Not in any of the usual ways, Mama," he said. "Look, I'm going to help Nita, and this is a serious one. I may not be back for a while."

"Okay, *brujito.*"

He had to smile at that. His mom had taken longer than his father to come to terms with Kit's wizardry; his father had been surprisingly enthusiastic about it, once he got over the initial shock. "Hey, my son's a *brujo,*" he started saying to Kit's mother. "What's the matter with that?" His pop wore his pride in a way that seemed to suggest that he thought he was somehow responsible for Kit's talent. *Maybe he is,* Kit thought. So far he didn't have any data on which side of the family his wizardly tendencies descended from; he'd been much too busy lately to look into it.

At least the situation was presently working in his favor. "Come on," Kit said to Ponch. As they went out into the backyard together, Kit glanced over in the general direction of Nita's house and in thought said, *Neets?*

There was no answer.

Kit stood still, hoping against hope that she was just distracted for a moment.

Nita!

Nothing.

It was the matter of a second to throw a transit circle around himself and Ponch, and it took no more than another second to make sure it would be silent in operation. A moment later Kit and Ponch were standing in Nita's bedroom.

It was empty. Kit stood there, listening to the sounds of an empty house, feeling for the presence of other human beings, and knowing immediately that Nita was already gone.

He felt just a flash of anger, replaced almost immediately by fear. *She left early because she was afraid for me,* he thought.

One more error in judgment. *Now what?* Kit thought, going cold with fear. *Go over to see Tom and Carl, get permission to follow her—*

Why? I can find her, Ponch said in Kit's head.

Kit looked at Ponch in astonishment. *How?*

The way I found the squirrels.

"But that was making a new universe," Kit said. "Neets is in an old one, a universe that exists already!"

"We can make some of *that* one as if it's new," Ponch said, in a tone of voice suggesting that he was surprised this wasn't obvious. "The part *she's* in."

Kit couldn't think of anything to say.

"I know her scent," Ponch said, impatient. "We can be where she's gone. Let's go!"

Kit was uncertain, but time was short. He reached

into his claudication and rummaged around it to find the wizardly leash, then slipped it around Ponch's neck and said, "Okay, big guy, give it your best shot."

Ponch stepped forward, and together they vanished.

They walked for a long time in the dark, an experience Kit was glad no longer unsettled him. Every now and then would come a flicker of light, and he could just see, or sense, Ponch putting his head out into that light and sniffing, the way he might have put his head out a dog door, then pulling back again, turning away. *Having trouble?* Kit asked silently, the third or fourth time this happened.

No. The world just twists, is all. And something doesn't want us to be where she is.

Kit swallowed. But finally they came out into the light and stayed there, and Kit looked around him in surprise, even though his experience of alternate universes had been expanded a lot lately. It was a huge place, a flat space, and its emptiness made it seem to echo in the mind. The sourceless lighting and the shining floor with the assortment of weird chairs, beds, hammocks, frames, and tables in the middle of it made it all look much like a furniture showroom.

Ponch pulled Kit toward the furniture, still sniffing. There were some people there: aliens, which didn't surprise Kit particularly—hominids were not at all in the majority in his home universe. As he approached, a few of them looked at him with slight surprise, and one of them pointed a greater than usual number of eyes at him. It was a Sulamid, Kit noticed, an alien native to the far side of his own galaxy, one of a people who—unusually—were almost all wizards, a fact that apparently had something to do with the way their brains were divided.

The looks they were giving him—furred people, one tall cadaverous hominid, a four-legged alien, another one that looked like five or six oversized blue ball bearings in company, and the Sulamid with its many stalky eyes—were speculative. "I'm on errantry," Kit said, "and I greet you."

Ponch barked. To Kit's bemusement, every wizard present looked in what seemed to be surprise at Ponch. The Sulamid bent over in half and then straightened up again, its eyes and various of its tentacles tying themselves in graceful knots.

"I'm looking for another of my species," Kit said. "My colleague thinks she was just here. Have you seen her?"

Various looks were exchanged. "You just missed them," said the ball bearings. "They were here with more of us: Pralaya. They just left. They were on an intervention. Pralaya was going to assist them."

The whole group of them were still looking at him. Kit started to feel uneasy, for he thought he knew what they were thinking: *This other wizard is trying to interfere somehow.* "Did she say anything about what she was going to be doing?" Kit said, somehow knowing that it was useless to do so. These other wizards were not going to help him; they were uncertain why he was here, uncertain whether he might somehow foul an intervention in progress.

"No," said first the ball-bearing wizard and then the others.

"She has gone into the dark," said the Sulamid, "all too accompanied. And her destination is an unknown."

The other wizards threw the Sulamid an odd look and began, one after another, to vanish. Shortly the space was empty except for Kit and Ponch and the Sulamid, which was standing not far away, its tentacles wreathing gently, looking at Kit with a lot of its eyes.

"How do you know?" Kit said after a moment.

"Vision is useless without comprehension," said the Sulamid. "Comprehension is bootless without compassion."

"Uh, yeah," Kit said.

The Sulamid bowed once again, if a bow was what it was. It was not directed at Kit but at Ponch. "Pathfinder, seer for the seer in the dark," said the Sulamid, "tracker in the night-places, wait."

And it vanished, too.

Kit could only stand there and look around him at the light and the empty furniture. "Well, thanks loads, guys," he said. *Why were they all so freaked out? What's the matter with them?*

But he and Ponch were not quite alone; not everyone who'd been there originally had left. Behind Kit someone coughed, or maybe it was more like a snort. He and Ponch both turned.

Behind them, looking at them thoughtfully, was what Kit had initially mistaken for a four-footed alien of some kind. But it was actually a pig.

Kit looked at it in astonishment. Ponch instantly

barked once, excitedly, and started to run toward the pig, possibly thinking that it could be chased like a squirrel. Kit hurriedly grabbed Ponch by the collar and made him sit down. And to the Pig he said, "What's the meaning of life?"

"You know, a friend of yours was asking me the same thing the other day," said the Transcendent Pig, ambling over, sitting down, and looking Ponch over in an amiable way. "*Is* asking," it added.

The statement was slightly confusing, even taking into account the multidirectional time tenses in the Speech. At least Kit knew that he wasn't the only one confused by the Pig. Every other wizard was, too, and even the Powers That Be weren't sure where the Pig had come from, and tended to describe it as a concrete expression of the universe's innate sense of humor, a sort of positive chaos.

"Is she?" was all Kit could think to say.

"Yes. And you know," said the Pig, "it's all just a big plot, isn't it? You're all just hoping that I might actually slip and answer the question, and *tell* one of you."

Kit blinked at that. "Uh, well—"

"Or else it's a practical joke planted by Someone high up," the Pig muttered, settling down with its trotters under it, a position that made it look peculiarly like a cat. "Wouldn't put it past Them. *Or* Their Boss."

Kit gave the Pig a look. "Oh, come on! The Powers..." His voice trailed off as the Pig gave him the same look right back. "I mean, the One...wouldn't play *jokes*—"

"Wouldn't It?" said the Transcendent Pig. "Been out in the real world lately?"

"Uh..."

"Right. Life being all the other things it is, if it's not funny sometimes, what's it worth? But you changed the subject."

"No, I didn't."

"Maybe you didn't," the Pig said. "I'll allow you that one. You were saying?"

Kit took a long breath. Beside him Ponch lay down but never took his eyes off the Pig. "You're really well traveled," Kit said.

"Omnipresence will do that for you," said the Pig, and it yawned.

"You said you'd seen Nita—" Kit wondered why such simple terms as *my friend* and *my partner* kept sticking in his throat. *What's the matter with me?*

Because one might not be true anymore. And— He absolutely refused to deal with the thought that the other might not be, either.

"Yes. I'm with her now, in fact."

"You are?"

The Pig gave Kit a wry look. "It wouldn't be a terribly useful kind of transcendence if I *wasn't*. Being everywhere at once is part of the job description."

"Where is she? What's she doing?" Kit said after a moment.

The Pig gave him another of those long dry looks. "Oh, come on, now. You know the drill, or you should. You tell me three truths that I don't know, and I tell you one."

Kit raised his eyebrows. "That doesn't sound real fair."

"If you knew how much trouble a human being can get into with just one truth," the Pig said, "you wouldn't be asking for more."

"Got a point there," Kit said. In a flash the thought went through his head that it was possible he didn't need to venture his time or his power on this gamble. Yet somehow he felt that the time spent would be worth his while. "So let's get going."

"An admirable attitude," said the Transcendent Pig. "First truth."

"I'm looking for the wizard who's meant to be my partner," Kit said.

"The first part I know perfectly well. The second part is conditional. 'Meant'? What exactly would it be that's doing the meaning?"

"I think the day we find that out for sure," Kit said, only half joking, "it might all be over."

The Pig raised its eyebrows. "I'm tempted to give you that one," it said. "From a member of Homo sapiens, the secondary insight is relatively unusual these days." It acquired a considering look. "But a half-truth is a half-truth. Give me a whole one this time."

Kit thought for a little while more, wondering what he would add on at the end of all this to make an extra half-truth. *Worry about it shortly.* He said, "My dog makes alternate universes, ones that no one's ever seen before. They're new."

The Pig blinked. "That *is* news. Continuous creation?"

"You've got me."

"Yes, but let's leave that issue out of it for the moment."

Kit blinked, too. "I thought continuous creation had been discredited, though."

The Pig smiled. "The moment any scientist says anything's impossible, you should start wondering. Science, like life, finds ways. But, anyway, you own a brain, and you still think continuous creation's been discredited? So where did *your* last bright idea come from?"

"Uh...," Kit said.

"Right," said the Pig. "Next truth."

"I think," Kit said, with the utmost reluctance, "that my partnership with Nita is about to get totally screwed up if I don't do something, and I'm not sure what to do. I have to find her, I know that. It's vital. But after that—"

"I'll grant you that," the Pig said. "So that's two and a half. What else have you got?"

Kit sat there scouring his mind for some moments, unable to think of even one truth, let alone two. The Pig started to get up.

"Wait a minute!" Kit said, and the Pig looked at him.

It was a desperate move, but it was all Kit could think of. "Here," Kit said.

He looked all around then. For some reason he felt like he didn't want anyone but the Pig to see this.

"It's all right," said the Transcendent Pig. "We're alone. Yes, I'm sure; don't give me that look. What is it?"

Kit pulled his personal claudication open, slipped

his hand into it, and came out with that little spark, carefully cupped in both hands. He held the hands just a little bit apart so that the Pig could see in.

It peered between his fingers, and looked at Kit with an odd, speculative expression. "Now, isn't that something," it said. "A glede."

"A what?"

"A glede. Or a dragon's eye, it's called sometimes." The Pig turned its head this way and that, looking at the little spark. "The idea was, you might draw a dragon, but the eyes were where the soul was—some people thought—and the drawing wouldn't come to life until the eyes were added."

The Pig let out a thoughtful breath. "Fine, put it away. Where'd you find it?"

"In the dark," said Kit. "When I stopped making things, and just let the night be what it was." He tucked the glede away.

When he finished doing that, Kit found the Pig watching him closely. "Over time," the Pig said, "and outside it, too, other beings have moved over and through that darkness one way or another. Some of them have found or brought back...objects like that— what the void brings forth in silence. The question, afterward, has always been what to do with them."

"What *do* I do with it?" Kit said.

The Transcendent Pig shrugged a transcendently porcine shrug, glancing away. "That's hardly one of the traditional questions."

Kit snorted. "Don't you get *tired* of the traditional questions?"

It glanced back at him, its eyes squinted closed a little in what Kit realized was the beginnings of a smile. "Tired? I can't get tired," the Pig said. "But bored? *Hoo*boy."

"So?"

The Pig was quiet for a little while. "Now, if I was a stinker," it said at last, "I would demand a whole third truth from you, and then tell you one of the truths you originally asked for: where she is. But there's the glede to consider; things like that don't turn up often. And besides, I've always been a sucker for young—well, for people in your situation."

Kit waited, not able to make much of this.

The Pig raised its eyebrows. "You got lucky today, but don't try to take advantage. So think for a moment, and then ask your question."

Kit thought for what seemed to him like hours but was probably no more than a matter of minutes. Finally he looked up and said, "How can I save her?"

The Pig rolled its eyes. "*Her* her, or *her*, her mother?"

Kit merely smiled.

The Transcendent Pig let out an exasperated breath. "The last time someone asked me a question phrased that way," said the Pig, "Atlantis sank. You know that story?"

"Several versions of it. And don't change the subject!" Kit said, severe.

The Pig gave him a shocked look, and then laughed out loud. "You simian-descended, equivocating, pronoun-starved little mortal twerp," it said. "Maybe the universe does favor young wizards because they haven't properly mastered the Speech's plurals yet. We really have to look into that."

It chuckled briefly, then composed itself. "All right. As you know," the Pig said, "Nita is attempting an intervention to save her mother's life. Unfortunately that intervention has been contaminated by the Lone Power from the start and therefore has little chance of succeeding, and much chance of backfiring. With results such as you should be able to imagine."

Kit swallowed, or tried to; his mouth had suddenly gone dry. "Oh, my God," Kit said.

"Yes," the Pig said.

Then all of a sudden something boiled over in the back of Kit's head. "Now just *wait* a minute," he said, annoyed. "First of all, I knew that. And second, you *knew* the Lone One was talking to her? And you didn't *tell* her?"

"She didn't ask," the Pig said. "Questions are important, and there's not a lot I can do without them. Don't look so shocked! The Powers That Be have the same problem. But it wasn't *my* business to tell her. For one thing, on some level, she *knows*. That One can never make Itself *completely* unrecognizable... and that's Its own fault. You set yourself apart from all previous creation, fine, but you're going to look and feel different to all creation afterward. What's more important is that the way she deals with the realization, when she comes up with it herself, is likely to be crucial to what she's working on. *That* I wouldn't interfere with, even if I could." It gave Kit a look. "And if you were smart, neither would you."

"So?" Kit said.

The Pig lay down with a thoughtful air. "Well," it said, "if I were you—which could happen, transcendence being what it is—I'd listen carefully to my hunches, when everything goes dark. You never know, you might hear something useful."

"Okay," Kit said. "Thanks."

"That's *it*?" the Pig said.

"Thanks a *lot*," Kit said.

"Well, I can't fault your manners," the Pig said. "Be being you, youngster. Go well!" And it got up and wandered away, the floor rippling uncertainly after it as it went. A moment or so later it was simply gone, without doing a transit or gating as such.

I guess if you're transcendent, you don't need to, Kit thought. He looked down at Ponch. "What do you make of that?" he said.

Ponch produced a feeling like a shrug. "I think maybe it's cheating. It shouldn't be *that* easy."

"I wish I felt better," Kit said. Yet there was something about what the Pig had said, something that was eluding him. . . .

"It's all right," Ponch said. "I know her scent. I got it fresh yesterday; it hasn't changed that much. And the trail is fresh. I can track her."

Changed, Kit thought, confused. *How could it change?*

"Come on!" Ponch said. "The longer we stand here, the farther away she goes."

"Let's go," Kit said. "There's not much time."

The leash was still around Ponch's neck. Kit picked

it up and wound it around his wrist. The two of them stepped into the darkness and were gone.

Grand Central was in shadow as Nita came out of the gate by track twenty-four, and as she put her foot down, she heard a splash. There was so little light in the space around her that Nita spent some power to produce a small wizard's candle, a glimmer of light that rode above her shoulder as she looked around.

The tracks were all under water, and water lapped at the piers that held up the platforms—a bizarre sight. Even the platforms were an inch deep or so in water, like black glass, the surface of it rippling gently, silent and intimidating. Beside her, Pralaya slipped into the water, ducking under it, and coming up again down by the place where the platforms tapered in, down where the tracks ducked more deeply under Forty-sixth Street. "This would be a wonderful swimmery," she heard him say from down in the darkness, "but I think perhaps it shouldn't be this way?"

"You got that in one," Nita said. Already she was trying to sense around her for this micro-universe's kernel, and she couldn't feel anything. *What's the matter? I should be able to at least get a hint. It's my mother, after all!* But it felt wrong somehow; she couldn't hear that faint buzz or whine that she'd learned to associate with a kernel, the sound of life doing its business. "Can you feel anything?" she said.

Pralaya surfaced in front of her, twisting and rolling in the dark water. "I'm not sure," he said. "There's...a darkness..."

Nita was all too aware of this darkness. Listening, watching, she could feel it all around her. It bent in; it pressed against her; and worst of all was the sense that at any moment Pralaya's innocent, merry personality could be twisted out of shape by the Lone Power suddenly looking out of his eyes at her, offering her the bargain she could not refuse.

It's here, she thought, feeling that heavy, dark presence leaning in all around her. *It's waiting for me to make a mistake.* And maybe she already had.

"Come on," she said to Pralaya, "let's get out into the open."

Together they made their way toward what would have been the Main Concourse in her own world. "What does this look like to you?" Nita said to Pralaya as they made their way through the wet.

"In my world? This is the Meeting of the Waters," Pralaya said. "The place where the rivers come together before they run to the Sea."

Nita thought of the Sea and immediately was sad, seeing in her mind's eye Jones Inlet, and the Sun over the water, leaning westward in the afternoon, and the long, broad golden sunset light over the Great South Bay, where she had screwed things up so seriously with Kit. But now they came out under what should have been the ceiling of the Main Concourse....

Nita stood there and took in a long breath of shock, and let out another long one of sorrow. The whole place was under water, five feet deep, and the beautiful cream-colored stone walls of the terminal, to the four compass points, were striped with green-brown tide-marks of high water from other times, and still flooded deep in an unhealthy dark water that lapped and sucked at the walls. The whole place smelled of damp and cold and weed and chilly pain, and Nita shuddered as she splashed out of the platform arcade into the center of the terminal. She looked up at what should have been a warm, summery, Mediterranean-sky ceiling, and instead saw nothing but watery stars and autumn constellations, all fish and dolphins and sea serpents—not to mention poor Andromeda shackled to the rock, waiting to be eaten by the monster from the waves. It was not a view that filled Nita with confidence.

"Is it always so dark here?" Pralaya said.

Nita thought of fire gaping out of the depths of this space, not so long ago; yet now that scenario seemed positively preferable, for it had put only her own life at stake, not her mom's. "Not usually," she said, and led Pralaya up out of the Main Concourse, up the ramp to what normally would have been the street.

It was no improvement. The sky was clouded, dark and heavy; this was a city in shadow and under threat, with the waters rising all around. Some of the skyscrapers around them were in good-enough shape, but many of them were crumbling. *Too many,* Nita thought, knowing that she was seeing what her own mind could most effectively make of her mother's physical condition. Things were already going wrong here, and her doubt rose up and choked her.

"We have to go where it's worst, don't we?" Nita said.

Pralaya nodded. "It would be the only way."

They stood there in the thunder-colored water, in the flooded street, and gazed up and down it. All of Forty-second Street was a river, and no traffic light, or any other light, burned on it anywhere; buildings cliffed out above the street, dark and forbidding, their lower stories wet and scummed with mold, their upper windows dulled with the residue of recent storms. Overhead, the roiling gray sky was like an unhealed wound, uncomfortable, unwell, unresolved. Nita closed her eyes and swallowed. Somewhere here was the kernel, the software of her mother's soul.

She held still and listened, listened.

"Do you have time for this?" said the voice behind her, a little provocative.

"Yup," Nita said, fierce. "Don't joggle my elbow, Pralaya, or I'll chew one of your legs off."

There was a pause. In a hurt voice Pralaya said, "I wouldn't have thought I'd have deserved that from you, Nita."

"Yeah, well," Nita said. "Sorry, cousin." *Assuming you're really my cousin at the moment, and not That One.*

The trouble was, there was no telling....*Never mind that.* Nita held still and listened with all of her. *It's my* mother, *for heaven's sake! I should be able to hear her.* But it was hard, suddenly.

And who's making it hard? Or is it just tough to sense your own mother when you're on business, as opposed to when you're at home? She becomes like water, like air, like anything else you get used to and take for granted.

Beside her, in the water, Pralaya paddled along as they worked their way down Forty-second Street. "Sorry," Nita said again. She would have said, *I didn't mean that,* except at the time she *had* meant it, cruel as it was, and a wizard did not lie in the Speech—that was fatal. *More fatal than what I'm about to do?*

Nita stood at the spot where Forty-second normally crossed the Vanderbilt Avenue underpass, saw the drowned canal that the under-running road had become, and wished that Kit were here. It seemed to her that if only he were here, everything would be all right.

Yet she had constructed the circumstances in which he *couldn't* be here. She stood there in the muddy, westward-flowing water...

...and something bit her in the leg.

Nita yelped and jumped. "What was *that*?" she said.

Pralaya had already clambered up onto a pillar of the west side of Grand Central, sticking up out of the water. "We're not alone here," he said. "What would these be? They have teeth—"

"Cancer viruses," Nita said. "I wouldn't let them get too friendly with your extremities, if I were you."

Peering down into the muddy water, Nita could see them: little dark blocky hexagonal shapes with fierce straight little tails or stingers, cruising around. The water was teeming with them, large and small, like the little dark minnows in one of the local freshwater creeks. *So many!* Nita thought. *How am I going to persuade all* these *things to do anything? The Lone Power was right. It was right.*

She considered using the spell that would let her

walk on water...but that took more energy than she now felt like using. *I'm going to need everything I can possibly save for later,* Nita thought. *Better use the low-power one I tailored earlier.* "I have a spell against these," she said to Pralaya. The spell would at least protect the two of them from the stings, but it couldn't stop the viruses from doing what they pleased with her mother.

She pulled the spell off her charm bracelet. With a little effort, she pulled the charm in two. It stretched like taffy then parted with a snap, leaving her holding two identical versions of the spell. Nita tossed Pralaya the clone, then dropped her version of it into the water.

Pralaya stretched out his version of the spell, adjusted it, and dropped it around him. Nita saw this happening and could not avoid thinking, *Here is the Power That invented these things, indirectly; and I'm protecting Its servant against them.*

Not that he knows...

Nita held still then, again, and listened. In this threatening light it was hard to think clearly. Everything seemed geared to leave you frightened, chilled, cowed, as slowly the livid sunset light behind those clouds shut down toward some final night.

Nita knew that day was waiting back there somewhere. If she could just find it, sense it, hear it. The sound of morning, of a dawn past all this leaden twilight. If she could just find it. If she could, it wouldn't matter if her wizardry departed her forever; it would be worth it.

And at the same time... She sloshed up Forty-second in the general direction of Fifth, listening with all of her, not hearing anything, and beginning, as predicted, to despair. *Kit...*

The bleak wind blew over the gray waters, and Nita walked on through it all, with Pralaya swimming beside her, and knew true desperation's colors at last.

Friday Afternoon

"I THOUGHT YOU SAID you were going to be able to find her."

"I should have been able to. But the scent's changed again."

"What?" Kit was confused, and stood still in the utter darkness where they had been walking. "How?"

Beside him Kit could feel Ponch gazing around him. "The One who doesn't want us to find Nita has changed it. The world she's gone to is twisted out of orientation with the usual ones."

Kit tried to put his own concerns aside; there was something more on his mind. "So where are they?" he said.

"Elsewhere."

"Thanks loads."

"You don't have the words for it," Ponch said, a little sharply. "You can't smell what's happening the way I do. We have to backtrack. There's a scent...but there's also trouble."

"What kind?"

Ponch shook himself. "Since we're not with Nita, it's going to be hard to convince the ones who guard the borders to let us in."

Kit let out a long nervous breath. "Never mind. Let's just keep going."

Nita and Pralaya kept making their way along through the dark waters, southward along Fifth Avenue. Nita had only a hunch to go on now, only the faintest sense of where her mother's kernel lay. Pralaya paused with her at the corner of Fifth and Fortieth, putting his head up out of the water and peering about him, while all around the two of them, the viruses darted and poked at their defense shields like angry little bees.

"Should we try it again?" Pralaya said.

Nita looked up and down the street—or rather the river, which the street had become—and nodded. "Yeah..."

She let her mind fall toward Pralaya's again, adding his viewpoint of this place to hers. Everything quivered, changed.

The darkness around them became even more oppressive, an inward-leaning, watching, sullen nest of shadows. Nita could feel how the place was full of death and the anticipation of death, and wanted them out of there.

But if Pralaya is the Lone One, why is It finding this so scary and upsetting? Nita thought. That was a question that she wasn't going to ask him out loud, though. She put it aside and did her best to feel around them for the kernel, listening.

A stronger hint this time. *South and west; and not too far.*

Nita let her mind drop away from Pralaya's again. He was lying there in the water, shivering. "You okay?" she said.

"Yes," he said, and shook himself all over, those big dark eyes troubled. "But, Nita, this is a terrible place. I wonder that you can bear it here."

She was shaking, too, but she couldn't let it stop her. "It's the one place I've been working to be," Nita said. "Let's go."

She set off westward, toward Sixth Avenue—splashing through water that was deeper and deeper—and Pralaya followed her, slowly, almost as if reluctant. Nita refused to spend any time trying to figure this out. She was tired, and very scared—both for herself and for her mother—and she simply wished that all this was over. The thought came to her: *You are now so tired, you will make some terrible mistake.*

And she was too tired even to care about *that.*

In the darkness between worlds, Kit felt Ponch pause and look at something.

"This is interesting," the dog said.

Kit couldn't see anything. "What is it?"

"Home," Ponch said in surprise.

"What?" Kit said, bemused. "Show me!"

"Here."

Suddenly they stepped out into Kit's backyard...except that the place had the feel of the universes that Kit and Ponch had been creating when Ponch first started taking Kit along on his walks—like something that Kit had made just now with whatever power lay between the worlds, ready to be used if you knew it was there. Kit looked around him in surprise at an utterly perfect summer day. Everything he could have wanted was there: the knowledge that school was out for the summer, the sound of Carmela's stereo blasting upstairs, his mother laughing with loving scorn at something his father was doing in the kitchen. The sky was flawlessly blue, the air just hot enough to make one think about going to the beach, but not having to *do* anything. The locusts were beginning to say *zzzeeeeeeee* in the trees. And just over there, the sudden *whoomp!* of air as Nita appeared out of nothing, turned toward him, grinning with excitement, her manual in her hand—

"Stop it right there," Kit said to the world. The image froze.

He stood there, now the only thing that could move in that whole still reality, and turned slowly, taking it all in: weeds and flowers, summer sunshine, peace. It was perfection, of a kind. The moment, held captive— heart's desire, caught in one place and unable to escape.

But moments aren't meant to be held captive. They're meant *to escape. That's what makes them matter.*

But I could make perfection, anyway, Kit thought as he turned, seeing a passing white cabbage butterfly caught in midair, in midstroke of its wings, trapped there as if in amber clearer than water. *I could go to live in it, if I wanted—the world where everything worked. I could even use this power to make myself believe that was where I'd always lived, the way things had always been.*

He swallowed. *I could* make *Timeheart.* Another *one.*

Kit held that moment for a long, long while, trapped in the grip of his mind, like a butterfly in his hand. He kept turning. The backyard with its backyard sassafras jungle, the long grass to lie in all through this lazy afternoon, looking up at the clouds—and standing there, frozen, but laughing, ready for anything: Nita. Not angry at him, not afraid, not troubled by any dark shadow hanging over her. Here it need never have happened. Here it was fine, had always been fine. He could be here the rest of his life if he liked, and everything, always, would be fine.

And if he could make that, then he could make anything. *Anything.*

Maybe this was how it had all started. The manual was "sketchy on the first hundredth of a second," Tom had said. "Privacy issues." Was it possibly something as simple as this—that in some other region of space-time, some other being, no more or less powerful than Kit, had stumbled across a spark such as the one he held now, and had created?

If it had happened that way, maybe it could happen that way again?

Here he was. Here was the power. All Kit had to do...was use it, and get everything right this time.

Everything: a whole universe of universes, innumerable, unfolding themselves as he watched—the essence of creation running riot, running rampant, life exploding through it. For a single moment that included and encompassed all moments, stretching out endlessly around him, time without beginning or end; Kit was lost in the vision—

—and then he had to laugh. He started to laugh so hard, he could hardly stand it; his sides started to hurt.

Oh, yeah, he thought. *Nice try. Gimme a break!*

When he was able to breathe again, Kit straightened up and gazed around him. No matter how he created such a perfect place—or had this one been left for him to find?—no matter that he might even be able to delude himself into believing that it was reality, the truth was that it *wouldn't* be. Elsewhere the real world would go on, people would hurt, life would be alternately happy and miserable...in the real places where wizards were needed to fight the fight, even if they might never see it won. And *this...This isn't real enough for me,* Kit thought. *I want the kind of reality that surprises me. And, anyway, wizardry isn't for getting out of reality, out of the world. It's for getting further into it.*

He gave that frozen pseudo-Nita one last glance, then turned away, back to the butterfly, embedded in air—and turned it loose.

The moment resumed. "Kit," Nita said, "Hey, whatcha—"

Kit squeezed his eyes shut and erased it all. A moment later he was standing in the darkness again, listening only to the silence … and having a little trouble breathing. *This isn't going to stop us,* he thought. *I know what the Lone Power trying to stop me feels like. We'll go all the way through. One way or another, we'll do what's necessary.*

They came to where the corner of Sixth and Thirty-eighth would have been if it hadn't been just an inter-section of two muddy, rushing rivers, and stopped there. Nita could feel the kernel more clearly now; it wasn't too far away. But somehow this wasn't making her feel any better. The darkness, that watching presence hidden in it, and the little swarming, biting viruses were all beginning to wear her down. Pralaya was always there, companionable enough, but not really that much help. And again and again the words of the Wizard's Oath kept coming back to Nita, as she slogged her way along through the dark, resisting water: *"I will guard growth and ease pain."*

But does there come a time when you stop growing?

And when you and the universe agree that you're going to stop?

"I will ever put aside fear for courage, and death for life, when it is right to do so."

Was there the slightest possibility, here and now, that it *wasn't* right?

How could you tell, without being one of the Powers?

And if people can't tell, then the game just isn't fair!

But that didn't matter right now. Nita stopped at the corner and looked down Sixth Avenue. The water seemed a little less deep down there; but that over-shadowing dark presence seemed much stronger. "The kernel's there," she said to Pralaya. "I'm sure of it."

"I think you're right," he said. "What is that—that tallest building there?"

"The Empire State," Nita said. It struck her as a poor place to hide anything. *But then, Its purpose isn't to keep the kernel hidden. It's to let me find it and use it and fail. So that I'll agree to the bargain—*

"Come on," she said, and splashed down Sixth Avenue with Pralaya swimming along beside her, uncertainty in his dark eyes.

Kit and Ponch were moving once more through the darkness. "It fooled us that time," Ponch said. "But not twice." The dog was angry.

"It's not your fault," Kit said. "It was after me."

"I should have expected it. But now we know something."

"What?"

"That you have something that can stop It."

Kit took a couple of long breaths. That thought had occurred to him.

"I'm telling the darkness," Ponch said, "to take us to where we'll learn best what to do to find Nita, to help her."

Kit's mouth was dry; he was getting more nervous by the moment. "Are we going to have time for this?"

"All the time we need."

How much longer they spent in the darkness, he wasn't sure. Kit could feel in Ponch a terrible sense of urgency, of the darkness resisting, pushing against him, trying to slow him down. But Ponch wasn't letting it stop him. He was pushing back, fierce, unrelenting. They slowed down, finally stopped, and Kit could feel Ponch pushing, pushing with all his strength against whatever was fighting him—

—until without warning they broke through into the light. Ponch surged forward, the leash wizardry extending away in front of Kit, while Kit stood still and rubbed his eyes, which were watering in the sudden brilliant light.

It was a beach. He was standing at the water's edge, and turning, he could see Jones Inlet behind him.

Is this another of Its tricks? Kit thought, confused. *Another place where I'm supposed to get distracted by what could have been?*

But somehow he knew it wasn't so. Though this was Jones Inlet, it was also something else.

Kit turned, looking south again. It was the Sea: darkness and light under the Sun, Life and the home of Life—all potential, lying burning and swirling under the dawn. "The Sea," Ponch was barking, shouting, as he ran down the beach and fought with the waves. "The Sea!" And it wasn't just what dogs always said—*Oh boy, the water!*—but something else, both a question and an answer, a reference to the beginning of things, the oldest Sea from which Life arose. *And our blood's like that Sea,* Kit thought. *The same salinity. The same—*

His eyes went wide. Ponch had been right. Here was the solution...the one that the Lone Power was counting on Nita not seeing, because she had messed it up so badly before.

"You're right!" Kit yelled to Ponch. "You're right! Come on, we've got to find her, before she starts!"

Ponch came running back, bounced around him a last few times, and then they leaped forward into the darkness together and vanished from the beach, leaving only footprints, which were shortly washed away.

Nita stood at the base of the Empire State Building and looked up at it. In this version of New York, there was a great flight of steps up to it, up from the water level, and she immediately went about halfway up them, glad to get out of the water, where the viruses were swarming and snapping more thickly than they had anywhere else. Pralaya came flowing up the stairs along with her, shaking the water out of his golden fur and scratching himself all over. "Those things," he said, "even though they didn't really bite me, they make me itch."

"Me, too," Nita said. She stood there and craned her neck upward, looking at the terrible height of the tower. Even in her own New York, when you were this close to it, the Empire State always looked as if it was going to fall on you. But here, she wasn't sure that it might not somehow be possible. And all around them was that terrible shadowy darkness, thicker in the air here than anywhere else, pressing in on them, looking at them.

"Let's go in," Nita said. She could hear the kernel now without actually having to listen to it: a buzz, that familiar fizz on the skin. Part of her was afraid; it shouldn't have been this easy to find. And she knew why it had been so easy....

They went in through the doors at the top of the steps and found themselves in a vast gray hall full of shadows. Standing up, here and there in the dimness, were many banks of steely doored elevators, which Nita saw were intended to go in only one direction: down. All around the great floor of the place were a number of square pools, and Nita looked at them and decided not to step into any of them. They had that black-water depth that suggested they had no real bottoms.

"Right," Nita said. She glanced once at her charm bracelet, made sure that the spells on it were active, and began walking through the place, listening.

Pralaya followed, pausing by each of the elevator banks and cocking his head to listen. "I'm not sure," he said.

"I am," Nita said. "Not up, but down." She paused by one of the pools, listening.

"Not here," she said softly. "But this is the right direction." She passed between two more of the great square pools, listening again. That faint fizz on her skin got more pronounced.

"That one," she said softly, and walked over to it. She knelt by the edge of the water, listening, then got up again and moved around to the other side of the pool. *Right there,* she thought. The kernel was well down in the black water, but not out of reach. Nita shook the charm bracelet around to check the status of her personal shields again, twiddled with one charm to adjust the shield just slightly, and then with the other arm reached down into the water.

It was freezing cold, so cold she could hardly breathe, and she could feel her fingers going numb. But she groped, and reached deeper, though she felt the buzzing and stinging of little dark lancets against her skin. None of them was getting through...yet.

There.

Slowly she reached under what she'd felt—the jabbing of the little black needles against her skin increased, but Nita forced herself not to rush—slowly she closed her fingers around what was waiting there for her. Slowly she drew it up.

It was an apple.

Nita stood up with it in her hands. It dripped black water, and as that water fell into the pool, the pool's surface came alive with more of the ugly little hexagonal virus shapes that had swarmed around her and Pralaya outside. These, though, were bigger, and somehow nastier. They had no eyes, but they were nonetheless looking at her and seeing prey, the kind they already knew the taste of.

"Okay," she said softly, and turned the "apple" over in her hands, feeling for the way its control structures were arranged. She found the outermost level quickly, let her hands sink into what now stopped being an apple and started being that familiar tangle of light.

All around, the shadows leaned in to watch what she was doing. Nita gulped and looked down into the pool, where those awful little black shapes had now put their "heads" up out of the water and were looking at her, hating her.

Guys, Nita said, *I'd like you to stop doing what you're doing to my mother.*

The buzzing, snarling chorus said, *No! We have a right to live!*

I mean it, Nita said. *It's really got to stop. It's going to stop, one way or another. It can be with your cooperation, or without it.*

No! they snarled. *We are her. We are of her. We live in her. She gave us birth.*

Not on purpose!

That does not matter. We have rights here. We were born. We have a right to do what we were created to do. The snarling was getting louder, more threatening. *You are also of her. What we do to her, we can do to you, given time.*

Nita didn't like the sound of that. *Guys,* she said, *last chance. Agree to stop doing what you're doing, or I must abolish you.* It was the formal phrasing of a wizard who, however reluctantly, discovers that he or she must kill.

The snarling scaled up; the waters in the pools all around her roiled. Shaking, Nita squeezed and manipulated the power-strands in the kernel until she found the one control sequence that managed the shapes of proteins in this internal space. She stroked it slowly and carefully into a shape that would forbid this kind of viral shape to exist in the local space-time.

One last chance, guys, she said.

The snarling only got louder.

Nita took a deep breath, flicked the charm bracelet

around to bring the power-feed configuration she'd designed into place, then brought it together with the kernel. *I'm sorry!* she said, and pushed the power in...

And nothing happened.

Nita stared at the kernel, horrified. She tried feeding the necessary power into the kernel again, twisted that particular strand of power until it bit into her fingers—

But that spell is now invalid, said a dark voice inside her. *It uses a version of your name that is no longer operational. Your name has changed; you have changed. When you were looking at your mother in the hospital last night, you made up your mind to pay my price, and therefore the spell cannot work.*

Nita stood still in utter shock and terror. She wanted to shout *No!* but she couldn't, because she was suddenly horribly certain that, just this once, the Lone Power was telling the truth. The fact that the spell hadn't worked simply confirmed it.

And because I agreed, I'm going to lose my wizardry... and my mom will die.

Standing there with the kernel, realizing once and for all that she'd done everything she could and there was nothing else she knew that would make the slightest difference, Nita's world simply started to come undone. She could do nothing to stop the tears of fear and grief and frustration that began to run down her face.

It told me it wouldn't work. What made me think I might somehow be able to manage it anyway?

"Pralaya," she said.

"This is beyond my competence," Pralaya said. "I wish I could help you, but..."

Nita nodded once, and the grief started to give way to anger. "Just what I thought," she said. "So much for any help from *you!*"

He looked shocked.

"But that would hardly be the Lone One's preferred method," she said. "No way It's going to give me any help at all, if it can be avoided."

Pralaya looked more stunned than before, if possible. "What are you talking about?"

"You don't know what's living inside you," Nita said. "Well, I bet you're about to find out. Come on," she said to the One she knew was listening. "This is the moment you've been waiting for, isn't it?"

"Not with any possible doubt of the outcome," said that huge dark satisfied voice.

The Lone Power was standing there looking at her; and for just the briefest second, Pralaya coexisted with Its newly chosen form. It looked human, like a young man—though an inhumanly handsome one—and shadows wrapped around It like an overcoat, shadows that reached out and now wrapped themselves around Pralaya, dragged him, struggling and horrified, into themselves, and hid him away.

"Now, you shouldn't really have said that," said the young man. "While he didn't actually know what was happening, I could have let him live. But you had to come right out and tell him, at which point his usefulness to me vanished."

Nita stood there horrified. "You just *killed* him!"

"No," the Lone One said, "*you* did. Not a bad start, but then you were intent enough on killing *something*."

All around Nita, the snarling of the viruses was getting louder and louder. "Anyway, don't be too concerned about Pralaya; I'll find another of his people to replace him if there's need. Now, though, matters stand as I told you they stood. All we need is your conscious answer to the question. Can we do business?"

Nita stood there, frozen.

And another voice spoke out of the darkness.

"Fairest and Fallen," Kit said, "one more time... greeting and defiance." Beside him, Ponch just bared his teeth and growled.

Nita stared in astonishment at Kit and Ponch. The Lone Power gave them an annoyed look.

"*You* again," the Lone One said. "Well, I suppose it was to be expected. You'll do anything to try to run her life for her, won't you?"

Nita's eyes widened in shock. "The chance that she might possibly pull something off without your assistance drives you crazy," the Lone Power said conversationally. "Well, fortunately you're not going to see anything like that today. She's decided to turn to someone else for her last gasp at a partnership." Its smile made it plain Who that was meant to be.

"We *know* better, so don't try this stuff on us," Kit said.

"*You* think you know better," It said.

It looked at Nita. "Does he?" It said. "Or are you perhaps a little tired of him ordering you around?"

Nita stood silent, trembling.

"Might you possibly, just this once, know better? Know best? Actually make the sacrifice?"

"Neets, don't pay any attention to It," Kit said. "You know why I came—"

"To keep her Oath from being contaminated," said the Lone One dryly. "Too late for that. The deal is done, and she's made her choice at last. Without *you*."

Nita saw Kit flinch at that, but he straightened up again. "I wouldn't write me off as useless just yet," Kit said. "And I wouldn't bet that Neets is just going to dump me."

"I would," the Lone One said. "I hold the only betting token that matters at all in the present situation. Only with my help can she save her mother's life."

"It's not true, Neets!" Kit shouted. "It tried pretty hard to keep Ponch and me from getting here. It must have a reason!"

"I can do without further interference," said the Lone One. "That's reason enough. Now, though, if I thought you might possibly accept a different version of the same bargain..." It stood musing. "Suppose Nita here keeps her wizardry—even despite the mistake she's just made. I even save her mother, in the bargain—"

Kit shook his head, and Ponch growled again. "I serve Life, and the Powers That Be That cast you out, and the One, the Power beyond Them. And so does Neets, whatever you've done to her. So just get used to it!"

The brief silence that followed was terrible. "I've been used to it for too long," said the Lone Power. "Here and there, I stop mortals from incessantly reminding me." The shadow wrapped around It, already huge, grew longer and darker; and inside it moved things that Nita emphatically did not want to see. It had been a long time since her bedroom shadows had been full of their little legs and their blind front ends, and their fangs, the little jaws that moved....

Kit, though, laughed. "Been there, seen them," he said. "Millipedes? Is *that* all you've got? What a yawn."

His tone was astonishing. It banished the shadows, all by itself. Nita remembered how she had dreaded those things when she was little, and now found herself thinking, to her amazement, *Can someone else really show you how to kill the fears? Is it that easy? I thought they always said you had to do it yourself.*

But maybe there was more to it than that. Maybe others' strengths weren't their own property—

—if they offered...

"Kit," Nita said. "I know what you want to do, and after how stupid I've been with you, it's great that you even tried, but you've got to get out of here—"

"And leave you alone with *That*? Not a chance."

The Lone Power laughed. "Well, anyone can see where *this* is going. Unless you throw him out of here yourself, it looks like you're going to let someone else die for you again. I wouldn't have thought you were such a coward."

The flush of fury and embarrassment and pain struck through Nita like fire. She opened her mouth to say, *You think I wanted it that way the last time? You think I'm not brave enough to do it now? Okay, here—*

She didn't get a chance, for another shape leaped through the shadows and hit Nita about chest high.

She came crashing down hard beside one of the pools. "Don't!" Ponch barked at her. "Don't do it!"

Nita rolled over and tossed Ponch off to one side. *Oh, the good pooch; I love him, but I can't let him stop me. There's still time, I can still save her.* Nita pushed herself up on her hands and knees, and opened her mouth again. But as she did, the greater darkness that had hung about her since she came to this place—that leaning, inward-pressing obscurity—came wrapping down around her, squeezing the breath right out of her, and it spoke.

Don't I get something to say about this?

That darkness leaned in ever closer around all of them, even the Lone One. It was a different kind of darkness than the Lone Power's enwrapping shadows. Nita stared up into it, confused, frightened…

…and then realized she had no reason to be. Nita knew this darkness…from a long time ago…from the inside. Some memories, she realized, are recovered only under very special circumstances. This dark, immense presence, completely surrounding her, owning the world, *being* the world…

"*Mom?*" Nita whispered.

"I *do* get something to say about this," said that voice, not just suspected now but actually heard.

"Nothing that matters," said the Lone Power, though it sounded just slightly uncertain.

"The *only* thing that matters," said her mother's voice.

"It's too late," the Lone One said. "She's made the bargain."

"She's made nothing," said Nita's mother's voice, "because this is *my* universe, and *I* say what goes here, and *she does not have my permission.*"

And Nita's mother was standing there, in the dark, between Nita and the Lone Power, in her T-shirt and her denim skirt, with her arms folded, and her red hair a spot of brightness even in this gloom. "This is *my* body," said Nita's mother. "If this is going to be a battleground, *I* make the rules."

"For a mortal," said the Lone One, "you're unusually assured. With little reason. You believe everything some part-time psychologist tells you?"

"For an immortal," said Nita's mother, "you're unusually dumb. The therapist, as it happens, was plainly more right than she knew. There they are, the nasty little things, just the way I imagined them." She glanced at the shadowy pools, roiling full of viral death. "In here somewhere, to match the darkness, there has to be light...and that's my weapon, for the darkness comprehendeth it not. On that point, I have sources of reassurance other than any therapist—much older ones. They say that you cannot command a soul that's firmly opposed to you."

"But bodies are not souls."

"At this level," Kit said, "just how sure are you?"

There was a slightly unnerved silence at that.

Nita's mother looked over her shoulder at Nita. "My daughter and I," she said, "are fighting the same battle. Maybe I do it in more ordinary ways. But we're on the same side. And you, if I recognize you correctly, are no friend of mine. *Get off my turf!*"

She talks a good fight, Kit thought. *But it's gonna take more than that.*

Nita was almost breathless with tension, yet she suddenly realized that this was the first time in a good while that she'd overheard Kit think. In any case, she had to agree with him. *She's tougher than she looks,* Nita thought. *But then she was a dancer. Dancers are tough. Maybe what we need to be doing is feeding* her *power—*

"You have no power to order me around," said the Lone One. "I've been part of 'your turf' since the beginning of things. I have my own rights here."

"I've heard that line before," Nita's mother said. "I reject it. *I* choose who shares my body with me…as I chose my children…and my husband. *I* choose! You think you have any rights here that I don't grant you? Maybe you can live inside people who don't look at themselves closely. But those who fight with you every day and have an idea of what they're wrestling with? Let's just find out."

She stood up tall. Nita gulped. She had seen her mother looking ethereal, in her tutu and swan feathers and dinky little crown, in the poster from a Denver Opera Ballet production—looking like something you could break in two. But looking over her shoulder one day and seeing Nita eyeing dubiously that old framed poster, her mother had said, "Honey, take my advice. Don't mess around with swans. One of those pretty white wings could break your leg in three places." And off she had gone with the laundry basket, sailing past, graceful and strong, with the danger showing only around the edges of the chuckle.

But just bravery isn't going to be enough. Not here—

"And just what do you plan to fight me with?" the Lone One said. "You have no weapons to equal my power. Not even the diluted form of it that's killing you now."

"She may not have anything but guts and intention," Kit said, "but that's half of wizardry to start with. And *we're* carrying." He reached into his claudication and came up with a long string of symbols in the Speech.

Nita looked at it, uncomprehending. The Lone One laughed.

"That won't work," It said. "Certainly not for *her.* And not even for Nita anymore, as you've seen. You think that by plugging an older version of Nita's name into this spell, she will no longer be mine? It won't work. It takes more power than either of you have to reverse the kind of changes she's been through. She knows me now. She's willing to pay my price to keep her mother alive...and, sorry, Mom, but permission or no permission, it's Nita's choice that finally counts."

"Oh yeah?" Kit said. "Neets," he said to her then, holding out his hand, looking at her urgently. "Quick—"

"Oh, of course, give him all your power, why don't you." The Lone One laughed. "So much for your doing anything useful by yourself."

Nita swallowed. In Its voice she heard too many

thoughts of her own, roiling in its darkness the way the viruses were boiling around in the pools.

Can't cope.

No independence.

Scared to make a move without her partner.

Doesn't have the nerve to strike out on her own—

Nita swallowed...and took off the charm bracelet.

—going to let him do all the dangerous stuff.

Going to prove him right again, and you wrong—

She hesitated one last time...

...and then threw the bracelet to Kit.

Kit caught it and quickly attached the old version of Nita's name he'd saved from the Jones Inlet wizardry. Then he reached into the air beside him and brought something else out.

A small pale spark of light—

The light it gave at first seemed little, but swiftly it lit up all that place, and even chased the shadows briefly from the Lone One's face...a sight that made Nita turn away—for the terror of It, to some extent, she could stand, but the beauty of It, seen together with that ancient deathliness, was difficult to bear. Around the Lone One, the darkness hissed with Its alarm, as if suddenly full of snakes. *A glede—*

"The dragon's eye," Kit said as he hooked the glede into an empty link of the charm bracelet, and the whole chain came alive with sudden fire. "Something brand new, something you've never touched. Something born after the change happened to *you*, the chance to be otherwise. Something you can't affect—"

"Not true!" It cried. "All creation, even the void

from which things are created anew, has my power at the bottom of it."

"Not here, it doesn't! Not in this! Whether you like it or not, even while you're killing people, the world is starting to heal... *and so are you!*"

Nita swallowed hard, watching Kit and suddenly remembering Tom and Carl's backyard and a fish looking up out of the water at her.

> *All the drawing lacks*
> *is the final touch: to add*
> *eyes to the dragon—*

She desperately wanted to shout to Kit that yes, this had to be the answer—but she didn't dare. She'd been wrong about so many things lately. What if her certainty, her desperation, got Kit killed, too? *And the Lone One's right, that's not who I am anymore—*

—but the other memory that came back to her, the amused piggy voice saying, "That is, assuming you're into sequential time... you can handle it however you like..."

That blazing spark of light on the bracelet Kit held glittered at her like possibility made visible.

Why in the world not?! Nita thought. *If you can't put together what you were with what you are now— so you can make up for your mistakes and not make the same ones again—then what's the point? This isn't about reversing anything. It's about going forward!*

"Kit!" she cried.

He threw her the charm bracelet. Nita snatched it out of the air, and almost dropped it as the added power of the glede jolted up her arm like an electric shock.

"I wouldn't do that if I were you!" the Lone One cried. "You'll destroy your mother, and yourself, here and now!"

Nita hesitated for just a second...then put the charm bracelet back on, taking hold of the two versions of her name that hung from it, side by side. "Well, guess what?" she said. "You're *not* me!" And in the single quick gesture she'd had entirely too much practice with lately, she knotted the names tight together with the wizard's knot.

The blast of power that went through her was like being hit by lightning. Whether because of her remade name or the presence of the glede, suddenly Nita could comprehend all those little darknesses in the water much more fully than just by using the kernel. Those stinging, buzzing little horrors were right about being, in their own twisted way, part of her mother. But now she could see exactly what to do about them. The solution was the same as what she had been trying to do with Kit and S'reee at Jones Inlet...

...except that, where she'd been wrong about how to use her part of the wizardry before, here and now she was right. Her wizardly fix for Jones Inlet had been too complicated. "This whole contrareplication routine would be great," Kit had said, "if the chemicals in the pollution knew how to reproduce themselves." Of course, they hadn't. But viruses were just very smart chemicals in a protein shell that *did* know how to reproduce themselves...which made the solution perfect for her mother.

It set me up, Nita thought in growing fury. *The Lone One made sure I came up against a problem where my solution would fail—and fail painfully—and where I fought with Kit. So that when I came to this moment, I'd be too hurt, too scared to try this solution again, too scared even to see it!*

She trembled with rage. But to waste time on being angry now would only play into Its hands. Nita's eyes narrowed in concentration as she channeled the power from the glede through both the kernel and her memory of her part of the Jones Inlet wizardry, and into the dark waters around her...

Every pool around them roiled in agitation as all the viruses thrust their heads up out of the lapping darkness, like blind fish gasping in the air, desperately crying *no!*

For many of them It was already too late. All around them, the sea of her mother's blood was churning as if in a storm with the power that washed through it— and from all around came countless little dark explosions as the viruses' shells unraveled. The wizardry was reminding the human blood of how it had once been part of an older, purer, uncontaminated Sea, one that was the outside of a world rather than the inside.

Yet Nita could feel through the kernel that there were some places where, for all the glede's power, that cleansing Sea didn't, couldn't quite reach. Scattered through her mother's inner world, little knots of darkness still lay, waiting... and there were many, many of them.

Too many...

Nita fell to her knees, defeated.

All for nothing...

"I told you," the Lone One said. "You should have done it my way. Too late now—" And it began to laugh.

Nita began to cry. It was all over... all over...

A deathly silence fell.

And an angry whisper broke it.

"With me," it said, "you can do what you like. *But not with my daughter!*"

And then another whisper.

"Mrs. Callahan—"

A moment later, someone took hold of Nita's bracelet. Nita looked up, gasping.

"You need this, sweetie," her mother said, her voice controlled despite her anger as she turned the bracelet past the new-made version of Nita's name. "But Kit's right. This is what I've been looking for!"

With a roar of fury, the Lone One moved toward the three of them, a terrible wave of shadow rearing up above It, ready to break. All around them, the waters of the pools rose up, to drown them, to destroy...

...and then suddenly fell back as if they had struck a wall. Everything kindled to blinding fire around them, the water glittering as it splashed away, the walls of the great hall shining, the Lone One standing there aghast in the blaze and terror of that light as Nita's mother pulled the glede free of Nita's bracelet, stood up, and squeezed the glede tight in her upheld fist, a gesture both frightened and fierce.

She was lost in the resultant violent blast of fire, and Nita tottered sideways and clutched at Kit, watching her mother in amazement and terror: a goddess with a handful of lightning, imperial and terrible, rearing up into the darkness and towering over them all, even over the Lone One, and—to Nita's astonishment and concern—paying It no mind at all. All her mother's attention now was on what she gripped in her hand, a writhing struggling knot of lightnings growing and lashing outward all the time, until it crowned her with thunder and robed her in fire, and there were no shadows left to be seen anywhere.

The fear and pain in her face were awful to see, as Nita's mother struggled with the glede, trying to keep from being consumed by its power as other mortal women had been consumed, in old stories, by fire from beyond the worlds. But her eyes were ferocious with concentration, and the look of terror and anguish slipped away as she started to get the better of the Power she held.

Slowly she straightened, looking down at all of them—a woman in a T-shirt and a faded denim skirt, blazing with the fire from heaven, and with sudden certainty.

"*The Light shone in the darkness,*" she said softly, and the whole little universe that was Nita's mom shook with it. "*And the darkness comprehended it not.* This *light!* But you never learn, do you? Or only real slowly."

The Lone Power stared at her with at least as much incredulity as Kit and Nita. After a second, It turned away.

"*Oh,* no you don't," Nita's mother said. And the lightning blasted out from her, and struck It down into the nearest pool.

Nita's mother looked at the Lone Power dispassionately as it struggled in the water. "If I am going to go anywhere," she said, "first *you're* going to find out up close and physical what the things you've done to me all this while have felt like." It struggled to get up out of the water. Nita's mom flung out her hand, and the lightning knocked It back in again.

"Having fun with *that*?" her mother said. "Doesn't feel like so much fun from inside my body, does it? You should have thought of that before you came in here. Just feel all those broken bones and strains, those six weeks off for tendonitis, the bruises and infections and herniated muscles and all the rest of it. Oh, we knew about pain, all right! Dance is two hours' worth of childbirth every weekday evening at eight, and a Saturday matinee!"

The Lone Power writhed and splashed in the water, stricken with the experience of her agony.

"And then how about this?" her mother said. "Now that I've got your attention—"

Nita flinched, for this was the phrase that most often preceded the tongue-lashing you got when you hadn't cleaned your room properly—and to a certain extent she could feel what her mother was imposing on the Lone One. Here the experience inflicted on It was

all the more intense for being recent, fresh in the suf-
ferer's mind—the blurred vision, the growing pain, the
uncomfortable and unhappy sense that, hey, this isn't
supposed to be happening, what's the matter with
me?—the loss of control, of mastery over a body that
was always precisely mastered in the old days; the
slowly growing fury, inexpressible, bottled up, that
things weren't working the way they should.

In fact, that nothing *was working the way it should.*

For in this place, under these circumstances, Nita's
mother now knew that if matters had somehow gone
otherwise, death itself wouldn't have happened. It was
an additive, an afterthought, somebody's "good idea."
And here was the somebody, right here, within
reach...and available, just this once, for spanking.

Not liking it, either, Nita thought.

"Fun, huh?" Nita's mother said softly. "But even
with your inventions, this Life that you hate so much is
still too much for you. It was always too much for you.
Whatever you do, it just keeps finding a way. Maybe
even this time."

The Lone One writhed and floundered in the water,
and couldn't get away. Nita's mom looked down at It
from what seemed a great distance. Under that majes-
tic regard, as It finally managed to drag itself out of
the pool, the Lone One seemed crumpled into a little
sodden shape of shadow, impotent in this awful blaze
of wrathful fire. *Beaten,* Nita thought, and her heart
went up in a blaze of triumph to match the blinding
light.

"But no," said her mother then, in a much more

mortal voice, and hearing it, Nita's heart fell from an impossible height, and kept on falling. "That's what you're expecting, isn't it? You want me to win this battle. And after that, when we're all off our guard, comes the betrayal."

The light began to fade. *No,* Nita thought. *No, not like this! Mom!*

But her mother had her own ideas … as usual. There was no longer any great distance between her and the much diminished darkness that was now the Lone Power in what she had made of her interior world. "No," Nita's mother said, "not even at *that* price. You've really been stuck playing this same old game for a long time, haven't you? And you just don't believe a mortal could refuse the opportunity."

From that sodden darkness there now came no answer. Nita's mother stood there looking down at the Lone Power as if at a daughter who'd turned up in particularly grimy clothes just after the laundry had all been done.

"No," Nita's mother said. "I can guess where this is going. How many times have I heard my daughters wheedle me to let them stay up late, just this once? It starts there, but that's never where it stops. And if I was firm with *them,* I have to be the same way with myself when my turn comes, too." She was looking entirely less like a furious goddess, entirely more like a slightly tired woman. "Because I'm up against my own time limit, now, aren't I? Override the body now, and we'll all be sorry for it later. If not personally, then in the lives of the people around us."

Nita was horrified. "Mom, *no!*"

"Honey." Nita's mother chucked the lightning away, careless, and came over to her. The lightning hit the floor, lay there burning, and then came slowly humping back toward Nita's mom, like some animate and terrible toy. "Believe me, if there was ever a time for the phrase 'Don't tempt me,' this is it."

"But, Mom, we're *winning!*"

"We're supposed to think so," she said. "Look at It there; what a great 'beaten' act." She gave the Lone Power a look that was both clinical and thoroughly unimpressed. "The point being to encourage us to go home in 'triumph,' and to distract me, at any cost, from doing what I know is right. If It can't ruin my life, and yours, straightforwardly, by killing me, It'll try it another way."

She walked a little way over to It, the lightning following her. "Can't you see it, honey? If we carry this to its logical conclusion, I live, all right. I survive this—and what the things in my body are doing to me now—because of what you kids have done here. And then I live and live, and live some more, and I get to like it so much that my whole life becomes about *not dying*. What kind of life is *that* going to be? Because sooner or later, no matter what any of us do, it's going to happen anyway. Finally—who knows how many years from now—I get to die, all bitter and furious and scared, and doing everything I can to make everybody around me miserable—including you, assuming you *are* still around, and I haven't driven you and Dairine and your dad away with the sheer awfulness of my wanting to keep on living. *That's* what that One has in mind. Well, I won't do it, sweetie. Not even for this." The persistent tangle of lightning was rubbing against her leg like a cat; she gave it a sideways nudge with her foot, and turned away from the Lone One, coming back toward Nita and Kit. "Not even because I love you, and I'm afraid to leave your dad and you and Dairine, and I don't know what comes afterward for me, and I love my life, and I hate the thought of leaving all of you alone, in pain, and I'm not ready, *and I just don't want to go!*"

It was a cry of utter anguish, and the air all around them trembled with it, rent as if by thunder. That shadow, crouched down off to the side, stirred just slightly, crouched down further. "Not even for that," her mother said, a lot more quietly, unclenching her fists. "It is not going to happen."

"Mom…," Nita said, and could find no other words.

Her mother just shook her head. For a moment, she seemed too choked up to speak. She pulled Nita close and held her, and then, her voice rough, she said, "Sweetie, I may not be what you are, but this I know. There's a power in what we are as mortal beings that even *that* One can't match. If we throw it away, we stop being human. I won't do it. And certainly not when doing it plays into the enemy's hands."

She let go of Nita and turned around. "So as for *you*," Nita's mother said to the Lone Power, her eyes narrowing in what Nita recognized as her mother's most dangerous kind of frown, "you'll get what you incorrectly consider your piece of me soon enough. But in the meantime, I'm tired of looking at you. So you just take yourself straight on out of here before I kick your poor deluded rear end from here to eternity."

The Lone Power slowly picked Itself up, towered up before them all in faceless darkness...and vanished without a sound.

"Mom..." Nita shook her head, again at a loss for words.

"Wow," Kit said. "Impressive."

Her mother smiled slightly, shook her head. "It's all in the documentation, honey," she said to Nita. "It says it plain enough: 'Have I not said to you, "you are gods"?' So we may as well act like them when it's obviously right to and the power's available."

They all turned to look around at the sound of a splash. Ponch had jumped into one of the now-cleansed pools and was paddling around.

Nita's mom smiled, then looked at the surroundings, once again dark and wet, then she glanced down at what Nita still held in her hands. "Is that what I think it is?"

Nita nodded and handed it over. Her mother tossed the apple in her hand, caught it again, looking at it thoughtfully, and polished it against her skirt. "Are we done here?" she said.

Nita looked around her sorrowfully. "Unless you can think of anything to add."

Her mother shook her head. "No point in it now," she said. She looked at the apple with an expression of profound regret, turning it over in her hands. For a moment Nita saw through the semblance, saw the kernel as it was, the tangle of intricate and terrible forces that described a human body with a human mind and soul inside it, infinitely precious, infinitely vulnerable. Then her mother sighed and chucked the apple over her shoulder into one of the nearby pools. It dropped into the waters and sank, glowing, and was lost.

Nita let out a long breath that became a sob at the end. There was no getting it back now, nothing more that could be done.

"Better this way," her mother said, sounding sad. "You don't often get a chance like this; be a shame to ruin it. Come on, sweetie." She looked around at the darkness and the water. "We should either call the plumber or get out of the basement. How do we do that, exactly?"

"I don't think you have to do anything but wake up," Kit said. "But Nita and I should go."

"Don't forget Ponch," Nita's mother said, as the dog clambered out of the pool he'd been swimming in and came over to the three of them. "If I come out of the anesthesia barking, the doctors are going to be really confused."

Ponch shook himself, and all three of them got splattered. "Kit needed me to get in," Ponch said. "Without me, I don't think he can get out. I'll see him safely home."

Nita's mother blinked at that. "Sounds fair," she said. "Meantime, what about this?" She bent over to pick up the dwindling knot of lightning that was all that was left of the glede.

The question answered itself, as it faded away in her hands. "One use only, I think," Kit said.

"I think I got my money's worth," Nita's mother said. "But thanks for the hint, Kit; you made the difference."

"Just a suggestion someone gave me," Kit said. "To listen to my hunches when it all went dark…"

"That one sure paid off. Go on, you kids, get out of here."

Nita hugged her mom while Kit put the leash on Ponch. Then Kit offered Nita his arm. She paused a moment, took it, and they stepped forward into the darkness.

The two of them came out in Kit's backyard. Nita saw Kit looking around him with an odd expression. "Something wrong?" she said. "Or is it just that reality looks really strange after what we've been through?"

"Some of that, maybe," he said. He took the leash off Ponch and let the dog run toward the house.

"Kit—"

He looked at her.

"You saved my butt," she said.

Kit let out a breath. "You let me."

She nodded.

"Anyway," Kit said, "you've saved mine a few times. Let's just give up keeping score, okay? It's a distraction."

Nita nodded. "Come on," she said. "Let's go to the hospital."

Between transit circles and the business of appearing

far enough away from the hospital not to upset anybody, it took them about fifteen minutes to get there. Down in that awful little waiting room, Nita found her dad and Dairine—and the look on her father's face nearly broke Nita's heart. There was hope there, for the first time in a long, long week.

Nita sat down while Kit shut the door. "Are they done?" Nita said.

Her father nodded. "They got the tumor out," he said. "All of it. It went much better than they hoped, in fact. And they think...they think maybe it hasn't spread as far as they thought. They have to do some tests."

"Is Mom awake yet?"

"Yeah. The trouble with her eyes is clearing up already, the recovery room nurses said, but they want us to leave her alone till this evening; it's going to take her a while to feel better. We were just waiting here for you to catch up with us." He looked at her. "What about you?"

Nita swallowed. "I think we did good," she said, "but I'm not sure how good yet. It's gonna take a while to tell."

Her dad nodded. "So let's go home...and we'll come back after dinner."

As much as Nita felt like she really needed a nap, she couldn't sleep. Kit went home for a while, but when Nita's dad was starting the car, Kit appeared again in the backyard, and Nita went downstairs to meet him.

As she was walking across the yard, there was another bang, less discreet: Dairine. She stalked out of the air with an annoyed expression. "Where've you been?" Nita said.

"The hospital."

"You weren't supposed to go yet!"

"I know. I sneaked in. They just found me and threw me out."

She looked at the two of them. "Have you seen the précis in the manual?" she said.

Nita shook her head.

"I have," Dairine said softly. "I owe you guys one."

Kit shook his head. "Dari, if you read the précis, then you know—"

"I know what's probably going to happen to her," Dairine said. "Yeah. But I know what you guys did. You gave it your best shot. That's what matters."

She turned and went into the house.

"She's mellowing," Kit said quietly.

"She's in shock," Nita said. "So am I. But, Kit— Thanks for not letting me go through it alone." She gulped, trying to keep hold of her composure. "I'm not— I mean, I'm going to need a lot of help."

"You know where to look," Kit said. "So let's get on with it."

In the hospital they found Nita's mother already sitting up in bed. She had a blackening eye and some bruising around her nose, but that was all; and the sticky contacts and wires and machines were all gone, though she now had an IV running into her arm. Nita thought her mom looked very tired, but as they came in, her face lit up with a smile that was otherwise perfectly normal.

She looked at Kit. "Woof," she said.

Kit cracked up.

"Does this have some profound secret meaning," Nita's dad said, sitting down and taking his wife's hand, "or is it a side effect of the drugs?"

Nita's mother smiled. "No drug on the planet could have produced the trip I've just been through," she said.

There was a long silence. "Did it work?" Nita's father said then.

"In the only way that matters," her mother said. "Thank you, kids."

Nita blinked back tears. Kit just nodded.

The head nurse came in and stood by the bed. "How're you feeling?"

"Like someone's been taking out pieces of my brain," Nita's mother said, "but otherwise, just fine. When can I go home?"

"The day after tomorrow," said the nurse, "if the surgeons agree. It's not like the surgery itself was all that major, and you seem to be getting over the post-op trauma with unusual speed. If this keeps up, we can send you home and have a private-duty nurse keep an eye on you for the first few days. After that, there'll be other business, and we'll be seeing a fair amount of each other. But there's time for you to deal with that when you're feeling better and the surgery's healed."

"You're on," Nita's mother said. "Now let me talk to you about dinner."

"No dinner tonight," said the nurse. "Just the bottle, until tomorrow."

"I want a second opinion," Nita's mother said, unimpressed.

The nurse laughed, and went out.

"And a cheeseburger!" Nita's mother called after her.

Nita chuckled; her mother got junk food cravings at the oddest times. Then she caught herself chuckling, and stopped abruptly.

"No," her mother said. "Don't. You're right; it's disgusting, and there's no reason you shouldn't laugh." This she said as much to Nita's dad as to Nita.

Her father didn't say anything.

"Would you two excuse us a second?" Nita's mother said to Kit and Nita.

They went out. "Back in a moment," Kit said, and walked away down toward the vending machine and the rest rooms—a little too quickly, Nita thought. She watched him turn the corner. *It didn't occur to me how much this was hurting him, too. If he's going to be watching out for me, I'd better keep a close eye on him.*

Might get to be a full-time occupation.

Nita leaned against the wall outside the room. She should not have been able to hear anything from where she was, but she could.

"Harry," she heard that soft voice say. "Cut it out and look at me. We've bought me some time. We have time to say our good-byes—enough for that, at the least. Beyond that, it's all a gamble. But it always has been, anyway."

Nita could hear her dad breathing in the silence, trying to let it in.

"But one thing, before I forget. You don't need to waste any more time worrying about Kit."

"No?"

"No."

I shouldn't be able to hear this, Nita thought. She closed her eyes and concentrated on not listening. It didn't work. *It has to have something to do with where I've just been.*

"But enough of that. We've got things to do. Listen to me! I don't want you to start treating me like someone who's about to die. I expect to spend every remaining moment *living.* There's little enough time left, for any of us."

Nita could have sworn she heard her father gulp. "Oh, God, sweetheart, don't tell me there's going to be some kind of . . . of disaster!"

"What? Of course not." Her voice went soft and rough again, in a way that Nita had last heard just after her mom had dropped a handful of lightning. "But, Harry, being where I've just been, do you think that sixty years looks any longer to me than six months? Or that anything that's just *time* looks like it's going to last? So shut up and kiss me. We've got a lot to do."

There was only silence then. Nita took herself away as quietly as she could. Down the corridor and around the corner, she found Kit leaning against the wall, his arms folded, waiting for her.

"What are they up to in there?" he asked after a moment.

"Don't ask." She gave him a thoughtful look. He didn't ask. *And I bet he doesn't have to.*

"So, what now?"

"Just for a little while," Nita said, "we leave them alone."

Kit nodded. Together, they headed out.

Dawn

NITA WENT HOME AFTER that, and slept the clock around. They would only need to go to the hospital once or twice more to pick up equipment that the visiting nurse would need, and to talk to the doctors about chemotherapy and so on. Nita was glad enough to let her dad take care of all that. For her own part, she and Dairine mostly just sat and held her mom's hands, and listened to her complain about the hospital food, which she had been allowed to start eating that morning. It was a peculiar kind of happiness that Nita and Dairine were experiencing, and Nita was being careful to say nothing that might break it. Just under the surface of it lay a lot of pain. But right now, the simple joy of knowing that her mom would be home the next day was more than enough for Nita...and she knew Dairine agreed.

They went home that evening, and Nita went off to her room and went straight to sleep again. She was getting caught up a little on her own weariness, enough to dream again, but the realization that she *was* dreaming coincided with a certain amount of confusion. The mountainous landscape towering all around her in a misty early morning sun wasn't anyplace she recognized. Neither were the forests running up and up those slopes, all golden, or—as she turned, and paused, amazed—the vast, glittering, many-spired city that was looming out of the mist a mile or so away from her. Beyond it was a faint glimmer, as of the sea unseen in the overshadowing light. Nita thought of the roil and shimmer of the light on Jones Inlet, and let out a long breath of wonder. "Where *is* this?" she said aloud.

"The inside, honey," Nita's mother said. "The heart of things…what's at the core. Don't you ever dream about this?"

"Uh…yeah, sometimes. But it never looked exactly like this."

"Oh, well, this is my part of the territory. That's yours over there; of course, it'd be here, too. It's part of me, like you are." Her mother, in that beat-up denim skirt and T-shirt again, waved a hand back at the glittering towers, half veiled in radiant mist. "I know you'll live there, eventually. Have your own children there." She smiled slightly. "What is it they say? Your grandchildren are your revenge on your kids?" And Nita's mother laughed. "Well, at least you'll know what to expect from them. Partly. But this…" She turned her back on the towers, looking toward the mountains. "This is mine. When you grow up at the edge of the Continental Divide, there's always this wall towering up over you... and when you're little, you look at it and say, 'I'm going to go there someday. Right to the top of that mountain.' Or else you imagine mountains that don't have any top. The places that just go right up and up, into the center of things... forever."

"Yeah," Nita said.

They stood there a while together, looking at those mountains, and then began to walk slowly down through the flower-starred meadow below where they'd been standing. "It's not fair," Nita said softly. "How come I only get to really know you now, when I'm going to lose you?"

"I don't know if you can ever lose me, honey. I'm your *mother*. There's a bond neither of us can break unless we want to. And it doesn't have to hurt."

Nita wasn't sure about that as yet. But still, there was no lying here....

"So this is it?" Nita's mother said, gazing around her with a look of awe and appreciation. "What you told me about: Timeheart?"

"Uh," Nita said. "I'm not sure. I'm not sure how nonwizards see it."

"After all *that*," Nita's mom said, "am I a nonwizard?"

Nita had no answer for her, but her heart lifted, and she felt a twinge of something that until now she had been afraid to feel: hope.

And it wasn't even hope that her mother would somehow miraculously survive. Nita would hurt for a long while every time she remembered all those dark little creatures dying, and the feeling of many of them *not* dying, hidden away where even the flush of power from the glede couldn't reach. But Nita had reason to believe that she and her mom would have enough time to get to know each other very well before the hardest moment—the moment of final parting—had to be faced.

And when that came...

...there would, eventually, be Timeheart, where no matter what you dreamed might await you, there was always more.

If she could just last through the testing that would follow, just keep faith long enough to find out *what* that more would be.

"I could definitely get used to this," her mother said.

You will, Nita thought...or heard. With the words came a pang of relief mingled with pain, the two impossible to separate. It would be a long time before Nita would get used to the pain, she knew. But the relief was there regardless, and here, in this place, there was no matching echo of grief to suggest that the relief was somehow false or illusory. Nothing that happened here could fail to be real. If she felt relief here, it was justified.

"No," Nita's mother said, "I don't think I'm going to let anyone throw me out of here."

"I don't think they can," Nita said, the tears coming to her eyes, even here. She knew, as all wizards know if they know nothing else, that in Timeheart everything worth having, everything that is loved, or of love, is preserved in perfection.

And everyone?...

As usual there were no concrete answers; the place was itself an answer before which all questions faded. Except, suddenly, one.

"Honey," her mother said, "not that I object to the idea, or anything. But can you tell me why there would normally be pigs in heaven?"

"Uh, Mom, this isn't—" But Nita stopped herself; she wasn't sure. And then there was still the question of the Pig, wandering along through the meadow not too far from them and gazing, as they did, at the mountains. The Pig looked, if anything, more transcendent than usual; it did not so much glow as seem to illuminate everything around it, if indeed the luminous surroundings could be any more illuminated than they already were.

"You're here, too?" Nita said to the Transcendent Pig.

"The annoying thing about omnipresence," the Pig said, "is that everybody keeps asking you that question. At least you didn't ask me what was the meaning of life."

Nita made a face. "I forgot."

It chuckled. "You're *here* and you need to ask?"

She smiled then. "Mom, this is the Transcendent Pig. Chao, this is my mother."

"We've met," said the Pig, nodding in a friendly way to Nita's mom.

Nita's mother smiled back. "You know, we have," she said, "but for the life of me I can't remember when."

"You will," said the Pig. It glanced at Nita. "She has

a lot of remembering to do. Not right away...but soon."

Nita's mother nodded as well, gazing at the Pig with an odd expression of slowly dawning recognition. It glanced at Nita. "They all remember me eventually," it said. "The way they all remember the Lone One. We have history."

The three of them walked along through the meadow together for a little ways. "Mom," Nita said, "I really don't want to lose you."

"I don't think we get much choice on this one," Nita's mother said. "Honey, our ways are going to part, one way or another." She looked at Nita with an expression that was sorrowful but tender. "Parents and kids do it all the time, as they both grow up. You and I are just going to have to do it faster than we planned... and more permanently. Since there's no way out of it, let's enjoy every day. Heaven only knows what may happen afterward, but they can't take away from us what we make, one day at a time, just all of us together. That, we keep...and anything else..." Her mother looked up at the mountains. "We'll find out soon enough."

Nita nodded. "But oh, Mom...I'm going to miss you so much! Always!"

"I'm going to miss you too, honey. But it won't be forever...not the kind of forever that matters. If this is where I'm going to be, I think everything will be just fine."

"It won't be the same, though," Nita said softly. "It won't be like being able to talk to you."

"You'll usually know what I would have said, if you think about it," her mother said. "We know each other that well, at least. Other than that, I'll always be around, even though you won't hear much from me. I mean, sweetheart, you started out inside me...Don't you think at the end of the process, things sort of go the other way around?"

Nita wiped her eyes and looked over at the Pig, which was looking at her mother with quiet approval. "Can't add much to that," it said.

Nita just hugged her mom; it was all she could do. "Go well," she said.

"As long as you do, sweetheart...I always will."

Nita's mother slowly let her go, then looked over her shoulder, up at those mountains, towering skyward into another kind of eternity, and began to walk toward them, through the mist.

Nita stood there with the Pig and watched her mom vanish, shining, into the mist. "What happens now?" Nita said.

"What usually does. Life...for a while. Then the usual brief defeat," said the Pig. "But victory's certain. Never think otherwise. There *is* loss, and there *is* pain, and in your home frame of reference, they're real enough, not to be devalued. But today the energy's running out of things just a little more slowly...for those who trust their hearts as a measure."

Nita swallowed hard. "You'll keep an eye on her," she said.

"Of course I will. I always do. But somehow," said the Pig, looking at Nita's mother, who was moving higher and higher up the hillside, almost lost in the ever-growing light, "I don't think she'll need it."

...The light on the bedroom ceiling woke Nita, glinting through her window from a car pulling into the driveway below. Nita sat up in bed, wiped her face, and tried on a smile. To her astonishment, it didn't feel like such a terrible fit.

She got up, threw on jeans and a T-shirt, and went downstairs to tell her mom hello.

Turn the page for a thrilling peek at

A Wizard Alone

The sixth book in the Young Wizards series

Chapter One

IN A LIVING ROOM of a suburban house on Long Island, a wizard sat with a TV remote control in his hand, and an annoyed expression on his face. "Come on," he said to the remote. "Don't give me grief."

The TV showed him a blue screen and nothing more.

Kit Rodriguez sighed. "All right," he said, "we're on the record now. You made me do this." He reached for his wizard's manual on the sofa next to him, paged through it to its hardware section—which had been getting thicker by the minute that afternoon—found one page in particular, and keyed into the remote a series of characters that the designers of both the remote and the TV would have found unusual.

The screen stayed mostly blue, but the nature of the white characters on it changed. Until now they had been words in the Roman alphabet. Now they changed to characters in a graceful and curly cursive, the written form of the wizardly Speech. In the middle of the blue screen appeared a single word:

WON'T.

Kit let out a long breath of exasperation. "Oh, come on," he said in the Speech. "Why not?"

The screen remained blue, staring at him mulishly. Kit wondered what he'd done to deserve this. "It can't be that bad," he said. "You two even have the same version number."

VERSIONS AREN'T EVERYTHING!

Kit rubbed his eyes and sat there staring at the blue screen, trying to sort through the different strategies he'd tried so far. The manual for the new remote said that the new DVD player was supposed to look for channels on the TV once they were plugged into each other, but the remote and the DVD player didn't even want to acknowledge each other's existence so far, let alone exchange information. The two pieces of equipment both came from the same company, they were both made in the same year and, as far as Kit could tell, in the same place. But when he listened to them with a wizard's ear, he heard them singing two different songs—in ferocious rivalry—and making rude noises at each other during the pauses, when they thought no one was listening.

"Come on, you guys," he said in the Speech. "All I'm asking for here is a little cooperation—"

"No surrender!" shouted the remote.

"Death before dishonor!" shouted the DVD player.

Kit covered his eyes and let out a long, frustrated breath.

From the kitchen there came a sudden silence, something that was as arresting to Kit as a sudden noise, and that made him look up in alarm.

"Honey?" Kit's mom said.

"What, Mama?"

"The dog says he wants to know the meaning of life."

Kit rubbed his forehead, finding himself tempted to hide his eyes. "Give him a dog biscuit and tell him it's an allegory," Kit said.

"What, *life*?"

"No, the biscuit!"

"Oh, good. You had me worried there for a moment."

Kit went back to trying to talk sense into the remote and the DVD player. The DVD player blued the TV's screen out again, pointedly turning its attention elsewhere.

"Come on, just give each other a chance."

"Talk to *that* thing? You must have a chip loose."

"Like I would listen!"

"Hah! You're a tool, nothing but a tool! *I* entertain!"

"Oh, yeah? Let's see how well you entertain when *I* turn you off like a light!"

"Listen to me, you two! You can't get hung up on the active-role-passive-role thing. They're both just fine, and there's more to life—"

"Like what?!"

Kit's mama came drifting in and looked over Kit's

shoulder. "It sounds like escargot," his mother said, leaning over him to look at the TV.

"What?"

"Sorry. Esperanto. I don't know why the word for snails always comes out first."

Kit looked at his mother with some interest. "You can hear it?" he said. It was moderately unusual for nonwizards to hear the Speech at all. When they did, they tended to hear it as the language they spoke themselves—but since the Speech contained and informed all languages, being the seed from which they grew, this was to be expected.

"I hear it a little," his mother said. "Like someone talking in the next room. Which it was..."

"I wonder if the wizardry comes from your side of the family," Kit said.

His mother's broad and pretty face suddenly acquired a nervous quality. "Uh-oh, the chicken broth," she said, and took herself back to the kitchen.

"What about Ponch?" Kit said.

"He ate the dog biscuit," his mother said after a moment.

"And he didn't ask you any more philosophical stuff?"

"He went out. I think he had a date with a biological function."

Kit smirked, then went rummaging through the paperwork on the floor for the DVD's and remote's manuals. *We're in trouble when even a remote control has its own manual,* he thought. But if a wizard with a bent toward mechanical things couldn't get this kind of very basic problem sorted out, then there really *would* be trouble.

He spent a few moments reading, ignoring the catcalls and jeers that the recalcitrant pieces of equipment were trading. Then abruptly Kit realized, listening, that the DVD *did* have a slightly different accent than the remote and the TV. *Now, I wonder,* he thought, and went carefully through the DVD's manual to see whether the manufacturer had actually made all the main parts itself.

The manual said nothing about this. Resigned, Kit picked up the remote again, which immediately began shouting abuse at him. At first he was relieved that this was inaudible to everybody else, but the DVD chose that moment to take control of the entertainment system's speakers and start shouting back.

He spent an annoying couple of moments searching for the volume control on the DVD, for the remote was too busy doing its own shouting to be of any use. Finally he got the DVD to shut up, then once again punched a series of characters into the remote to get a look at the details on the DVD's core processor.

"Aha," Kit said to himself. The processor wasn't made by the company that owned the brand. He had a look at the same information for the remote. It also used the same processor, but it had been resold to the brand-name company by still another company.

"Now look at that!" Kit said. "You have the same processors. You aren't really from different companies at all. You're long-lost brothers. Isn't that nice? And look at you, fighting! Now I want you guys to shake hands and make up."

There was first a shocked silence, then some muttering and grumbling about unbearable insults and who owed whom an apology. "You both do," Kit said. "You were very disrespectful to each other. Now get on with it, and then settle down to work. You'll have a great time. The new cable package has all these great channels."

Reluctantly, they did it. "Thank you, guys," Kit said, taking a few moments to tidy up the paperwork scattered all over the floor. "See, that wasn't so bad. But someday all this will be so much simpler," Kit said, patting the top of the DVD player.

"No it won't," the remote control said darkly.

Kit rolled his eyes. "*You* just behave," he said to the remote, "or you're gonna wind up in the Cuisinart."

He walked out of the living room, ignoring the indignant shrieks of wounded ego from the remote. This had been only the latest episode in a series of almost constant excitements lately, which had begun when his dad broke down after years of resistance and decided to get a full-size entertainment center. It was going to be wonderful when everything was installed and everything worked. Meanwhile, Kit had become resigned to having a lot of learning experiences.

From the back door at the far side of the kitchen came a scratching noise: his dog letting the world know he wanted to come back in. The scratching stopped as the door opened. Kit turned to his pop, who had just come into the dining room, and handed him the remote. "I think it's fixed now," he said.

"What was the problem?"

"Something cultural."

"Between the remote and the DVD player?! But they're both Japanese."

"Looks like it's more complicated than that."

Kit realized how thirsty all this talking to machinery had made him. He went to the fridge and rummaged around to see if there was some of his mom's iced tea in there. There wasn't, only a can of the lemon soft drink that Nita particularly liked and that his mom kept for her.

The sight of it made Kit briefly uncomfortable. But neither wizardry nor friendship were exclusively about comfort. He took the lemon fizz out, popped the can's top, and took a long swig.

The phone rang. *"IgotitIgotitIgotit!"* his sister shrieked from upstairs. *"HolaMiguelque—"* A pause. "Oh. Sorry. *Kit!!"*

"What?"

"Tomás El Jefe."

"Oh." Kit got up and went into the kitchen, where the extension phone was. Ponch, Kit's big black Labrador-cum-Border-collie-cum-whatever, was now lying on the floor with his head down on his paws, carefully watching Kit's mother debone a chicken. As Kit stepped over him, the dog spared him no more than an upward glance, then turned his attention straight back to the food.

Kit smiled slightly and picked up the phone.

"Hi, Kit," said Tom. "Am I interrupting anything?"

"I just finished dealing with a hardware conflict," Kit said, "but it's handled now, I think. What's up?"

"I wouldn't mind a consultation, if you have the time."

He wants a consultation from me? *That's a new one.* "Sure," Kit said. "No problem. I'll be right over."

"Thanks."

Kit hung up, and saw the look his mother was giving him. "When's it going to be ready, Mama?" he said. "I won't be late. Not too late, anyway."

"About six. It doesn't matter if you're a little late... It'll keep." She gave him a warning look. "You're not going anywhere sudden, are you?" This had become her code phrase for Kit leaving on wizardly business.

"Nope," Kit said. "Tom just needs some advice."

His father wandered back into the kitchen. "The remote working okay now?" Kit said.

"Working?" his pop said. "Well, yeah. But possibly not the way the manufacturer intended."

Kit looked at his pop, uncomprehending. His father went back into the living room. Kit followed.

Where the TV normally would have showed a channel number, the screen was now showing the number 0000566478. The picture seemed to be showing a piece of furniture that looked rather like a set of chrome parallel bars. From the bars hung a creature with quite a few tentacles and many stalky eyes, not in the usual places. The creature was talking fast and loud in a voice like a fire engine's siren, while waving around a large shiny object that might have been an eggbeater, except that, in Kit's experience, eggbeaters didn't usually have lasers built into them. Characters flashed on the screen, both in the Speech and in other languages. Kit stood and looked at this with complete astonishment. His father, next to him, was doing the same.

"You didn't hack into that new pay-per-view system, did you?" his father said. "I don't want the cops in here."

"No way," Kit said, picking up the remote and looking at it accusingly. The remote sat there in his hand as undemonstratively as any genuinely inanimate object might...except that Kit was increasingly uncertain whether there really *were* any such things as inanimate objects.

He shook the remote to see if anything rattled. Nothing did. "I told you to behave," he said in the Speech.

"But not like *what*," the remote said in a sanctimonious tone.

His father was still watching the creature on the parallel bars, which pointed the laser eggbeater at what looked like a nearby abstract sculpture. This vanished in a flare of actinic green light, leaving Kit uneasily wondering what kind of sculpture screamed. "Nice special effects," Kit's father said, though he sounded a little dubious. "Almost too realistic."

"It's not special effects, Pop," Kit said. "It's some other planet's cable. Shopping channel, looks like." Kit handed the remote back to his father.

"This is a *shopping* channel?" he said.

Kit headed for the coat hooks by the kitchen door and pulled his parka off one of them. "Popi, I've got to get to Tom's. I'll be back pretty soon. It's all right to look at it, but if any phone numbers that you can read appear—do me a big favor, okay? *Don't order anything!"*

Kit opened the back door. Ponch threw one last longing look at what Kit's mama was doing with the chicken, then threw himself past Kit, hitting the screen door with a *bang!* and flying out into the driveway.

Kit followed him. At the driveway's end he paused, looking up briefly. It was almost dark already, the bare branches of the maples showing black against an indigo sky. January was too new for any lengthening of days to be perceptible yet; the shortness of the daylight hours was depressing. But at least the holidays were over. Kit could hardly remember a year when he'd been less interested in them. For his own family's sake, he'd done his best to act as if he was, but his heart hadn't been in the celebrations, or the presents. He hadn't been able to stop thinking about the one present Nita most desperately wanted, one that not even the Powers That Be could give her.

Kit sighed and looked down the street. Ponch was down there near curbside in the rapidly falling dark, saluting one of the neighbor's trees. "Back this way, please?" he said, and waited until Ponch was finished and came galloping back up the street toward him.

Kit made his way into the backyard again, with Ponch bouncing along beside him, wagging his tail "Where did that whole 'meaning of life' thing come from all of a sudden?" Kit said.

I heard you ask about it, Ponch said.

The question had, indeed, come up once or twice recently in the course of business, around the time Ponch

started talking regularly. "So?" Kit said, as they made
their way past the beat-up birdbath into the tangle of
sassafras at the back of the yard, where they were out
of sight of the two houses on either side. "Come to any
conclusions?"

That your mama's easy to shake down for dog biscuits.

Kit grinned. "Didn't need to start talking to her to
find that out," he said. He reached into his pocket, felt
around for the "zipper" in it that facilitated access to
the alternate space where he kept some of his spells
ready, and pulled one out—a long chain of strung-
together words in the Speech that glowed a very faint
blue in the swiftly falling darkness. "I'd keep it in the
family, though," Kit told Ponch. "Don't start asking
strangers complicated philosophical questions...It'll
confuse them."

It may be too late, Ponch said.

Kit wondered what that was supposed to mean, then
shrugged. He dropped the spell-chain to the ground
around them in a circle. The transit wizardry knotted
itself together at the ends in the figure-eight wizard's
knot, and from it a brief shimmering curtain of light
went up and blanked the night away as displaced air
went *thump!* A moment later he and Ponch were standing together in Tom's backyard, behind the high privet
hedge blocking the view from Tom's neighbors' houses.
Across the patio, lights were on in the house, and banging noises were coming from the kitchen.

Kit pushed the patio door to one side and went into
Tom's dining room. That space flowed into the living
room area, where Tom's desk sat in a corner, past the

sofas and the entertainment center. But all the action at the moment was in the kitchen, off to the left, where big, dark-haired Carl was doing something to the strip lighting that ran below the upper kitchen cupboards. Tom was leaning against the refrigerator, holding a cup of coffee with the expression of a man who wants nothing to do with whatever's happening. "Hi, Kit," he said, as Ponch ran through the kitchen and out the other side, heading toward the bedrooms, where the sheepdogs Annie and Monty were presently barking at something. "Coke?"

"Yeah, thanks." Kit sat down at the table and watched Carl, who was bent over sideways under the upper cupboards and making faces.

"I told him to call an expert," Tom said as he fished a can of Coke out of the refrigerator and sat down with Kit at the dining room table, where a number of volumes of the Senior version of the wizard's manual were piled.

"We're expert enough to change the laws of physics temporarily," Carl muttered. "How hard can wiring be?"

With a *clunk!* all the lights in the house went out.

Carl moaned. Kit could just see Tom make a flicking motion with one finger at the circuit-breaker box near the kitchen door, and the lights came back on again. "You should stick to physics," Tom said.

"Just one more time," Carl said, and went down the stairs to the basement.

"This will be the sixth 'one more time' in the past two hours," Tom said. "I'm hoping he'll see sense before he blows up the transformer at the end of the street. Or maybe the local power station."

"I *heard* that!" said the voice from the basement.

Kit snickered, but not too loudly.

"Anyway," Tom said, "thanks for coming over. Briefly, one of our wizards is missing, and I'd like you to look into it."

This was a new one on Kit. "Missing? Anybody I know?"

"Hard for me to tell. Here's the listing." Tom pulled down the topmost manual and opened it; the pages riffled through themselves to a spot he had book-marked. It was a page in the master wizards' address listing for the New York area, and one block of information glowed a soft rose. Kit leaned over to look at it. In the Speech, it said:

DARRYL McALLISTER
18355 Hempstead Turnpike
Baldwin, NY 11568
(516) 555-7384
power rating 5.6 +/– .3
status: On Ordeal
initiation: 4777598.3
completion:
duration to present date: 90.3
resolution: nil

Kit stared at the duration figure for a moment: There was something wrong with it. "That doesn't look right," he said at last. "Did a decimal point get misplaced or something? That looks like months."

"It *is* months," Tom said. "Just a whisker over three,

which is why it came up for attention just today. The manual normally flags such extended Ordeals to be audited by a Senior."

"I thought nobody was allowed to interfere with a wizard's Ordeal," Kit said. "It's what determines whether you ought to be a wizard in the first place. Whether you can run into the Lone Power and survive..."

"Normally that's true," Tom said. "But Ordeals aren't always so clean-cut; they do sometimes go wrong. A resolution can get delayed somehow, or there can be local interference that keeps the resolution from happening. An area's Seniors are allowed a certain amount of information about Ordeals among probationary wizards who'd be in their catchment area if things went right, especially if something goes wrong in a specific sort of way—a 'stuck' Ordeal, or a contaminated one. We have some latitude to step in and try to kick that Ordeal back into operation again. While interfering as little as possible."

Kit nodded, glancing to one side as Carl came up from the basement with a very large roll of duct tape. "Ah," Tom said. "The substance that binds the universe together."

"We'll see," Carl said, and bent himself over sideways again.

"It's a brute force solution," Tom said. "The phone's right there!"

Carl ignored him and started doing something with the duct tape.

"So now we come to this kid," Tom said, indicating

the highlighted listing again. *Clunk!* went the circuit breaker, and the house went dark again; only the text on the page in front of them continued to glow, while in the back bedroom the dogs paused, then went on barking. Tom gestured once more at the breaker box, and the lights came on. "It's not like he's been physically absent from the area for all this time, as far as I can tell," Tom said. "If he were, certainly there would have been something about it in the news, and there's been nothing. But at the same time, this is not a normal duration for a human Ordeal. We need to find out what's going on, but quietly. Do you or Nita know him well enough to look in on him and see what's happening? Or do you know anyone who does?"

Kit shook his head. "I can check with Neets, but she's sure never mentioned him to me," Kit said. "Why bring me in on this, though? You're a Senior; you'd probably be able to tell a lot better than I can what's going on with him."

"Well," Tom said, "in this particular situation, if people start noticing *you* in the neighborhood around the object of our mutual interest, they won't think too much about it—it's not far enough from your own stamping grounds to provoke suspicion. If Carl or I went to investigate personally, notice might be taken. This kind of initial fact-finding is better suited to a wizard of your age."

"Besides," Carl said, peering up at the bottom of the cupboard, "lately you've been evincing a certain talent for finding things."

"Well, Ponch has," Kit said.

"I'm not sure he'd be producing these results without you as part of the team," Carl said.

"Anyway, are you willing?" Tom said. "To go over there during the next couple of days? See what the kid's doing, physically, talk to him if you can, try to get a sense of what his state of mind is."

"Sure," Kit said. "Am I allowed to tell him I'm a wizard, if he asks?"

"I'll leave that up to you," Tom said. "Normally I would suggest that you try to avoid it if possible. You don't want to take the chance of altering his perception of his Ordeal, maybe even making him think you're supposed to be involved in it somehow. But if you can come by any sense of why his Ordeal's taking him so long, I'd be glad to hear it."

Carl straightened up. "Okay," he said. The strip lights under the cupboards were now actually on. He looked at the light they cast on the counter with some satisfaction. "At least now I'm going to be able to see what I'm cooking without getting blinded." He went over to the wall, turned the dimmer switch.

Clunk!

"I could stop by the supermarket on the way home and get you some candles," Kit said as he got up. "Fire still works."

"Very funny," Carl said.